Praise for *USA TODAY* bestselling author Marie Ferrarella

"Marie Ferrarella is a charming storyteller
who will steal your heart away."
—*RT Book Reviews*

"Great romance, excellent plot,
grabs you from page one."
—*Affaire de Coeur* on *In Graywolf's Hands*

"As usual, Ferrarella's dialogue is crisp and moves
the story along without ever bogging down in the
emotional angst each brings to the relationship. *Once
a Father* is a hearty recommend for a skilled writer."
—*The Romance Reader*

"A pure delight."
—*Rendezvous*

"Once again Ms. Ferrarella demonstrates a mastery
of the storytelling art as she creates charming
characters, witty dialogue and an emotional story line
that will tug at your heartstrings."
—*RT Book Reviews* on *In the Family Way*

MARIE FERRARELLA

is a *USA TODAY* bestselling author and RITA® Award
winner. She has written two hundred books for
Silhouette and Harlequin Books, some under the name
of Marie Nicole. Her romances are beloved by fans
worldwide. Visit her website at www.marieferrarella.com.

USA TODAY Bestselling Author

Marie Ferrarella

LABOR OF LOVE

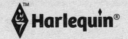
Harlequin®

TORONTO NEW YORK LONDON
AMSTERDAM PARIS SYDNEY HAMBURG
STOCKHOLM ATHENS TOKYO MILAN MADRID
PRAGUE WARSAW BUDAPEST AUCKLAND

Recycling programs
for this product may
not exist in your area.

ISBN-13: 978-0-373-68835-7

LABOR OF LOVE

Copyright © 2011 by Harlequin Books S.A.

The publisher acknowledges the copyright holders
of the individual works as follows:

MOTHER IN TRAINING
Copyright © 2006 by Harlequin Books S.A.
Marie Ferrarella is acknowledged as the author of this work.

A BILLIONAIRE AND A BABY
Copyright © 2003 by Marie Rydzynski-Ferrarella

Printed in U.S.A.

TABLE OF CONTENTS

MOTHER IN TRAINING

To
Patience Smith,
the kind keeper
of my sanity.
Thank you

Chapter 1

The short, squat man moved his considerable bulk between her and the front door, blocking her line of vision. The look on his round, florid face fairly shouted of exasperation.

"You know how a watched pot don't boil?" he asked her. "Well, a watched door don't open, neither. So stop watching the door and start doing somethin' to earn the money I'm paying you, Zoo-ie."

Zooey Finnegan grimaced inside. Milo Hanes, the owner of the small Upstate New York coffee shop where she currently clocked in each morning in order to draw a paycheck, seemed to take an inordinate amount of pleasure mispronouncing her name.

Most likely, she thought cynically, it was a holdover from his days as the schoolyard bully.

That was okay, she consoled herself. It wasn't as if waitressing at the coffee shop was her life's ambition. She was just passing through. Just as she'd passed through a handful of other jobs, trying them on for size, searching for something that would arouse a passion within her, or at least awaken some heretofore dormant potential.

Her parents had been certain that her life's passion would be the family furniture business. As the firstborn, she'd been groomed for that ever since she was old enough to clutch a briefcase. They and her uncle Andrew had sent her off to college to get a business degree, and after that, an MBA.

The only problem was, Zooey had no desire to acquire a degree—not in business, at any rate.

Her family had made their money designing and selling stylish, affordable furniture. What had once been a small, single-store operation had branched out over the years to include several outlets, both in state and out. Proud as she was of their accomplishments, Zooey couldn't picture herself as a company executive, or a buyer for the firm, or even a salesperson in one of their seven showrooms. As far as she was concerned, Finnegan's Fine Furniture was going to have to remain fine without her.

She loved her parents, but she refused to be browbeaten by them into living a life of not-so-quiet desperation. Stating as much had led to "discussions," which led to arguments that indirectly resulted in her breaking up with Connor Taylor. Her parents felt he was the perfect man for her, being two years older and dedicated to business. What he was perfect for, it turned out, was the company. He'd upbraided Zooey when she'd told him her plans, saying she was crazy to walk away from such a future.

That was when she'd realized Connor was in their relationship strictly for the money, not out of any all-consuming love for her. If it had been the latter, she'd informed him, he would have been willing to hike into the forests of Oregon and subsist on berries and grubs with her. Declaring that she wanted to be mistress of her own destiny, she'd had a huge fight with everyone involved—her parents, her uncle and Connor. When her parents threatened to cut off her funds, she'd done them one better. She'd cut them off and left to find her own way in the world.

So far, her "way" had led her to take up dog walking, to endure a very short stint as a courier, and now waitressing. None of the above proved to be very satisfying or fulfilling. As a dog walker, she'd managed to lose one of her charges. As a courier she'd gotten lost three times in two days, and her first week's pay as a waitress went to repay Milo for several cups and saucers she'd broken when she'd accidentally tilted her tray.

A lesser woman might have given up and gone home, but Zooey had her pride—and very little else. Cut off from the family and the family money, she was running out of options as well as cash. The rent on her closetlike apartment was due soon, and as of right now, she was still more than a hundred dollars short.

She supposed she should have been worried, but she wasn't. Zooey was, first and foremost, a die-hard, almost terminal, optimist. She refused to be beaten down by circumstances, or a scowling boss who could have doubled as a troll in one of *Grimm's Fairy Tales.*

Something would come along, she promised herself.

After all, she just didn't have the complexion to be a homeless person.

In the meantime, she still had a job, she reminded herself.

Offering Milo a spasmodic smile, she went back to mechanically filling the sugar containers on each of the small tables and booths scattered throughout the coffee shop. As she worked, Zooey tried not to look toward the door. Or at least, not to appear as if she was looking toward the door.

He was late.

Rubbing away a sticky spot on the table with the damp towel she had hanging from her belt, Zooey couldn't help wondering if anything was wrong.

Jack Lever, the drop-dead-gorgeous blond criminal lawyer who came in every morning for coffee and a blueberry muffin—and secretly lit her fire—hadn't turned up yet. It wasn't like him.

She'd met Jack her first day on the job. He'd been sitting at her station, with an expression that indicated he had the weight of the world on his shoulders. Being of the opinion that everyone could use a little friendly chatter and, at times, a shoulder to lean on, she'd struck up a conversation with him.

Or, more accurately, a monologue. She'd talked and he'd listened. Or appeared to. After about a week of relative silence on his part, Jack finally offered more than single-word responses to her questions.

Given something to work with, she let her questions grow lengthier and progressively more personal than just inquiries about how he liked the weather, the Mets, his muffin. Week number two had actually seen the beginnings of a smile on his lips. That was when her heart had fluttered for the first time. That was also when she'd almost spilled coffee on his lap instead of into his cup.

She began to look forward to Jack's daily stops at the shop. A couple of times, he put in more than one appearance, dropping by around lunchtime the two days he was in the area because of a case. The county courthouse was only two blocks away.

He was a creature of habit as much as she was a free spirit. And he always, always came into the shop around the same time. Eight-thirty. It was almost nine now.

"Maybe Mr. Big Shot's cheating on you with another coffee shop," Milo said, chuckling into his two chins as he changed the industrial-size filter for the large steel coffee urn. Steam hissed, sending up a cloud of vapor as he removed the old filter.

Milo had caught her looking again, she realized, averting her eyes from the door and back to the sugar container in her hand. Zooey shrugged, her thin shoulders moving beneath the stiff, scratchy white cotton uniform. It chafed her neck a little.

She saw no point in pretending she didn't know what her boss was talking about. "Maybe he took a vacation day."

"Or maybe his wife did," Milo commented.

Zooey was about to tell the man that Jack was a widower. It was the latest bit of personal information he'd shared with her. Eighteen months ago, his wife had been killed in a hit-and-run car accident, leaving him with two small children to raise: a girl, Emily, who was about seven now, and a little boy, Jack Jr., still in diapers. The boy was almost two.

But the information never reached her lips. Milo was nodding toward the door.

Zooey turned around in time to see Jack Lever

walking in. He was herding a little girl before him, while holding tightly on to a boy who looked as if he was ready to explode in three different directions at once. Jack was also trying to hang on to his briefcase.

Zooey's heart went out to him immediately. The man was obviously struggling, and while she would have bet even money that Jack Lever was a formidable opponent on the courtroom floor, he looked as if he was in over his head at the moment.

Kids did that to you, she thought. She had a younger brother who'd been a pistol when he was around Jack Jr.'s age.

Abandoning the sugar dispenser, Zooey made her way over to Jack and his lively crew. She flashed her brightest smile at him, the one her father had once said could melt the frown off Satan.

"Hi. Table for three?" she asked, her glance sweeping over the two children before returning to Jack.

"More like a cage for two," he murmured wearily under his breath.

Zooey's eyes met his. He would have looked more refreshed wrestling alligators. "Tough morning?"

He gazed at her as if he thought she had a gift for severe understatement. "You might say that." Jackie tried to dart under a table, but Jack held fast, pulling him back. "My nanny quit."

"You don't have a nanny, Daddy." Emily giggled shyly, covering her small, pink mouth with both hands.

The sigh that escaped his lips measured 5.1 on the Richter scale. "And as of seven this morning, neither do you."

Zooey deliberately led the three to a booth, feeling that the enclosed space might make it easier for Jack to restrict the movements of his children. Just before she turned to indicate that they should take a seat, she grabbed hold of two booster seats stacked in the corner and slid one on each side of the table. Then, because Jack seemed to be having more trouble with the boy, she took him by the waist and lifted him in the air.

"Up you go, young man."

Because she added a little bounce to the descent, Jack Jr. laughed gleefully, his eyes lighting up. He clapped his hands together. "Again," he cried.

Zooey winked at him, leaning over to make sure that he was securely seated. "Maybe when you leave."

The little girl was tugging on the short apron Zooey wore. When she looked at her quizzically, Emily said shyly, "You're pretty."

Straightening, Zooey beamed. "Well, thank you, honey."

The smile on Emily's lips faded just a little as sadness set in. "My mommy was pretty, too," she added quietly.

Poor baby, Zooey couldn't help thinking. She deliberately avoided looking at Jack, feeling that the moment had to be awkward for him.

"She would have had to have been," Zooey told her, running a hand over the girl's vivid blond hair. "Because you are."

Jack saw his daughter all but sparkle in response.

It suddenly hit him. For the first time since they'd opened their eyes this morning, his children were quiet. Both of them. At the same time.

Stunned, he looked at the young woman he'd been exchanging conversation with for the last six weeks, seeing her in a brand-new light. That of a sorceress. "How did you do that?"

Looking up from the children, Zooey smiled at him beatifically. "Do what?"

"Get them to quiet down like that. They've been making noise nonstop all morning." Even Emily, whom he could usually count on to behave herself in his company, had been more than a handful today. When it rained...

The waitress's green eyes were smiling as she looked at the two children again. "Maybe they're just worn-out," she suggested modestly.

The truth of it was she had a way with kids. She always had, having gotten her training early in life while learning to keep her brothers and sisters in line. The fact that it had resembled more of a conga line than anything drawn using a straight edge was the secret of her success.

Zooey raised her eyes to Jack's. He was, after all, the customer. And undoubtedly running late. "The usual?" she asked.

It took him a second to get his mind in gear. And then he nodded. "Yes, sure."

Emily cocked her head, trying to understand. "What's the usual, Daddy?"

"Coffee and a blueberry muffin," Zooey answered before he had the chance. The little girl made a face. Zooey laughed. "How does hot chocolate with marshmallows bobbing up and down sound to you?"

The grimace vanished instantly, replaced by a wide grin. "Good!" Emily enthused.

"Messy," Jack countered.

"The nice thing about messy," Zooey told him, giving the towel hooked on her belt a tug, "is it can always be cleaned up." And then she looked from one child to the other. "But you guys aren't going to be messy, are you?"

Emily shook her head solemnly from side to side. Watching her, Jack Jr. imitated the movement.

Zooey nodded, trying hard to match the children's solemnity. "I didn't think so. By the way, my name's Zooey." She held her hand out to Emily.

The little girl stared at it, stunned, before finally putting her own hand into it. "Emily," she said with the kind of pride and awe a child felt when she suddenly realized she was being treated like an adult.

"Jackie," the little boy announced loudly, sticking his hand out as if he was gleefully poking a snake with a stick.

Zooey shook the little boy's hand and never let on that the simple gesture made her own hand sticky. Without missing a beat, she took her towel and wiped off his fingers.

"Pleased to meet you, Jackie. You, too, Emily. I'll be right back with your hot chocolates," she promised, backing away. "And the usual," she added, looking at Jack before she turned on her heel to hurry to the kitchen.

Jack leaned back in the booth, blowing out a long breath. Trying to get his bearings. And focus.

He didn't often believe in miracles. Actually, he didn't believe in them at all. They weren't real and, contrary to popular belief, they just didn't happen. Miracles belonged in legends, something for the desperate to cling to in times of strife.

And then he smiled to himself at the irony of it. God knew he certainly fit the desperate criteria today. More so than usual.

At exactly five minutes after seven this morning, just as he was preparing to call her to ask why she was running late, the children's latest nanny had called to tell him that she wasn't coming back. Ever. And then she'd hung up.

He could only assume that the soured old woman had spent the night mulling over this declaration of abandonment, brought on by the disagreement they'd had yesterday evening regarding her strict treatment of the children. Emily had tearfully told him she'd been punished that morning because she'd accidentally spilled her glass of milk at the table. Since there wasn't a single truly willful bone in the little girl's petite body, he knew Emily hadn't done it on purpose.

But apparently Agnes Phillips did not tolerate anything less than perfection. This wasn't the first time she and Jack had locked horns over her uptight behavior. He'd taken her to task on at least two other occasions. And she'd only been in his employ a little over two months.

Obviously, the third time was *not* the charm, he thought cynically. He'd been planning on replacing the woman as soon as he could get around to it. Agnes had undoubtedly sensed it and, reject from a military camp though she was, had beaten him to the punch by calling up and quitting.

Leaving him in a hell of a bind.

He felt like a man in the middle of the ocean, trying to survive by clinging to a life raft that had just sprung a leak.

Jack had a case due in court today and he didn't think that Alice, the receptionist at his law firm, was going to be overly thrilled about his need to turn her into a babysitter for a few hours.

But observing the way both his children seemed to light up the moment the young waitress returned with their hot chocolates gave him food for thought.

"Zooey?"

She placed his coffee and muffin down on the table and very carefully pushed the plate before him. She raised her eyes to his, wishing she could clear her throat, hoping she wouldn't sound as if something had just fluttered around her navel at the sound of his deep voice saying her name. "Hmm?"

He leaned forward across the table, his eyes never leaving hers. "I'd like to offer you a bribe."

"Excuse me?" Zooey withdrew the tray from its resting spot on the table and held it to her like a bulletproof shield that could protect her from everything, including handsome lawyers with drop-dead-gorgeous brown eyes.

"Maybe I'd better backtrack."

"Maybe," she agreed firmly.

He slanted a glance at his children. Jackie was already wearing a hot chocolate mustache on his cheeks. "Look, I told you their nanny quit this morning."

Out of the corner of her eye, Zooey saw several other customers come through the door and take seats. She knew that she should be easing away from Jack, turning a deaf ear to his problems. But the kids looked as if they were about to drive him over the edge.

Jack delivered the final, hopefully winning, salvo. "And I'm due in court today."

More customers came in. Zooey caught the eye of Debi, the other waitress, mouthing, "Can you get those tables?"

"And there's no room for short assistants?" she asked out loud, turning back toward Jack.

He didn't crack a smile at her comment. "None."

Zooey paused, thinking. But it was a foregone conclusion as to what she'd come up with: nothing. "I'd like to help you out," she told him apologetically, "but I don't know of anybody who could watch them."

He hadn't wanted a substitute. "I was thinking of you."

"Me?" She glanced toward Milo. He was behind the counter, pretending not to listen. She knew better. The man had ears like a bat on steroids. "I've already got a job. Such as it is," she couldn't help adding.

Her lack of enthusiasm about her job was all the encouragement Jack needed. "I'll pay you double whatever he's giving you."

That still didn't amount to all that much, she thought. But this really wasn't about money. It was about time. "Double? I don't th—"

"Okay." He cut in, not letting her finish. "Triple. I'm a desperate man, Zooey."

And gorgeous. Don't forget gorgeous, she added silently. And triple her pay would go a long way toward helping her with her bills.

Jack could see that he had her. All he needed was to reel her in. "It'd only be for the day," he assured her. "You could take them to the park, the mall, wherever—"

Something suddenly hit her. She put her hand up to stop him before he could get any further.

"Mr. Lever. Jack. You're talking about leaving your kids with me. Your *children*," she emphasized. "And you don't even know me." What kind of a father did that make him—besides desperate?

He knew all he really needed to know about the young woman, he thought. It wasn't as if she had kept to herself. She'd been open and forthright even when all he'd wanted with his coffee and muffin was a side order of silence.

"We've talked for six weeks." He picked another point at random. "And I know you like jazz. And," he added, his voice growing in authority, "you're conscientious enough to point out that I don't know you."

A smile crept over her lips, even as she stooped to pick up the spoon Jackie had dropped. "Isn't that like a catch-22?"

Jack nodded. "And you're intelligent," he added, then played his ace. "And I'm desperate."

Zooey couldn't help the laugh that rose to her lips. "Intelligent and Desperate. Sounds like a law firm in an Abbott and Costello routine."

Jack looked mildly surprised. He didn't expect a twenty-something woman to be even remotely familiar with the comedy duo from the forties and fifties. "Anyone who knows things like that is above reproach," he told her.

He didn't need to flatter her, Zooey thought. The man had her at "hello."

"Okay, if I'm going to do this, I'm going to need some information," she told him, mentally rolling up her sleeves. "Like where you work, where you live, how to reach you in case of an emergency, where and when to meet you so that you can take your children home...."

She was thorough; he liked that. She was asking all the right questions, questions he would have given her the answers to even if they'd been unspoken. "I knew I wasn't wrong about you."

"The day is young," she deadpanned. Then, because she'd never been able to keep a straight face for long, she grinned. "Just give me a few minutes to clear it with my boss."

Jack was aware of every second ticking by as he automatically glanced at his watch.

"I'll make it fast," she promised, already backing away from the table.

"I like her, Daddy," Emily told him in a stage whisper that would have carried to the last row in Carnegie Hall.

"Lucky for us, she feels the same way," he told his daughter.

Zooey returned to their table faster than he'd anticipated. Jack rose to his feet, scanning her face. Looking for an unspoken apology. To his relief, there was none.

"All set," she announced.

He glanced toward the counter. The man behind it was scowling and sending him what could only be referred to as a dark look. "Your boss is all right with this?"

"He's fine with this," she replied. Jack noticed she was carrying her jacket and that she was now slipping it on. "He doesn't care what I do."

Jack raised an eyebrow. And then it hit him. "He fired you."

Zooey shrugged dismissively. She wasn't going to miss the itchy uniform. "Something like that."

Jack hadn't meant for this to happen. "Look, I'm sorry. Let me talk to him."

But Zooey shook her head. "You're running late, and besides, I was thinking of leaving soon, anyway. This is just a little sooner than I'd originally planned," she admitted. And then she smiled down at the two eager faces turned to her. The children had been following every word, trying to understand what was going on. "You two ready to have fun?"

Chapter 2

The last word Jack Lever would use to describe himself was *impulsive*.

It just wasn't his nature.

He was thorough, deliberate and didactic. Born to be a lawyer, he always found himself examining a thing from all sides before taking any action on it.

It was one of the traits, he knew, that used to drive his wife, Patricia, crazy. She'd complain about his "stodgy" nature, saying she wanted them to be spontaneous. But he had always demurred, saying that he'd seen too many unforeseen consequences of random, impetuous actions to ever fall prey to that himself.

It was, he thought, just one of the many stalemates they'd found themselves facing. Stalemates that had brought them to the brink of divorce just before she was killed.

However, he thought as he slipped case notes into his

briefcase, this was an emergency. Emergencies called for drastic measures. Tomorrow was going to be here before he knew it. Tomorrow with no nanny, with Emily needing to be dressed and taken to school, and Jackie still a perpetual challenge to one and all.

Walking out into the hall, Jack made his way to the elevator and pushed the down button. He needed a sitter, a nanny. A person with extreme patience and endless fortitude.

The express elevator arrived and he got on, stepping to the rear.

Desperate though he was, it seemed that fate—the same fate that had sent him three ultimately unsatisfactory nannies, one worse than the other—had decided to finally toss him a bone.

Or, in this case, a supernanny.

So when he stepped out of the fifteen-story building where the firm of Wasserman, Kendall, Lake & Lever was housed, and saw Zooey sitting on the stone rim of the fountain before the building, one child on either side of her and none looking damaged or even the worse for wear, Jack decided to go with his instincts. And for once in his life, do something impulsive.

The moment she saw Jack exiting the building, Zooey rose to her feet.

"Daddy's here," she told the children. A fresh burst of energy sent Jackie and Emily running madly toward their father.

Jackie reached him first, wrapping his small arms around his father's leg as high as they would reach. "Hi, Daddy!" he crowed. For a little boy, he was capable of a great deal of volume.

"Hi, Daddy." Emily's greeting was quieter, but enthusiastic nonetheless.

He'd dropped his briefcase to the ground half a beat before Jackie and Emily surrounded him. "Hi, yourselves," he said, wrapping an arm around each child.

Jack did like being a father. He just had no idea how to exercise small-person control.

Finding himself in a large conference room with a collection of the state's greater legal minds, or in a tiny briefing area with a known hardened criminal, Jack knew how to handle himself. Knew how to maintain control so that the situation never threatened to get away from him.

But when it came to dealing with the under-fifteen set, especially with small beings who barely came up to his belt buckle, he was at a complete loss as to what to do.

Not so Zooey, he thought. Being with the children seemed to be right up her alley. As a matter of fact, she appeared to be as fresh as she always was when he walked into the coffee shop each morning.

He had no idea how she did it. His children had worn out three nannies in the last eighteen months, and seemed destined to wear out more.

Unless his instincts were right.

Slipping his arms free, he nodded at the short duo. "Did they give you any trouble?" he asked, almost afraid of the answer.

Zooey looked at him, wide-eyed. "Trouble? No!" she replied with feeling.

The way her green eyes sparkled as she voiced the denial told Jack that today had not been a boring one by any means.

Though he didn't spend all that much time with them,

he knew his kids, knew what they were capable of once they were up and running.

"Should I be writing out a check to anyone for damages they or their property sustained?"

She grinned. "You really do sound like a lawyer. No, no checks. No damages. Emily and Jackie were both very good."

He stared at her. The trip to the parking structure that faced his office building and presently contained his car was temporarily aborted. "You sure you're talking about my kids?"

She laughed, and it was a deep, full-volume one. "I am sure," she assured him. "We went to the park, then saw that new movie, *Ponies on Parade,* had a quick, late lunch and here we are."

Ponies on Parade. He vaguely remembered promising Emily to take her to that one. He guessed he was off the hook now. And damn grateful for it. He looked at Zooey with awe and respect. "You make it sound easy."

"It was, for the most part."

Zooey thought it best to leave out the part that while she was taking Emily to the ladies' room, with Jackie in tow, the latter had gotten loose and scooted out from under the stall door. He'd managed, in the time it had taken her to leave Emily and go after him, to stuff up a toilet with an entire roll of toilet paper he'd tossed in and flushed.

Moving fast, Zooey had barely managed to snatch him away before the overflowing water had reached him.

Jack had always been very good at picking up nuances. He studied her now. "Something I should know about?"

The man had enough to deal with in his life, Zooey thought. He didn't need someone "telling" on Jackie. "Only that they're great kids."

"Great kids," Jack echoed, ready to bet his bottom dollar that that wasn't what had been on her mind at all.

But, when he came right down to it, he knew Emily and Jackie were that. Great kids.

They were also Mischievous with a capital *M*. Kids who somehow managed to get into more trouble than he could remember getting into throughout his entire childhood.

Reflecting back, Jack had to admit that he'd been a solemn youngster—an only child whose father had died when he was very young. For years, Jack had thought that it had somehow been his fault, that if he'd been a better person, a better son, his father would have lived.

His stepfather did nothing to repair the hole that doubt had burrowed into his soul. He was never around during Jack's childhood. He'd been, and still was, a terminal workaholic, laboring to provide a more than comfortable lifestyle for Jack's mother, a woman who absolutely worshipped money and everything it could buy. Growing up, Jack supposed it could be said that he'd had the best childhood money could buy.

Everything but attention and the sense that he was truly loved.

He studied Zooey's expression now. "You mean that?"

"Of course I do." Why would he think anything else? she wondered. "I wouldn't say it if I didn't mean it." Truth was something she had the utmost respect for. Because once lost, it couldn't be easily won back. Like with Connor, she thought, then dismissed it. No point in wasting time there.

About to grasp Jackie's hand to help lead him across the street to the parking structure, Zooey saw that the little boy had both arms raised to her, a silent indication that he wanted to be carried. She scooped him up without missing a beat.

Holding him to her, she glanced toward Jack. "Nothing worse than lying as far as I'm concerned." She would have expected that, as a lawyer, he should feel the same way. But then, she'd always been rather altruistic and naive when it came to having faith in people, she reminded herself.

Holding Emily's hand, Jack waited beside Zooey for the light to turn green. He read between the lines. "Somebody lie to you, Zooey?"

Connor, when he said he loved me, and all the while he was in love with the family business. And the family money. She wasn't about to share that with Jack no matter how cute his kids were.

Instead, she shrugged her shoulders. "No one worth mentioning."

The slight movement reminded her that the uniform she had on still chafed. She hadn't had a chance to go home and change before taking on the task of entertaining Jack's children.

One movement led to another, and it was all she could do to keep from scratching. "I guess I'd better get out of this uniform and give it back to Milo."

The light turned green and they hurried across the street.

Reaching the other side, Jack glanced at her. "So, you really are fired?"

Zooey nodded.

In his estimation, she didn't look too distressed about it. Which he couldn't begin to fathom. From what she'd told him, he knew that Zooey lived by herself and didn't have much in the way of funds to fall back on. If it had been him, he would have been sweating bullets. But then, if it had been him, he wouldn't have been in that position to begin with.

Jack was nothing if not pragmatic. "What are you going to do for money?"

"I guess I'm going to have to hunt around for another job." She looked up at him brightly, tongue-in-cheek. "Know someone who wants to hire a go-getter who makes up in enthusiasm what she lacks in experience?"

He surprised her by answering seriously. "As a matter of fact, I do."

Zooey had asked the question as a joke, but now that he'd answered her so positively, she was suddenly eager. This meant no hassles, no scanning newspapers and the Internet. No going from store to store in hopes that they were hiring.

It was nice to have things simple for a change.

"Who?"

And this was where Jack allowed himself to be impulsive. "Me."

The parking garage elevator arrived and they got on. Zooey stared at him, dumbfounded. "You?"

He nodded, wondering if she was going to turn him down, after all. Until this moment, he hadn't considered that option.

"I need a nanny." He heard Emily giggling again. "The kids need a nanny," he corrected. "And you need a job. Seeing as how you got fired doing me a favor, the least I can do is hire you." He paused, then added the required coda. "If you want the job." The last thing he wanted was for her to feel that he was trying to railroad her, or pressure her into agreeing. He might be desperate, but she had to *want* to do this.

Zooey narrowed her eyes, trying to absorb what he was saying. He'd always struck her as being a cautious man, someone who believed in belts *and* suspenders. Normally, she found that a turnoff. But there was something about Jack Lever, not to mention his looks, that negated all that.

"You'll pay me to watch your kids?"

"It's a little more complex than that, but yes."

Zooey looked at him guilelessly. "Sure."

He really hadn't expected such a quick response from her. All the women he'd previously interviewed for the job had told him they would have to think about it when he made an offer. And they'd wanted to know what benefits would be coming to them. Zooey seemed to be the last word in spontaneity. Patricia would have loved her.

"You don't want to think about it?"

Zooey waved her hand dismissively. "Thinking only clutters things up." And then she hesitated slightly. "One thing, though."

Conditions. She was going to cite conditions, he thought. Jack braced himself. "Yes?"

A slight flush entered her cheeks. She looked at him uncomfortably. "Could you give me an advance on my salary?" He gazed at her quizzically, compelling her to explain the reason behind the request. "I sort of owe a couple of months back rent and the landlord is threatening me with eviction."

From out of nowhere, another impulsive thought came to Jack. He supposed that once the gates were unlocked, it seemed easier for the next idea to make its way through.

He refrained from asking her the important question outright, preferring to build up to it. "Do you like where you live?"

The elevator had reached the fourth level. Zooey got out behind Jack and Emily. A sea of cars were parked here.

Like was the wrong word, she thought, reflecting on his question. She didn't like the apartment, she made do with it. Because she had to.

"It's all I can afford right now," she admitted. "More than I can afford," she corrected, thinking of the amount she was in arrears. A whimsical smile played on her lips as she added, "But that'll change."

Did she have a plan, or was that just one of those optimistic, throwaway lines he knew even now she was prone to? "It can change right now if you'd like."

Zooey's smile faded just a tad as she looked at him. A tiny bit of wariness appeared. She was not a suspicious person by nature—far from it. For the most part, she was willing to take things at face value and roll with the punches.

But she was also not reckless, no matter what her father had accused her of that last day when they'd had their big argument, just before she'd taken her things and walked out, severing family ties as cavalierly as if they were fashioned out of paper ribbons.

"How?" she asked now.

"You can move in with me. With us," Jack quickly corrected, in case she was getting the wrong idea. "As a nanny." He moved Emily forward to underscore his meaning. "There's a guest room downstairs with its own bath and sitting area. From what you mentioned, it's larger than your apartment."

She rolled his words over in her head. It wasn't that

she minded jumping into things. She just minded jumping into the *wrong* things.

But this didn't have that feel to it.

Zooey inclined her head. "That way I could be on call twenty-four–seven."

"Yes." And then he realized that might be the deal breaker. "No." He shook his head. "I didn't mean—"

Zooey couldn't help the grin that rose to her lips. Here he was, a high-priced criminal lawyer, actually tripping over his tongue. Probably a whole new experience for him.

He looked rather sweet when he was flustered, she thought.

She was quick to put him out of his misery. "That's all right, Jack. I don't mind being on call twenty-four–seven. That makes me more like part of the family instead of the hired help."

Jack wasn't all that sure he wanted to convey that kind of message to Zooey. Right now, he had all the family he could handle. More, really, he thought, glancing at the deceptively peaceful-looking boy she held in her arms.

But as Jack opened his mouth to correct the mistaken impression, something cautioned him not to say anything that might put her off. He was, after all, in a rather desperate situation, and he wanted this young woman— the woman his children had taken to like catnip—to accept the job he was offering her. At least temporarily.

If things wound up not working out, at the very least he was buying himself some time to find another suitable candidate for the job. And if things *did* work out, well, so much the better. There was little he hated more than having to sit there, interviewing a parade of nannies and trying to ascertain whether or not they were dependable. So far, every one he'd hired had turned out to be all wrong for his children. Neither Emily nor Jackie *ever* liked who he wound up picking.

This was the first time they had approved.

And he had a gut feeling about Zooey. He had no idea why, but he did. She was the right one for the job.

Emily was becoming impatient, tugging on his hand. He pretended not to notice. His attention was focused on Zooey. "So does that mean you'll take the job?"

She wasn't attempting to play coy, she just wanted him to know the facts. "Seems like neither one of us has much choice in the matter right now, Jack. You've got your back against the wall and so do I."

She smiled down at Emily. The little girl seemed to be hanging on every word. In a way, Emily reminded Zooey of herself at that age. As the oldest, she'd been privy to her parents' adult world in a way none of her siblings ever had. There was no doubt in her mind that Emily understood what was going on to a far greater extent than her father thought she did.

Zooey winked at the little girl before looking up at Jack. "Lucky for both of us I enjoy kids."

As a rule, Jack liked having all his *i*'s dotted and his *t*'s crossed. She still hadn't actually given him an answer. "Then you'll take the job?"

He was a little anal, she thought. But that was all right. As a father, he was entitled to be, she supposed. "Yes, I'll take it." And then she looked at him, a whimsical smile playing on her lips. "By the way, how much does the job pay?"

She was being cavalier, he thought. Her attitude about money might have been why she'd found herself in financial straits to begin with. He was annoyed with himself for not having told her the amount right up front. He told her now, then added, "According to the last nanny, that's not nearly enough."

Zooey did a quick calculation in her head, coming up with the per hour salary. She had always had a gift for math, which was why her father had been so certain that getting an MBA was what she was meant to do. Zooey liked numbers, but had no desire to do anything with them. The love affair ended right where it began, at the starting gate.

Jack was going to be paying her more than twice what she'd gotten at her highest-paying job so far. She wondered if that was the going rate, or just a sign of his desperation.

"That should have been your first clue," she told him glibly.

He didn't quite follow her. "Clue?"

"That the woman was all wrong for the job." Still holding the sleeping Jackie, she ran a hand over Emily's hair. Zooey was rewarded with sheer love shining in the girl's eyes. "Nobody takes this kind of job to get rich," she informed him, "even at the rates you're paying. They do it because they love kids. Or at least, they should."

Reaching his car, Jack dug into his pocket for his keys. Once he had unlocked the vehicle, Zooey placed the sleeping boy in his arms.

This time, Jackie began to wake up, much to his father's distress. The ride to his Upstate New York home wasn't long, but a fussing child could make it seem endless.

"You're leaving?" Even as he asked her, he was hoping she'd say no.

But she nodded. When she saw the distress intensify,

she told him, "Well, I do have to get my things from my place."

But Jack wasn't willing to give up so easily. "Why don't you come home with us tonight, and then I'll help you officially move out on the weekend?"

Zooey raised her auburn eyebrows and grinned. "What's the matter, Jack, afraid I won't come back?"

"No," he told her adamantly. And then, remembering her comment about the truth, admitted, "Well, maybe just a little." Once the words were out, he was surprised by his own admission. "You know, what with time to think and all."

"You don't have anything to worry about," she assured him. "This is the best offer I've had since I left college."

He noticed that she'd said "left" rather than "graduated." He wondered if lack of funds had been responsible for her not getting a degree. If she worked out, he might be tempted to help her complete her education, he decided. That would definitely get her to remain.

"Give me your home address, Jack. And your home phone number," Zooey added. "Just in case I get lost." Her eyelid fluttered in a quick wink. "I'll be at your house bright and early tomorrow morning, I promise. By the way, when is bright and early for you?"

"Six-thirty."

"Ouch." At that hour, she'd be more early than bright, she thought. "Okay, six-thirty it is."

Setting Jackie in his car seat, Jack wrote out his address and number. Reluctantly. Wondering, as he gave her the piece of paper and a check for the advance she'd asked for earlier, if he was ever going to see her again.

Chapter 3

October

Zooey could still remember, months later and comfortably absorbed into the general routine of the Lever household, the expression of relief on Jack's handsome face that first morning she'd arrived on his doorstep. She'd had her most important worldly possessions stuffed into the small vehicle, laughingly referred to as a car, that was parked at his curb.

Funny how a little bit of hair coloring could throw a normally observant man for a loop. When she'd taken the job at the coffee shop, she'd been at the tail end of her experimental stage. Auburn had been the last color in a brigade of shades that had included, at one point, pink, and several others that were more likely to be found in a child's crayon box than in a fashion magazine.

Going back to her own natural color had seemed right as she opted to assume the responsibility of caring for a high-powered lawyer's children.

It was the last thing she'd done in her tiny apartment before she turned out the lights for the last time.

It had certainly seemed worth it the next morning as she watched the different expressions take their turn on Jack's chiseled face.

Finally, undoubtedly realizing that he'd just been standing there, he had said, "Zooey?" as if he were only seventy-five percent certain that he recognized her.

She'd drawn out the moment as long as she could, then asked, "Job still available?"

"Zooey," he repeated, this time with relief and conviction. A second later, he moved back, opening the door wider.

She had only to step over the threshold before she heard a chorus of, "Yay! Zooey's here." And then both children, Jackie in a sagging diaper and Emily with only one sock and shoe on, an undone ribbon trailing after her like the tail of a kite, came rushing out to greet her.

Jack had continued staring at her. "Why'd you dye your hair?" he finally asked.

"I didn't," she'd replied, laughing as two sets of arms found her waist, or at least made it to the general vicinity. Neither child seemed the slightest bit confused by the fact that she had golden-blond hair instead of auburn. "I undyed it." Raising her eyes from the circle of love around her, she'd looked at him. "It just seemed like the thing to do, that's all." She couldn't explain it to him any better than that. "This is my natural hair color."

Jack had nodded slowly, thoughtfully, as if the change

in color was a serious matter that required consideration before comment.

And then he'd said something unexpected. And very nice. "I like it." It was the first personal comment he had addressed to her.

Hard to believe, she thought now, as she threw on cutoff jeans beneath the football jersey she always wore to bed and slipped her bare feet into sandals, that nearly ten whole months had gone by since then. Ten months in which she'd discovered that each day was a completely new adventure.

She'd also discovered that she liked what she was doing. Not that her life's ambition had suddenly become to be the best nanny ever created since Mary Poppins. But Zooey did like the day-to-day life of being part of a family—a very important part. Of caring for children and seeing to the needs of a man who went through life thinking of himself as the last word in self-sufficiency and independence.

The very thought made Zooey laugh softly under her breath. She had no doubt that Jack Lever was probably hell on wheels in a courtroom, but the man was definitely *not* self-sufficient. That would have taken a great deal more effort on his part than just walking through the door and sinking into a chair. Which was practically all he ever did whenever he did show up at the house.

There were days when he never made it back at all, calling to say that he was pulling an all-nighter. There was a leather sofa in the office that he used for catnaps.

She knew this because the first time he'd called to say that, she'd placed dinner in a picnic basket and driven down to his office with the children. He'd been rendered speechless by her unexpected appearance. She and the kids had stayed long enough for her to put out his dinner, and then left. He was still dumbstruck when she'd closed the door.

Zooey wondered absently if her employer thought the house ran itself, or if he even realized that she was not only "the nanny," but had taken on all the duties of housekeeper as well.

It was either that, she thought, or watch the children go hungry, running through a messy house, searching for a clean glass in order to get a drink of water. Taking the initiative, she did the cooking, the cleaning, the shopping and the laundry, when she wasn't busy playing with the children.

She was, in effect, a wife and mom—without the fringe benefits.

As far as she knew, no other woman was on the receiving end of those fringe benefits. Jack Lever was all about work.

So much so that his children were not getting nearly enough of his company.

She'd mentioned that fact to him more than once. The first time, he'd looked at her in surprise, as if she'd crossed some invisible line in the sand. It was obvious he wasn't accustomed to having his shortcomings pointed out to him, especially by someone whose paychecks he signed. But Zooey was nothing if not honest. There was no way she would have been able to keep working for him if she had to hold her tongue about something as important as Emily and Jackie's emotional well-being.

"Kids need a father," she'd told him outright, pulling no punches after he'd said he wasn't going to be home that night. That made four out of the previous five nights that he'd missed having dinner with Emily and Jackie.

He'd scowled at her. "They need to eat and have a roof over their heads as well."

Men probably trembled when he took that tone with them, Zooey remembered thinking. But she'd stood up to her father, reclaiming her life, and if she could survive that, she reasoned that she could face anything.

"And the food and roof will disappear if you come home one night early enough to read them a story before bedtime?" she'd challenged.

He'd looked as if he would leave at any second. She was mildly surprised that he remained to argue the point. "Listen, I hired you to be their nanny, not my conscience."

She'd gazed at him for a long moment, taking his full measure. Wondering if she'd been mistaken about Jack. Then decided that he was worth fixing. And he needed fixing badly. "Seems like there might be a need for both."

Her nerve caught him off guard. But then, he was becoming increasingly aware that there was a great deal about the woman that kept catching him off guard, not the least of which was that he found himself attracted to her. "If there is, I'll tell you."

"If there is," she countered, "you might not know it. Takes an outsider to see the whole picture," she added before he could protest.

Jack blew out a breath. "You take an awful lot on yourself, Zooey."

In other words, "back off," she thought, amused. "Sorry, it's in my nature. Never do anything by half measures."

He'd made a noise that she couldn't properly break down into any kind of intelligible word, and then left for work.

He'd come home earlier than planned that night. But not the night that followed or any of the nights for the next two weeks.

Still, she continued to hope she'd get through to him, for Emily and Jackie's sake.

Jack was a good man, Zooey knew. And he did love his kids in his own fashion. The problem was, he seemed to think money was a substitute for love, and any kid with a heart knew that it clearly wasn't.

Someone, she thought, heading out of her bedroom toward the kitchen, had given the man a very screwed up sense of values. There was no price tag on a warm hug. That was because it was priceless.

She smelled coffee. Zooey knew for a fact that she hadn't left the coffee machine on last night.

Walking into the kitchen, she was surprised to see that Jack was already there. Not only had he beaten her downstairs, he was dressed for the office and holding a piece of burned toast in one hand, a half glass of orange juice in the other.

Not for the first time, she saw why he'd always come into the shop for coffee and a muffin. The man was the type to burn water. From the smell of it, he'd done something bad to the coffee.

"Good morning," she said cheerfully, crossing to the counter and the struggling coffeemaker. Taking the decanter, she poured out what resembled burned sludge—she'd never seen solid coffee before—and started to clean out the pot. "Sit down," she instructed, "and I'll make you a proper breakfast."

He surprised her by shaking his head as he consumed the rest of the burned offering in his hand, trying not to grimace. "No time. I'm due in early."

She glanced at her wristwatch; this was way ahead of his usual schedule. "How early?"

He didn't bother looking at his own watch. He could *feel* the time. "Half an hour from now." He washed down the inedible toast with the rest of his orange juice and set the glass on the counter. "Traffic being what it is, I should already be on my way."

"Without saying goodbye to the kids?" This was a new all-time low. She thought that pointing it out to him might halt him in his tracks.

Instead, he picked up his briefcase. "Can't be helped."

Zooey abandoned the coffee she was making. "Yes, it can," she insisted. Grabbing a towel, she dried her hands, then tossed the towel on the back of a chair. "I can get them up now." She saw impatience cross his face, and made a stab at trying to get through to him. "They go to sleep without you, they shouldn't have to wake up with you already gone as well."

An exasperated sigh escaped his lips as he told her, "Zooey, I appreciate what you're doing—"

If time was precious, there was none to waste. Zooey cut to the chase. "No, you don't. You think I'm a pain in the butt, and I can live with that. But the kids shouldn't have to be made to live without you. For God's sake, Jack, they see the mailman more than they see you."

He didn't have time for her exaggerations. "I have to leave."

Zooey stunned him by throwing herself in front of the back door, blocking his exit. "Not until you see the kids."

There were a hundred things on his mind, not the least of which was mounting a defense for a client who was being convicted by the media on circumstantial evidence. Jack didn't have time for this.

"This is a little too dramatic, Zooey," he informed her, "even for you."

He'd come to learn very quickly into her stay with them that the young woman he'd hired to watch over his children was not like the nannies who had come before her. Not in any manner, shape or form.

It seemed to him that if Zooey had an opinion about something he'd done or hadn't done, he heard about it. And if he was doing something wrong as far as the children were concerned, he'd hear about that, too. In spades.

While he found her concern about the children's welfare reassuring and their love for her comforting— absolving him of whatever guilt he might have for not taking a more active part in their lives—there were times, such as now, when Zooey went too far.

He glanced at his watch. "Zooey, I'm due in court in a little over an hour."

She stared at him, unfazed. "The longer you argue with me, the more time you lose."

His eyes narrowed as his hand tightened on his brief-case. "I could physically move you out of the way."

Zooey remained exactly where she was. "You could try," she allowed. And then she smiled broadly. "I know moves you couldn't even begin to pronounce."

He knew of her more than just passing interest in martial arts. Late one evening, he'd come across her on the patio as he investigated the source of a series of strange noises he'd heard. He'd found her practicing moves against a phantom assailant, and remembered thinking that he would feel sorry for anyone stupid enough to try anything with her.

Looking at her now, Jack had his doubts that she would use those moves against him. But he wasn't a hundred percent sure that she wouldn't. She was adamant when it came to the children.

He tried to appeal to her common sense. This was way before the usual time when Emily and Jackie got up. "You'll be waking them up."

Zooey appeared unfazed by the argument. "They'll be happy to see you. Besides, they have to get up soon anyway. I've got to get Emily ready for school."

He'd forgotten. The months seemed to swirl by without leaving an impression. It was October already. School had been in session for over four weeks now. There were times he forgot that his daughter went to school at all.

Maybe because he hadn't really become involved in her life, he still tended to think of Emily as a baby, hardly older than Jack Jr.

But even Jackie was growing up.

Jack blew out a breath. "Okay, let's go. I don't have time to argue."

Zooey beamed. She was generous in her victory. "That's what I've been saying all along." Still standing in the doorway, she gestured toward the rear of the house. "After you."

He eyed her, picking up on her meaning immediately. "Don't trust me?"

Growing up around her parents and uncle had taught her the value of diplomacy. Her parents were experts at it. So Zooey smiled, declining to answer his question directly. "Better safe than sorry."

They went to Emily's room first.

The little girl was fast asleep. Fanned out across her pillow, her hair looked like spun gold in the early morning sunbeams. Coming to the side of the bed, Zooey gently placed her hand on Emily's shoulder. She lowered her head until her lips were near her ear. "Emily, honey, your daddy wants to say goodbye."

One moment the little girl was asleep, the next her eyes flew open and she bolted upright.

Her expression as she looked at her father was clearly startled. And frightened. She clutched at his arm as if that was all there was between her and certain oblivion.

"You're leaving, Daddy?"

I knew this was a bad idea, Jack thought darkly. He ran his hand over the silky blond hair. "I've got to go, honey. I've got an early case in court today and Zooey seemed to think you wouldn't be happy unless I said goodbye."

Instantly, the panicky look was gone. The small, perfect features relaxed. She was a little girl again instead of a tiny, worried adult.

"Oh, that kind of goodbye." A smile curved her rosebud mouth. "Okay."

Jack was completely confused. He looked at Emily uncertainly. "What other kind of goodbye is there, honey?"

"Like Mommy's," his daughter told him solemnly.

This time, he raised his eyes to Zooey's face, looking for some sort of explanation that made sense. "What is she talking about?"

Zooey's first words were addressed to Emily, not him. "I'll be back in a few minutes to help you get ready, honey. In the meantime, why don't you lie down again and rest a little more."

"Okay." Emily's voice was already sleepy and she began to drift off again.

Turning toward Jack, Zooey hooked her arm through his. "C'mon," she whispered, as if he'd been the one to wake Emily up, and not her. Tugging, she gently drew him out of the room.

"What's she talking about?" he asked again the moment they cleared the threshold.

Instead of answering, Zooey looked at him for a second, searching for something she didn't find. He didn't know, she realized. But then, he hadn't been there during Emily's nightmares, hadn't seen the concern in the little girl's eyes whenever he was late getting home without calling ahead first.

"Emily is afraid that you're going to die."

Her answer flabbergasted him. He stared at her incredulously.

"What? Why?" he demanded. He hadn't done anything to make Emily feel that way. What had Zooey been telling her?

"Because her mother did," she answered simply, then went on quickly to reassure him in case he thought there was something wrong with Emily. "It's not an uncommon reaction for children when they lose one parent to be clinging to the other, afraid they'll die, too, and leave them orphaned. That's why I wanted her to see you before you left. So she knows that you're fine and that you're coming home to her. She needs that kind of assurance right now."

"So now you're into child psychology?" Jack didn't quite mean that the way it came out. His tone had sounded sarcastic, he realized. But it wasn't in him to apologize, so he just refrained from saying anything.

She treated it as a straightforward question. To take offense would be making this about her, and it wasn't. It was about the children.

"I dabbled in it, yes. Took a couple of courses," she added.

Jack was silent for a moment, then nodded toward his son's room. "And what's Jackie's story?"

"He picks up on Emily's vibrations," Zooey told him frankly. "Except at his age, even though he's very bright, he doesn't know what to make of them." And then she smiled. "Mostly, he just wants his daddy around. Like any other little boy."

Jack had never been one of those fun parents, the kind featured in Saturday morning cartoon show ads. He hadn't the knack for children's games, and his imagination only went as far as drafting briefs. He couldn't see why his children would care about having him around.

"Why," he demanded, "when they have you?"

"I'm more fun," Zooey admitted, "but you're their daddy and they love you just because of that. It's only natural that they'd want you to be part of their lives," she continued, when he didn't look as if he understood. "And for them to want to be part of yours. An important part," she emphasized, "not just an afterthought."

Jack shook his head. The lawyer in him was ready to offer a rebuttal to what she'd just said. But he held his tongue. Because deep down, part of him knew that Zooey was right. That he should be part of their lives far more than he was.

But right now, it wasn't possible. The demands on his time were too great, and he had to act while he could. That was how careers—lasting, secure careers—were made.

Lucky for his children—and him—he'd struck gold when he'd found Zooey.

He supposed that made a good argument for going along with impulse—as long as it could stand to be thoroughly researched, he added silently. Old dog, new tricks, he mused.

Standing before his son's door, Jack paused for half a second as he looked at Zooey over his shoulder. The harsh expression on his face had softened considerably. "Am I paying you enough?"

"Probably not," she responded, then waved him on. "Now go say goodbye to your son if you don't want to be late."

Now she was looking out for him as well. Jack shook his head. "Anyone ever tell you that you're too bossy?"

The list was endless, she thought, but out loud she said, "Maybe. Once or twice. I wouldn't have to be if you did these things on your own. Now open the door," she told him.

"Yes, ma'am," he murmured, amused, as he turned the doorknob.

Chapter 4

"See, that wasn't so hard, now was it?" Smiling broadly, Zooey shot the question at him three minutes later as she walked with him to the front door.

He stopped in the entry, a less than patient reply on his lips. It froze there as something seemed to crackle between them. It wasn't dry enough to be static electricity, but certainly felt like it.

And like something a little more...

Feeling like a man who was tottering on the brink, Jack pulled himself back. "I didn't say it would be hard, I said that it was—oh, never mind." He waved a hand in the air, dismissing the exchange he knew he'd be destined to lose. "I guess I should just be grateful that you're not with the D.A.'s office."

Her eyes crinkled as she grinned. She was going to get lines there if she wasn't careful, he thought.

"Attaboy, Jack. Always look at the positive side of things."

He didn't believe in optimism. The last time he'd felt a surge of optimism, he'd asked Patricia to marry him—hoping, unrealistically, for a slice of "happily ever after." What he'd wound up getting were arguments and seemingly irreconcilable differences—until her life, and their marriage, was abruptly terminated.

"I deal in facts," he told Zooey tersely.

Was that pity in her eyes? And what was he doing, anyway, staring into her emerald-green eyes.

"Facts can be very cold things," she told him. "At the end of the day, dreams are what get you through, Jack. Hopes and dreams are a reason to get up and strive tomorrow."

Had he *ever* been that idealistic? He sincerely doubted it. If he had, it was far too long ago for him to remember. "Mortgage payments and college tuition are reasons to get up and strive tomorrow."

Zooey cocked her head, her eyes looking straight into him. Into his soul. The touch of her hand on his felt oddly intimate.

"Don't you ever have any fun, Jack?"

He tried to shrug off the feeling undulating through him, the one she seemed to be creating. "You mean I'm not having fun right now?"

The expression on her face told him she took his flippant remark seriously. "You are if you love your work."

"I'm good at it." There was no pride in his answer. It was just another fact.

Zooey shook her head. He could have sworn he detected a whiff of jasmine.

"Not what I said. Or asked." Her eyes seemed to search his face. "Do you love your work, Jack?"

Love was too damn strong a word to apply to something like work, he thought. "When everything comes together, there is a surge of...something, yes."

The answer did not satisfy her.

He was a hard man to pin down, she realized. She wondered if he knew that, or if this verbal jousting was unintentional.

"A 'surge' isn't love, Jack." Zooey's voice softened a little and she leaned forward to smooth down his collar. "Love is looking forward to something. To thinking about it when you don't have to because you want to. Love is anticipation. And sacrifice."

She was standing too close, he thought. *He* was standing too close. But stepping back would seem almost cowardly. So he stood his ground and wondered what the hell was going on. And why. "For a single woman you seem to know a lot about love."

"Don't have to have a ring on your finger to know about love, Jack." The smile on her lips seemed to somehow bring her even closer to him. "Do *you* know about love?"

Okay, now he knew where this was headed. She was trying to get him to spend more time at home. Which would have been fine—if somehow his work could do itself. But it couldn't. "If you're asking me if I love my children, yes, I love my children. I also don't want them doing without things."

Again she moved her head from side to side, her eyes never leaving his. Where did she get off, passing judgment? Telling him how to be a father when she'd never been a parent? The desire to put her in her place was very strong, almost as strong as the desire to take her in his arms and kiss her.

Exercising the extreme control he prided himself on, Jack did neither.

"The first thing they shouldn't be doing without," she told him softly, "is you."

Okay, it was time to bail out. Now. "This conversation is circular."

His harsh tone did not have the desired effect on her. "That's because all roads lead to 'Daddy.'"

Retreat was his only option. So with a shrug, Jack turned to leave.

"Wait," Zooey cried, just as he crossed the threshold.

"Somebody else I forgot to say goodbye to?" he asked sarcastically. The woman was definitely getting under his skin and he needed to put distance between them. Before he did something that was going to cost him.

To his surprise, Zooey was dashing toward the living room. "No," she called over her shoulder, "but you did forget something." The next moment, she was back at the front door with his briefcase in her hands. She held it out to him with an amused smile on her face. "Here, you might need this."

Jack wrapped his fingers around the handle, pulling it to him with a quick motion she hadn't expected. The momentum had her jerking forward. And suddenly, there was absolutely no space between them. Not for a toothpick, not even for a sliver of air.

The foyer grew warmer.

Zooey could feel her heart accelerating just a touch as she looked up at him. Something threatened to melt inside her, as it always did when she stopped thinking of him as Emily and Jackie's father, or her boss, and saw him at the most basic level—a very good-looking man who did, on those occasions when she let her guard drop, take her breath away.

It was so still, she could hear her pulse vibrating in her ears.

"Wouldn't want you to go into the office without your briefcase," she finally said, doing her best to sound glib. Not an easy feat when all the moisture had suddenly evaporated from her mouth.

Damn it, it had happened again, Jack thought, annoyed with himself. From out of nowhere, riding on a lightning bolt, that same strong sense of attraction to her had materialized, just as it already had several times before. Each time, it felt as if a little more of his resolve was chipped away.

He had no idea why it overwhelmed him, when other times he could go along regarding her as his children's supernanny, a woman who somehow seemed to get everything done and not break a sweat. A woman his children seemed to adore and who could, thank God, calm them down even in their rowdiest moments.

All he knew was that every so often, every single pulse point in his body suddenly became aware of her as a woman. A very attractive woman.

He took a breath, trying not to appear as if his lungs had suddenly and mysteriously been depleted of the last ounce of oxygen.

"No, can't have that," he murmured, then nodded his head. "Thanks."

She smiled that odd little smile of hers, the one that quirked up in one corner. The one he wanted to kiss off her lips.

"Don't mention it."

Jack merely grunted, then turned and walked quickly

to the safe haven of the garage. He never looked back. Even so, he knew she was watching him.

She made him feel like a kid. The last thing he should be feeling, given the responsibilities weighing so heavily on his shoulders.

Damn it, what was wrong with him? He shouldn't be letting himself react to her.

But he had. And not for the first time.

This was going to be a problem, Jack thought, getting into his BMW. He couldn't act on his feelings. For the first time since Patricia had died, his children appeared to be happy. And thriving. If he gave in to the flash of desire—damn, it had been desire, he admitted with exasperation—and things went badly, what would he do? He hadn't the first idea how to conduct a successful relationship. He had no blueprints to follow, no natural ability of his own—Patricia had been the first to point that out to him.

Once things *did* turn sour between himself and Zooey, he mused, recapturing his train of thought, he'd be out one perfect nanny. And right back where he'd been in January, when he'd first asked Zooey to watch the kids.

No, whatever was going on inside of him would have to remain there, swirling and twisting, and he was just going to have to deal with it.

Heaven knew, he thought, driving away from his house and Danbury Way, dealing with "it" was a lot easier than sitting and interviewing another endless parade of less than perfect nannies.

Out of the blue, the realization hit him right between the eyes.

My God, he'd almost kissed her back there.

What the hell was the matter with him? Jack upbraided himself.

Sex, that was what was the matter with him, he decided. Sex. Or, more accurately, lack thereof.

Jack swerved to avoid a car that was drifting into his lane, coming from the opposite direction. He swore roundly under his breath, feeling as if someone was pushing him onto a very thin tightrope.

Or maybe that was just the pent-up hormones doing the talking.

He hadn't been with a woman since Patricia was killed. And hadn't been with her in a while, either, except for that one time that resulted in Jackie.

No wonder he felt so tense, Jack realized. He was an average male who had hormones roaming through his body like midnight looters. He needed an outlet.

For a second, as he approached the end of the long cul-de-sac, he all but came to a stop. It occurred to him just what he needed. It was, God help him, a date. He needed to spend time with a woman who would take his mind off Zooey.

Glancing into his rearview mirror, he saw Rebecca Peters standing outside her house. And she, as she turned around, saw him. Or at least his car.

The wide smile was unmistakable.

And it was also, he thought, a sign.

But one, he told himself, he was going to have to deal with later. Right now, he had a case to pull together.

"My stomach aches," Emily complained half an hour later as she sat at the breakfast table, staring into her bowl of cereal. The little girl pressed her lips together as if to keep from crying. "Can I stay home from school today?"

This was not the first time Emily had complained of a stomachache. There had been a number of other ailments cited as well, deployed as valid reasons for not going to school.

Zooey felt a slight tug on her heart. It brought back memories of early school days and those harsh feelings of not quite fitting in.

Glancing toward Jackie to make sure the boy was still securely belted into his high chair, she drew her chair closer to Emily's and sat down. "Do you have a test today?"

Avoiding her eyes, Emily continued to stare into her bowl and shook her head. "No."

Zooey took another stab, although she had a feeling she knew what lay at the bottom of Emily's sudden maladies. "A book report due?"

"Did it," Emily told the sinking golden balls of cereal in her bowl. "Miss Nelson says it's due next Friday."

Zooey looked at her closer. "Somebody picking on you in school?"

Emily's frown grew deeper. Sadder. She raised the spoon, only to tilt it and watch the milk and little golden balls go cascading back into the bowl.

"No."

There was too much hesitation, Zooey thought. She was on the right trail. "Are you sure nobody's teasing you?" she coaxed gently. "Emily, you can tell me. I want to help."

The little girl raised her head, and Zooey saw the glimmer of tears as she fought them back. "Nobody's teasing me, Zooey. They don't even see me. They're like Daddy. I'm not even there."

Wow, and wasn't that a mouthful? But at least they'd reached the heart of it. Big time. Emily was suffering from a case of loneliness—on all fronts, it appeared. She thought her dad was ignoring her, and nobody had time for a shy little girl at school.

Time for a change, Zooey decided.

She put her arm around the girl. Emily laid her head against her shoulder. Moved, Zooey stroked the child's silky hair with her free hand. If she had a little girl, she thought, she'd look like this. Like Emily. Small and delicate. And vulnerable.

She was going to change the last part, Zooey promised herself. "Sure they see you, honey. And I bet they're wondering why you won't talk to them."

Emily raised her head, her eyes frightened. "Talk to them? What'll I say?"

"Well, 'hi' for openers." Zooey thought for a moment, trying to remember what it was like being seven. "If they're playing a game, you could ask to join in."

"I don't know any games," Emily murmured. "The nannies Daddy hired kept us in the house. They said it was easier than following Daddy's rules."

Ah, yes, Zooey thought. *Daddy's rules.* The very same rules she completely disregarded. For an absent parent, the man had a myriad of rules to take the edge off his guilt. He was going to have to learn that it didn't work that way.

And, when it came to going out, she had noticed a certain reluctance, at least on Emily's part. The little girl seemed to be happiest sitting in front of the television set, a video game control pad in her hand. Since she'd heard that playing video games helped improve dexterity and hand-eye coordination, Zooey hadn't protested too much.

But it was definitely time to make a few changes.

Zooey thought of the kids in the house directly across the street. There were two boys and a girl living there—Anthony, who was nine, Michael, five, and Olivia, age seven—Emily's age. They belonged to Angela Schumacher, a single mom who worked as an office manager. The woman was a regular supermom, to the extent that when her younger sister, Megan, needed a place to stay, she'd taken her in as well.

But it was Olivia Zooey was interested in at the moment.

"Emily," she began slowly, "aren't you in the same class as Olivia—?"

Emily abandoned her cereal and looked up at Zooey, puzzled. "Yes."

"Do you like Olivia?" Zooey asked her innocently.

Emily nodded, her blond hair bobbing. "Everyone likes Olivia." There was a wistful note in the little girl's voice.

All systems are go, Zooey thought. Now they just had to wait for liftoff. She nodded at the bowl of cereal. "You about done with that?"

"Uh-huh." Emily pushed the bowl of soggy golden balls to the center of the table. "My stomach hurts," she repeated.

"We're going to fix that stomach," Zooey promised. Getting up, she crossed to Jackie and unstrapped him from the high chair. He all but bounced up, pivoting on the footrest and straining for freedom.

This boy has too much energy, Zooey thought. Lifting him out of the chair, she felt his legs immediately begin to wave back and forth as if he was attempting to propel himself upward.

All things considered, Zooey decided that it was

more prudent to hang on to the boy than to set him down. She tucked him against her hip.

"You're riding in style right now, fella." She turned toward his sister. "Emily, go get your backpack."

"Now?" she asked, even as she hurried to the corner by the counter where she had deposited her backpack on the way into the kitchen.

"Yes, now." Zooey grabbed her purse and slung the strap over her shoulder as she led the way to the front door.

"But we're early," Emily cried. This was definitely *not* what she had in mind. She wanted to avoid school, not get there early.

"We're not going to school just yet," Zooey told her. She held the door open, then locked it behind them. Pocketing her key, she bypassed the car in the driveway and continued walking. "First we have to make a stop at the house across the street."

Emily scrunched up her face, completely confused as she hurried to keep up with her nanny and her brother. "Why?"

"We're going to ask Olivia's mom if she'd like us to take Olivia to school with us."

"Olivia?" Emily repeated the name with hushed reverence. "In our car?"

"Why not?" Zooey stopped just shy of the neighbor's front door and looked at Emily, a whimsical smile playing on her lips. "Does she have cooties?"

Emily's face scrunched up again as she desperately tried to follow the conversation. "What's that?"

Zooey merely shook her head. Boy, things certainly changed a lot. Fast.

"Sorry, wrong generation, I guess." And then, because Emily was still looking up at her with a quizzical expression on her face, she explained, "Cooties are something that boys say girls have so they don't have to play with them."

Emily frowned, looking at her little brother. Jackie made a face at her, then laughed, secure in the sanctuary provided by Zooey's arms. "Boys are stupid."

Zooey laughed. "I'm sure your father will appreciate you holding that thought until you're at least thirty. Maybe older."

Standing in front of Angela Schumacher's door, Zooey shifted Jackie to her other hip and rang the doorbell. A minute or so later, she was about to ring a second time when the door finally opened.

She expected to see Olivia's mother in the doorway. Instead, it was Megan.

Even better, Zooey thought. She had gotten friendly with Olivia's aunt.

"Oh, hi." Megan's gaze swept over Zooey, taking in Jackie and Emily. She seemed mildly surprised to see them at this hour. "Are you looking for Angela?" Even as she asked, Megan glanced over her shoulder into the house.

Zooey stopped her before she could call out to her sister. "No, actually, we're looking for Olivia."

Turning back, Megan glanced at the little girl who was all but hiding behind Zooey. She smiled at her. Painfully shy, Emily shifted even farther behind Zooey. "My niece?"

"Yes. I thought that since both Olivia and Emily here—" she nodded at the child, who was attempting to morph into her own shadow "—go to the same school—"

"The same class," Emily told her in a stage whisper. "Miss Nelson's, remember?"

"Sorry," Zooey replied in the same stage whisper. "The same class," she said in a normal voice to Megan, "we thought we'd ask if your sister would like us to take Olivia to school with us this morning."

Megan looked a little taken aback by the unexpected offer. "Um, sure. I don't see why not." She held up her finger, as if to pause the action. "Just let me go and ask her. Come in, won't you?"

Zooey nodded and stepped in the door, Jackie still in her arms. Emily was right there behind them, clinging to the hem of Zooey's jacket.

Megan disappeared, calling out to Angela, loudly repeating the offer that had just been made.

It was a nice house, Zooey thought, looking around. But it felt a little lonely.

Both Megan and Angela appeared in less than two minutes. Olivia was between them, striding to keep up with the adults.

"Thank you," Angela said warmly. "Your offer is much appreciated." She flushed slightly. "I'm running behind this morning."

Zooey smiled. "Isn't everyone? Emily, why don't you take Olivia to the car? I'll be there in a second."

As Emily shyly took Olivia's hand and led her outside, Zooey turned toward Angela and quickly explained the sudden request for a carpool.

This morning was going to mark the beginning of the end of Emily's painful shyness.

Chapter 5

It dawned on Zooey in the middle of a left turn fifteen minutes later that she was beginning to have definite parentlike feelings when it came to dealing with the Lever children. Especially Emily.

These last few months she'd become closer to the little girl, ached for her when she seemed to be so alone or when Emily longed for her father to pay some attention to her. Zooey had become acutely aware of just what her own mother must have gone through raising *her*.

Of how her mom must have felt. And what had been going through her mother's mind when she'd wanted her to join the family firm.

Zooey had never thought of either of her parents as particularly bad people. She'd never felt rage, or gone through that I-hate-you period that some teenagers experienced, turning life into a living hell for themselves and their parents.

But she hadn't exactly been the easiest person to get along with, either. Admittedly, the last few years she'd been perverse, saying "day" when her parents and Uncle Andrew had said "night" just because she didn't want to be agreeable. Didn't want to walk the same path they walked. The one they wanted her to take.

She still didn't want to be part of the family business, but it suddenly dawned on her that her parents hadn't pushed for it because they wanted to be mean or didn't care about her dreams. They just wanted what they thought was the best for her.

Zooey's epiphany inside the silver SUV brought with it a slash of guilt that came equipped with big, sharp teeth. Said teeth took a sizable chunk out of her. There were words she did regret saying, people she did regret hurting.

She supposed that part of the trouble was that she knew, despite her seemingly breezy attitude, that she'd never thought she would measure up to what was expected of her. And, coming from two parents who were as close to perfect as was possible, she hadn't wanted to disappoint them. The best way to avoid certain disappointment was not to try in the first place. Not to get involved in what they wanted her to be involved in.

So she'd chucked it all—school, Connor, everything—in order to avoid presenting them with the ultimate disappointment: a daughter who was a failure on all fronts.

In its own circular way, that made sense to her. But probably not to anyone else.

"Sorry, Mom," she murmured under her breath, just as she glanced in the rearview mirror.

Emily was sitting in the middle of the backseat, with Jackie strapped into his car seat on one side and Olivia belted in on her other, directly behind the driver's seat.

Emily, Zooey noted, no longer had that distant-because-I'm-scared expression on her face. Good. She'd even heard Emily say a few words to Olivia. What was more important, Olivia had said a few words back. And they hadn't sounded as if they'd been squeezed out of the clogged end of a used tube of toothpaste. They had flowed freely. So freely that within a few minutes, Olivia began to chatter. And soon there was an actual conversation going on back there.

Zooey smiled to herself.

They were making progress. And it was probably a toss-up as to who was happier about it—her or Emily. Maybe it was a tie, Zooey thought, her smile spreading into a wide grin.

"Hey, Olivia?" Zooey raised her voice in order to be heard above the din. Politely, Olivia immediately stopped talking to listen. She'd chosen a good playmate for Emily, Zooey thought, congratulating herself. "Emily and I are thinking of going shopping this weekend."

"Shopping?" Olivia uttered the word with reverence and wistfulness.

"You know, for some new clothes for the fall." Not risking turning around, Zooey raised her eyes to the mirror again. Emily appeared surprised, but Olivia was fairly beaming. "Think you and your mom or your aunt Megan might be interested in joining us?"

As of yet, Emily hadn't developed any particular interest in acquiring new clothing. Zooey had a strong hunch that Olivia, even at this young, tender age, was a shopper.

The sparkle in the child's eyes told her she'd guessed correctly. "Sure," Olivia cried enthusiastically. "I'll ask my mom," she promised, then turned to Emily. "But she'll say yes. I know she will."

Emily nodded. Things were happening a little too fast for her to assimilate. She'd never had a friend before, other than her brother. But slowly, a smile slipped across her lips.

Zooey saw it and felt a surge of triumph. "Okay, then we'll consider it a date," she said to Olivia.

Now all she had to do, Zooey thought as she approached the school, was get Jack to sign off on this.

For once, Jack was getting home earlier than he'd expected. Or at least he'd left the office earlier than he'd been doing for the last few weeks.

He felt drained and yet wired. Wired because the morning's near-miss with Zooey hadn't quite faded from his mind, despite all the effort he'd put into forgetting it since he'd driven away from his house. Something seemed to be stirring inside of him. Something he didn't want stirring.

But he couldn't exactly go into hiding, either. He lived here, for God's sake. A man shouldn't feel uneasy coming home at night. Uneasy not because of what was waiting for him, but because of what he might be tempted to do.

As he turned the corner onto his street, he saw Bo Conway working on the car that stood in the driveway of Carly Anderson's house.

Bo's house pretty soon, Jack thought.

The house had been dubbed the McMansion by the other residents of Danbury Way because, for one thing, it was almost twice the size of the other homes on the block.

When Carly and her ex-husband moved in, the house had been like all the others along the cul-de-sac. And then they had bought the house next door as well because Carly wanted to merge the two houses together to create one great big one.

Bo Conway had been the last contractor on the scene, coming in to augment and tinker with the McMansion at the tail end of Carly's crumbling marriage. He'd stayed on to offer a shoulder to cry on. And that turned into an offer to love, honor and cherish. Or words to that effect.

The words themselves would be uttered soon, Jack knew, because what Bo had ultimately repaired was Carly's broken heart and very damaged self-esteem. When her husband suddenly declared that he was leaving because he was no longer in love with her, Carly Anderson's entire world had crashed and burned. She had, according to rumor, lost all hope, all faith that life held anything for her but emptiness. Amid all the wealth she had surrounded herself with, she was very poor.

But Bo had fixed all that, Jack thought as he pulled his BMW into the driveway and set the hand brake.

Too bad there wasn't some kind of magic around to fix him, he mused. Because he felt he was just as much a member of the walking wounded as Carly had been.

Except that he wasn't able to divert himself by adding on to the house or turning bedrooms into dens. His answer, he knew, was to work. Because work was something he was good at. Life, apparently, was not. His marriage had been doomed even before the accident. Oh, he'd had all sorts of hopes when he'd married Patricia. Delusional hopes, he now realized.

He had absolutely no idea how to love someone, how

to conduct a satisfying and satisfactory relationship. There were no examples to follow in his life, no blueprints to emulate. He hadn't a clue.

All he knew was work. So he'd buried himself in it again, only to be told that he was shortchanging his kids.

Getting out of his car, Jack called out a greeting to Bo. The tall, muscular, brown-haired man was everything he wasn't, Jack thought—warm, friendly, outgoing. And, from what he'd heard, Bo came from a close-knit family. Jack had no idea how that felt, what that meant. To him, "close" meant standing next to one another—certainly not sharing feelings or fears or thoughts, all of which he now found himself unable to do.

It was a sad, vicious cycle. God, but he envied Bo.

About to walk into his house, Jack was surprised when the man waved him over. Welcoming the diversion, Jack crossed the yard to the McMansion and nodded at Bo, who was doing something with the car he was working on that Jack wouldn't have understood if his life depended on it.

"Hi, what's up?"

Bo wiped his hands on the back of his jeans, his biceps rippling as he did so.

I've got to get back to the gym, Jack thought.

Coming closer, Bo asked in a low voice, "Can you keep a secret?"

Jack thought it was an odd question. They were friends, granted, but it wasn't exactly as if they'd become close. Still, he felt a little pleased at being approached.

"I'm a lawyer," Jack reminded him. "I'm supposed to be closemouthed."

Bo grinned, inclining his head. "Yeah, but this doesn't exactly come under the heading of attorney-client privilege."

Jack saw his point. He nodded and said, rather solemnly, not knowing what to expect, "Yes, I can keep a secret."

Bo looked around, just in case someone was listening, but for once, and probably only for a moment, Danbury Way was devoid of people, young or old. "Carly and I are getting married."

Jack laughed. "Hate to rain on your parade, but that's not much of a secret, Bo. Everyone around here kind of suspected that."

Bo shook his head. "No, I mean next week." He lowered his voice even more, although it was obvious he found it hard to contain his enthusiasm. "We're eloping."

"Eloping?" Jack repeated the word skeptically. "Are you sure Carly wants that?"

Bo was a down-to-earth kind of guy, but everyone knew Carly liked all the trimmings. If something could be done on a small scale or a grand one, she'd choose grand every time. According to what Patricia had once told him, twelve bridesmaids had been in attendance at Carly's wedding to Greg. Jack fully expected there to be fourteen this time around.

But Bo seemed to have other ideas. "Definitely. Carly said she wants this to be as different from her first wedding as possible. It's going to be just her, me and a preacher to make it legal. And a couple of witnesses off the street," he said. "Would you mind looking after the place while we're gone? I've installed a great security system, but you never know. Burglars always seem to be one step ahead."

Jack thought it odd that Bo should ask him instead of Molly Jackson or Rebecca Peters, the people who lived in the houses on either side of Carly's. But then, he supposed that Bo felt more comfortable asking a guy to look after things.

"I'm not around that much, but sure, I'll keep an eye out for you when I'm here. I can get Zooey to pick up the mail and hold on to it until you two get back." It occurred to him that he was volunteering Zooey's services as if they were a set, and hoped that Bo didn't get any wrong ideas.

But Bo seemed too blissfully happy to notice. "Perfect." He nodded, pleased. "Knew I could count on you. I'd offer to bring you back a souvenir from Maui, but I don't think Carly and I will be leaving the hotel room very much." Bo grinned broadly as he looked at him. "There's nothing like being in love, Jack."

"I really wouldn't know," Jack murmured.

"That's because all you do is work." Bo hit the back of his hand against Jack's chest, as if to remind him that there was a heart there whose function was to do more than just pump blood. "You really need to get out more often, buddy."

Jack knew Bo meant well. People who were in love wanted the rest of the world to join them, but the last thing he wanted was romantic advice. In his case it was as useless as offering a pair of earmuffs to a frog.

"Yeah, well…" His voice trailed off.

Bo apparently wasn't about to let the matter drop so easily. "I'm sure Rebecca wouldn't mind if you asked her out."

"Rebecca?" He wasn't a man who noticed women looking at him, but he would have had to be blind not to notice the interest in the freelance photographer's eyes whenever their paths crossed.

"Sure." Bo nodded toward the woman's house. After him, Rebecca was the "new kid" on the block, having moved here from New York City, and she stuck out like a sore thumb. She moved fast, talked fast and was in general fast. "Haven't you noticed the way that woman all but drools whenever you drive by?" Bo winked. "Try walking by instead. As a matter of fact, I know she's home now. I saw her car pull up less than twenty minutes ago. Why don't you stop by, ask her out for coffee sometime."

This was going a lot faster than Jack was comfortable with. "I don't know..."

But Bo was not about to let him back away. "That's just the point. You can't know, until you do something about it. You know what they say—all work and no play makes Jack a dull boy."

Jack had never liked that cliché. Besides, he wasn't sure if he actually wanted to go out with Rebecca. Oh, the woman was extremely attractive in a smoldering, sexy sort of way, but when he came right down to it, that wasn't really his type.

Hell, he didn't know what his type was. Lately he'd found himself feeling attracted to Zooey—the nanny, for heaven's sake. It wasn't as if his experience had taken him far and wide. Once he'd left high school behind, there'd only been Patricia. He'd always been too busy trying to make something of himself to go the partying route in college. After graduation, he'd really buckled down.

Bo picked up the two rags he'd dropped on the ground and placed them on the hood of the car. "Since you seem to have lead in your feet, why don't I just walk you over there?"

Jack stared at him. "And I do what—knock on her door and ask her out?"

The look on Bo's face said he expected him to do exactly that. "Sure, why not? Hey, Jack, it's done all the time."

He had no doubt that it was, yet that didn't make him comfortable with the notion. "Maybe, but not by me."

Bo looked at him seriously. "Maybe it's time to start."

"If I run into her, perhaps," Jack allowed. "But if I have to go to her house, then no, it doesn't seem casual enough. I—"

Bo was looking at something over his shoulder. And grinning. "Guess what."

"What?" But even as he asked, Jack had a feeling he knew exactly what was coming.

Putting his hand on Jack's shoulder, Bo turned him around.

While they'd been talking, Rebecca had come out of her house. She was standing on her porch, hands on her hips as she scanned the area. The crisp fall wind was weaving sensuously through her hair.

Bo inclined his head toward Jack, so his voice wouldn't carry. "She just stepped out of her house. Casual enough for you?" And then he straightened, looking pleased. "It's fate, man," he assured him. "Nothing less than fate stepping in."

Maybe it was at that, Jack thought. After all, hadn't he been thinking about some sort of a diversion, something to get his mind off Zooey's being anything more than a fantastic nanny? If he started seeing someone else, then maybe that would take the edge off the way he was feeling. Maybe those damn "stirrings" that were going on in his gut would subside and disappear.

It was worth a try.

Zooey looked toward the door for possibly the tenth time in as many minutes. It was still not moving, still not opening. She sighed.

She was certain she'd heard Jack's car pull up in the driveway a full ten minutes ago, but there was no sign of him yet. What was taking him so long? She didn't want to seem as if she was standing around, listening for the sound of his car, but on the other hand, what if something was wrong? What if he was sitting out there, wrestling with something he wanted to say to her?

There'd definitely been something humming between them this morning. Neither one of them had acted on it, but it had been there.

Had it put him off? Made him reconsider having her live on the premises? Or was he just being a typical male, not knowing how to react?

Or was it something simpler than that? Did it have to do with the kids? Had she been too pushy this morning, all but marching him up the stairs to say goodbye to Emily and Jackie? She wondered if he expected her to apologize for that.

Zooey chewed on her lower lip, thinking. She couldn't very well apologize to the man for wanting him to take a more active role in his kids' lives. As their nanny, she was *supposed* to have their best interests at heart.

Damn it, where *was* he?

She had an excuse, she told herself, to go to the window and look for him. She wanted to tell him about the progress Emily had made today and about the proposed shopping trip this Saturday.

Her mouth curved in a smile. Technically, she did need his permission for that, especially since she was going to be spending his money on Emily's new fall wardrobe.

Zooey blew out a breath and headed for the door with long, purposeful strides. She was just about to pull it open when she heard a key being inserted in the lock. The next second, the door opened and Jack walked in.

"Hi." She offered him a sunny smile, taking his brief-case from him and placing it at the base of the coatrack, the way he always did when he first walked in. "You're home early. Taking my advice? Or did your firm suddenly run out of clients?"

"Neither." He shrugged out of the light topcoat he had on, hanging it up. "Court got out early."

"Hungry?" She was already turning toward the kitchen. "I made pot roast."

That was what was different, he realized. It was quiet. Whenever he came home early—in Jack's world, that meant anytime before 7:00 p.m.—it took exactly five seconds before he was surrounded by short people. But there was no sound of running feet, no greetings of "Daddy!" echoing through the air.

He looked at Zooey. "Where are the kids?"

"Jackie fell asleep right after dinner, so I put him to bed." She smiled fondly. "Emily is still at Olivia's house."

He tried to place the name and couldn't. "Who's Olivia?"

"The little girl across the street. Her mother's Angela Schumacher. Her aunt's Megan Schumacher, the woman

Greg Banning is seeing. Carly Anderson's ex," she added for good measure.

Zooey certainly kept up on the neighborhood gossip a lot more than he did. And then he replayed her words in his head. "Emily's at someone else's house?" Since when did that happen?

"She's playing," Zooey declared triumphantly. She backtracked a little. "Haven't you noticed how shy Emily is?"

His shrug was careless. "She's a little girl." As far as he knew, because he had no experience, all little girls were shy.

Zooey laughed. The man needed to have his stereotypes updated. "Don't know many little girls, do you? They're shy for a minute and a half, until they get to know you, then they're live wires. Emily's precocious and she makes a lot of waves at home, but when it comes to being around girls her own age, she is *painfully* shy."

He didn't follow. "So what's she doing at someone else's house?"

Zooey paused to fluff up a pillow that had been flattened earlier by Jackie. "Hopefully, getting over her shyness. I volunteered to take Olivia to school today. They're in the same class," she added, guessing that he probably wouldn't know that. "After school, they did their homework together here, had dinner together and then went to Olivia's to play." It was hard to keep the note of triumph out of her voice. So far, things were going swimmingly. "And, this coming Saturday, the four of us are going out to shop."

"Shop?" He frowned. He would rather endure a root canal. "I can't go shopping."

She was getting ahead of herself. "Sorry, not the four of *us*—" she vaguely pointed to him and then herself

"—the four of us. Emily, Olivia, her aunt Megan and me," she elaborated.

He was probably going to have to go into the office at some point Saturday. He couldn't do that if no one was home to watch his son. "What about Jackie?"

"Arrangements are being made," Zooey assured him complacently. She wasn't about to tell him that she was planning on asking her mother to watch the boy, not until she was certain it was possible. She hadn't spoken to her mother in over ten months, just before she'd taken that job at the coffee shop. They'd had a huge fight over it and Zooey had stormed out of the house.

She regretted that now.

She cocked her head, looking at Jack curiously. "You sounded adamant about not being able to go with us. Is it just the typical male phobia about malls and shopping in general, or are they chaining you to the courthouse over the weekend?"

"Neither. Actually, I do have to do some work in the early afternoon, and after that…" Jack paused, searching for the right words to phrase this, then told himself he was being ridiculous. What he did or didn't do with his social life shouldn't matter one way or another to Zooey. She was just making conversation. "I have a date Saturday night."

It was one of the very few times in her life that Zooey found herself at a loss for words.

Chapter 6

It took her several very long seconds before she could locate her tongue, and several more before she could get it in gear well enough to form words. The numbness that had descended over her body felt like an encasing plastic garment bag, sucking away her air.

"A date?"

"Yes. With Rebecca Peters." Even as he said it, he was having doubts. Had he just allowed himself to be railroaded into something? Or was this the only course he could take, under the extenuating circumstances he found himself grappling with?

Zooey continued to stare at him. When had all this happened? "From down the block?"

"Yes." If he'd ever been more uncomfortable in his life, Jack would have been hard-pressed to remember when. "Is that a problem?"

Yes, it's a problem, you big, dumb jerk. "No." She

forced a smile to her lips. "Why should it be a problem?" God, but her voice sounded hollow. *Why aren't you asking me out if you feel the need to go out with someone?*

"No reason, you just looked like—" Jack shook his head.

He'd thought she looked upset, but maybe he was projecting his own feelings onto her. He didn't want her to think that he felt she was attracted to him. It was the other way around that was the problem.

He cleared his throat, desperately searching for something to send the conversation in another direction. "You said something about pot roast?"

Yes, how'd you like to wear it? She'd hoped, as little as a few minutes ago, that they could enjoy a quiet meal together. Now her appetite had completely vanished.

"It's in the kitchen. I'm going to go get Emily," she murmured.

She didn't mean to slam the front door as she left; the handle just slipped out of her hand.

Hands clenched at her sides, more from anger than the nippy October evening and the fact that she'd left the house wearing only her pullover sweater, Zooey made her way across the street.

As she went down the walk, she heard very distinct, plaintive cries: Jackie was waking up from his premature nap. She could almost visualize the distressed look on Jack's face.

Zooey just kept walking. *Good, call your girlfriend and ask her to handle that.*

Despite her enthusiasm and zest, Zooey had always been a good poker player, able to maintain an expressionless mask on her face even when holding a winning hand. And that skill was coming in handy now. There was no way she was going to let Jack see that his newly invigorated social life had any effect on her at all.

So instead, she went about life for the next three days as if he hadn't dropped a bomb on her. As if she didn't want to do the same, literally, on number 4 Danbury Way, where Rebecca Peters had taken up residence.

Even so, it took everything Zooey had to keep her temper in check and to go about business as usual. For one thing, it wasn't as usual. Jack was going out. He had a date. With someone else.

Damn it.

She'd hoped, fantasized, that when the time came that Jack Lever could be torn away from his court cases and his legal briefs, she'd be the one he'd do the tearing for, not some brown-haired, blue-eyed, curvy ex-fashion magazine contributor.

She'd been fooling herself, she supposed, but damn it, she'd felt certain that there was chemistry between them. Was positive when he looked at her, he felt the same way.

Get with the program, Zooey, she upbraided herself. Jack Lever's social calendar wasn't supposed to be the dominant thing in her life. She had responsibilities, things to do.

She blew out a breath. Right now she needed to confirm that Saturday's shopping trip was a "go."

Pressing her lips together, Zooey looked up at the five-story building she was parked in front of. The building that housed the corporate offices of Finnegan's Fine Furniture.

She couldn't put this off any longer. She could take Jackie tomorrow, but that would definitely put a crimp in Emily's day, and the little girl deserved to enjoy it without having her rambunctious brother in tow. Although Zooey loved Jackie as if he were her own, she knew he could be one huge pain when he wanted to be.

Not for nothing did they call it the terrible twos, she thought.

Zooey frowned. Time to get with it.

She turned in her seat to look at the little boy in the car seat behind her. "Well, I guess we can't stay here all morning, huh?"

"No," Jackie declared, using his newly acquired favorite word.

She laughed at him, shaking her head, then turned around again and looked back at the building as she released her seat belt. How had so much time managed to slip by? she wondered, still mentally dragging her feet.

"Okay, here goes nothing."

"No."

"Easy for you to say."

With her fingers on the door handle, ready to open it, she still hung back a second longer. This was a first, she supposed. She'd never felt nervous before, not about seeing her own mother. But then, she had never teetered on the edge of estrangement, either.

Getting out of the car, Zooey rounded the back and went to the rear passenger side, where Jackie sat strapped in his car seat.

It was chilly this morning, she thought, hunching her shoulders. Or maybe she just felt cold because she was nervous.

The second she opened the door, Jackie's waving feet went into double time. He really wanted to get out, Zooey realized. "Settle down, Jackie," she soothed.

The feet went faster as he grinned, looking like an angelic little devil. "No!"

She sighed. "Have it your way."

Unbuckling him, she took the boy out and planted him firmly on her hip. She knew that taking his hand and having him walk on his own would have been better for the boy, but she was in a hurry, and the only time those little legs of his pumped fast was when he was fleeing the scene of his latest crime.

Zooey walked through the front door of the building and looked slowly around the lobby. There were a handful of paintings on the wall.

It looked, she thought, just as she remembered it. Of course, not a whole lot of time had gone by, but somehow, part of her had expected that it would look different. Because she *felt* different. Wiser.

She nodded to the guard at the front desk and crossed to the elevator. She could tell by the old man's expression that he was trying to place her and was unsuccessful. She hadn't exactly been a regular visitor here even when things had been going fairly well at home.

When she'd actually thought she had a shot at being the person she felt everyone in the family wanted her to be.

The elevator car arrived and she stepped into it. A second later, it was time to step off again. The aluminum doors opened onto a plush, airy second floor. There was a receptionist sitting at a desk that seemed to run half the length of the hall.

It all looked so classy. She could remember when everything had been operated from their garage. She couldn't have been more than Emily's age. Seventeen years had brought about a lot of changes.

Her parents had done very well for themselves, she realized. The rush of pride was a surprise, and she savored it.

"Excuse me, do you have an appointment?" the young woman called as Zooey walked right by her toward the offices in the rear of the building.

"Don't need one," Zooey stated over her shoulder.

"No," Jackie sang out.

"You tell her, kid," she laughed.

The receptionist was on her feet immediately, hurrying after her. "Wait," she cried. "You can't go in there without an appointment."

Zooey made it to her mother's office door and smiled to herself. For a young thing, she certainly wasn't in very good shape, Zooey thought.

"Mrs. Finnegan, I'm sorry," the young woman panted breathlessly, "but she—"

Frances Finnegan looked up from the computer monitor and last quarter's financial statements that she was reviewing. Surprise washed through her as the sight of her daughter registered. Zooey was the last person she'd expected to see walking in. And what was she doing with a baby?

She looked at the child carefully. There was no resemblance. Not to Zooey, or to any of her other children when they were that age. Did he look like his father?

Had Zooey gotten married to a man with a ready-made family?

"That's all right, Liz." Frances slowly rose to her feet, her eyes never leaving her daughter and the little boy riding her hip. As an afterthought, Frances waved the receptionist away. "This is my daughter, Zooey."

"Oh." The woman looked as if she could have been knocked over with a sneeze. "Then it's all right," she murmured, backing away.

"Is it?" Zooey asked, gazing at her mother. Her mom

made no answer as the receptionist left, closing the door. "You look good, Mom."

"You look thin," Frances responded. "You're not eating enough." It wasn't a criticism, it was an observation. By now, she was standing in front of Zooey. "May I?" she asked.

"Sure. Careful," she cautioned as her mother took Jackie into her arms, "he's a live wire."

Frances glanced at her daughter. She did love Zooey. Very much. And she'd missed her these past months. It had almost killed her to give Zooey the space she'd wanted. "And you weren't?"

Zooey shrugged carelessly. "I can't remember that far back."

"Trust me," Frances assured her, her voice now warm, "you were." A wide smile replaced the cautious look. "What's his name?"

"Jackie. Jack Jr. John, Junior, really," Zooey corrected. Since Jack never used his legal name, she tended to forget what was actually entered on their birth certificates.

Frances nodded. It had been a long time since she'd held a child in her arms. Every maternal bone in her body woke up and rejoiced at the contact with this soft bundle of perpetual motion. She made the boy comfortable against her. He cuddled close and she savored the feeling.

"Jackie," Frances repeated. The little boy began to wiggle again in response to his name. "Hi, Jackie," she murmured with a smile. She looked up at her daughter again. "Whose is he? Not yours, right?"

There was a hint of longing in her mother's voice. Zooey felt a smattering of guilt. Had she married Connor the way her parents had both hoped, she might have been well on her way to giving them their first grandchild.

Zooey banished the thought from her brain. No point in thinking about things that mercifully never came to pass.

"No, he's not mine." She stroked the boy's hair. It was getting rather long, she thought, absently. Time for a haircut soon. "I'm just responsible for him."

There was no emotion in Frances's voice, but her eyes gave her away. "You're babysitting now?"

Long ago, when she'd left college, Zooey had tried to make peace with the fact that she was going to be a disappointment to her parents. Still, it hurt to be in the same room as that disappointment, to see it take form.

"It's a little more professional-sounding than that, Mom. I'm a nanny."

"A nanny," Frances echoed. "With a near-genius IQ." She supposed it was a step up from dog walking, and tied with waitressing, but when she thought of the hopes she'd had for Zooey, the dreams…

Frances caught herself. This wasn't the way she wanted things to go with her daughter. "Sorry. I swore the next time I saw you, I wouldn't be judgmental." She looked down at Jackie. "Is this your way of trying to reconcile? Bringing me a baby to hold?"

"No baby!" Jackie declared.

Frances raised her eyes to Zooey's in barely suppressed amusement.

"He's two," Zooey told her with just a hint of exasperation.

Frances smiled, remembering. Relieved that those years were long gone. And yet, in hindsight, things had been simpler back then. And the world a great deal smaller.

She nodded, looking at the boy. "That would explain it."

Her mother was a natural at this, Zooey thought, watching her. Funny how she'd never realized that until now. "I was wondering if you could watch him for me."

"Now?" Her tone indicated that it wouldn't have been out of the question, even if the answer was yes.

"No," Zooey told her quickly. She peered at her mother's face. "It would be just for a few hours. This Saturday."

"Why me?"

"Because you're the best person for the job," Zooey told her honestly. There was more she needed to say. Years to apologize for. She wasn't sure just where to start. Taking a breath, she plunged in. "Look, Mom, I've been doing this for a while now—"

Curiosity got the better of Frances. "What's 'a while'?"

"Ten months." Her momentum breached, Zooey began again. "And it's taught me something."

Frances offered the keys to her Porsche to Jackie, who was immediately fascinated. His eyes sparkled as he took them in his chubby hands.

"Patience?" Frances guessed, looking over his head at her daughter.

"Among other things," Zooey allowed, veering back on track again. "Mainly it's taught me that you and Dad went through a lot raising me. Raising Kim and Ethan and Tyler, too," she added, lest her mother thought she was singling herself out. "And…" Oh, what the hell. She could go on for hours with this. In the interest of brevity, she got to the bottom line. "Look, Mom, I'm sorry."

Puzzled, Frances stopped making funny faces at

Jackie, who was a very receptive audience, and looked up at her daughter. "Come again?"

"I'm sorry," Zooey repeated, this time with more feeling. "I'm sorry for the grief I gave you, and for all the hard times."

Frances could hardly believe what she was hearing. This didn't sound like her headstrong, stubborn daughter. She treaded lightly.

"Does this mean you're coming back? That you'll work in the business?"

That was a little further ahead than she'd intended on going right now.

Zooey smiled. "No. It means I don't want to be estranged anymore."

Shifting Jackie to her hip as easily as Zooey had, Frances laced her free arm around her daughter's shoulders, bringing her closer and kissing her forehead. "I never was. Your father and I just let you have that 'space' you kept clamoring for."

"And I appreciate it," Zooey told her honestly. "I also don't want as much of it as I thought I did." Her mother stared at her, surprised and pleased. "I know that you just want the best for me."

Jackie had latched on to her necklace. Gently, Frances disengaged his fingers and held them. She was nothing short of astounded at this epiphany her daughter had gone through. "That must be some job you have."

"It has its moments," she admitted.

Zooey went to take Jackie from her mother, thinking that she'd probably had enough for a first dose. To her surprise, she shook her head. Her mom had more endurance than she'd remembered.

After being cut off for over ten months, Frances was hungry for details. "How many children are there?"

"Two." Zooey knew better than to say, "just two." At times Emily and Jackie seemed more like an army. "Jackie and his sister, Emily. She's seven and very shy. I'm trying to get her to come around a little."

Frances shook her head. "Can't force these kinds of things."

"I know." Zooey was working from memory here, realizing what it was like to be seven. She couldn't remember what it was like to be shy because she'd never been that way a day in her life. "But there's a little girl across the street who's in Emily's class. I'm taking the two of them shopping tomorrow. That's why I need someone to watch the baby." She stroked Jackie's hair again.

"What's wrong with leaving him with his parents?" Frances asked matter-of-factly. Seemed to her that parents should want to spend time with the children they'd brought into the world. She'd had a career and still managed to make time for four children in various stages of growth. Never once did she think she was doing anything out of the ordinary. "I can't see them not wanting to be with this huggable sweetie."

"Parent," Zooey corrected. "There's only one."

She saw curiosity in her mother's eyes. "Divorced?"

Zooey shook her head. "Widower."

"So then you're working for a single father?" Frances asked with interest.

"Yes." She knew her mother. She needed to give Jack's credentials quickly before Frances Finnegan allowed her imagination to run wild. "He's a partner at a law firm—a criminal lawyer," she added, not knowing if that was a good thing in her mother's eyes.

A slight frown flickered across Frances's face. Obviously not a good thing, Zooey thought.

"I certainly hope he doesn't bring his work home."

Zooey sighed. "He rarely brings himself home."

Frances made the natural leap, given the information. "Then you live there?"

"Yes," Zooey said slowly, wondering if that was going to be a problem for her mother. She'd once thought of her mom as an extremely closed-minded woman—before she'd realized what it was like to worry about someone you cared about.

Jackie threw down the keys. Frances scooped them up and set them aside, jiggling the child ever so slightly to keep him quiet. It was second nature to her. "And what's this criminal lawyer's name?" she asked.

Oh, God, she wasn't going to sic a P.I.on Jack, was she? "Mom, don't get all maternal on me—"

Frances gave her a serene smile. "Isn't that why you came?"

Zooey paused. "I came to mend fences and to ask for help. Limited help," she stressed. "He's a very nice man, Mom."

Now just a hint of suspicion appeared in her eyes. "Exactly how nice?"

"Up to your standards nice," Zooey told her. And then, because she could see her mother needed a little more convincing, she added, "Like Connor, except without the greed."

Frances had always been quick to defend those she'd taken a liking to, and she was not yet disenchanted with her firstborn's ex-fiancé.

"Connor wasn't greedy."

"You never knew the real Connor, Mom." Zooey's engagement had long been a thing of the past, and she wanted to keep it that way. "But I didn't come here to talk about him—"

Frances looked at her. There was something Zooey needed to be told. "He's dating Kim, you know."

The information caught Zooey off guard. Kim had always been competitive, wanting everything her sister had. There were times when Zooey thought her sibling didn't have the sense to come out of the rain—not if she was trying to beat someone out. Zooey also knew that there was no way Kim would listen to anything she had to say.

Kim was at that age, Zooey realized. How did their mom stand it?

"Tell her to run for the hills" was Zooey's only comment. And then she smiled brightly, getting back to the reason for her visit. "So, will you do it? Will you watch Jackie for me tomorrow?"

"How could I say no to such a handsome young man?" Frances laughed, giving Jackie one last hug before she surrendered him back to Zooey. "Come to the house and leave him as long as you like." She paused for a moment before adding, "On one condition."

Zooey knew better than to say yes before she knew all the details. Uncle Andrew had taught her that, too. "And that condition is?"

"You say hello to your father."

Well, that wasn't really a hardship, especially seeing as how she wanted to get back into the fold. "Done," Zooey declared.

Frances took the hand she offered and shook it. "Done."

Chapter 7

"Look, Daddy, look!" Emily cried excitedly as she erupted through the door like a stick of TNT that had just been discharged.

Standing in the living room, Jack swung around to peer at his daughter, not quite knowing what to expect.

He had gotten in from the office less than half an hour ago and had been surprised to discover that no one was home yet. The silence was deafening and he found himself feeling restless. For more than one reason. Restless because he was accustomed to the feeling that his children were somewhere in the house, sleeping or causing havoc, and there was an odd sort of comfort in that knowledge.

Restless, too, because of the evening that still lay ahead of him.

He wasn't really comfortable about this "adventure" he was embarking on.

Jack's social skills began and ended in his professional world, where there was a safety net in place and where whatever went on could touch him only so far and no further. He had control over his professional life. *Felt* in control.

On a personal level, however, a completely different set of boundaries and parameters came into play. He felt as if he was out in the open, exposed. He didn't like that feeling, and that was exactly what dating did to a man—it put him out in the clearing, away from any sort of protective covering. Like a buck at the height of deer hunting season.

If he'd had a choice, Jack knew he wouldn't be going through this.

But he didn't have a choice. Not really.

He needed to find some sort of outlet for these pent-up feelings or else something regrettable could happen. Something that, once done, couldn't be undone or taken back.

But right now, for this small segment of time, he focused his attention exclusively on his little girl, who was pirouetting in front of him.

Emily looked like a little doll, he thought, and yet there was a hint of the young woman who was to be.

He had no idea where that strange, unexpected ache in his heart came from.

"Who is this vision?"

He addressed his question regarding his daughter to the woman coming in behind her. Glancing up, he saw that Zooey was herding his son before her. Both of her wrists were adorned with a multitude of rope handles attached to several shopping bags.

"Here, let me help," Jack offered, trying to take the bags from her.

Since they were all looped together over her wrists, it wasn't as easy a matter as it sounded. Jack found himself entangled with the handles and Zooey before she could successfully uncouple herself from the shopping bags.

He shook his head as he finally succeeded. "What did you do, buy out the whole mall?"

"No, just whatever came in her size," Zooey answered breezily. "I'm kidding," she quickly added when she saw the expression on his face. Jack was taking her at her word. The man *had* to lighten up. Didn't humor have any place in his world?

Not her concern, she told herself. Shrugging out of her coat, she quickly removed Jackie's jacket before he could escape. He wiggled to and fro, then made a break for freedom the second his arms were free.

"Daddy, you're not looking," Emily cried, tugging on his sleeve.

Putting the shopping bags down by the sofa, Jack looked at his daughter and smiled. "That's because I'm blinded by your beauty."

Emily beamed from ear to ear. Again he thought that his little girl was blossoming right before his eyes. "Really, Daddy?"

"Really."

Jack raised his eyes toward Zooey once more, to find that she was watching for his reaction. He was grateful for what she'd done for his daughter. None of the other nannies he'd employed had ever taken such an interest in either of his children. They saw their positions as a job, nothing more. Zooey was different. She effortlessly meshed everything together, acting more like family than an employee.

He'd gotten lucky, finding her. "She looks very pretty."

"Zooey did my hair." Emily turned her head so that he could get a better view of her French braids. "Do you like it?"

"Very much. You look very grown up," he told her, knowing that was what she wanted to hear. And to an extent, it was true. The little girl who had been running around the house just yesterday seemed to have disappeared. He felt a pang. Jack squatted down to her level. "Don't grow up too fast, Emily."

"Just a year at a time, Daddy," she told him solemnly, as if this was a plan she had carefully laid out for herself.

Jack laughed and hugged her to him. The next moment, he heard a crash behind him. Turning, he saw that there were books scattered on the floor. It was obvious that Jackie felt too much attention was going to his sister, and he wanted some of it diverted to him. The little boy had sent several books flying off the built-in bookcase flanking the flagstone fireplace.

Zooey looked toward Jack. "I think someone's cranky."

Jack began to protest, then realized she wasn't making a comment about his own disposition. "Oh, you mean Jackie."

"This time," she allowed.

She supposed that sounded a little edgy and sarcastic, but she wasn't feeling as charitable as she had at the mall. That had all been about Emily, and about the little girl forming a closer bond with Olivia. But now Zooey's mood had become a little testy. Because Jack was going out.

Telling herself she had no business reacting this way,

that Jack was just her employer and nothing more, had no effect. Common sense and reason refused to penetrate the blanket of hurt that seemed to be wrapped around her.

"What do you want for dinner?" she asked as she replaced the books on the shelves. "Oh, I'm sorry, I forgot. You're going out with Rebecca tonight." She pushed the last book onto the shelf, then looked at him over her shoulder. "It is tonight, isn't it?"

She didn't quite carry off the innocent air she was attempting to project. She knew that because Jack frowned at her.

"Yes," he replied. She could have gone ice-skating on his tone of voice.

Allowing a sigh to escape, Zooey bit down on the inside of her cheek in an effort to think before she spoke. She really didn't want to say anything she was going to be sorry for. Sitting back on her heels, she couldn't help giving him the once-over. "Is that what you're wearing?"

He was wearing the dark gray suit he'd worn to the office that morning. Despite the fact that today was Saturday and there was hardly anyone there, he still hadn't dressed casually. Being one of the partners of a high profile law firm dictated that he always dress formally, at least to his way of thinking.

After glancing down at his suit, he looked back at Zooey. "Yes, why? What's wrong with it?"

"Nothing." And there wasn't. He looked good. Too good. "I was just curious, that's all." She glanced at her watch. "Shouldn't you be going?"

His eyes were steely. "Shouldn't you be minding the children and not me?"

Zooey rose to her feet and straightened her shoulders.

For the life of him, he couldn't read her expression. Not a comforting thought for a man who made his living by juries.

"I never mind you, Jack," Zooey replied with a smile that was paper-thin. And then she turned away, looking at the little girl who was quietly observing all of this. "Emily, why don't we take your things into your room?" Zooey scooped up the shopping bags again.

Emily came alive, sunshine radiating from her small face. "Okay! Can I try them on again?"

Zooey laughed at the joyous enthusiasm. At least she'd been successful with part of her day, she thought. "Sure. But then we have to hang everything up," Zooey told her. "Cuts down on ironing."

Emily nodded solemnly, as if she was the recipient of another heretofore forgotten commandment.

"Me, too?" Jackie demanded, obviously not wanting to be left out of whatever it was that his sister was going to be doing.

"Sure, you, too. Grab a bag, sport," Zooey encouraged, then picked out one for him to carry that had only a blouse in it. With that, she led the way out of the room, Jack watching every step she took.

When she returned to the living room more than forty minutes later, leaving Emily to revel in her new finery, and having put Jackie down for a quick nap, Zooey really didn't expect to find Jack still in the house, much less in the living room, where she'd left him.

It was getting late and she was going to have to see about throwing together some kind of dinner for herself and the kids. Or at least for the kids. To a great extent, her appetite had seemed to evaporate.

Her lips pulled into a tight smile. "You're still here."

Jack shoved his hands into his pockets. He was actually supposed to be leaving. But a general reluctance to begin that phase of the evening held him in place. "Yes."

Zooey paused and quietly studied him for a long moment. "Cold feet?" she guessed.

He didn't care for that assessment. Especially since it was so close to the truth. "What makes you say that?"

She forced herself to bank down her attraction to him and just think of Jack Lever as someone she was friendly with. Someone who looked a little lost right now.

"By my calculation, Rebecca is the first woman you've gone out with since you lost your wife."

Her assessment was too close for his comfort. He found himself wishing that he hadn't allowed Bo to catch him at a weak moment and talk him into this date.

"Very observant. Maybe you should be a private investigator."

Zooey kept her face as expressionless as his. "Maybe." She began to head for the kitchen, then stopped and turned toward him again. God, but he looked ill at ease. It took some of the edge off this strange, hurt feeling that kept assaulting her. "Would you like some advice?"

Knowing that he might not like what she had to say, he still said, "All right," because he was curious.

"Just be yourself and everything will be fine." It was the gold standard, given to everyone who had ever faced a "first date." She had no idea why she was saying that to him, except that Jack did look uncomfortable and she had this damn capacity for empathy. There were times, such as now, when that capacity seemed to be at cross-purposes with what she would have liked to be happening.

He laughed shortly, shaking his head. "I'll try to keep that in mind."

He turned to leave, and she called after him, "Your collar's up."

Jack stopped and glanced at her over his shoulder. Lost in thought, all he'd heard was the sound of her voice, not the words.

"What?"

Rather than repeat herself, Zooey crossed to him and took care of the problem herself, carefully smoothing down the upturned corner of his collar.

That brought her up close and personal to him. So close that she could feel his breath on her face. Could feel her pulse quickening from the contact.

Zooey meant to drop her hand to her side, but somehow, she couldn't quite seem to make herself do it. Everything around her seemed to stand still. It was like being in a living photograph, where the moment was forever frozen in time.

His eyes were on hers, holding her in place.

And then his lips were on hers, and everything inside of her sighed, then exploded.

Except that it was more. Much more. More intense. More everything.

The hand that had refused to leave his collar now slipped along the back of his neck, joined there by her other hand.

Zooey leaned into the kiss and was thrilled to feel Jack's palms moving along her spine. Drawing her to him. Her heart began to pound. Hard.

She felt the outline of his body against hers.

Her head began to swirl as the kiss deepened,

growing until it blotted out everything else in the room. All thought, all time. Everything.

Zooey gave herself up to it, knowing she'd never felt anything close to the reaction she was having to Jack right this moment.

He had no idea what came over him.

One minute he was wrestling with his thoughts, with the stirrings he felt inside of him, trying to distance himself from everything. And the next moment, there was no distance at all. At least, not between him and this woman who somehow kept infiltrating his days, his life, his nervous system.

Jack gave in to the overwhelming curiosity that had dogged him even before he took her into his home. He had wondered what her lips would taste like ever since the day he'd watched them curve into a wide smile across the coffee shop counter.

They tasted the way he'd imagined—and felt soft, silky. They filled his senses, enflamed his blood.

He shouldn't be doing this. Shouldn't be giving in to curiosity and to desire and kissing his children's nanny. He was just minutes away from going out with another woman. Of course, the only reason he was going out with Rebecca Peters was so that he wouldn't be tempted to do exactly what he was doing right now....

"Daddy, are you kissing Zooey?"

The small, curious voice came out of nowhere and had them springing apart as if they'd been struck by lightening.

Out of the corner of his eye, Jack saw Zooey taking in several deep breaths. This kiss had left her just as breathless as it had him, he realized. There was a certain amount of satisfaction in that, but he was going to have to savor it some other time.

There was damage control to see to.

"Um, no. I'm not. I wasn't." Why was it that when he was in court, he could withstand the onslaught of even the most ruthless, well-seasoned lawyer, but the innocent question of a wisp of a girl could rattle him to his very bones? "Zooey had something in her eye and I was just trying to help get it out."

The expression on Emily's face told Jack his daughter knew when she was being lied to. Her next words confirmed it.

"Daddies aren't supposed to fib, Daddy. You were kissing Zooey."

It was time to jump into the fray and save his butt, Zooey thought.

She put her hand on Emily's shoulder. The little girl looked up at her. "I was feeling sad, honey, and your daddy was just trying to make me feel better. You know, the way I kiss your hurt when you get one."

Emily's delicate eyebrows drew together in a perplexed blond line. "Why were you sad, Zooey?"

"Zooey no sad," Jackie declared, making his entrance by pushing his sister out of the way and rushing into the room.

And baby makes four, Zooey thought. Nap time had obviously been terminated. Jackie had more energy than any three children his age. If there was only some way to harness it.

Emily was still looking at her, waiting for an answer.

Zooey's mind raced, searching for something plausible to tell the little girl. And then she looked at the dress Emily was wearing. It was one they had picked out today.

"Because I didn't have time to get a whole bunch of pretty dresses, like you did."

Emily took her hand and wrapped her small fingers around it in a mute sign of comfort and camaraderie. "Next time," she promised solemnly.

Damn, how did some kids get to be so wonderful? Zooey could feel her heart overflowing with love. She wondered if Jack knew how very lucky he was. If she ever had a daughter, she hoped the girl would be half as sweet and generous as Emily was.

Using a laugh to cover the sudden desire to cry, Zooey hugged Emily to her. "Next time," she agreed.

Shaken to his roots by being caught in a compromising situation by his seven-year-old daughter, Jack restlessly ran a hand through his hair. That had been close. What if he'd allowed his control to slip even further? What if Emily had walked in on them not just kissing but— He couldn't allow his mind to go that route.

The way he saw it, he *needed* to go out with Rebecca more than he'd thought. Something had to cool his jets. Otherwise...

He didn't want to think about otherwise. There were too many consequences if he went down that path.

He cleared his throat. When Zooey looked in his direction, he murmured, "I'd better be going."

She was still on her knees, hugging Emily.

"Yes, you'd better go." On a scale of one to ten, there was a minus-two level of enthusiasm in her voice. And then she forced a smile to her lips as she rose to her feet. "We'll keep a candle burning in the window for you," she joked. She saw Emily raise her head to stare at her, a quizzical expression on her face. "So you find your way home," Zooey concluded.

That's just the trouble. I know my way home. All too

well. "Thanks," he said without emotion. And then he looked at his children, clustered around Zooey as if she were the center of their life.

She's just the nanny, nothing more, he insisted silently. "You two be good and listen to Zooey."

"Yes, Daddy," Emily said dutifully. Jackie made some kind of animal noise. Jack had no time to press for more of an answer; he was already late.

Emily turned away from the door the moment her father closed it and looked at Zooey. "Is Daddy going to get lost?" she asked.

Zooey knew she'd picked up on the candle in the window reference. Nothing got by this girl, she thought. "Let's hope not, Emily. Let's hope not." Then she took her hand. "C'mon, you can help me whip up something for dinner."

"Can we have mashed potatoes?" Emily asked.

"Just mashed potatoes?" Her brother Ethan had had an attachment to peas when he was a little boy. Just peas. Platefuls of peas for lunch and dinner. The phase had lasted almost four months.

"Gravy?" Emily added hopefully.

"Mashed potatoes and gravy it is," Zooey agreed. Luckily, she'd bought a bag of potatoes at the grocery store the other day.

Emily smiled broadly. She was a very picky eater, but the little girl loved mashed potatoes. Whatever worked, Zooey thought, desperately trying not to think about Jack and the woman three doors down.

What she had was a crush, Zooey insisted, nothing more. Women got them all the time and they usually lasted about as long as they sounded they would. Ten minutes. Twenty, tops. She'd be over him by morning.

But the imprint on her lips was not going to fade

away by morning, she feared. Neither would the imprint on her soul.

It would if she ignored it, Zooey promised herself.

Just as Emily began to walk into the kitchen, she
turned on her heel and beckoned for Zooey to bend
down. When she did, Emily threw her arms around her
and hugged her. Hard.

"Not that I didn't like that, Emily, but what's it for?"
she asked once Emily's little arms had slipped from
about her neck.

"You looked like you were being sad again," Emily
told her simply.

That's because I was, Zooey thought. "I'm going to
work on being happy," she vowed. And then she put
her arm around Zooey's shoulders. "Unless, of course,
I want another hug from you."

"You can have one, they're free," Emily assured her.
And then the little girl looked at her for a long moment,
as if she was trying to work something out in her head.
"Zooey?"

"Yes?"

"Will you be my mommy?"

If she'd been eating or drinking anything at the
moment, Zooey felt certain she would have begun to
choke.

"Mommy, Mommy," Jackie repeated in a singsong
voice. Zooey vaguely realized that the little boy had
never called anyone by that name.

Mostly, though, she was stunned by Emily's question.
That made twice in one week that she'd found herself
at a loss for words.

She hoped this wouldn't get to be a habit.

Chapter 8

When she could finally move her lips and engage part of her brain, Zooey asked the little girl, "What did you say?"

Emily repeated, "Will you be my mommy?" in the same tone of voice she'd used the first time.

Listening closer, Zooey realized that what Emily had said wasn't a request. She wasn't *asking* her to be her mother. It was a question regarding the chain of events that might take place, as in "Will you be my teacher next year?"

Still, where had this come from?

"Why would you ask me that, Emily?" she inquired softly, not wanting Emily to think she was upset or rattled by the question.

It was apparently all very logical to her. "Because Daddy was kissing you. And you were kissing Daddy."

This girl was definitely going to go far, Zooey

decided. If Emily was this observant now, there was no telling how astute and aware of things she was going to be when she grew up. Emily was also bright enough to disregard the excuse Zooey had given earlier about Jack attempting to cheer her up. There was no pulling the wool over this kid's eyes.

"Mommies and daddies kiss," Emily was saying, driving her point home. "I see it in the school yard sometimes."

For just the tiniest moment, Zooey entertained the idea. What would it be like, being Emily's mother? There were times when she felt she was more than halfway there. All that was missing from the picture was Emily's father.

Zooey's mouth curved. Not exactly a small point. "*People* kiss, Emily. If they like each other and the moment is right, they kiss."

Emily was very receptive to that explanation. It just helped to further her own version of things. "Is that what happened?" she demanded eagerly. "Do you like my daddy?"

Uh-oh. Quicksand dead ahead. Zooey deliberately chose an evasive way out. "Your daddy's a very nice man, Emily."

She was not about to be put off with vague answers. "Does my daddy like you?"

If that kiss is any indication of the way he feels, then yes, he likes me.

Again, Zooey remained nebulous. "He thinks I'm a good nanny." Opening the pantry, she took out the sack of potatoes and placed it on the counter before undoing the tie at the top.

Emily's small face scrunched up as she debated the merits of that endorsement. For now, she appeared to settle for what she could get. At least this meant Zooey would get to stay.

"Good. Because he didn't like the other nannies and they went away." She lowered her voice, like one adult confiding in another, and kept her eyes on her brother to make sure he wasn't listening. "I didn't like the other nannies, either. But I like you."

Moved, Zooey hugged Emily to her with one hand, while counting out potatoes on the counter with the other. "And I like you." She paused to kiss the top of Emily's head. "A lot."

"Me, too?" Jackie abandoned the truck he'd been making sound effects for, and wiggled in between them.

Annoyed, Emily began to push her brother away. Zooey stopped counting potatoes and knelt down between the two warring siblings, separating them and draping an arm around each child. She hugged them to her and tried hard not to notice the maternal stirrings that insisted on rising up within her.

"Yes, Jackie, you, too. I like both of you." She listened to herself. Since when had she been this careful? "I love both of you," she exclaimed.

With a small cry, Emily threw her arms around her, hugging her hard.

It was one of those nights when sleep absolutely refused to come or even make a token appearance.

Ordinarily, Zooey only had to get ready for bed and then crawl into it. Once there, she'd close her eyes and within seconds be dead to the world.

The last time she'd tossed and turned this much she'd been searching for the right way to tell her parents that she was dropping out of school. Dropping out of their plans for what amounted to the rest of her life.

Sighing, Zooey stared up at the ceiling and thought about today and how well things had gone.

Up to a point.

The shopping trip had turned out to be even better than she'd hoped. Emily and Olivia had bonded in that special little-girls-discovering-fashion-and-their-budding-power sort of way. The two really liked one another.

And Zooey and Megan had had a good time as well. Before today, she'd only exchanged a few words with Olivia's aunt. She'd discovered that Megan was a very nice person, not at all like some of the rumors claimed—that she was a home wrecker and worse. The woman was fun, loved her niece and was easy to talk to. It seemed as if Emily hadn't been the only one who had made a new friend today.

The personal highlight of Zooey's day, of course, had been the stop she'd made at her parents' house before the shopping trip began. She hadn't really looked forward to that. In fact, she'd been dreading it. She and her father hadn't exchanged a single word since she'd dropped out of college. She was sure today would only be more of the same.

She was wrong.

Oh, there'd been a frosted moment or two when her mother had ushered her into her father's workshop, and the two of them had just stood there, looking at each other. Two statues with pulses.

But all she'd had to say was, "Dad," and suddenly, he was there, hugging her and saying it was all right.

It was as if the silence of the last year and a half had never existed.

Zooey smiled to herself now. All that was good. But

none of those things, separately or together, would have kept her awake like this.

It was waiting for Jack to come home that was doing that.

Waiting to hear his key in the lock, to hear the door opening and then closing again, telling her that he had come home. Alone.

Oh, God, what if he didn't come home alone? What if he brought *her* with him?

Or what if he'd decided to spend the night, or a good portion of it, at Rebecca's house? Zooey sincerely doubted that they'd spend the entire night quietly sipping tea and discussing lawn fertilizer. Rebecca was much too much woman for that.

Well, what was *she?* Zooey wondered. Chopped liver? He'd kissed her for God's sake. In front of his children, or at least in front of his daughter. Not that he'd planned it, but that was the way it had turned out. Didn't that mean anything?

Zooey pressed her lips together. Sure, it meant something. It meant Jack was using her to warm up for the main event.

Turning over on her belly, she dragged the pillow over her head in frustration. Damn it, she needed to get to sleep. She was going to be a wreck tomorrow. She had to stop driving herself crazy like this.

There was nothing between her and Jack except her wishful thinking. End of story.

Exasperated, Zooey sat up, throwing her pillow on the floor. She'd given up the larger room downstairs that Jack had initially told her was hers for a smaller one on the second floor. She'd wanted to be closer to Emily and Jackie so that she could hear them if they needed her during the night.

That left her straining to hear sounds that could have been coming from downstairs.

This was pathetic.

She needed a book, she decided, something to *put* her to sleep, since she couldn't seem to get there on her own power. Kicking the covers aside, she got up. The wooden floor felt cold against her feet. Zooey wiggled her toes into slippers, tugged on the robe she normally kept at the foot of the bed, and made her way downstairs.

She didn't bother tying the robe. Her mind wasn't on details. It felt restless and disoriented. Like the rest of her.

No sooner had she reached the bottom of the stairs than she heard the front door being unlocked. For a split second, she thought of running back up, but no matter how fast she moved, she knew that Jack would see her the moment the door opened.

The alternative was to make a mad dash for the shelter of the kitchen, but that seemed cowardly to her. So Zooey remained exactly where she was, her hand tightly wrapped around the banister, half expecting to see Rebecca walking in with Jack, most likely hanging on his arm or half draped along his body.

When he came in alone, Zooey's heart began to beat again.

Yes!

Lost in thought, thinking how he had done smarter things in his time than what he'd done tonight, Jack didn't realize he wasn't alone when he first walked in.

He wasn't sure exactly what it was that caught his attention, but he looked up. And saw Zooey standing at the foot of the stairs. She was wearing a football jersey that should have been at least six inches longer, and a robe that should have been closed. For his sake if not for hers.

Now there was irony for you. Rebecca had worn a dress that almost wasn't there. And what there had been of it was as skintight as the laws of physics would allow. And yet seeing her like that hadn't aroused him half as much as seeing Zooey in her damn football jersey, with her damn robe hanging open, offering no protection, no barrier.

His mouth felt dry, as if he'd had an entire cup of sand to drink. He pocketed his key, attempting to distance himself from his thoughts, his reactions. He succeeded only marginally.

"What are you still doing up? Something wrong?" He cleared his throat to keep from croaking.

She shook her head. Movement was easy. Talking, or at least making sense, was the hard part. He wasn't home early, but at least he was home. Without *her*. "I just came down looking for a book."

"A book?" He glanced over her head up the stairs, listening for the sound of one of his children calling or fussing. He heard nothing. "To read to the kids?"

"To read to me," she told him with a smile. Had the date gone badly? God, she hoped so. "I couldn't sleep." But even as she tendered her excuse, Zooey found herself stifling a yawn. Chagrined, she flashed a quick, embarrassed smile. "I guess maybe I'm more tired than I thought I was."

She knew she should either go get a book or turn around and head back upstairs. She did neither. Clearing her throat, Zooey crossed to him, her hands buried deep in the pockets of her robe. "So," she began, trying to sound cheerful, "how was your date?"

Now here was something he wasn't prepared

for—being quizzed by his children's nanny about his evening out. "You know, I'd ask you if you were my mother—except that my mother never asked questions like that."

Zooey laughed softly. Memories, embarrassing ones, came flying back to her from all sides. "Lucky you. My mother *always* asked questions like that. No matter what time I got in."

She'd once gotten in at four in the morning, only to find her mother still waiting up. The woman had incredible tenacity. The last Zooey had heard from Kim, their mom was still at it.

"Not so lucky," he commented, surprising her. Was that a sad note in his voice? "At least your mother cared."

Zooey knew she had no right to ask, to probe, but it wasn't in her nature to back away. It never had been. "Yours didn't?"

He slid the topcoat off, draping it on the coatrack, and shrugged in response to her question. "Not that I ever noticed."

Mothers cared, she thought. Most mothers cared too much, getting in their sons' way. "Maybe she just wanted you to think she didn't, while trying to give you your space."

He'd had space, all right. A whole continent of it. "She did that. Gave me my space from across the ocean." He saw Zooey looking at him oddly, as if he'd lost her. "Most of my high school years, my mother was away 'touring' Europe."

There was a cynical expression on his face, Zooey noted. If she scraped the surface, she was certain she'd find anger. "As in performing?"

He laughed at her question, but there was no real humor in the sound. "Who knows? Maybe." His mother liked to associate with famous people, people with blood-lines and pedigrees. Maybe she'd slept with a few, as well. "But the official version was that she was 'vacationing.' My stepfather was away so much, I don't know if he ever realized she wasn't around."

That sounded absolutely awful to Zooey. But she kept her pity under wraps, knowing he wouldn't appreciate it. "Not much of a home life."

She led the way to the kitchen. Because they were talking, Jack followed automatically. He shrugged in response to her comment. "The servants were cool. Sometimes."

Taking the pot from the coffeemaker, she poured water into it and transferred that into the urn. She didn't bother with the filter or coffee; she was going to make him some herbal tea. He looked as if he needed to be soothed.

"So that's where you get it from," she murmured. That explained a lot.

Jack lowered his frame onto a stool at the counter, watching her. Watching the way the open robe moved and caught, allowing the outline of her body to take his imagination hostage.

"Get what from?" he demanded. "Zooey, what are you talking about?"

The coffeemaker began to make crackling, hissing sounds as the water found its way through the machine, heating in the process.

"You're imitating a pattern. The only one you've ever known. Your stepfather was a workaholic, so now you are, too."

Jack looked at her, annoyed, a stinging protest rising to his lips. But the words never emerged, because he realized she was right. Even though he'd hated his adolescent years, he was reliving them from the other side—doing the same thing to his children that his own parents had done to him. Getting lost in his own world, while mouthing platitudes that this was all for them. That he was working all these long hours for them.

It was himself he was doing it for. To feel worthwhile. To feel as if he was in control of some small part of his life.

Blowing out a breath, Jack ran a hand through his hair. He didn't like the fact that she was right. But that didn't change anything.

He eyed Zooey as she reached up to get cups from the cabinet. Her short jersey rode higher, lighting a fire within him. He looked away, trying to maintain some semblance of decorum.

"What was it you said your degree was in?" he murmured.

"I didn't." Placing a tea bag in each cup, she took the pot and poured hot water into both. "And I don't have a degree," she corrected. "I dropped out during the last semester before graduation."

He winced as if he'd just received a physical blow. He knew how he would have felt if Emily pulled that kind of stunt on him. "I'll bet that didn't go over very well at home."

He had the gift of understatement, she thought, setting the pot back on the burner. "That would be a bet you'd win."

Curiosity got the better of him. "Why did you drop out?"

Ah, the million dollar question. Too bad she didn't have a million dollar answer. Just a whole bunch of little ones that didn't seem all that good when she said them out loud.

"Because I could," she told him. "Because I didn't want to be dictated to, even by my family. Especially by my family," she amended, remembering the period she'd been through. "Because I didn't want to 'conform.' And maybe," she concluded quietly, "because I was scared."

"Scared?" He said the word, but it really wasn't registering. Jack couldn't picture Zooey being afraid of anything. She struck him as being absolutely fearless, even when common sense would dictate caution. "You?" he scoffed. "Of what?"

She set his cup of tea before him, knowing he didn't care for cream or sugar. As far as she was concerned, the more cream and sugar, the better.

"Of what was expected of me once I had that degree," she told him, saying something she hadn't even admitted to herself until this moment. "If I didn't have the degree, they couldn't expect me to be like them. Perfect."

"So, if I'm following you correctly, in order not to disappoint your parents, you decided to disappoint them big time."

He made it sound stupid. Hell, maybe it was at that, she thought.

Zooey grinned with a dismissive shrug. "I don't exactly do my best work when I'm feeling desperate."

He was still thinking about the unfinished degree. It seemed a shame to put in so much work, only to walk away from the finish line a second before the race was over. He took a sip of tea, his eyes never leaving her face. "Why don't you go back and finish up? Get your degree," he coaxed. "You know what they say. A mind is a terrible thing to waste."

"Maybe," she allowed. "But as far as my going back to finish up my degree, I can't. You see, I have this job

I like, and the guy, he kind of depends on me to be there for his kids."

Jack laughed. He hadn't forgotten about that part. It wasn't as if he wanted her to leave. "There are always evening classes."

"The kids are there in the evenings, too," she said with a perfectly straight face.

His deadpan expression faded before hers did. "Yes, but the 'guy' could be, too."

Her eyes met his. This was new, she thought. Usually she had to beg him to put in an appearance once a night in the children's rooms. "That would mean he'd have to make an effort to come home earlier."

Jack stopped being so vague. "I could make it home earlier than I have been." He gazed into her eyes, even as he told himself to stop doing that. "For a worthy cause."

It was a struggle not to feel flattered. Zooey knew he didn't mean it that way, but she still felt warm. And touched. "What about your cases?"

He laughed. The woman certainly did know how to throw up obstacles. "Ever hear about bringing your work home with you?"

She'd heard of it, but hadn't expected him to do it. Not when he hadn't before. She wondered if something was up, and told herself to stop being so suspicious.

Sliding her cup beside his, she settled on the stool next to his. "You'd do that? For me?"

God, but Zooey's eyes were wide. And beautiful. He'd never noticed that before. It was difficult trying to focus on the conversation. Hard fending off this urge that had only gotten stronger since his date with Rebecca.

"You had a good point. I should be spending more time with the kids," he agreed. "And if I *am* home, there's no reason why you couldn't take a few classes until you satisfy your degree requirements."

She laughed, shaking her head. This had to be the *last* thing she'd ever expected to hear from him. "My mother would really like you. She's already crazy about Jackie," she added. Instead of being worn-out, her mother had been reluctant to give the boy up at the end of the day.

Jack was looking at her quizzically, waiting for clarification. "I left Jackie with her today when I took Emily and Olivia shopping."

He nodded. He'd almost forgotten about the shopping spree. He took a sip of the tea she'd prepared for him, but it was going to take more than herbal tea to quell what was going on inside of him. Still, he appreciated the effort, even if he couldn't say so out loud. "Emily seemed a lot happier than I've seen her in a long time."

She was very pleased with herself for that, she decided. "Well, she's got a new best friend and a new wardrobe. At seven, her world is just about perfect."

"Thank you." The words came out of nowhere.

Zooey tried to second-guess what he was talking about. "For the tea?"

He shook his head. "For my daughter's happiness." He moved the cup away and studied her. "You're really a very special person, Zooey."

Compliments embarrassed her. She never knew what to say. Declaring, "No, I'm not," didn't quite seem the way to go here. Still, the situation begged for something. "Your kids make it easy."

Which just made her that much more unique in his book, Jack thought.

"Not to hear the other nannies talk about it. They thought the kids were hell on wheels. Of course, they weren't very thrilled with me, either. Said I was too demanding. And 'too invisible,'" he said, quoting one of the women. "Whatever that means."

Zooey leaned her chin in her hand, gazing at him. "You look pretty visible to me." Then she stopped. Taking a napkin out of the holder on the counter, she draped it over her index finger and wiped it along the corner of his mouth. When he pulled his head back, she said, "Pink isn't your color," and held up the corner of the napkin with traces of lipstick on it.

He cleared his throat. "Rebecca kissed me."

"Well, I didn't think she tried to brand you with it."

Zooey was sitting too close. And his resolve was only so strong. He wasn't going to be able to resist her much longer. Wasn't going to keep his curiosity about what she looked like beneath that jersey under lock and key more than a couple more minutes.

Squaring his shoulders, he stood up. "I'm going to turn in," he said abruptly.

"I'll stay down here and clean up," she murmured, more to herself than to him.

She sighed as she heard him go up the stairs. For every step she took forward, there was another step back, waiting to be taken.

And in the end, she was standing in the same place where she'd begun. And damn confused about how she got there.

Chapter 9

Zooey closed the front door behind her. She'd just ushered her charges into the house after picking up Emily and Olivia at school and dropping the latter at her house.

There was homework to get to and dinner to start, but Zooey firmly believed in balancing out work with play. She had milk and chocolate chip cookies waiting for the children in the kitchen. Leaving the treats out without having Jackie get into them had been the tricky part.

Under Zooey's watchful eye, both children took their turn at getting up on the wooden step she had butted up against the sink and washing their hands before sitting down at the table.

Zooey paused to wipe the area around the sink after Jackie had finished. There was enough water there to fill half a duck pond.

"Are you excited about Halloween?" Zooey asked Emily as she hung up the towel again.

"Halloween, Halloween," Jackie cried, providing the excitement that was missing from Emily's face.

He was like a three-foot-tall tape recorder, repeating everything he heard, Zooey thought. But the little boy wasn't her main concern at the moment. Emily was. Granted, Zooey had gotten the child started. Once or twice in the last few weeks she'd even heard Emily begin a conversation when she was around Olivia. But she needed more. Something to give her more confidence, make her feel as if she blended in better.

The displays of Halloween candy in the supermarket—the displays Jackie had made a beeline for before she managed to grab him—had given her an idea. Emily could have a Halloween party, one for the children in the neighborhood and their parents. It wouldn't hurt Jack to do a little mingling, either—with someone other than Rebecca.

Getting permission for the party was going to require some finessing on Zooey's part when it came to Jack. But before she undertook that, she needed to get Emily on board. If the little girl regarded the holiday in the same manner that most kids regarded broccoli, there was no point in knocking herself out.

Still, she couldn't picture any child not liking Halloween.

"Maybe," Emily finally said. The single word was accompanied by a vague, careless shrug of her small shoulders.

When Zooey and her siblings had been little, they couldn't wait for Halloween to come around. To them, it was almost as big a holiday as Christmas. She didn't understand Emily's lack of enthusiasm.

She sat down at the table, taking a cookie. There was already a circle of crumbs around Jackie's plate, along with splotches of milk. She was letting him sit on a booster seat instead of his high chair today, and was beginning to doubt the wisdom of that move.

"Don't you like dressing up for Halloween, going trick-or-treating?" Zooey pressed.

Emily looked at her for a long moment as if she was talking about something entirely foreign. "We don't go trick-or-treating."

This might be easier to pull together than she'd thought. "Because you have a party?" Zooey asked.

Emily shook her head. "No."

And then again, maybe not. "Do you dress up?" Again, Emily shook her head. "Why not?"

Emily sighed, and it was clear to Zooey that it was a wistful sound. "The last two nannies we had said it was silly."

How had Jack managed to find such heartless creatures? What kind of an ad had he put out? Wanted: one nanny, completely devoid of a sense of humor or any memories of childhood.

Zooey dunked her cookie in milk and held it out to Emily. "You're a kid. You're supposed to be silly. And anyway, dressing up for Halloween isn't silly," she said defensively. "It's a tradition. It's fun."

Emily now appeared to be hanging on every word. Her eyes were wide. Hopeful. "Do you dress up on Halloween, Zooey?"

"Absolutely." She leaned closer to the girl. "How would you like to have a Halloween party this year?"

If eyes could truly sparkle, then Emily's did. "A real party?"

Zooey grinned broadly. "A real party."

There was awed disbelief on Emily's small, heart-shaped face. "With balloons and everything?"

"With balloons and everything," Zooey echoed, making a note to find the biggest, prettiest balloons she could. She didn't believe in scary Halloweens, but ones filled with princesses and unicorns and everything magical.

And then suddenly, the enthusiasm that had been building in Emily's voice all but vanished. As did the light from her face. "Daddy won't like it."

"You leave your daddy to me," Zooey told her. "He's going to love it."

Emily obviously still had her doubts, but it was also obvious that she thought Zooey could walk on water and work miracles whenever she needed to. "You think?"

"I think." It was more than a statement, it was a promise.

Emily jumped up from the table and threw her arms around her. Her heart bursting, Zooey hugged the girl fervently.

"You're the best, Zooey."

"Yes, I am," she laughed, squeezing Emily a little harder. And praying that the man she'd hardly seen in the last week—ever since his so-called date with the neighborhood vixen—could be convinced to come around.

"Best!" Jackie crowed, scrambling off his chair and sending the booster seat flying as he tried to claim his share of his nanny.

Zooey's heart stopped for half a second as she grabbed him in time to keep him from crashing to the floor.

"You are going to be the death of me, boy," she told him.

"Death!" he yelled.

"But not before the Halloween party," she added, looking at Emily.

"Not even after," Emily said fervently.

There was no stopping the warm feeling once it took hold. Zooey wrapped her arms around the children and hugged them hard.

That night she waited up for Jack to ask him about the party. Loaded for bear, she intended to give him both barrels if necessary, use every trick she could think of to get him to agree, including guilt.

So, after she had put Emily and Jackie down for the night and made sure they'd fallen asleep, she went back to the living room and planted herself in the oversize chair that faced the doorway. It was extremely seductive in its comfort.

Zooey sighed as she sank into it. She'd put in a long day with the children. Teachers were giving second graders a lot more homework these days than they had when she was Emily's age, she thought grudgingly. Emily was very bright, but Zooey wasn't about to fluff off the job of checking the little girl's work by just assuming everything was correct—which, of course, it had been.

The next moment, Zooey found herself wondering if Jack would soon be married to someone else who would help Emily with her homework.

The thought brought a pang with it, a sharp one that went straight to Zooey's heart even as she struggled to dismiss it. It wasn't supposed to matter to her whom the man married, whom he finally selected to act as a mother to his children.

It wasn't supposed to, but it did, she admitted with

another sigh as she checked her watch. It was getting late.

She had Jack's dinner prepared, covered and waiting for him in the warming oven. By her count, it had been there for several hours.

Didn't the man remember his way home anymore?

That was the last thought that passed through her head before she nodded off to sleep.

The sound of the front door closing had Zooey jerking her head up. Blinking, she automatically looked down at her watch. It was a habit, a holdover from her college days, when she'd had a tendency to oversleep and miss her early classes.

She'd been asleep for almost an hour. Grabbing the armrests, Zooey pushed herself up out of the chair. A second later, she realized that she'd gotten up too fast. A wave of dizziness, something that plagued her occasionally whenever she forgot to eat right, had her head spinning. She swayed just as Jack was entering the room.

"Zooey, what's the matter?"

She felt his arms close around her, catching her before she could sink back down to the chair. His voice held a note of concern. Forcing herself to focus, she took a deep breath, then let it out again.

"Nothing. I fell asleep in the chair and got up too fast," she explained simply.

Jack searched her face to assure himself there wasn't more going on that she wasn't mentioning. Her color began to return.

"What are you doing up?" he asked. He'd deliberately come home at this hour to avoid seeing her. The last thing he'd expected was to have to rush forward and catch her in his arms before she fell. "It's late. You should be in bed."

She took another breath. It was hard to get her bearings when he was this close to her. "That's what you're supposed to say to your daughter, not me."

"She's not up," he pointed out. "You are." Jack realized that he was still holding her. And that he liked it far too much. "Can I let go of you? Can you stand on your own?"

"Yes and yes."

He dropped his hands, and something inside of her felt bereft.

"As for what I'm doing up, I'm waiting for you to come home."

Concern returned, driving a chariot straight into the arena. He looked toward the stairs and the children's bedrooms. "Is something wrong?"

Turning back, he watched her work her lower lip between her teeth. "Only if you say no."

Clear as mud. His day had been long and his nerve endings were raw. That didn't leave a lot of room for patience. "I know why the kids like you so much. You talk in riddles."

Zooey needed him to be in a receptive mood. A full stomach helped. She backtracked. "There's dinner in the warming oven."

"I ate."

She looked at him, not ready to give up. "What?"

"I ate," he repeated.

Zooey shook her head. "No, not what did you say, what did you eat?"

He thought for a moment. He could remember chewing, but nothing had actually registered on his palate.

"I'm not sure," he admitted. "Some chickeny thing one of the law clerks brought in from a fast food place."

There had been three of them staying late, working on their individual cases. When the intern had volunteered to make a food run, Jack had given him a ten, but no instructions beyond getting something that wasn't too greasy. He vaguely recalled being told they were chicken strips. Fries had come with that, but he'd skipped them.

Jack started for the stairs, and was surprised when Zooey hooked her arm through his and tugged him in the direction of the kitchen.

Now what? "What are you doing?"

"Taking you to the kitchen for a real meal." She wasn't about to take no for an answer. "I made meat loaf. The kids loved it."

He frowned as he crossed the threshold into the kitchen. The lights were all on. Instead of appearing lonely, the room seemed welcoming. He was overtired, he decided.

"I don't like meat loaf."

Zooey picked up two pot holders. "You'll like this one."

He didn't seem to have a say in anything anymore. What was worse, he was too tired to be annoyed about it. "Anyone ever tell you that you're damn pushy?"

She looked at him over her shoulder, her mouth curving. "I might have heard a rumor to that effect. You'll like the meat loaf," she repeated, taking a plate out of the oven. "Honest." She closed the stove door with one swift movement of her hip, then brought the plate to the table. "It has carrots, two kinds of peppers, onions, scallions and sour cream in it, not to mention a whole bunch of other things. It's a meal all by itself."

He had to admit that it did smell tempting.

But then, so did she. Despite her rapid-fire delivery,

there were still traces of sleepiness around Zooey's eyes, and he found that exceedingly sexy for some reason. He had another date set with Rebecca, their third, but that didn't take the edge off the way he was reacting to Zooey. It should have, but it didn't. Just as he'd been afraid it wouldn't.

He'd kept away from the house, from her, for most of the last ten days, and that still didn't negate or even blunt the attraction he felt toward her. If anything, it sharpened it. Zooey intrigued him, amused him, attracted him.

Any way he sliced it, Jack felt doomed.

And there wasn't a damn thing he could do about it, because he needed a nanny and the kids were wild about her. And she seemed to be the only one who could keep them from being wild, period.

Doomed.

"Here, try some." Zooey moved the plate closer to him and handed him a fork. "Sit," she instructed, when he still remained standing.

He did as she asked, his knees bending mechanically until he made contact with the chair. Under her watchful eye, he sank his fork into the meat loaf, corralled a piece and brought it to his lips. He fully expected not to taste anything at all, because his mind was definitely not on food at the moment.

But the moist, flavorful forkful managed to break through the barriers around him. Surprised, he took another sampling. And then another. It tasted better each time.

"Well?" she asked when he said nothing. That he was eating it was certainly testimony that he liked it, but she wanted him to say the words. The man needed to express himself, so that he could verbalize his feelings to his children, who needed to hear them a lot more than she needed to be complimented on her cooking. But a start had to be made somewhere.

"Not bad," he murmured.

"Not bad?" she echoed. If he'd been one of her brothers, he would have been on the receiving end of a head-rattling shove. Curbing the impulse, she demanded, "Did they repossess your taste buds, too?"

He laughed then, at her expression, at her choice of words and at her exasperation over his so-called indifference to what he had to admit was probably the best meal he'd had in a while. Which was saying a lot, seeing as how she'd been doing all the cooking since January.

"This is good," he admitted.

Damn straight it's good. She waved for him to keep moving his fork. "Eat up," she told him. "There's plenty more where that came from."

"So what is it that you want to talk to me about?" he asked after three more forkfuls had found their way into his mouth.

Sitting down again, Zooey took a deep breath, bracing herself for an argument. Knowing she needed to win it. "I thought you might have a party for Emily."

"A party?" he echoed in surprise. "Why? It's not her birthday." And then he paused for a second, trying to remember what month it was. "Is it?"

Zooey stared at him, stunned. Just how wrapped up in his work was he? "You don't know when your daughter's birthday is?"

"Of course I do." He was annoyed that she could even suggest such a thing. "It's June. June 11th. Working late, I just lose track of time sometimes," he admitted. "The weeks and months get jumbled up." This wasn't the first time he'd had to stop to get his bearings, unable to recall what month it was.

"Dusty books will do that to you." Not wanting to alienate him, she turned to the business at hand. "I'm talking about a Halloween party," Zooey specified. "I think you need to throw a Halloween party for Emily."

"Need?" he echoed. The woman used the strangest words sometimes. What he *needed* was peace and quiet, neither of which seemed to be in his immediate future. "Zooey, I don't know the first thing about throwing a party."

She hadn't really meant that he was going to be the one in charge of it. That would have been a disaster waiting to happen. "Lucky for you, I do."

Finished with the meat loaf, he set down his fork and took another sip of water. "I never doubted it. But before you get carried away here, why do I 'need' to throw my daughter a Halloween party? I thought things were going well for her and Odette—"

"Olivia," Zooey corrected. "The girl's name is Olivia. And they are, but Emily needs to branch out a little more. She needs to learn how to have fun."

"That's why I have you." That did *not* come out the way he'd meant it, Jack thought, afraid that Zooey might take offense. "I mean, that's what you're supposed to provide for her."

"Which I'm trying to do," she emphasized, bringing the conversation back full circle. "As soon as you say yes to the party."

He was not the kind of man anyone ever accused of leaping first and looking later. Before he jumped into a pool, he not only looked it over but asked to review the building specs on it as well. Giving his permission for the party came under the same heading. He needed to have more input before he agreed. Who knew what Zooey thought constituted a party?

"Just how many people are you planning to invite to this so-called party?"

She could almost see the way his mind worked. "Not the immediate world," she assured him. "Just the kids in the neighborhood— and their parents."

Zooey had her mind made up, he could see that. He could also see why this would be good for Emily. He'd never had a party of his own when he was a kid, and maybe that was part of the reason that socializing without a legal brief in his hand had always been difficult for him. "When's Halloween?"

"Same day it's always been—October 31st. In two weeks," she added, in case today's date escaped him.

"Sure, go ahead." Pushing back his chair, he rose from the table. "I suppose I can stay late in the office even if I'm not on a case—"

"No, no, no!" Zooey interrupted with such feeling that Jack stopped in midsentence and stared at her. "You have to be here."

He saw absolutely no reason for his presence to be required. "Why?"

"Because it's for the *parents* as well," she emphasized, "and the last I looked, you're Emily's parent."

The thought of attending a party with a bunch of kids running around sent a shiver up his spine. Mingling with adults he didn't know all that well held no attraction for him, either.

"You can take my place."

"I don't look mean enough." The words were out of her mouth before she could stop them.

"Mean?"

He'd never thought of himself as being mean,

especially not around the children. Granted, he wasn't around them all that much, but when he was, he never raised his voice, never lost his temper no matter how rambunctious Jackie became.

Zooey backpedaled tactfully. "Okay, maybe *stern* is a better word. You do scowl a great deal," she pointed out. He looked surprised. Didn't he know? "Of course, you can do that on Halloween because it'll go with the costume."

This was getting out of hand very quickly. "What costume?"

"The pirate costume you'll be wearing," she answered innocently.

The hell he was. Jack knew he had to lay down the law to Zooey very succinctly. "I will not be wearing a pirate costume."

"Oh?" She could easily envision him as a pirate. There was a hidden, rakish side to him. Otherwise, she wouldn't be so attracted to him. But she wasn't going to push that if he wanted to go another route. "Then what kind of costume do you want to wear? I've got to get to the stores soon to find one in your size. They run out fairly quickly."

She said that as if she was familiar with the supply and demand of Halloween costumes. He had no doubt that she probably was. "A jacket, matching trousers and a tie," he answered.

She should have known. Zooey shook her head. The man had to get with the program. "The object is to dress like something other than what you are. If we don't find a costume to your liking, I can sew one."

That caught him off guard. "You sew?"

She knew she didn't look like the domestic type.

Yet she loved to cook, loved caring for children, she'd discovered. And sewing relaxed her, she'd told him.

She did *not* strike him as a relaxed woman. "You haven't sewn much lately, have you?"

She laughed. "That's the first time I've heard you make a joke."

"I wasn't joking." It was merely an observation on his part. "Look, Zooey, you can do whatever you think is necessary to make my daughter happy. I'll give you my credit card and you can get anything you want for this party—"

"Good, because the first thing I want is you." That came out a little too quickly, with a little too much feeling, she thought. "For Emily," she added. "How do you think she'll feel when all the other kids have their parents there and she's the only one without a mother or father in attendance?"

He supposed she had a point, even though he hated to admit it. "You're an expert at this guilt thing."

Zooey laughed, taking his plate to the sink and rinsing it before putting it in the dishwasher. "I had a great teacher."

"Your mother?" he guessed.

"My father." She closed the dishwasher door, then turned to face him. "So, you'll come?"

He really didn't want to, but she had his back against the wall. "You make it sound like Emily will spend the next ten years in therapy if I don't."

Then her work here, Zooey thought, was done. At least for the time being. Before turning off the light, she smiled at Jack. "I'm glad we understand each other."

Not hardly, he thought as he followed her out of the

kitchen. He really doubted that he would ever understand the way her mind worked.

A pirate. He sighed inwardly. There had to be a way around that. He had two weeks to find it.

Chapter 10

Caches of candy began showing up throughout the house in strange places. There were three bags on the top shelf above the built-in cabinets in his three-car garage. There were four hidden inside his bedroom closet, where even Jack couldn't reach them without first pressing a stepstool into service.

When he groped for a seldom-perused book on the uppermost shelf in his study and was unexpectedly showered with a hailstorm of M&M's that had torn loose from their bag, he figured it was time for an explanation.

It only took calling her name twice to get Zooey to put in a personal appearance.

"You bellowed, sir?" she asked, wiping her damp hands on her apron.

"I didn't bellow, I called," he informed her coolly.

"Forcefully," he added when she gave him a penetrating look. "What's this?" He nodded at the floor.

Crossing the threshold, Zooey made her way to the scene of the crime. She looked down where he indicated and pretended to study the items in question earnestly. Then she looked up at him, a tranquil smile on her lips. "M&M's, I believe. Orange and black," she added.

"I know what they are," he muttered between gritted teeth. "What are they doing on my bookshelf? And in my garage? And behind the wineglasses in the kitchen? And God only knows where else." Exasperated, he paused. "Have you acquired some kind of a sugar fixation in the last few weeks that I should know about?"

Zooey didn't answer immediately. Instead, she smiled at him. He was familiar with that smile. It was the one she used with the children when she was patiently allowing them to prattle on until they tired themselves out. Ordinarily, he found it rather endearing.

Aimed at him, he found it irritating as hell.

"No," she finally replied as she bent down and began to gather up the scattered candy, depositing the pieces into her apron.

He found himself addressing the top of her head, a completely dissatisfying way to conduct an inquisition, in his opinion. "Then why are there stashes of candy all over the house?"

The fallen candy secure in the artificial fold of her apron, Zooey rose to her feet. "Halloween, Jack," she reminded him.

"Is a week away," he responded.

He knew that because he was keeping track of the date, despite all the other things he had on his mind. He was still trying to come up with a viable reason why he couldn't attend the party, or at least not attend it wearing some ridiculous costume. He'd never worn one as a kid and saw no reason to start now, at his age.

But for some reason, saying no didn't seem an option in this case.

Zooey looked at him as if she couldn't fathom his not comprehending her reasoning. "I don't like leaving things to the last minute. Most of the good candy is gone by then."

He blew out a breath, mystified. The woman came up with the oddest explanations. "I had no idea that there was good candy and bad candy."

When she raised her eyes to his, Jack could have sworn there was a hint of pity in them. He resented it, and squared his shoulders.

"Weren't you ever a kid?" she asked.

He didn't see what that had to do with it. "Yes, but I didn't spend my time grading candy."

She had a feeling that he'd never gone trick-or-treating as a kid, either. Otherwise, he'd know.

"Good candy," she explained patiently, "is the kind that all the kids are familiar with, the name brands. Bad candy is what the stores try to pass off at the tail end of a holiday like Halloween or Easter. It's cheap and tastes that way."

He wasn't about to argue with her, not over something so trivial. "If you say so." He sighed, looking at the ripped bag. "How much of this stuff do you have stashed around the house?"

"Not enough yet," she told him frankly. "But I'm getting there."

In his opinion, they had more than enough to rot the teeth of every kid in the neighborhood. "And you're hiding the bags because…?"

"I don't want to have to rush either of your children,

especially Jackie, to the emergency room for a chocolate overdose," she answered patiently. "Or spend the day cleaning up after him when he throws up. In case you didn't know, your son absolutely cannot resist chocolate."

Actually, Jack didn't know that. He supposed there was a great deal he didn't know about his children that Zooey did. But then, she was with them more than he was.

"I see your point." About to say something else, he stopped. Zooey was reaching toward him. The next moment, her fingers were in his hair. "Zooey?"

She grinned as she held a small, round object up for him to see. "You had an orange M&M in your hair." Without thinking, she popped it into her mouth.

Why the hell he found that unnervingly sensual, he had no idea.

Maybe he was undergoing a brain meltdown, Jack thought. Whatever the reason, it took him a second to get his mind back into gear.

Clearing his throat, he nodded toward the doorway, hoping she would take the hint. He needed some space. "Okay, you've explained it. Sorry to take you away from whatever it was you were doing."

She wasn't moving, Jack noted. "Just washing dishes."

That didn't make any sense. "We have a dishwasher for that."

Zooey shook her head. "There aren't enough dirty dishes to make it worthwhile running it." It unsettled her sense of order.

Moving toward his wastebasket, she formed a funnel with her apron and sent the candy she'd gathered up raining into the container. Finished, she raised her eyes to his. "Have you given it any more thought?"

Jack gave up trying to ignore her so he could get back to perusing the textbook that had started all this in the first place. There *was* no ignoring Zooey, at least not when she was within a few feet of him. He sighed, putting the book down on his desk. "Given what any more thought?"

Zooey cocked her head and looked at him. She was wearing that tolerant smile again. "Your costume," she prompted.

He wondered what it took to get the word *no* across to this woman. "Yes, I've given it some more thought and the thought is no."

She shook her head, indicating that his response was unacceptable. "What other thoughts have you had on the subject?"

He could feel his temper heating up. Why amusement seemed to be hovering at the same time, he had no clue. Being around Zooey always seemed to put him at cross-purposes.

But lines had to be drawn, boundaries had to be re-established, since they had obviously gotten blurred. She was taking far too much upon herself. "That all the other nannies I've hired for my kids had enough sense not to bother me with trivia like this."

Zooey seemed unfazed by his words and his tone. "Well, too bad. They're gone, I'm not."

There was that amusement again, he noted, shaking his head. "You really don't have the proper employee mentality, you know that?"

She squared her shoulders, an indication that if he meant to put her in her place, he had failed. Miserably.

"You're within your rights to fire me anytime you want, Jack."

He realized that she was sticking out her chin. Obviously a symbolic gesture, he thought, exasperated. "I don't want to fire you, Zooey."

"Good," she said, nodding her head. "Because I don't want to have to look for another job." And she didn't. For the first time since she'd left school, she really liked what she was doing. It wasn't just a way to pay the bills, but a way to make a difference in the lives she touched.

He seized his opportunity. "Keeping that in mind, maybe you could see your way to cutting me some slack on this."

She looked surprised that he could even say that. "I am. I haven't said anything to you about the costume for a whole week."

"And I appreciate it. Now if you could just continue that way…"

Her expression told him he was living in a fool's paradise even before she said anything to confirm it. "Sorry, can't. Time's getting short. Halloween is next Sunday, and like I said, you wait too long, there's nothing left to pick over."

She'd just made his point for him, he thought. "Exactly."

Zooey continued as if he hadn't said anything at all. "Seeing that you're so busy and in such demand, I decided to pick up a costume for you to try on." Then, just in case he thought he was stuck with it no matter what, she quickly added, "I know the guy who runs the shop and he said if this didn't fit, I could bring it back."

It was like watching a snowball descend down a hillside, gaining speed and girth. And waiting for it to swallow him up. Well, he had no intention of being swallowed up.

"Just exactly what part of 'I don't want to dress up' do you not understand?" he demanded.

"All of it," she answered cheerfully, as she exited the room.

Zooey was back in less than three minutes, holding a large box in her hands with the logo Fantasy written across it in big, bold red letters. When Jack made no move to take it from her, she thrust the box at him.

"Here. Try this on for fit," she urged. "I took my best guess, but I'm not all that good when it comes to sizing up men." There was amusement in her eyes as she said it.

Part of him wanted to stand firm, to tell Zooey that she probably knew damn well what she could do with the costume. But the part of him that had urged him to become a lawyer, that believed in order and prescribed ways of doing things, figured if he put the damn thing on and let her see how ludicrous he looked, she would finally leave him in peace.

Or so the theory went.

So he took the box from her and walked into the powder room down the hall to change, and finally put this verbal tug-of-war between them to rest once and for all.

Anticipation hummed through Zooey as she waited for Jack to return. It was, she supposed, like waiting to see if reality lived up to her fantasy. Since staying still was not something she had ever managed to do with aplomb, she began to straighten up the study, carefully stacking the books he'd left scattered all over on his desk.

It was rather ironic that she took better care of Jack's

house than she ever did of the tiny apartment she'd lived in before moving here. She supposed that there was something about Jack and his children that brought her nesting instincts to the surface, that made her want to take care of the three of them, because, in different ways, they all needed to be taken care of.

It was an entirely new sensation for her, a new emotional grouping to reckon with.

And, if she moved fast enough, she didn't have any time left over to dwell on the fact that she had the same need within her. The need to lean on someone, to have someone who was willing to take over.

Not all the time, of course, but once in a while. When the burden on her shoulders grew too heavy. Even just the knowledge that there was someone willing to take over would have been enough.

She supposed that what it boiled down to was having someone to love. Someone who loved her back.

Zooey sighed.

She was getting maudlin. She was going to have to watch that. Being maudlin was ordinarily as foreign to her as shoes were to a duck.

The slight noise behind her had Zooey instantly turning toward the doorway. Since she'd moved into Jack's house, her reflexes had become razor sharp. They had to be. She never knew when Jackie might decide to take a dive from one of the bookcases.

For a second, her heart stopped.

Because her fantasy had taken on flesh and blood.

Humoring her, Jack had put on the entire costume, down to the shoulder-length wig and wide hat with its colorful scarlet plume.

He looks magnificent.

This wasn't a garden-variety cheap costume made to

last a night before it began to fall apart. She had gone out of her way to find an exact duplication of what a well-heeled pirate might have worn three hundred years ago while plundering his way across the seven seas.

There was no doubt about it, Zooey thought. In another life, Jack Lever had been a swashbuckler. Every woman's fantasy come to life.

"Well?" he finally asked, when she made no comment. He was feeling progressively more stupid by the nanosecond.

Zooey swallowed, searching for saliva so that her lips wouldn't find themselves sealed together midword. Her mouth remained annoyingly dry. "You need a sword," she finally said.

Her comment seemed to come out of left field. "What?"

"A sword. To complete the outfit. You need a sword," she repeated. *And I definitely need oxygen before I make an idiot of myself.* As subtly as she could, Zooey drew in a lungful of air.

"If I had a sword, I might be tempted to use it." It was a warning. Holding his arms out at his sides, Jack turned around full circle until he was facing her again. Well, at least she wasn't laughing, he consoled himself. But she had to see how absurd he looked in this outfit. "Okay, say it."

Zooey looked at him, puzzled. "Say what?" *Uncle? Okay, I say uncle, or whatever it is someone says when they surrender.*

Because she did. She surrendered. Completely and utterly. She'd always thought that Jack was good-looking in a dark, distinguished sort of way, but seeing him like this made her kneecaps melt, along with most of the rest of her.

Did he have to pull the words from her mouth? he wondered in exasperation. "That I look like an idiot."

That was the very last thought that would have passed through her mind. Very slowly, never taking her eyes off him, she moved her head from side to side. "Not any idiot I know."

"But an idiot," he pressed.

She was about to make a very vocal denial of that completely unmerited description. He looked gorgeous, not idiotic, but how did she phrase that without sounding as if she was willing to jump into bed with him? He was far too straitlaced to be on the receiving end of that kind of sentiment.

Even if it did vibrate in every vein in her body.

But she was mercifully spared from making any kind of a reply because, just then, Emily came running in in her nightgown. The look on her very serious young face fairly shouted that Jackie had done something unforgivable to her. Again.

However, whatever complaint was hot on her tongue vanished as she came to a skidding halt just inside the study, where she had tracked down both adults in the house.

Her eyes were wide as she looked up at her father. Recognition mingled with confusion, making her entirely uncertain. "Daddy?"

"Yes, it's me." Jack bit off the curse that hovered on his tongue, not wanting to subject Emily to the less than flattering thoughts that were now thriving inside his head. He'd begun to pull off the hat and wig when the awestruck look on Emily's face froze his hand in midmotion.

She looked every bit the little girl who had inadvertently stumbled into Neverland, only to find a dashing pirate in place of the malevolent Captain Hook. "Daddy, you look beautiful," she cried.

Zooey grinned, relieved that the pressure was off her. "Out of the mouths of babes." Her comment earned her a slightly confused look from Jack. Their eyes met and held for a long, pregnant moment. Zooey could have sworn the temperature in the room went up a whole ten degrees. She turned her attention to Emily, not because she was the girl's nanny, but because right now it was easier to look at her than at Jack. "Your daddy's going to be Jack Sparrow."

Emily seemed to accept the explanation, but it only raised another question for him. "And who the hel—heck is Jack Sparrow?"

You, Zooey thought. "He's a magical pirate in *Pirates of the Caribbean*," she explained.

The reference was vaguely familiar, but raised still more questions. Nothing, it seemed, was straightforward when it came to the children's nanny. "The Disney ride?"

"The movie," she corrected. "Johnny Depp played him." Maybe that would do it for him, Zooey thought. But judging from Jack's expression, very little had been cleared up. The man probably didn't watch movies, she thought. Something else to address. Eventually.

Zooey turned toward Emily. Time to bring in the big guns, she thought. "Your daddy doesn't think this is a good costume for him. He doesn't want to wear it."

Emily reacted just as she'd hoped the little girl would. "Oh, please, Daddy, please wear it. You're beautiful," she repeated.

Zooey bent down to her level. "Yes, he is, isn't he?" And then she straightened again, confident that the battle of the pirate costume had gone her way. "Go on up back to bed, Emily," she instructed. "I'll be there in a few minutes to tuck you in again."

Forgetting why she'd come down in the first place, still looking at her father, Emily nodded, then hurried out of the room.

Jack looked at Zooey as Emily disappeared down the hall. She couldn't begin to read his expression. "You don't play fair."

Zooey relaxed and grinned. She'd won the battle. "I never claimed I did. You do look very good, you know." And then a thought struck her and she sobered just a shade. "I'm sure Rebecca will think so."

"Rebecca?" he repeated, puzzled. "How is she going to see me?" He had no intention of leaving the premises in this outfit, even if the house caught on fire. He'd just resign himself to dying in the blaze.

"I invited her to the party." It hadn't been easy, but Rebecca did live only three doors down. Inviting everyone *else* on the block and omitting her would have made her seem petty and jealous.

Jack stared at her. "But she doesn't have any children."

Which was a technicality Zooey had almost given in to. But then, she was also inviting Bo and Carly to the party, and neither of them had children, either.

"No, but she is a neighbor and the party is for the adults in the neighborhood as well as the children." Zooey smiled up at him. "I thought that maybe Emily wasn't the only one who needed help with social skills."

She'd gone too far again. "You're their nanny, not mine."

His dark tone did not succeed in scaring her off. "Consider it a bonus."

Maybe being blunt was the only thing she'd understand, the only way to make her retreat. "I consider it irritating."

She paused for a moment, debating backing off. But that went against her grain. So, for the second time within the space of a few minutes, she stood up to him.

"You're within your rights to—"

Jack closed his eyes for a second, gathering strength and being grateful that he wasn't facing her in a courtroom. Because he'd be sorely tempted to wring her neck.

"Fire you—yes, I know." He opened his eyes again and gave her a meaningful look. "I just might take you up on that someday."

Her expression never changed. "I know."

"And still you continue." She was either very dumb or a hell of a poker player. He had a hunch it was the latter.

To her, it was a simple matter. "Have to be true to my nature."

"Of being a pest?" he demanded.

Zooey never blinked an eye. "Of doing what I think needs doing."

The woman was nothing short of infuriating, eating up his entire supply of patience.

Damn, but he wanted to kiss her.

To kiss her and shut that mouth of hers with his own so that he could just lose himself in her.

What the hell was the matter with him? This wasn't like him. The hat and wig were probably cutting off his circulation, he thought darkly.

That didn't change the fact that he wanted Zooey. That he wanted to make love with her.

He needed space. Needed to open a window and air out her scent, which was driving him crazy. It was raining outside, but the damp, dank breeze would be welcomed right about now.

"You promised to tuck Emily in."

"I know."

"I think you'd better go do that," he told her, his voice strained.

Go, leave. Before I do something stupid, Zooey, he pleaded silently.

Zooey smiled serenely at him, as if she'd heard his thoughts.

"On my way," she responded.

She left the room and Jack immediately crossed to the window, opening it and trying to erase her presence.

Chapter 11

Emily burst into Jack's study the following Saturday morning. "Daddy, Daddy, we're going shopping for stuff. You wanna come with us?" she asked him excitedly as his door banged open.

Jack winced inwardly, anticipating the hole in the wall that the doorknob probably made. He was going to have to start locking his door, he decided as he set down the brief he was reviewing. "Now why would I want to do that?"

"Because it's for the party. We're going to the *super*-market!" she announced, emphasizing *super* because today that seemed to her like a particularly funny thing to call the grocery store.

Having raced into the room like gangbusters, Emily was now tugging on his arm with all her less than considerable might, trying to get him to stand up.

His daughter seemed a lot happier these days, Jack

mused. A lot more lively. In true you-never-know-what-you're-missing-until-it's-gone fashion, he found himself missing the quieter Emily. But he knew that this change was actually for the best as far as the little girl was concerned.

Looking over her head, he saw Zooey standing in the doorway, a firm grip locked around Jackie's hand. For once, it appeared as if this invasion was not of her making.

"We have to go, Emily. Your daddy's busy," Zooey told her kindly.

"No, I'm not."

He could see that his response completely floored Zooey. In what was undoubtedly an unguarded moment, surprise registered on her face. Though he knew it was probably childish, he felt a small sense of accomplishment for being able to get to her. It seemed only fair, seeing as how the woman kept getting to him.

"You're not?" She was looking at the papers in his hand.

"Less than usual," he acknowledged.

Letting Jackie into the room ahead of her, Zooey crossed to Jack's desk. The same desk Jackie was attempting to scale. She caught the little boy up in her arms without missing a beat and set him down again, blocking his access.

She looked at Jack uncertainly, wondering what had brought this sudden change. "And you're willing to come to the supermarket with us?"

Emily was standing next to him, closer than a shadow. He passed his hand over her silky hair and she looked up at him, beaming. Emily, like her brother, had been unplanned. But he was beginning to understand why people wanted children.

"Might be interesting."

"Might be," Zooey echoed, still a little stunned. And then, because she couldn't help herself, she asked, "Are they putting something extra into your coffee these days?"

He was toying with her, he realized. And enjoying it. "Can't a man want to go with his family to the grocery store without being held suspect?"

With his family.

Had he just lumped her into the group by accident, or by design? Zooey felt her pulse accelerating.

Don't get ahead of yourself, Zooey. You don't want to go on a toboggan ride and find out there's no snow on the hill.

"Absolutely," she answered. Getting Jack to come along would have been her idea, except that she remembered what today was. And where he was going to be in a few hours. And with whom. "But I thought you might be wanting to get ready."

She couldn't mean for the party. That was tomorrow. Which left him fresh out of guesses. "For?"

Why was he making her say it? He couldn't possibly be that absentminded. Which only meant that he was having fun at her expense. And yet he didn't seem like the type. He wasn't cruel, just removed.

"Your date with Rebecca," Zooey finally said, once again taking Jackie away from a source of temptation— this time the coffee table. It had a glass top and she could almost see the thoughts going through the two-year-old's head. "It is today, isn't it?"

He'd canceled his date several days ago. It didn't seem fair to him to take up Rebecca's time when his head was elsewhere and his heart just wasn't in it. But he'd had no intention of making a major announcement about his change of plans. "It was."

"Who's Rebecca?" Emily asked, looking from her father to Zooey.

"Was?" Zooey echoed. *Don't start celebrating, he's probably just rescheduling, that's all.* Still, even though she managed to keep the smile off her face, she couldn't quite manage to keep it out of her voice. "What happened?"

He was not about to go into detail, especially not around his children. "Can we talk about this later?" This time he was the one who took Jackie down from the sofa, where the child was attempting to build up momentum bouncing up and down on the cushions.

"Who's Rebecca?" Emily asked again, a little more forcefully.

"Just a lady in the neighborhood," Zooey told her. "She lives three doors down, close to Olivia. She'll be at the party."

Planting his son on the floor, Jack went to retrieve his coat. "I wouldn't count on it." He tossed the comment over his shoulder on the way.

Zooey caught Jackie's hand and drew the boy out of the room, following Jack. Emily came skipping along behind.

Now he'd done it, Zooey thought. The man had stirred up her curiosity until it was practically at the explosion level—and then just walked out. And he knew it. He'd been around her long enough to know that she was insatiably curious.

How could he do that to her?

But she knew that he wasn't about to discuss the matter around Emily and Jackie. She was just going to have to contain herself until she got him alone.

The next few hours, she thought, were going to be a mixture of ecstasy and agony.

He felt drained.

But oddly satisfied.

Pulling into his driveway, Jack realized that he was smiling to himself. He'd actually enjoyed the exhausting afternoon. Looking back, he couldn't remember the last time he'd been inside a supermarket. Foraging for groceries had never really numbered among his required tasks.

The last time he'd gone questing for food without intentionally winding up with a menu propped in front of him had been back in college. Before then, in his mother's house, there had been housekeepers to take care of that kind of thing. And afterward, there'd been Patricia. Grocery shopping was just something she took care of without involving him. After Patricia had died, the nannies he'd hired had taken care of stocking the refrigerator and the pantry.

This afternoon, with his squeaking grocery cart and his marauding children, had been nothing short of a near-life-altering experience.

He glanced at Zooey as he turned off the ignition. The music coming from the radio died down. His kids didn't. It seemed to him that they had been going nonstop since they left the house.

Unbuckling his seat belt, he got out of the car and went to open the trunk. He liked the sound of Zooey's laugh, he decided as he picked up four bags and carted them into the house. Jack made his way to the kitchen, where he deposited the bags on the table.

Behind him, Emily and Jackie were bringing up the rear, each proudly carrying a small plastic bag. Zooey had given Jackie the sack with the Halloween napkins. Emily had been awarded the colorful paper cups and plates to take in.

Looking at them now, he caught himself thinking that it felt very much like a family effort.

Or what a family effort would have felt like if he'd been familiar with such a thing, he amended. When Patricia was still alive, they'd never done anything as a family unit. She'd taken care of the kids, and on those rare occasions when he had some free time available, he and Patricia would get together to do something. It never extended beyond that, never included the children.

He'd been very close to being a stranger to his own children when Patricia died, he thought. The fault was his, he knew, but it didn't change the facts.

Today had been different.

What would it be like, he wondered as he went back to the car to retrieve the rest of the bags, if Zooey really was part of the family? If she was more than just the kids' nanny?

She *was* more than just the nanny, he reminded himself. Because they hadn't been a family until she'd come along. Just a man with two children he'd inherited from his late wife. It was Zooey who'd orchestrated things to get him closer to the kids. Pulling him into it, something that Patricia had never managed to accomplish. If that had ever been her goal.

Looking back now, he wasn't sure. He'd married Patricia with the greatest of hopes that he'd found someone who could finally make him feel. But ultimately, that wasn't enough, and somehow, somewhere down the line, those feelings he'd thought he had just seemed to vanish. Fading slowly until he gradually became aware of the fact that they weren't there at all.

That maybe he had just imagined them.

But now—now they seemed to be back. Stronger than they had ever been before.

And, ironically, he needed to bank them down. Because whatever it was he was feeling couldn't be allowed to go any further. Couldn't be allowed to thrive and grow. For so many reasons.

He'd never liked complications, and at the very least, getting involved with Zooey promised a whole host of complications.

Walking in with the last four grocery bags, he deposited them on the table. Miraculously, Zooey had unpacked all the others and put the contents away, except for one. He watched her now as she placed four cans of pumpkin pie mix on the counter, right beside the stack of unbaked pie crusts.

"You're really going to bake all those pies?" he asked skeptically.

"Sure. And I'm going to have help, aren't I?" Her question was addressed to Emily and Jackie, who both nodded vigorously.

"Yes!" Emily cried.

"Yes!" Jackie echoed with deafening enthusiasm.

"Well, that should set you back a few hours," Jack commented with a laugh. In his opinion, Zooey was undertaking a monumental task. "'You're a better man than I am, Gunga Din.'"

She began to take bowls out of the cupboards below the counter. "Rudyard Kipling notwithstanding, it will go very smoothly." Measuring cups came out of another cupboard. Mixing spoons emerged from a drawer in the corner. "The key to getting things done when you have children around is utilizing them, not trying to get them to stay out of your way."

"If you say so."

Zooey grinned. "You're welcome to pitch in if you like."

He looked at the items she was setting out. The closest he ever came to cooking was eating. He knew nothing about what it took to transform raw goods into edible offerings. "I thought I already had, by agreeing to wear that ridiculous costume."

If an inch was offered, she felt confident that somewhere there was a mile waiting to be taken. Or at least coaxed into the open. "That was a start."

Wasn't she ever satisfied? "You don't want much, do you, woman?"

"No more than I think I can get." An enigmatic smile played on her lips. She turned toward Emily and Jackie. "Kids, why don't you go change your clothes and wash your hands so you can help me bake the pies? Emily, help your brother," she added.

With a patient sigh, Emily took his hand. "Come on, Jackie."

To Jack's surprise, the little boy docilely followed her out. Miracles apparently came in all sizes these days.

He glanced at the preparations Zooey was making. "Party's tomorrow," he pointed out. "Why bake the pies today?"

Opening the pantry, she took an apron from its hook and slipped the loop over her head, then began tying the strings behind her back. "Because I don't like leaving things—"

"To the last minute." He laughed, shaking his head. "Yes, I'm beginning to get the idea."

The second Jackie disappeared down the hall behind his sister, Zooey turned to look at Jack. She had been patient long enough, and not knowing was killing her. "Why aren't you going out tonight?"

Jack looked at her, stunned. They'd been shopping for close to two hours. He'd forgotten all about the conversation he'd left hanging earlier in the study. Obviously, she hadn't.

"You're like a junkyard dog, aren't you? Once you clamp down, you don't stop."

Zooey shrugged. She'd been called worse. "I would have preferred a more flattering comparison, but, okay, I won't argue with the image," she stated, then focused on him. "Why?"

He wasn't comfortable discussing his social life with her. Especially since she was both the reason why he'd first gone out with Rebecca and the reason he'd canceled his date tonight. "Don't you think that's a little too personal for you to ask?"

"Probably," she agreed. But that didn't stop her from wanting to know. "Why?" she repeated for the third time, pinning him with her eyes.

He knew by now that she wasn't going to let up until he gave her some kind of reason. "Because I don't believe in wasting a person's time."

Zooey's eyes narrowed. "Yours or hers?"

He paused for a second before answering. Wondering if he should. "Both."

Zooey studied the man standing beside her at the counter for a long moment. She read what she needed to into his answer. And then she smiled. Broadly.

"I see."

"No, you don't," Jack informed her firmly. He didn't want her to get the wrong—or in this case, right—idea. This was a matter between him and him, and no one else.

The more he denied it, the more certain Zooey was that she was right.

"Yeah," she countered, feeling immensely pleased. "I do." As she waited for Emily and Jackie to return, she folded the last of the grocery bags and put them away for future use, then crossed to the sink to wash her hands. "How are you at grating cheese?" she asked nonchalantly. *He's not going out with Rebecca. He's staying in. Home team 1, Vixens 0.*

"Cheese?" he echoed uncertainly. "For the pie?"

He really didn't know anything about cooking or baking, did he? She refrained from pointing out that there was no cheese in pumpkin pie. She didn't want to alienate him or insult him, especially not since he was back on the market.

"No," she replied sweetly, "for the stuffed tenderloin I'm making."

No more enlightened now than he had been a minute ago, Jack lifted his shoulders and then let them drop again in a mute indication of helplessness. "I don't know, I've never tried."

She would have guessed as much. "Now's as good a time as any to learn." Taking the cheese grater out of the utility drawer, she presented it, a cutting board and a hunk of mozzarella cheese to Jack. "Have at it," she urged. She put the grater into his right hand, the cheese into his left and slipped the board closer to him on the counter. "Just be sure to watch your fingers," she cautioned. "Blood isn't part of the recipe." As Jackie and Emily ran in, making their return appearance, she switched her attention to them. "Okay, everyone's here," she announced cheerfully. "Let's get to work."

Jack thought of the brief he had waiting in the study. It wasn't urgent, just something he'd planned on getting done before Sunday night and the much-dreaded Halloween party.

But it would keep, he thought as thin slivers of cheese began to make their appearance at the bottom of the grater, forming a small, growing mound. It would definitely keep.

The doorbell started ringing a little after five the next evening as party guests began to make their appearance.

Coming down the stairs, feeling awkward as hell, Jack hardly recognized his own house. Zooey and the kids had spent all morning and part of the afternoon decorating. Now there was hardly any space that didn't have a friendly ghost, a warm fuzzy spider or some mythical, equally happy looking creature hovering against a backdrop of balloons.

There was candy everywhere, and somehow, miraculously, Zooey managed to keep Jackie out of it. To that end, she'd enlisted Emily's help. Honor bound, Emily had to refrain from eating the candy herself.

His daughter apparently had more willpower than he gave her credit for.

As for Zooey, the woman was nothing short of a witch, despite the harem girl costume she'd slipped on at the last minute. Even though she had all but forced him to parade around in his costume, she hadn't shown him hers. So when he caught a glimpse of her coming out of the kitchen carrying the punch bowl, Jack had found himself in dire jeopardy of swallowing his tongue. Or of carrying on a flirtation with cardiac arrest.

He'd never seen material arranged so sensuously. Everything essential was covered, but alluringly so. The costume fired up his imagination to the point that he found himself indulging in fantasies. Fantasies he knew he couldn't bring to fruition, but that nonetheless gave him no respite.

"Wow."

When he heard the single word, he realized that he hadn't just thought it, he'd uttered it. The flash of an appreciative grin as she turned to look at him told Jack that Zooey had heard his verbal error.

"Thank you. Right back at you. You look very dashing," she countered.

He scowled. His scalp was itchy beneath the wig, and the hat was making him perspire. "I look ridiculous," he declared.

It wasn't vanity prompting him, Zooey thought. He actually believed what he was saying. And obviously hadn't taken a look at the cartoon figures and comic book heroes milling around in his living room, which was growing progressively more festive.

"No, you don't," she insisted. Spying Emily, she called her over. When the little girl came running up, Zooey placed her hands on the child's shoulders and turned her around to face her father. "Doesn't your daddy look handsome, Emily?"

Emily nodded vigorously, the ringlets that Zooey had spent half an hour setting into her hair bobbing like golden springs. But before she could say anything, the doorbell rang.

Emily's eyes widened. Shifting from foot to foot, anxious to be gone, she asked hopefully, "Can I get it?"

As a rule, Zooey never allowed either of the children to open the door, evoking the do-not-trust-strangers mandate.

"We're all home," Zooey told her, emphasizing her point. "So it's okay."

But even though they lived in a neighborhood that was deemed to be one of the safest in the state, that did not automatically give Emily a green light to open the door whenever someone came knocking or ringing. Zooey firmly believed it was better to teach good behavior than to have to negate and "unteach" bad habits.

Dressed as a fairy princess, Emily ran over to the door, the veil from her small, pointed hat flapping behind her like a pink cape.

"Nice job," Jack observed.

Zooey thought he was referring to the costume she'd made. She'd finished it just this morning. Actually, she had sewn all three of their costumes, including Jackie's Robin Hood outfit. Only Jack's was left up to professionals. She'd tried to control as much as she could, making sure that Jack had no viable excuse why he couldn't dress up for his children's party.

"Thanks," she responded, watching the door to see who Emily was admitting. She watched Olivia bounce into the room, wearing a poodle skirt and saddle shoes, with her hair pulled back into a swinging ponytail. Cute. "It was remarkably simple to make," she said, referring to Emily's costume.

"No, I meant telling her about when she could open the door and when she couldn't." There was an admiration in his eyes as he looked at her. "You've been very good for the kids."

No hardship there, she thought. Part of the trick was just remembering how she'd wanted to be treated when she was Emily's age. With respect, not ordered around as if she didn't have her own set of brains.

"They've been very good for *me*," she told him. "Actually, they have a rather calming influence," she confided.

Jack could only stare at her, unable to comprehend how that was possible. And then he laughed, really laughed. He judged that, combined, his children probably had more energy than was typically generated on an average day at the nuclear power plant. That was *not* conducive to having a calming influence.

Zooey was one very strange, intriguing young woman. Not to mention sensual.

He banked down the last thought and went to greet his guests. Hoping no one would laugh.

Chapter 12

When he finally got to the front door and opened it, Jack wasn't prepared for what he saw standing there.

Instead of the trick-or-treaters who had been ringing his bell throughout the evening, it was yet another guest. He'd thought that everyone who was coming to the party had already arrived.

He hadn't counted on Rebecca attending after he'd canceled their date without rescheduling.

And he definitely hadn't counted on her looking like this.

There was an amused expression on her face, undoubtedly in reaction to the surprised, unsettled one on his. But he could hardly be faulted for that.

At first glance, Rebecca appeared to be wearing a very long, flowing blond wing. And nothing else.

The hair extended down to her knees and was, mercifully, strategically arranged to cover everything that was supposed to be covered. Just barely. The operative word here, he thought, being *barely.*

His first impulse was to grab one of the coats from the coatrack and throw it over her.

"Aren't you going to invite me in?" Rebecca's amusement grew by the moment.

"Um, yes. Sure." Jack moved back awkwardly, as if all his joints had suddenly been fused together.

Entering, Rebecca moved aside so that he could close the door again. She was very aware of the looks she was garnering. And reveling in it.

"I thought lawyers were never at a loss for words." And then, since she'd gotten the hoped-for reaction from him, her smile became benevolent. "Relax, Jack. I've got a body stocking on. A very thick body stocking," she emphasized mischievously. "In case you haven't figured it out yet, I'm supposed to be Lady Godiva." The look in her eyes became positively wicked. "I just seem to have misplaced my horse."

From out of nowhere, and to his eternal gratitude, Zooey materialized with a tray of hors d'oeuvres. She placed the tray between him and Rebecca, her smile never fading as she greeted the party's newest guest.

"I'm sure your 'horse' will turn up somewhere, Rebecca. Maybe he's just taking a breather for a moment," she suggested, never taking her eyes off the other woman. She thrust the tray closer to her. "Crab puff?"

Rebecca glanced down at the tray, but then shook her head. Her hair moved ever so slightly. "Maybe later."

"They're going quickly," Zooey told her, addressing her words to Rebecca's back as the woman melted into the gathering. "There might not be any left later." Turning to look at Jack, Zooey asked mildly, "Would you like a tank of oxygen?"

Having collected himself, and relieved that the woman wasn't actually wearing an X-rated outfit—because there were children to consider, especially his own—Jack shrugged away her question as casually as he could. "I just didn't think that she was coming."

Obviously, Zooey thought. She was surprised when he didn't crane his neck, following Rebecca's progress. Maybe there really *wasn't* anything going on between them. Zooey found that extremely heartening.

She laughed softly at his naive assumption about Rebecca's attendance. "And miss a chance to mingle with the men in the neighborhood? Don't know much about women, do you?"

"No," he admitted, popping a crab puff into his mouth. It was gone in one bite. "I don't."

His admission took her by surprise. One of the guests reached over to snare a crab puff and Zooey raised the tray a little to make the transfer easier. "An honest lawyer. Wow, you are unique."

"And hungry," Jack told her, taking two more crab puffs. He nodded appreciatively. "These are good."

The compliment pleased her, though she tried not to show it. She'd baked them from scratch. "If you want something more substantial, there's the tenderloin," she reminded him. "It's on the table in the dining room. I could get you some."

"That's okay." He indicated the last crab puff in his hand. "This'll hold me for a while."

"Okay, then, time to push the crab puffs some more," she quipped.

Jack watched as she made her way through the colorful, milling groups of guests in the family room and beyond. Without missing a beat, Zooey had easily taken on the duties of a hostess for this party. He would have said it was her waitressing training rising to the fore, except that, by her own admission, she'd been a fairly poor waitress.

No, it was something more. Something inherent. Because there she was, effortlessly weaving in and out of the crowd with a tray of food in her hands, stopping to exchange a few words with this neighbor or that, as if she'd been throwing and hostessing parties all of her life.

He heard her laugh at something that Megan Schumacher, Olivia's aunt, said to her. The sound managed to travel to him above the din of mingled adult voices and squealing children. It seemed to go right through him, burrowing into all the corners of his being.

With effort, he turned his attention elsewhere. Anywhere but where Zooey was.

Carly and Bo were over in a corner. The newlyweds had their heads together, talking, touching, laughing like two teenagers in love. They seemed oblivious to everyone else around them.

Jack popped the last crab puff into his mouth, hardly aware of what he was doing. Aware only that he envied Bo, envied the man what he had to be feeling right now. He had no doubts, judging by Bo's expression, that his gut was probably tightening and he was finding breathing to be a challenge because his heart was pounding so hard.

Startled, Jack stopped. *He* had experienced those very same symptoms recently. Not at the door just now when Rebecca made her appearance. Not even when he'd taken the woman out those two times, or on their second date, which had ended with an unambiguous invitation to come inside her house and remain for breakfast. It had nothing at all to do with Rebecca.

He'd felt all those things, and more, when he had kissed Zooey.

He needed, he decided, a drink.

And something to take his mind off Zooey and the way her hips moved as she continued to make her way through the crowd.

Jack went in search of someone to talk to. Preferably someone with a major supply of testosterone.

"This was a wonderful idea, Zooey," Angela Schumacher enthused as she took the next to last crab puff on the tray Zooey offered. She looked toward her three kids, or rather, looked around for them. Each was with his or her own peers, and for once, no one was arguing. Moments like this were close to perfect for her. "The kids are having a great time."

Zooey had never doubted it for a moment. All she'd really needed to do was provide the refreshments and the games. The kids took it from there. And most were generally well behaved. She was keeping an eye on the ones who tended to disrupt things.

"And the adults?" Zooey prompted, glancing from Angela to her sister. Megan had temporarily left her fiancé, Greg Banning, second in command at Banning Enterprises, talking over the merits of forsaking daylight saving time with one of the other men while she got some punch.

Taking a cup, Megan ladled the fruity drink into it. "We're holding our own," she told Zooey. Reaching for a second cup, she nodded toward another couple. Adam Shibbs only had eyes for the very pregnant Molly Jackson, whose side he seldom left. "Molly certainly looks happier these days than she has in a very long time."

"People in love generally tend to look that way," Angela commented a bit tersely.

Her tone was not lost on Zooey. "That sounded a little cynical."

Angela flushed, shifting uncomfortably. She hadn't meant to call attention to herself. But having been abandoned by her husband brought out something less than charitable within her.

"Did it?" she asked innocently. She decided to have a glass of punch herself, and waited for her sister to be finished. "Sorry," she murmured. "Old wounds just rising to the surface."

Zooey looked at her knowlingly. It was no secret what had happened to the woman. He husband had walked out. Once out of the picture, the man became lax with his child support payments, forcing Angela to work extra hours in an effort to make up the difference. Which meant that her time with the children at what amounted to a vulnerable period in their lives had to be cut down. Fortunately, Megan was there to take up the slack, but when you got right down to it, it just wasn't the same thing.

Angela's kids wanted Angela. And she knew it.

"They only become old wounds if you let them heal," Zooey murmured. "Otherwise, they remain ongoing, open wounds."

"So now you're dispensing medical advice along with hors d'oeuvres?" Jack's voice came from directly behind her.

She swung around, surprised by his unexpected appearance and trying her best not to show it. It didn't jibe with the cool, calm and collected image she was attempting to portray tonight.

"Whatever it takes," Zooey replied nonchalantly. She

set the now empty tray on the nearest flat surface and faced Jack. "Do you need me for something?"

He almost laughed out loud. If ever he'd been asked a loaded question, this was it. A dozen different answers, all variations of the same feeling, the same desire, materialized in his head in response to her innocent query.

Or maybe not so innocent, Jack amended, looking into Zooey's eyes. She seemed to know exactly what she was asking, he realized. Exactly what kind of response her question aroused.

He doubted it was possible for her to be ignorant of what she was doing to him just by breathing.

But because he hoped no one else was privy to this, he said, "I thought maybe you'd want to get the kids started playing their games. It looks to me like everyone's here."

Not trusting his assessment, Zooey conducted her own quick survey, and discovered he was actually right. There was surprise and admiration in her eyes. "You do keep track."

He saw Angela and Megan struggling not to laugh as they moved off to another area of the room.

"I'm a lawyer, Zooey," he said to her. "Credit me with a little bit of awareness."

"Oh, but I do," she told him, the soul of innocence. "Very little." And then she laughed at her own joke. The dark look on Jack's face brought her up short. Now what?

She didn't have long to wait. "Don't do that," he told her.

He'd lost her. She hadn't done anything. Not for the last five minutes. "Do what?"

"Laugh."

Okay, now he was getting just plain weird, she thought.

Just because he had trouble curving his mouth into a smile didn't mean she had to become solemn as well. This was a party. He *needed* to loosen up.

"Why?" she retorted, propping one hand on her waist.

His answer totally floored her, leaving her without a comeback.

"Because it gets to me," he told her tersely, just before he turned on his heel and walked toward a gathering comprised of a cowboy, an alien, a futuristic space traveler and Fred Flintstone. The group, all neighbors that he recognized and spoke to on occasion, looked very eclectic. It suited his mood.

Stopping only long enough to collect the last of the hors d'oeuvres from the kitchen and replenish her supply, Zooey made her way over to Molly Jackson and her fiancé, Adam Shibbs. The duo were dressed as Romeo and his ever-so-slightly pregnant Juliet.

Molly reached over to the tray without looking. Her attention was riveted to the boyish-looking, blond-haired Adam. Zooey had known the woman since starting her job with Jack, and had never seen Molly looking happier.

Why shouldn't she be? Zooey thought, retreating again. Molly was getting a baby *and* a husband, almost at the same time. What could be better than that?

She watched as Rebecca approached the couple, moving to hug Molly and say something to Adam. Both greeted her warmly. Zooey recalled that Rebecca had thrown Molly a baby shower just last month.

That meant the woman wasn't all bad, Zooey supposed. Actually, Rebecca wasn't really bad at all. Just in her space.

Her space.

Listen to her, Zooey mocked herself. As if Jack Lever

was hers. As if the man would actually have anything to do with an ex-waitress, an ex-dog walker, currently a nanny who, if the truth be told, was having trouble finding where her head really belonged.

Her heart, however, was another matter. Zooey knew where her heart belonged, or at least was.

Even if it shouldn't be.

Rousing herself, she abandoned thoughts that were going to lead her nowhere, and got back to overseeing the party and making sure everyone was having fun. Even Rebecca.

Zooey had no concerns as to whether Megan, Angela's sister, was enjoying herself. It was obvious she was, even to the casual observer.

Megan had arrived dressed as a fairy godmother, right down to the wand.

"Actually," the graphic artist had confided a few minutes earlier, "I feel more like Cinderella. Especially every time I look at Greg." A contented sigh, tinged with a hint of disbelief, accompanied the admission. "I'm surprised I'm not black-and-blue from pinching myself."

"That's supposed to be a figurative statement," Zooey had told her with an amused laugh.

Megan appeared lost in her own thoughts as she continued gazing toward Greg. Even dressed as one of the Musketeers, he looked very Ivy League.

"Who would have ever thought that a plain Jane like me would have landed someone like that?"

The one thing Zooey couldn't abide was listening to people run themselves down. Especially someone she liked.

"Me, I would have thought," Zooey told her. "And just take a look at yourself." For lack of a mirror, she directed Megan toward her reflection in the sliding glass door that led out to the patio. "You're not a plain Jane anymore. And even when you thought you were, you weren't," she insisted. "There was always an inner glow about you, Megan," she pointed out. A shy, appreciative smile bloomed on Megan's face. "You just relaxed long enough to let it surface and come out."

Megan knew better than to offer any denials to what Zooey was saying; she just wouldn't accept them. But something else struck her. "You're a great one for dispensing advice."

"Yes," Zooey agreed, sensing something more was coming. "I am."

"What about you and Pulse-Accelerating Man?" Megan nodded toward where Jack was standing with a group of men.

"Jack?" Puzzled, she wasn't sure where Megan was going with this. "What about him?"

"He has his eye on you, you know," Megan told her.

"No, he doesn't," she said quickly. Because to entertain the hope that Megan might be right, and find out otherwise, would have been too cruelly disappointing. Better not to hope at all than to be crushed. "And even if he does, it's just to make sure that I'm doing what he pays me for."

Humor curved Megan's mouth. "You're taking money for that?"

"No!" Zooey retorted with feeling, then lowered her voice when she saw that she'd attracted attention she definitely didn't want. "I mean—he pays me for watching his children."

"Mothers watch children, too, you know."

The word "mother" stirred up an entire myriad of feelings inside of her, setting off thoughts she didn't feel equipped to deal with at the moment. Because in the dead of night, when restlessness plagued her, she'd found herself entertaining the idea of being Emily and Jackie's mother.

And Jack's wife...

Still, she was confident that no one would ever guess she thought about that. Zooey raised her head. "What are you saying?"

The smile on Megan's lips was kind. Understanding. "What do you think I'm saying?"

She didn't trust herself to answer, so she diverted the conversation by pointing out the obvious. "Jack was going out with Rebecca."

There were next to no secrets in the neighborhood. Everyone took a great deal of interest in everyone else. "But he's not anymore, is he?"

"No."

Megan put her hand over Zooey's and squeezed it warmly. "That's because someone closer to home has his attention."

No, she wasn't going to go there. She wasn't going to begin building castles in the air, much as she wanted to. "The only thing that has his attention on an ongoing basis are his briefs."

Laughter entered Megan's eyes. She'd changed a great deal in the last month or so, come out of her shell and grabbed life with both hands.

"Tell me about them."

"Not *those* kinds of briefs," Zooey hissed.

Megan stood back as if to get a better view of her. "I never thought it was possible."

"What?" Zooey demanded.

"You're blushing."

She could feel the heat rising along her neck, her

cheeks. She had no doubt that Megan was right, but she wasn't about to admit it. "There are a lot of people here. The room's getting warmer."

Megan glanced to where Jack was standing. He was in the center of a group of men, yet completely separated from the conversation going on around him. And he was looking over toward them.

Toward Zooey.

"And with any luck," Megan commented, "it'll get warmer still after everyone leaves."

Zooey looked at her sharply. For one of the very few times in her life, she was flustered. "You don't know what you're talking about."

Her friend inclined her head, lowering her voice. "Trust me, Zooey, the people involved are sometimes the last to know." She glanced toward Greg. He was coming over to join her. Her eyes shone with love. "Believe me, I should know."

Zooey shook her head. Megan meant well, but her instincts were off.

She was happy for Megan. Very happy for all the couples here who had found love and were making the most of it. But you didn't find what you weren't looking for, and she wasn't looking for love. First she needed to get her life in order and on the right track, *then* she could find a place for love. Not before.

She realized that she was looking toward Jack and clutching the tray extra hard. With effort, she forced herself to blow out a breath and then take another one in. Slowly.

It was an evening that seemed to go on forever. Not that Zooey found it a hardship to endure. The party was nothing short of wonderful. She enjoyed people, and the folks who lived along Danbury Way were a very special lot, with the possible exception of the always-bickering Martins.

But they hadn't shown up, which was just as well. They weren't really missed, and everyone else, with or without children, had responded positively to the Halloween party invitation. So much so that the original planned sit-down dinner had to be turned into a stand-up buffet. The kids loved it, gathering together whenever they wanted and eating when the mood hit.

That eventually translated into an incredible amount of paper plates, cups, napkins and miscellaneous garbage strewn around the entire first floor of the house, and the grounds outside by those hardy enough to brave the sudden drop in temperature. It was all worth it.

The exodus began at eight and continued until almost eleven. The discrepancy in time depended on whether or not guests had children to take home.

Cleanup was an ongoing process that didn't seem to get done, despite the help Zooey received from Angela, Megan, Carly, Molly and, surprisingly, from Rebecca. Before they left, the women did, however, put a sizable dent in what she was going to have to face tomorrow.

She was still finding stray glasses and plates to pick up even as the last of the guests walked out.

"Leave it," Jack told her after he closed the door.

Emily and Jackie had long since been put to bed, and the house suddenly seemed almost eerily quiet.

Zooey continued gathering. "I just thought I'd do a little more now—"

Crossing over to her, Jack physically took the paper plates out of her hands.

"I said leave it, Zooey," he repeated. "You've done more than enough." He glanced around. The house looked almost clean to him. "Call in one of those cleaning crews tomorrow to handle the rest."

She hated wasting money. "There's no need, Jack, I can—"

He frowned, stopping dead in his tracks. "Do you feel an overwhelming need to contradict everything I say?"

"No. Not an overwhelming need," she replied, a smile creeping over her lips. "Just when you're wrong—"

He cut her short. "Humor me. Call in a cleaning crew. Your time is far too valuable to waste picking up paper plates."

She liked that he thought so, but wasn't sure if that was the punch or the man talking. She needed to be clear. "I thought that was what you were paying me for. Being the nanny-slash-housekeeper."

He laughed shortly. "I don't want to wear you out before your time."

There was little chance of that. If the kids hadn't done it by now, a little elbow grease wasn't about to do the job.

"I'm more resilient than I look."

He gazed at her for a long moment. When he spoke, his voice was low. "I already know that."

Damn, there went her heart again. In double time. "Oh?"

"Yes, 'oh,'" he echoed.

How she came to be in his arms the next minute, Jack couldn't have explained. He had no memory of making the first move, no memory of folding his arms around her. All he knew was that time seemed to suddenly stop of its own accord.

Because her presence was filling the room.

Chapter 13

Even as he kissed her, Jack knew it was wrong. Knew that he should have more control over himself, more willpower than this.

But the sad truth of it was, he didn't. When it came to the feelings that Zooey stirred up, his willpower, his resolve, his whatever it was that ordinarily kept him on the straight and narrow, unwavering path, were badly corroded. Moreover, the very foundations of that willpower had been turned, by this mere slip of a woman, from concrete to Swiss cheese, so that simply taking her into his arms, simply kissing her, was setting off an entire chain reaction inside him that he couldn't control. He could only stand here in mystified confusion and feel it unfold.

The effects were heightened when Zooey rose up on her toes, wrapped her arms around his neck, leaned into him and deepened the kiss. It was as if she'd been waiting for this to happen all evening long.

If so, that made two of them.

But still, it shouldn't *be* happening. He wasn't some reckless teenager, governed by mindless impulse, by raging hormones. Hell, he'd never *had* raging hormones. He hadn't behaved this way when he actually was a teenager, so why was he doing so now, surrendering to his emotions as an adult? He was a lawyer, for God's sake, a man whom his colleagues said was the last word in steely control.

Where was that steely control now, when he really needed it?

With what felt like his last ounce of swiftly dwindling strength, Jack managed to take hold of Zooey's shoulders and pull back.

His brain vainly searched for a way to frame an apology. Because he owed her one for misleading her this way. For making her think that this was about something other than just gratifying a physical urge. Because it couldn't be about anything else.

He searched her face, looking for a sign, for a way to ease into this. But all he saw was exactly the opposite. "Zooey, I didn't mean—"

The look in Zooey's green eyes told him she had his number, but good.

"Yes," she whispered, "you did. And so did I."

She was right. But going forward, as everything inside of him begged him to, could very possibly destroy that newly constructed haven that not only he, but more importantly, his children, had taken up residence in. He needed to make Zooey understand that. To understand that while she was precious to him, to all of them, nothing could be allowed to happen here.

He threaded his fingers through her hair. Desire pounded its fists against him. He was having trouble trying to ignore everything but the right course to take. "Zooey, you've come to mean a great deal to Jackie and to Emily, of course—"

And they, Zooey thought, had come to mean a great deal to her. Almost from the first moment in the coffee shop that morning he'd brought them in. More than she could even put into words.

But this wasn't about Emily or Jackie, this was about Jack. About them.

Or was she just deluding herself?

She'd never been one to hang back, to wonder if there was rain or sunshine outside her door. She wasn't the type to find out by listening to a weather report, or staying safely indoors while looking through a window. Zooey was proud of the fact that she'd always thrown open the door and braved whatever it was that was waiting outside for her.

This was no different.

"And you?" she pressed, her eyes never leaving his. "Do I mean a great deal to you?"

How did he answer that and stay true to the goal he'd set for himself? And how could he accomplish that without hurting Zooey? He felt like a man in an uncharted minefield.

"Having you here… Having you here…"

He was trying to say that having her here, taking care of his children the way she did, afforded him peace of mind. It allowed him to function and do what he did best. But right now, having her here *didn't* allow him to function. It didn't even allow him to think, or talk like a man with half a brain. Having her here at this moment was scrambling his thoughts, his pulse, setting absolutely everything on its ear.

His voice had trailed off and he didn't look as if he was going to finish what he'd begun to say. "Yes?" Zooey murmured.

Frustration all but exploded in his veins. "Oh, the hell with it," he growled. The next second he lowered his mouth back to hers.

Oh, the hell with it. The words echoed in her head. Not exactly an endearment, Zooey thought, surrendering to the feeling Jack summoned from within her. And definitely not the tender words a woman waited to hear. But in an odd way, she understood the sentiment behind the frustration that had caused him to say it.

Understood it because it was rampaging through her own body.

She wanted to make love with him. Desperately. To have him touch her and take what was already his.

But even as everything suddenly went on overload inside of her, Zooey knew that they couldn't give in to the demands raging within them. Or at least, not where they currently were, standing beside the buffet table. They were right out in the open down here, and Emily and Jackie had a habit of popping up where least expected. Zooey didn't want to take a chance on setting their sex education back by a couple of decades.

But God, she wanted him. Wanted Jack so much that in another moment there wasn't going to be a shred of logic left in her head.

"Wait." It took everything within her to voice the cry, to make him stop just as he cupped her breast and sent all sorts of delicious sensations coursing madly through her system.

At the sound of her voice, everything pulled up short

inside of him. He knew it. Damn it, he knew. Knew he should have somehow harnessed himself. Knew he'd gone too far.

He jerked back as if someone had jabbed a red-hot poker in his chest. "Zooey, I'm sorry. I shouldn't have—"

Why did he think she was saying no? Did he think she was some kind of mercurial tease? Someone who ran hot and cold almost simultaneously? She just wanted a change of venue, not of agenda.

"My room," she instructed breathlessly.

Jack stared at her. His brain wasn't processing. "Your room?"

Maybe he had something against doing it there. It didn't matter where they did it as long as the children couldn't see them.

"Or yours. I don't care, but please, take me somewhere." *Before I implode or explode, or go all to pieces.* "Just not here," she added. She ran the tip of her tongue along her bottom lip, tasting him. "The children might…"

Damn it, how could he have been so stupid? So self-absorbed and overwhelmed that he had forgotten Emily and Jackie could wake up and come wandering out of their rooms and down the stairs at any second?

He might be a hell of a lawyer, but he was one sad example of what a father should be.

"I—"

Zooey put her finger to his lips, silencing anything he might have to say. She didn't want to hear any further attempts at an apology, didn't want anything to take away from the magic of the moment. Grasping his hand, she led Jack to the staircase.

At the foot of the stairs, just as she was about to lead

the way up, Zooey suddenly found her feet leaving the floor. Jack had lifted her into his arms. She looked at him in surprise.

He resisted the temptation to kiss her again. The fact that her weight barely registered was a source of concern to him.

"Don't you eat?" he demanded. He hardly ever saw her take more than two bites in succession before she was up on her feet, attending to something. "You don't weigh anything."

Zooey winked at him. "I do it all with smoke and mirrors." She slipped her arms around his neck, thinking how nice this felt. Still, something within her prompted her to make a token protest. "I can walk."

"I know. I've seen you." He also knew that given half a chance, Zooey would take complete charge of the situation, and a man needed to take the lead sometime.

This was that sometime.

Because this was going to happen. There was no point in pretending it wouldn't. It was almost as if it was meant to, and the longer it was put off, the larger the resulting explosion threatened to be.

If his logic proved to be faulty, he'd examine it tomorrow, in the light of day, when all secrets were exposed. All he knew was that in the soft glow of evening, he couldn't resist her any longer.

There was something about Zooey, some undefinable X factor that spoke to him, that jumped up and seized him by the throat, threatening to cut off his air supply permanently if he didn't immerse himself in her.

A man couldn't live very long without his air supply.

Jack brought Zooey into his bedroom, closing the door with his elbow. The click echoed in the quiet room as he set her down at the foot of his king-size bed.

The moment he did, they came together, sealed to one another. Their bodies sent waves of heat shooting in all directions as his mouth once again closed over hers.

His hands roamed her body as if to reassure him that she was actually there, that he was actually touching her.

There was a breathlessness to it, to just being with her like this. Drowning in her.

Anticipating more.

There were no buttons on his shirt, Zooey realized. That made it easier. The material was loose and billowing and she managed to get it up over his head and off his body with a minimum of effort. His vest was already mysteriously gone, shed somewhere between the family room and the front door.

The moment she dropped his shirt from her fingers, Zooey was certain she understood what a piece of toast unable to pop out of the toaster felt like. Just looking at him caused heat to radiate, nonstop, all over her. Doubling her body temperature and threatening to turn her into a piece of charcoal.

Her breathing was quick, shallow, and growing more so as she felt his hands on her. He was removing her veils, trying to get down to her bare skin.

"How many layers does this thing have?" There was exasperation in Jack's voice.

"Just one less than enough to make you insane," she told him.

One by one, the veils came off, leaving her vulnerable and wanting. The colorful scarves floated to the floor, creating a rainbow of fabric around them.

Zooey shivered as she felt his strong, capable hands on her bare hips. She caught her breath as he tugged down the harem pants, leaving her in thong underwear that was all but transparent.

And then in nothing at all, wearing only his hot gaze.

He had the same feeling he'd had when he'd first looked at a sculpture of Venus while on a forced field trip to the Metropolitan Museum of Art years ago. Overwhelmed. Awed.

Zooey's body, devoid of clothing, was tight and sleek and firm. And he wanted her so badly he could barely breathe.

This time when he kissed her, each kiss was more powerful than before, collecting momentum from the last, flowering into the next. Unable to keep still, his hands continued to roam almost worshipfully over her, touching, sampling, wanting.

And all the while, Jack kissed her over and over again, completely absorbed by what he was doing. Immersed in the sight, the sound, the scent of her. Nothing else existed beyond that. Nothing else registered, save how soft her skin felt, how pliant her body was, and how, as she twisted and turned beneath him on his large, lonely bed, she sent tongues of fire shooting into his every single pore.

Fueling him.

Inspiring him.

Unaccountably, Jack found himself doing things he'd never thought of doing, not even with Patricia.

Patricia had been a good woman. A good wife. But their lovemaking had been unimaginative, right from the very beginning. He blamed himself for that. Pursuit of his career had taken all his energy. To appease the woman he'd married, he'd gone through all the required motions, the tried-and-true steps. They'd brought him to the desired conclusion, but left him unsatisfied. As they'd probably left her.

But with Zooey, it was different. With Zooey, there were firecrackers. There were sparklers going off, lighting up the dark skies with wonder and an endless fountain of elation.

He was certain he was dreaming. Imagining all of it.

And yet it was real. As real as the woman of flash and fire here with him in his bed.

He knew, by the frantic way she clawed at the silken, chocolate-colored comforter beneath her, by the way she twisted and arched, moaning in pleasure, that he had brought Zooey to more than one climax. He'd used everything at his disposal—his tongue, his lips, his fingers—doing things with her that he'd never attempted with Patricia.

Yet here, with Zooey, it seemed right.

And then, because each time she lifted her hips, grasping for him, he wanted nothing more than to be with her on this journey, he found he couldn't hold back any longer. He'd stretched his endurance, his control, until it was a long, thin thread, threatening to snap.

Moving her legs apart with his knee, while her eyes held him prisoner, Jack drove himself into her. Passion and desire slammed into him with the force of a hydrogen bomb. As she began to move, to moan his name against his mouth, Jack realized he was twice as lost within her as he'd been before.

The journey to fulfillment was quick, euphoric, and he found himself wanting both the sensation and the anticipation of that sensation to exist at the same time. Wanting it to continue forever, or as much of forever as he could manage to hang on to.

Because he knew that logic and remorse waited for

him just around the corner. More than anything, he
wanted to elude both for as long as humanly possible.

Longer.

So after the last glorious sensation had shuddered
through him, Jack gathered Zooey to him on the bed
and held her for a very long time. Losing himself in the
scent of her body, the silky way her hair felt against his
skin.

So this was paradise.

This was what perfect felt like, Zooey thought, a
sweet, dreamy sensation swirling through her as she
curled her body into his.

Jack wasn't her first lover, but, she realized, he was
her first love.

She'd been engaged to Connor, coming together with
him because at the time it seemed as if it was the thing
to do. It was what everyone else wanted from her. She'd
remained engaged to Connor, even though something
inside of her had resisted, because she knew it would
make her parents happy. Connor had not been without
appeal. But you could only take a relationship so far because of a sense of responsibility. After that, it began to
fall apart if its foundations weren't based on anything
solid. Anything real.

Tonight was real. Very real. As were her feelings for
Jack.

She didn't want to leave. Not his bedroom, not the
moment. She knew that for the rest of her life, she was
going to be trying to recapture this sensation. And the
promise of finding it, of having it again, no matter how
briefly, was what was going to sustain her.

But even now, Zooey could feel Jack withdrawing.
Pulling away from her. He wasn't actually moving aside,
but she could feel his body tightening. As if he was

physically attempting to reconstruct the barriers that had disintegrated tonight. The barriers that normally stood between them.

Too late, she crowed silently. You couldn't unring a bell, and hers had been rung. Over and over again. What had happened between them *had* happened. And every wonderful, delicious, unexpected moment was forever sealed in her memory.

Raising her head, Zooey looked at the man who was the father of the children she adored. An enigmatic smile played on her lips. She had no idea how that aroused him.

"So," she began, tracing her fingertip along his chest, "about the Christmas party…"

How could she talk about parties, about anything, after what they'd just done? After what they'd just shared? "You're kidding."

"Am I?"

There was mischief in her eyes, and even though he knew he should be getting up, should somehow be trying to rummage through the ashes to find the bits and pieces of his life the way it had been only an hour ago, he couldn't help being drawn to her again. Wanting her again.

Zooey was strumming her fingers down his chest, stroking it lightly with the familiarity of a longtime lover, not someone who had only breached the wall a scant few minutes ago.

He felt as if their souls had been together forever, even as he told himself he was being insane.

Zooey gave him the benefit of her thoughts. There really was logic behind her teasing question. "Parties seem to bring out the best in you." It certainly had tonight. "Or maybe it's the costume." Her eyes crinkled as she grinned. "How do you feel about putting on a Santa Claus suit?"

Jack grabbed her hand to keep her from distracting him, and held on to it as he talked.

"Oh, no," he declared firmly. "This time, I mean it," he added, in case she was actually serious. With Zooey, he had no clue, no way to second-guess her. Had she been on a jury he was pleading a case before, he would have been entirely uncertain how the verdict might go.

She was unpredictable. He was the predictable one. Or at least, he would have said he was—until tonight. Until she'd taken his hand, led him to the stairs and managed to send him over the brink, into a land he had no previous knowledge of. He had nothing to help guide him. Nothing to light his way as he tried to navigate to a safe harbor.

Being with Zooey didn't make him feel safe. Didn't make him feel complacent. But he discovered that for the first time in his life, being safe wasn't all that important to him.

Because of Zooey, inspired by Zooey, he found himself wanting to be reckless, daring.

Wanting, he realized, to make love to her again. Because while he was making love with her, he didn't have to think. All that was required of him was to react. And he could do that. With her.

He gave her an alternative to her plan, just in case she was seriously entertaining the idea he was fairly certain she'd tossed out on a lark. "You can be Mrs. Claus, or one of the elves."

She wasn't ready to give up her suggestion. "You'd look cute dressed up as Santa." And then the gleam in her eye became positively wicked. "But I have to admit, you look even cuter not dressed at all."

Grasping her hips, he drew her over him until she was on top. "Funny, I was thinking the very same thing."

Her hair rained down around his face like golden sunbeams. "What else were you thinking?"

He could feel himself hardening again. Wanting her. "Guess."

Zooey shifted ever so slightly, just enough to arouse him further. "I don't think I have to. I think I might have a clue," she told him, right before she brought her mouth down to his.

Chapter 14

"Morning!"

Zooey sang out the greeting cheerfully when Jack finally walked into the kitchen the following morning. She was surprised he'd taken so long to come down. Even the children were up and ready and at the table before him.

Maybe last night had worn him out, she thought with a smile. He'd been sleeping when she'd slipped out of his room, taking the precaution just in case Emily or Jackie woke up and went looking for either her or Jack. She'd been tempted just to lie there, watching him sleep, but sense won over temptation. This time.

Zooey turned down the flame beneath the frying pan and the newest batch of French toast. She felt remarkably cheerful for a woman who had slept a total of six and a half, maybe seven, minutes the entire night. But she was still flying high on adrenaline and a double dose of euphoria.

Last night had been like a dream come true. Jack had been everything she'd always thought a lover should be. Tender, kind and completely involved in ensuring her pleasure above his own. Given that, along with the fact that he was handsome and successful, she had no idea why this man didn't have droves of women following him wherever he went.

Whatever the reason, she was glad he didn't, because she hated having to worry about how she measured up against another woman.

As of this moment, she thought, watching Jack come in, life was absolutely perfect.

She saw his eyes dart in her general direction. Jack barely nodded his head. Something that sounded like "Morning," emerged from his lips, but it could have just been that he was clearing his throat. He also only vaguely acknowledged the children at the table, only after Emily said something to him twice, repeating it when he didn't respond to her the first time.

Taking the mug of extra black coffee she'd poured a second ago, Zooey placed it in Jack's free hand. With a smile, she stepped back and indicated the French toast that was still in the frying pan.

"I made breakfast."

She noticed that he didn't release his hold on his briefcase.

"I don't have time." He didn't even look at her as he said it. His attention seemed to be riveted to the back door. And escape.

Maybe not so perfect, Zooey silently amended. But then, just because the earth had moved for her last night didn't necessarily mean that it had for him, even though, until just this moment, she would have sworn on a stack of Bibles that Jack had been as swept away by what had happened last night as she was.

"Breakfast is the most important meal of the day, Daddy," Emily informed him. Her tone of voice indicated that she felt she was imparting important information that could also be classified as breaking news. As a clincher, she added, "My teacher says so."

"And she's right," Zooey agreed. She kept one eye on Jack, who was frowning. She didn't want him to feel as if she was trying to be pushy, or at least pushier than she'd been. The last thing she wanted was for him to think that she felt last night gave her special privileges, such as the right to tell him what to do. "But sometimes, people don't have time to eat breakfast at the table. They eat it on the run."

Anticipating that he might be in a hurry because it was Monday and because he was Jack, she'd wrapped up a serving of French toast, complete with syrup in a small, airtight container, and packed it to go.

"Here." Smiling, Zooey handed him the bag she'd prepared. "Run."

Jackie's eyes lit up. "Run, Daddy, run!" he exclaimed excitedly, waving his feet back and forth for added momentum.

Draining the last of the coffee, Jack put the mug down and looked down at the bag she'd put in his hand. "What's this?"

"Breakfast," she told him simply. Since he hadn't been down here first thing in the morning as usual, she was pretty sure he'd overslept. Which made him late. "I had a feeling you might be in a hurry this morning."

He was. But he was fairly sure it wasn't the way she thought.

He was in a hurry to get away from the feelings that had insisted on rising up and haunting him in his dreams all night, no matter how hard he tried to ignore them or banish them.

Feelings that he felt entirely unequal to dealing with. He had no idea what to make of them or how to react.

All he knew was that he felt as if he was coming unraveled. And he didn't like it.

"Yeah," he mumbled. "Thanks." Without any further communication, either to his children or to her, he made his way out the back door to the garage.

"See you tonight," she called after him just as he was about to shut the door.

He paused only long enough to give her fair warning. "I might be late."

The way Jack said it, she had a feeling he was planning on it.

And she was right.

Jack didn't come home. Not at the usual time, or the time he often walked through the door when he was late. By eleven, Zooey gave up waiting. She turned off the warming tray with his dinner in the kitchen and went upstairs to bed. Despite her disappointment at his no-show, she was still desperately clinging to the shred of euphoria that continued to hover around her, telling herself that this was business as usual for Jack. At this point, she should have been more than used to it.

Except it wasn't supposed to be business as usual, she argued with herself as she lay in the bed a few minutes later, watching shadows on the wall. Some part of Jack should have been affected by what had happened last night, shouldn't it?

Okay, she didn't exactly expect him to start grinning

from ear to ear and singing silly love songs, but she also didn't expect him to audition to play the phantom of Danbury Way.

The last thing she remembered thinking before she fell asleep was that tomorrow would be better.

But it wasn't. It was more of the same. If anything, Jack became even more of a nonentity than he had been before.

As each day went by, it progressively became worse. Instead of just working long hours, he seemed to be working around the clock, gone before Zooey got up in the morning, back after she'd gone to bed. It got to the point that if it hadn't been for the wet towels in his bathroom and the dishes that magically appeared in the sink, testifying that he had come home, showered and had something to eat before making good on another escape, she would have thought she'd made him up.

The second day he was gone, Jack left a voice message on the phone, telling her that he was involved in preparing a high profile case for trial, one that required all of his attention.

She knew in her heart it was more than that. There might have been a case, all right, but that wasn't making him turn into the invisible man. It was her.

Zooey thought of waiting up for him, of confronting him when he came home and making him own up to what was going on. And then make him explain to her why he was doing this. But while she felt perfectly justified in cornering him when it had something to do with the children's welfare, because this merely involved her—*them*—she couldn't get herself to do it. Because she shouldn't *have* to do it, she thought, fighting back tears. After one night of lovemaking with her,

Jack Lever shouldn't suddenly have turned into Upstate New York's version of a hermit.

Had her techniques been that bad? she demanded silently in the privacy of her own room late at night. Had the idea of the two of them being intimate for any given length of time appalled him that much?

She had no answers.

All she had was a heart that was aching more and more. She couldn't make herself shrug this off, couldn't find a way to just lie low and wait it out. It hurt too much to be living in the same house, knowing that Jack was avoiding her like the plague.

And because of that, avoiding his children as well. That hurt just as much as his sudden abandonment of her.

"Is Daddy gone away on a trip?" Emily asked Friday morning as she and Olivia were being driven to school.

"Yes," Zooey answered quickly.

It was easier saying that than explaining to the girl that something had happened to make her father stay away. More than likely, Emily would want details.

"Is he going to be back soon?"

Zooey could tell by her tone of voice that the little girl sorely missed her father.

This had to stop, Zooey vowed. Before he completely destroyed whatever relationship he had left with his children.

"Soon," she promised Emily.

Zooey knew of only one way to end Jack's self-imposed exodus and get him to start keeping regular hours at home again. It was a drastic step, but she had no choice other than to take it. Not if she wanted to keep her conscience clear. There was something far greater at stake here than her supposed love life.

Frances Finnegan sat very quietly at her desk. She tended to do that when she was in shock. Finally, she raised her eyes to her firstborn and formed the question she wished she didn't have to ask. Not when it followed a request that not only made her heart glad, but would make both her husband and her brother-in-law extremely happy.

"Zooey, are you sure?"

Zooey hadn't allowed herself to think. Once she'd decided on this course of action, she hadn't looked back, hadn't left herself the option to reconsider. She tried to sound as positive as she could as she replied, "Yes, I'm sure."

Frances wasn't buying it. She knew her daughter too well, even if Zooey didn't think so. Though it wasn't really necessary, she took her for a trip down memory lane.

"But you said you didn't want to work here," she reminded her. "You even left college a month before graduation because you said you didn't fit into the business world." Frances gestured around the office. "And this is the business world, Zooey. Make no mistake about that."

Not wanting to go into her reasons for this sudden change, Zooey zeroed in on something minor her mother had said. "If you need me to have a degree to work here, I can complete the classes—"

Frances waved her hand dismissively. She was too savvy to allow herself to be snowed. "That's not my point, Zooey. My point was that you were adamant you didn't want to go into the family business."

Rather than sit on the chair in front of her mother's desk, or on the leather sofa off to one side, Zooey prowled around the room restlessly. She shrugged off her mother's words. "I was young."

Frances laughed. "You were a little more than a year younger than you are now."

Zooey paused to take a deep breath. She shoved her hands into the pockets of her jeans. The emptiness that haunted her, that in part prompted her to do this, refused to go away. "A year is a long time."

Frances rose to her feet and rounded her desk until she was standing in front of her daughter. "Zooey, what happened?"

Zooey pressed her lips together, willing herself to sound cheerful, or at least not upset. "Nothing. I just grew up."

Her mom placed her hands on her shoulders, holding her still. Frances wanted to hug her, to hold her the way she had when Zooey was little and she could make her problems go away with a few comforting words, accompanied by a bowl of strawberry ice cream. But she knew Zooey was in a fragile place right now. Hugging would not be welcomed. It would be confused with pity. "That's not what I'm seeing in your eyes."

Zooey flashed a grin. "You always did let those eye doctor appointments slip by," she said fondly. Very gently, she separated herself from her mother's hold. "Really, Mom, I'm okay." And then, because she knew her mother could read her like a book, she added, "This is just for the best, that's all."

Whose best? Frances wondered. It certainly didn't seem as if it was Zooey's. "What about those children you were taking care of?" she pressed. "Emily and

Jackie. It seemed to me they were very attached to you."

Leaving them would be one of the hardest things she'd ever done, if not the hardest. But she had to go, for their own good. Because who knew how long Jack would avoid staying home if she was there?

So she shrugged carelessly and murmured, "They're young. They'll get attached to someone else." *Far easier than I will.*

As if she could read her mind, her mother asked, "Do you want them to?"

Zooey wasn't up to discussing this right now. The last thing she wanted was to was let her mother see her cry. "Mom, this is a very simple question. Do you have a place for me or not?"

Frances slipped an arm around her shoulders. She couldn't remember them ever feeling this stiff. She pretended not to notice, but found herself wanting to box Jack Lever's ears even if she didn't know the man. Because he had to be at the bottom of this. Zooey was too crazy about those kids to want to leave on her own.

"Zooey, there's always a place for you here, you know that. Your father'll be overjoyed when I tell him. So will your uncle. And what I feel about you coming back goes without saying, but—"

Zooey turned and looked at her, stopping her mother before anything further could be said. "All right, then it's settled."

Frances studied her firstborn for a long moment. There was no reasoning with her now. But then, that was nothing new. "If you say so, Zooey."

"You're leaving?"

The sparsely written note that she had slipped under

his door in the middle of the night and that he had just discovered a minute ago on his way out, was crumpled in his hand as Jack burst into the kitchen the following Monday morning.

Zooey looked up from the scrambled eggs and ham she was making for the children. Jackie was in his high chair, making confetti out of his toast, while Emily sat primly at the table, nibbling on hers. Both children looked surprised to see their father.

"Yes," Zooey replied quietly, taking a spatula and dividing the contents of the pan between two plates. She hadn't bothered to make three portions. She had no appetite, and she hadn't been sure if she would even see Jack.

Emily looked stunned, then upset. "No!" she cried, staring at her.

"No!" Jackie echoed, without the slightest clue why his sister had uttered the word.

Damn it, she wasn't going to cry. Zooey tried to keep herself together as best as she could. "It's time, sweetheart," she told Emily.

"Why? Why is it time?" the child demanded, tears springing to her eyes. Trapping Zooey's soul there. "You can't go. You can't leave us." Zooey had just enough time to put down the pan before Emily flung herself at her, wrapping her arms around her waist and holding on tight. "You can't! I won't let you go."

This was ripping her apart, Zooey thought. Very gently, she removed Emily's arms and then stooped down to the little girl's level. It took everything she had not to drag her into her arms and hold her tightly. But it was reason that was needed right now, not emotion.

Zooey was painfully aware that Jack wasn't saying

anything, which just proved to her that this was ultimately the right course to take.

She kept her eyes on Emily. "Just because I won't be living here anymore doesn't mean that I'm leaving you or your brother. I'll always be around if you need me," she promised, her voice low, husky, as she struggled to keep it from breaking.

Reaching into her pocket, Zooey took out a business card with the company logo embossed on it. It had the address of Finnegan's Fine Furniture's corporate offices. She'd written her cell phone number, too, in preparation for this moment.

Nothing could have prepared her, though, she realized, her heart feeling like lead in her chest.

She placed the card in Emily's hand and closed her fingers over it. "All you have to do is call this number and I'll come."

Emily grasped the card. Tears began to spill down her cheeks. "It's not the same," she whispered.

"No," Zooey agreed. "It's not the same. But it's almost the same. It's close. Just like I'll be." She pointed to the address on the card. "This isn't really all that far away."

"It's farther than your room," Emily sobbed.

"It is," Zooey agreed heavily.

Jack had not said anything at all beyond the first initial expression of surprise. He was still standing there, looking at her, not even trying to alleviate his daughter's distress.

She was right, Zooey thought, feeling lost. Feeling alone. He wanted her to leave. Wanted her to leave so much that he wasn't even willing to offer up a token protest to make Emily feel better.

How could she have been so wrong about someone? Zooey wondered.

Served her right for dreaming. For hoping. There was no such thing as perfect men, no such thing as perfect moments. If ever she'd had any doubts, Jack had just shown her that there weren't.

Jack remained walled in his silence, not trusting his voice, not trusting his emotions.

He didn't want Zooey to leave. More than anything, he didn't want her to go. But he'd known in his gut that this was coming. Known as surely as the sun would rise that this had to be the natural consequence of what had happened between them Halloween night. He should have found a way to maintain control.

Too late. Damage done.

He couldn't blame her. Only himself. The situation had turned awkward between them almost instantly. He'd certainly felt it. Because that one night had not satisfied him, it had just shown him what had been missing from his life. Had shown him that he wanted more. And all of this had placed Zooey in a terrible dilemma. Her "employer" had made love with her and he wanted to do it again. If she gave in, would she do so because she didn't want to lose her job? Because she didn't want to leave the children? Or because she had feelings for him?

Jack was certain that the last, if it factored in at all, came a very distant third. So, as much as he wanted her, he'd been trying to give Zooey as much space as was humanly possible. To make her feel that he wasn't going to crowd her, wasn't going to demand repeat performances of the other night if she didn't want any to take place.

And still she was leaving. Because she was undoubtedly afraid that he would put more moves on her.

Her fear had to be tremendous, since he knew how much she loved his children. It was there in everything she did for them and with them. For her to leave them meant she just couldn't cope with the idea that things might heat up between them again. The fear that perhaps, some night, he might force himself on her.

He thought of telling her he'd never do that, but it would be a matter of protesting too much. It would only convince her that she was right in the first place.

So, as much as he wanted to tear up the note she'd left for him, refuse to accept her resignation and to have her remain here permanently, his hands were tied. He couldn't impose his will on her.

The best thing he could do for Zooey would be to let her go. Even though doing it twisted a knife in his gut.

"How soon?" he finally asked, his voice devoid of all emotion.

God, he couldn't wait to get rid of her, could he? Zooey thought, fighting back tears. Well, if he didn't care, she wasn't going to let him see that she did. She didn't want him thinking even less of her.

"As soon as you can line up someone to watch the children," she said in a voice that matched his own.

"Don't worry about that." There were temporary agencies he could turn to until he could find someone suitable. "I don't want to interfere with your plans." And then he paused, searching her face. Maybe this was a ruse for some reason. "You are going somewhere after this, aren't you?"

"Yes." She bit off the word wanting to use the frying pan behind her for more than just making eggs. She struggled to get hold of her temper. "Yes," she repeated more calmly, "I have something lined up."

"All right," he agreed, his voice calm, distant, "then I'll make the arrangements and you can be on your way by tomorrow."

Zooey felt as if her stomach had dropped out. He was all but giving her the bum's rush. Why? Was he that appalled at being involved with her?

"Perfect," she replied tersely.

"Perfect," he echoed.

He'd been hoping, even as he made the offer, that Zooey would change her mind at the last second. That she would tell him she needed more time. Stall. Give him some kind of sign, *any* kind of a sign, that maybe she wanted to stay. Stay with the children. Stay with him.

But since she was saying yes almost eagerly, he knew he'd just been deluding himself. She wanted to leave. Quickly.

Served him right for giving in to his impulses, for having the audacity to think that someone as bright, as outgoing as Zooey would want to be with someone as settled, as set in his ways, as he was.

"If you need references—" he began.

"I don't need references," she almost snapped. Zooey raised her chin. She kept one arm around Emily, wishing she could take the kids with her. Jack didn't deserve to have children. "I'm all set, actually."

He nodded, picking up his briefcase. "Then I guess there's really nothing more to be said on the subject."

"No," she agreed in the same tone, "nothing more."

Chapter 15

Every day seemed that much worse than the one before.

Zooey didn't know how much more she could take. It was supposed to be getting better, not worse. She'd never felt like this before—like a drowning victim dragged back from the brink of death who couldn't seem to suck in enough air to make her feel as if survival was an actual option.

She couldn't shake it, couldn't seem to work her way past it. She just kept moving through the pea soup fog, waiting for it to clear up.

It didn't.

Because she'd taken all her things with her when she left Danbury Way, Zooey was figuratively among the homeless when she reported in for work at the corporate offices the first day. That was quickly remedied by her mother, who immediately threw open the door of her old room. To make the invitation to take up residence in the house where she'd been born more appealing and less off-putting, Frances, clever soul that she was, had told her she was welcome to stay there until she found something more to her liking.

The trouble was, Zooey thought as she prowled around her office, restless and exhausted at the same time, she wasn't out looking. There seemed to be no energy in her veins to prompt her to go from apartment to apartment, looking for someplace to make her own. She of the boundless energy suddenly had barely enough to get out of bed and dressed in the morning.

Zooey told herself that she was coming down with something. "Something" kept coming for an entire two weeks without ever taking shape, hovering in the background. Making itself known just enough so that she felt as if each limb weighed a thousand pounds and could be moved only with the greatest of effort.

One day loosely worked into another. Like a prisoner sentenced to life without parole, she lost track of time.

Days no longer meant anything to her. They were just something to get through, nothing more.

"Not that I don't love having you around, Zooey, but I just don't know what to do with you."

Frances Finnegan looked at her daughter over the tops of the glasses nature and her ophthalmologist had forced her to wear in order to read words smaller than a billboard. She'd summoned Zooey into her office this morning after reviewing the halfhearted report that had come from her daughter's computer concerning the next six months' sales projections. It was obvious that not only was Zooey's heart not in it, her mind appeared to be AWOL as well.

Thinking that it was time to shake her up and have

a serious heart-to-heart, Frances said as much to her daughter.

"This report was written by someone whose mind kept wandering away from its subject." Even her brother-in-law, who was awful when it came to report writing, could do a better job than what she had lying on her desk. This just wasn't her Zooey, and Frances meant to find out why.

A rueful expression passed over Zooey's face. Reaching for the report, she took it from her mother's desk. "I'll do better."

"You'd have to work hard at doing worse," Frances said honestly, then sighed. "Zooey, I'm trying to figure out what you are doing here. Your coming to work for the family business is certainly not working out."

Zooey raised her chin defensively, a spark of her old self returning, much to her mom's relief. "I need a period of adjustment."

But Frances shook her head. She'd never expected to hear herself say this. "You need to go back to where you came from."

Zooey's eyes widened. She hadn't envisioned this. "Are you firing me?"

"I'm freeing you," Frances corrected.

She didn't want to be freed, Zooey thought, a slight edge of panic slicing through her. She *needed* to work, not so much for the money but because it gave her someplace to be, something to do, however badly. If she just sat at home, she'd lose what little mind she still had.

"Mom, I'm sorry, I'll do better," Zooey promised.

She saw the look in her mother's eyes. The same look that had been there when she was growing up. The look that said the truth was required from her. So the truth came. Or at least the part she could put into words.

"It's just that...I keep wondering if they're okay. Emily and Jackie," she added, realizing she was verbally jumping around.

There was more to it than that and they both knew it, but for now, Frances played along. "If that's all that's on your mind, why don't you just call them and find out?"

"I don't want to—" Zooey stopped herself. She'd almost said that she didn't want to take a chance on having Jack pick up the phone, but that was something she didn't want to share yet. Maybe never. "Interfere," she finally said. "I don't want to interfere," she repeated. "They're adjusting to a new nanny. Having me call and talk to them will just set them back to square one."

An almost amused expression played on her mother's lips. "Maybe they're not adjusting to the new nanny. Maybe they hate her."

Zooey looked at her for a long, poignant moment, as if that thought hadn't crossed her mind a hundred times already. "You know, I never realized how much you and I think alike."

Frances laughed. "Your best qualities come from me, Zooey. The other ones, blame your father." And then she grew serious. "Zooey, you're going to have to move on or move back." It wasn't anything that Zooey hadn't told herself more than once since she'd walked out of Jack's house. "This wavering in the middle—"

"Move on," Zooey declared fiercely, in case her mother had any doubts. "I want to move on. It's just taking me longer than I thought, that's all." Crossing to her mother's desk, she perched on one corner, feeling helpless. She'd never been in this kind of position before and didn't know how to get out of it. "The moment I decided to put Connor behind me, he was history. So was college and every job I ever had."

"Except for this last one."

"Except for this last one," Zooey echoed. She looked down at her mother. "I just need you to be patient with me, Mom."

"I have infinite patience." And it was true. She'd proved it more than once while Zooey was growing up. But there was a time to cut her daughter some slack and a time to tighten the reins. "The business, however, would like you to get up to speed a little faster than you've been doing. A lot faster, actually," she amended. "Quarterly reports are just around the corner—"

Zooey nodded vigorously. "I know, I know." She slid off the desk. "I promise I'll do better."

"Good." Frances rose to her feet as well. She slipped an arm around her daughter's shoulders, walking her to the door. "You'll make your father very happy—if that's what you want."

What I want isn't going to happen, Zooey thought.

She did her best not to make the smile she forced to her lips look as if it was merely painted on. "Always like to see you and Dad happy."

Frances gave her a penetrating look. "You know what I mean."

"Yes, I know what you mean." Before leaving, Zooey paused to kiss her mother's cheek. She'd never really appreciated her before, she thought. "Thanks, Mom."

She was aware that her mother continued watching her as she walked down the hall.

Moving at a quicker pace than she had for the last two weeks, Zooey started back to the office she'd been given, silently vowing to do better. She owed it to her mom, if not both her parents.

As she hurried past the receptionist, the woman half rose in her chair. "I put them in your office."

Confused, Zooey looked at her. As far as she knew, nothing was being delivered to her. "Put what into my office?"

"The kids. I didn't think you wanted me to interrupt you when you were in with Mrs. Finnegan, and I didn't know what to do with them—"

The last part of her statement was addressed to Zooey's back.

Zooey flew the rest of the way to her office. She didn't need to ask "What kids?" She knew. Emily and Jackie. Alone?

Her heart lodged itself in her throat as half a dozen scenarios, none of them good, flashed through her mind like a doomsday kaleidoscope.

The second Zooey opened the door, Emily and Jackie rushed toward her. She dropped to her knees just in time to have the children fling themselves at her, surrounding her with small arms and huge doses of affection.

"We missed you, Zooey," Emily cried, hugging her as hard as she could.

"Missed you!" Jackie echoed, the words thundering into her left ear.

"And I missed you." Zooey kissed them both more than once and held them to her tightly for a long moment before finally releasing them. She drew back to look at their faces. She needed answers. Lots of answers. "What are you doing here?"

Emily's lower lip quivered, as if she expected to be rejected and sent away. "You said to come if we needed you."

"No," Zooey corrected gently, "I said to call and *I'd* come if you needed me." This had *desperate* written all over it, she thought.

Rising, she took each child by the hand and led them over to the love seat against the wall. It was just large enough for the three of them.

Zooey sat down with a child on either side. To her surprise, instead of squirming, Jackie curled up beside her and laid his head in her lap. She'd never seen him so docile before. She stroked his hair as she posed questions to Emily.

"How did you get here? Did your dad bring you?"

"No." Emily looked up at her with big, innocent eyes. "We took a taxi."

Zooey stared at the little girl, stunned. "A taxi?" Taxis here didn't roam the streets the way they did in the city.

Emily nodded. "Olivia helped me find one in the telephone book and we called it together. I showed the man the address on the card you gave me."

"How did you pay for it?" Was there a driver outside, waiting for his money and getting progressively angrier?

"I used the money in my piggy bank," Emily told her. "And he brought us here."

This wasn't right. A seven-year-old and an almost-three-year-old weren't supposed to be out, wandering around alone like that. Why didn't the cab driver ask about adult supervision? "Where's your nanny?"

"Sleeping." Emily leaned closer and confided, "She sleeps a lot. The yellow medicine from the bottle she keeps in her pocket makes her sleep when she takes it."

Damn it, what kind of people was Jack leaving his kids with? Why didn't he do a thorough check into the woman's references before he hired her? "Did you tell your daddy that she sleeps so much?"

Emily shook her head. "Daddy's so sad, I didn't want to make him sadder." The little girl looked up at her. "I saw him looking at your picture."

Emily was making this up. Zooey had never given Jack a photograph of herself. "Your daddy doesn't have a picture of me, Emily."

"Yes, he does," she insisted. "It's the one that Olivia's mommy took at the Halloween party. Daddy was in it, too."

As soon as Emily said it, Zooey remembered Angela aiming the camera at them and ordering, "Smile." Zooey recalled being surprised that Jack hadn't turned his head away at the last minute. Until that moment, she would have said that he wasn't the type to pose for photographs.

"Olivia's mommy came to the house last week to give it to him. Daddy looks sadder every time he looks at it. He has it on his desk." Emily wiggled up to her knees on the cushion, lowering her voice as she whispered into her ear. "He told me he misses you."

Emily's warm breath grazed her cheek even as her words grazed her heart. Zooey resisted believing the girl. Resisted because more than anything in the world, she wanted it to be true. She wanted Jack to have missed her half as much as she'd missed him these last two weeks.

But she knew that Emily was very bright, very creative for her age. It wasn't beyond her to fabricate the story to get what she wanted.

Tucking one arm around the girl's small waist, Zooey told her seriously, "Your nose grows when you fib, Emily."

Instead of feeling to see if her nose had gotten any larger, Emily looked like the personification of innocence as she insisted, "He misses you, Zooey."

Then why didn't the big jerk call?

Beginning to feel like her old self, Zooey made up her mind on the spur of the moment. Moving Jackie into an upright position, she rose to her feet.

"C'mon," she declared.

Emily instantly hopped off the love seat. "Where are we going?"

Not waiting for Jackie to clamber to his feet, she picked him up. Stopping only long enough to get her purse from her desk and to slip her poncho over her head, she reclaimed Emily's hand. "To see your dad and let him know where his children are."

Zooey hurried past the receptionist again. The woman looked on in confusion. "Where are you going, Ms. Finnegan?"

Possibly to hell, Zooey thought. "I need to tell Jack Lever that he picked a lousy nanny to watch his kids."

There was a meeting scheduled for four o'clock. A meeting that the woman knew Zooey was supposed to be attending. "You can't—" the receptionist began, rounding her desk to try to catch up to the threesome.

"Oh, yes, I can," Zooey retorted as she turned the corner toward the elevators.

For the first time in more than two weeks, Zooey felt like smiling.

The inner-sanctum quiet of the law firm of Wasserman, Kendall, Lake & Lever was shattered the moment the elevator doors parted. Office doors all along the corridor were opened by occupants curious to see what the commotion was all about. It sounded as if a busload of children had been deposited there.

Not bothering to attempt to get Jackie to lower his voice, Zooey slowed down only when she reached Jack's office.

Lost in thought, a state aided and abetted by a malaise that threatened to completely undo him, Jack rose from his desk and opened the door when the vaguely familiar noise sounded as if it was growing louder.

His face almost came in contact with Zooey's fist.

He would have been less stunned to see Noah saying he was there to collect two of everything. "Zooey."

About to knock, she dropped her hand. She set Jackie down inside the threshold, then took his hand as well as Emily's and held them up.

"Missing something?" she asked Jack.

The sarcastic question had a simple enough answer. Or so she thought. The answer she received wasn't the one she was expecting.

"Yes," he told her quietly, finally finding his tongue. "You."

With the wind suddenly sucked out of her sails, Zooey was left completely stunned. Positive that her mind had put words into his mouth, she hoarsely asked, "What?"

Aware that everyone on the floor had suddenly volunteered to become unofficial witnesses to his every word, Jack drew Zooey and his children into his office and shut the door behind him.

Because it was his nature to be orderly, he backtracked. There were blanks that needed filling in. "What are you doing here?"

Now that sounded more like Jack, she thought. The other had been a momentary out-of-body experience.

There couldn't be any other explanation for what she thought she'd heard.

"Showing you that while you might be a great lawyer, you're lousy when it comes to finding a nanny for your own children." It was very hard trying to remain angry with him when everything inside of her ached to be with him again.

Where was her pride? she demanded silently.

Since his mind had been focused on her all this time, it was only natural that he thought she was referring to herself, not the lackluster woman in the sensible shoes he'd taken on to fill the vacancy Zooey's departure had left. He couldn't bring himself to think of the woman as taking Zooey's place because there was no way she could manage to do that. Zooey was an impossible act to follow, on all counts.

"Oh, I don't know—"

Zooey didn't let him get any further. She wasn't about to get snowed by lawyer rhetoric.

"Well, I do. Emily and Jackie came to my office. In a cab," she stressed heatedly. "Emily told me the nanny was asleep, something she apparently does with a fair amount of regularity after drinking." Zooey's eyes were blazing now as she came at him. "Don't you check references?"

God, but he wanted to kiss her. For the first time in more than two weeks, he felt alive. It took effort to hold himself in check. To not at least touch her face. "She was just a temp."

That was a lousy excuse and he knew it, Zooey thought. "And the damage she could have done to the kids might have been permanent." She blew out a breath. Her exasperation mounted. "You obviously need help."

He couldn't take his eyes off her. Part of him was

afraid that if he did, she would vanish like a dream and this had to be a dream, because both of his children were here—and quiet, something he knew was a complete impossibility.

"Yes," he agreed, keeping a straight face, "I do."

She made another impulsive decision. One she'd been longing to execute ever since she'd walked out of his house. "Okay, I'll come back to work until you can find a new nanny."

Jack summoned his best poker face. "That might be hard."

Wasn't he going to allow her to come back? Was he that angry at her for quitting? "Why?"

The corners of his mouth rose just the slightest bit. Or maybe that was her imagination again. "Because I won't be looking for a new one."

Did he want her to handle that, too? Didn't he see how necessary it was to get involved in his children's lives? Selecting the right nanny was crucial to their development, not to mention their happiness. He had to be made to understand that.

"I know you're busy, Jack, but these are your kids we're talking about."

He took a deep breath before answering. Not to fortify himself, but to fill his head with the scent of her shampoo. He'd never realized he was so partial to jasmine until she was no longer there.

"I know. But the kids don't want a nanny," he informed her. "They want you."

Damn, but he was making her feel awful. Zooey shook her head. "That's not going to work out," she told him solemnly.

"Why?" he asked. "Why won't it work out?" Because he intended to make it work out, no matter what it took.

She told him the truth. "Because I can't work for a man who's not there."

And the way she saw it, since he hadn't tried to get in contact with her, it meant he was glad she was gone, no matter what Emily said to the contrary. And if he was relieved to have her gone, he'd revert to playing those awful games of hide and seek again if she did come back. Forget that it hurt her; it was awful for the children.

He nodded, his expression indicating that he thought her protest was reasonable. "What if I promise to be there more often?"

She wasn't about to get captured by a lawyer's rhetoric. "How often?"

Suppressing a grin, he lobbed the ball back into her court. "How often would you like?"

She thought a moment. He was coming across as extremely accommodating. Maybe she'd misjudged him. Maybe he was partial to his children, after all.

"Normal hours would be nice. To see you in the morning and at some reasonable hour at night so that Emily and Jackie don't forget what you look like."

"Done."

There hadn't even been a moment's hesitation. She couldn't help being suspicious. "Just like that?"

"Just like that," he assured her. "Whatever it takes to get you back into our—into my life," he amended.

Jack watched as surprise washed over her face. He knew that if he wanted her, he was going to have to be willing to step up to the plate, to say what she wanted to hear. What had resided silently in his heart up to now.

He needed to tell her what he felt, not what he thought sounded right.

"Your life," Zooey repeated, certain that she had to be hearing things.

As his children watched, Jack took her hand in his. "My life."

"You need a nanny, too?" She thought that might amuse the children, but this time, she didn't hear Emily giggling. Instead, she could have sworn she heard the little girl suck in her breath and then hold it in what seemed like anticipation.

"I don't know about a nanny," Jack replied, "but I need you."

Maybe she was hallucinating. "You need me," she repeated, mystified.

His eyes never left hers. "Yes."

She was going to need clarification. To have everything spelled out before she was going to allow her imagination to run away with her.

"For what?"

"To make the sun come up in the morning. To make my day."

It was her turn to look amused. "Like Clint Eastwood?"

Jack was still holding her hand, afraid that if he released it, she'd walk out on him again.

"You're a hell of a lot prettier than Clint Eastwood." He took a breath, then plunged in. "The kids need a mother. I need a wife…"

Her heart slammed against her chest. She had no idea how she managed to even frame a sentence. "You make it sound like a want ad."

"The key word is *want*," he told her. "The kids want you back, and God knows I do. I love you, Zooey. I've been thinking of nothing else since you left."

She was afraid to let herself believe that. Afraid of getting hurt again.

"You knew where to find me. It wasn't exactly a secret. Emily had the card with the address on it," she reminded him.

"I didn't want to make you do anything you didn't want to do." And in putting what he thought were her wishes ahead of his own, he'd wasted valuable time. Because it didn't look as if those had been her wishes at all.

She laughed softly to herself. "A noble lawyer. What a concept."

"Yes," he agreed, slipping his arms around her. To his relief, she didn't back away. God, but it felt good to hold her again. "But nobility only goes so far. When I saw you just now, with the kids, I decided I didn't want to be noble anymore."

A smile played along her lips. "What do you want to be?"

"Married." And then, in case he wasn't making himself clear, he said, "Zooey, will you marry us?"

Zooey could feel tears forming. "I always did love package deals."

"Then it's yes?" Emily cried.

Zooey spared her a glance. "Absolutely."

"You're supposed to kiss Daddy now," Emily told her, "so it's official."

Zooey laughed. "How do you know that?"

"I watch TV," the little girl replied with an air of one who wasn't to be argued with.

"Kiss Daddy," Jackie echoed.

"Not a hardship," Zooey murmured as she wrapped her arms around Jack's neck, whispered, "I love you, too," and did as the children had instructed.

* * * * *

A BILLIONAIRE AND A BABY

To Brenda and Frank Corl,
with affection.

Chapter 1

"Don't I know you from somewhere?"

The question was finally directed at Sherry Campbell after ten minutes of covert and not-so-covert staring on the part of the new office assistant as she copied a file. The assistant, standing at the *Bedford World News*'s centrally located copy machine, wasn't even aware that the state-of-the-art machine had ceased to spit out pages and was now content to sit on its laurels, waiting for her next move.

The assistant's next move, apparently, was to continue staring. Her brow furrowed as she attempted to concentrate and remember just where and when she had seen her before.

Sherry stifled a sigh of annoyance.

It wasn't that she was unaccustomed to that look of vague recognition on a person's face. Sometimes Sherry was successfully "placed," but as time went on, not so often. There was a time, at the height of her previous career, where that was a regular occurrence. She couldn't say that she really minded. Then.

These days, however, people were just as apt to rudely stare at her swollen belly as they were at her face, that being the reason why her former career was a thing of the past. It was her unscheduled pregnancy that had gotten her dismissed from her anchor job and brought her to this junction in her life. Not in so many words, of course. Television studios and the people who ran them had an almost pathological fear of being sued because of some PC transgression on their parts. So when she had begun to show and told Ryan Matthews of her pregnancy, the executive producer of the nightly news had conveniently found a way to slip her into something less visible than the five o'clock news anchor position.

Within a day of her notifying Matthews that her waistline was going to be expanding, he had given her place to newcomer Lisa Willows and transformed her into senior copy editor, whimsically calling the move a lateral one. When she'd confronted him with his transparent motives, he'd lamely told her that demographics, even in this day and age, wouldn't have supported her "flaunting her free lifestyle." People, he'd said, still found unmarried pregnant women offensive and weren't about to welcome them into their living rooms night after night.

Matthews's words, even after five months, still rang in her ears. The fact that Sherry delivered the news behind a desk that was more than equal to hiding her increasing bulk from the general public, and that she'd never had a so-called free lifestyle—the pregnancy having arisen from her one and only liaison, a man who took no responsibility other than giving her the name of an abortion clinic—carried no weight with Matthews. With his spine the consistency of overcooked spaghetti, Matthews bent in the general direction of the greatest pressure. In this case it was the studio heads.

"If they can shoot around pregnant actresses on sitcoms to hide their conditions, why not me?" Sherry had insisted, but even then she knew it was no use. Matthews's mind had been made up for him. She was politely and firmly offered her new position or the door.

She took the door.

Her first inclination to "sue the pants off the bastard" faded, even as her friends and family rallied around her, echoing the sentiment. The last thing Sherry wanted was to draw negative attention to the baby she was carrying. She'd come to the conclusion that the less attention, the better.

In mulling over her options, she'd decided to take her circumstance as a sign that she should return to her first love: the written word. This meant following in her father's footsteps. Connor Campbell had been a well-respected, Pulitzer Prize-winning journalist before his retirement. It was because of him that she had gone into the news business in the first place.

Determination had always been her hallmark. So, after allowing herself an afternoon to grieve over her late, lamented career, Sherry moved full steam ahead, firing all torpedoes. She went to Owen Carmichael, her father's best friend and her godfather and asked for a job. Having started out with her father in the days before electric typewriters, Owen Carmichael was now the editor in chief of the *Bedford World News*.

Owen had been glad to hire her. Of course, she'd thought that he'd start her out with something a little more meaty than lighter-than-air fluff.

That was where her mind was right now, on the latest puff piece she was facing, not the assistant who stared at her with intense blue eyes and a puzzled frown on her face.

Sherry didn't feel like going into her previous life, or the reasons for the change. She felt too irritable for anything beyond a polite dismissal. Also the woman had the look about her that said she lived to gossip.

"I get that a lot," she told the other woman cavalierly. "I've got one of those faces people think they've seen before."

The assistant looked unconvinced. "But—" And then the woman paused, thinking. Suddenly, her whole face lit up as if a ray of inspiration had descended on her. "Say 'Hello, from the L.A. Basin.'"

That was her catchphrase, certainly nothing profound, but different enough to be remembered upon daily repetition. And she had been nightly anchor for four years before Matthews has ushered her out the door.

Sherry shook her head, her light-auburn hair swaying like a velvety wave about her oval face. "Sorry, I have to get upstairs to see Owen. Posthaste." She made it sound as if Owen was sending for her rather than the other way around. She was preparing to beard the lion in his den. Glancing at the dormant copy machine, Sherry pointed at it. "I think it needs feeding."

With that she hurried off, aware that the woman was still staring after her.

Hurrying these days was no small accomplishment for Sherry. She felt as if she was carrying around a lead weight strapped to her midsection. A lead weight that felt as if it was in constant flux.

On her way to the elevators, she tried not to wince as she felt another kick land against her ribs. At this rate she was going to need internal reconstructive surgery once her little squatter moved out.

"Don't you ever sleep?" she muttered to her stomach. She'd dragged herself into the office this morning because she'd been up half the night. Little whosit-whatsit was apparently learning the rumba. Either that or the baby had found a way to smuggle a motorcycle in there and had entertained itself through the wee hours of the night by constantly revving it up.

She'd been in no mood for what she found on her desk when she'd arrived. This week's assignment was even worse than last week's and she'd been convinced that that was the pits.

Breezing past Rhonda, her godfather's secretary, a woman whose curves detracted from the fact that she had a razor-sharp mind and practically ran the department in Owen's absence, Sherry walked straight into the managing editor's office.

"Owen," Sherry announced with more drama than she'd intended, "we have to talk. Please," she tagged on. As a further afterthought, she closed the door behind her.

Owen Carmichael barely glanced up from his computer. Mind-numbing statistics and figures were spread across the screen, bearing testimony to various polls conducted by the paper's PR department. He was scanning the figures while on his feet, his hands planted on the desk, his body leaning forward at an uncomfortable angle. It was an idiosyncrasy of his. He claimed he thought better in this position.

Of average height and far-less-than-average weight, he wore a shirt that was almost the same light color as his pants. With his semibald head, Owen gave the impression of an oversize Q-tip that someone had been nervously plucking at.

He glanced in his goddaughter's direction with almost no recognition. His mind was clearly somewhere other than in the room.

"Not now, Sherry."

She'd known the man as long as she'd known her own parents and was just as at ease with him as with them. Others might cower when he took on that low tone, but Sherry wasn't among them.

"Yes, now." She plunked the assignment on his desk, feeling that it spoke for itself. "It's not that I'm not grateful for the job, Owen," she began.

He raised his eyes to her face before lowering them back to the screen. "Then do it."

All right, maybe the assignment wasn't speaking, maybe it was whispering. She moved the sheet closer to him on the desk until the edge of the page touched one of his spread-out fingers. "Just what the hell is this?"

He spared it a glance. The title jumped out at him. "An assignment."

"No," Sherry corrected slowly, her voice deceptively low. "It's a fluff piece." By now she'd thought she would have graduated out of that classification, moved on to something with teeth, or muscle or an iota of substance. Her voice rose an octave as frustration invaded it. "It's less than fluff. If I wasn't holding it down, it would float away in the breeze, it's that lightweight."

Owen sighed, looking up from the computer in earnest now. "There're no breezes in the office—other than the ones generated by overenergetic junior journalists flapping their lips. Aren't women in your condition supposed to be tired all the time, Sherry? Why aren't you tired?"

He didn't know the half of it, but she felt this need to prove herself, to lay the groundwork for a stellar career. Her parents had raised her not to do anything by half measures.

Loving Drew fell under that category. Had she not leaped in with both feet, she would have realized that he wasn't the type to stick around once the going got the slightest bit difficult.

"I am tired," she told Owen, doing her best not to sound it. "Tired of standing on the sidelines, tired of doing pieces people line their birdcages with."

One painfully thin shoulder rose and fell with careless regard. "Then write them snappier and they'll read them before lining the birdcage."

She wasn't in the mood for his humor. "Owen, I'm a serious journalist."

"And I'm a serious managing editor." He temporarily abandoned his search and looked at her. "Right now there's no place I can put you but in this department. The first opening that comes up for an investigative reporter, I promise you'll have first crack at it. But right now, Sherry, I need you to be a good scout and—"

She didn't want to hear it. Sherry splayed her hands on his desk, carefully avoiding the almost stereotypically grungy coffee mug filled with cold black liquid. "Owen, please. Something to sink my teeth into, that's all I ask. Something more challenging than searching for a new angle on the latest local school's annual jog-a-thon and/or bake sale." Sherry leaned over the desk, her blue eyes pleading with his. "Please."

"So, you think you're up to a challenge?"

"Yes, oh, yes," she cried with enthusiasm. "An exposé, something undercover. I'm perfect for it." Straightening, she waved both hands over her far-from-hidden bulk. "Who'd suspect a pregnant woman?"

"All right, you want a challenge, you got a challenge."

Opening up the side desk drawer that the people who worked with him laughingly referred to as no-man's-land, Owen took out a canary-yellow file folder and handed it to her.

Sherry took the folder from him, noting that it felt as if it hardly weighed anything. Opening it, she discovered that there was a reason for that. It was empty.

"What am I supposed to do with this?" She raised a brow, waiting.

"Fill it," he told her mildly.

Pregnancy had all but eradicated her normally ample supply of patience. It was difficult to keep emotion out of her voice. "With what?"

"With a story on St. John Adair."

Second verse, same as the first, she thought. This wasn't what she'd been talking about. "But—"

Knowing what was coming, Owen cut her off. "Not just a story, a biography." For emphasis, he spread his bony hands out in the air, as if touching the pages of a phantom newspaper. "I want everything you can find on this man. More."

And here, just for a moment, she'd thought he was being serious. Instead, he was asking for one of those simpering write-ups in the People section. Frustration threatened to cut off her air supply. She tossed the folder on his desk in disgust. "Owen, this is just a dressed-up fluff piece on steroids."

"Oh, really?" He picked up the folder. "St. John Adair, raider par excellence of the corporate world, the mere mention of whose name sends CEOs dashing off the sunny golf course and to their medicine cabinets in search of the latest high-tech antacids. The man who's fondly referred to as Darth Vader by even his closer associates. The man who has no biography, is said to have arrived on the scene full-grown, springing out of some shaking multi-mega business corporation's worst nightmare."

She was aware of the man's name, but not his awesome power. The focus of her interests lay elsewhere. "Business corporations don't have nightmares."

Owen's thin lips curved. "They have Adair," he contradicted. "And we have nothing on him. No one does." He held out the folder to her. "You want a challenge, there's your challenge. Find out everything you can on Adair—find out more than everything you can on him," he amended. "I want to know what elementary school he went to, what his parents' names are, does he even have parents or was he suckled by wolves in the Los Angeles National Forest like Pecos Bill—"

Sherry struggled to keep back a smile. This was way over the top, but she had to admit, Owen had her curious. "Pecos Bill didn't grow up in the Los Angeles National Forest—"

"Good, that's a start." He tendered the folder to her again. "Give me more."

Eyeing him, she took the folder from Owen. "You're serious."

"Yes, I'm serious. Nobody else has managed to get anything on him or out of him other than 'Veni, vidi, vici.' I came, I saw, I conquered."

"I don't need the translation, Owen. Julius Caesar, talking about his triumphs," she added in case he was going to clarify that for her, as well.

Owen had launched into his coaxing mode, one of the attributes that made him good at his job. "You can be the first on your block to find something out on him." He pretended to peer at her. "Unless, of course, you think it's too hard—" He reached for the folder.

It was a game. She knew what he was up to and because of the friendship that existed between them, played along. She backed away to keep him from reaching the folder. "No, it's not too hard."

The grin transformed what could charitably be called a homely face into an amazingly pleasant one. "That's my girl."

She looked at the folder, already planning strategy. "When's the deadline?"

"The sooner the better. You tell me."

Now that she thought of it, she remembered her father saying something about Adair. Something along the lines of his coming out of nowhere and creating quite a sensation. Her first impulse was to call her father and ask if he had any connections that could lead her to the man, but she quickly squelched that. She wasn't about to walk a mile in borrowed shoes unless there was no other way. She didn't want to be her father's daughter, she wanted to be Sherry Campbell, use her own devices, her own sources.

She turned the folder around in her hand. "And you really think of this as an investigative piece?"

Owen gave her his most innocent expression. "Is this the face of a man who'd lie to you?"

She couldn't help but laugh. "As I recall, you're the one who told me about the Tooth Fairy."

To that, he could only plead self-defense. "Your tooth had fallen out. You were crying your eyes out." He spread his hands out. "You were five years old. What was I supposed to do?"

"Exactly what you did." Wheels began to spin.

Mentally she was already out of the office. Sherry slapped her hand across the folder, her eyes sparkling. "Okay, you're on."

"Great." He was already back looking at the computer screen. "Don't forget to shut the door on your way out." The assignment she'd brought in was still on his desk. He held it up. "And give this other piece to Daly."

She darted back to retrieve the paper. "I'll do it in my spare time."

He nodded, satisfied. "Good." The familiar sound he was waiting for didn't register. Owen glanced up from his screen. "The door?"

Sherry nodded as she crossed the threshold and eased the door closed behind her.

A smile sprouted and took root as she deposited the assignment into the yellow folder and tucked it under her arm. It wasn't the kind of thing she'd been after, but if it was a challenge, then she was more than up to it. God knew she needed something meaty to work on before she completely lost her mind.

The woman's voice, crisp, clear, with "no nonsense" written over every syllable, echoed in Sherry's ear, "No, I am afraid that Mr. Adair is much too busy to see you. Try again next month. At the moment he's booked solid."

The woman sounded as if she was about to hang up. "The man has to eat sometime," Sherry interjected quickly, hoping for a break. "Maybe I could meet with him then."

She could almost hear the woman sniff before saying, "Mr. Adair has only working lunches and dinners. As I've already said—"

Undaunted, Sherry jumped back in the game.

"Breakfast, then. Please, just a few minutes." That was all she needed for openers, she thought, but there was no reason to tell the guardian at the gate that.

Unmoved, the woman replied, "I'm sorry, I can't help you."

"But—"

The next moment Sherry found herself talking to a dial tone.

With a sigh she hung up. She was getting lazy, she thought. The way to get somewhere was in person, not over the telephone. She knew that. If the mountain wouldn't come to Mohammed, then Mohammed damn well was going to come to the mountain. With climbing gear.

Although these days, she thought, pushing herself up out of her chair, she wasn't sure just which part she would be cast in, Mohammed or the mountain.

The meeting had run over. It was within his power to call an end to it at any time, but Sin-Jin Adair liked to choose his moments. Authority wasn't something he believed in throwing around like a Frisbee; it was a weapon, to be used wisely, effectively. So he had sat and listened to the employees that he'd culled over the past few years, as he'd taken over one corporation after another. Keep the best, discard the rest. It was a motto he lived by.

A bastardization of his father's edict. Except that his father had applied it to women. Sin-Jin never did.

"Leaving early, I see."

He nodded at his secretary. Like everyone else around her, Edna Farley was the soul of efficiency. He and Edna had a history together, and her loyalty was utterly unshakable. It was another quality he demanded, but one he could be patient about. He valued the kind that evolved naturally, not one that was bought and paid for. If you could buy loyalty easily, then it could just as easily be sold to a higher bidder, thereby rendering it useless. That he paid his people top dollar ensured that they would not be tempted to look elsewhere in search of worldly goods.

"Not as early as I'd like. Go home, Mrs. Farley."

"Yes, sir." The woman peered out into the hall as he strode out. "Don't forget the Cavannaugh meeting tomorrow. And Mr. Renfro said he would be calling you at eight tomorrow morning."

"Good night, Mrs. Farley."

Walking away, he smiled to himself as the less-than-dulcet tones of Mrs. Farley echoed behind him, reminding him of appointments he didn't need to be reminded of. Everything he needed to know about his schedule was not tucked away in some fancy PalmPilot, but in his mind. He had a photographic memory that had never failed him.

Reaching the elevator, he pressed for a car. Just as he stepped inside, he was aware that someone had slipped in behind him. The floor had appeared deserted a moment earlier.

"Sorry," a woman's voice apologized a second after he felt someone bump into him from behind.

Turning around, he was about to say something when he saw that it had been the woman's stomach that had made contact with him.

Rounded with child. The phrase came floating to him out of nowhere.

So did the smile that curved his lips ever so slightly. "That's all right."

Sherry looked down innocently at the bulk that

preceded her everywhere these days. She placed her hands on either side of the girth.

"Can't wait for this little darling to be born so I can move it around in a stroller instead of feeling as if I'm lifting weights every time I get up."

Because pregnancy, children and loved ones existed on an unknown plane, Sin-Jin could only vaguely nod at her words. A rejoining comment failed to materialize. The only thing he noted was, pregnant or not, the woman was extremely attractive.

His father had said there was no such thing as an attractive pregnant woman, but then, his father had demanded perfection in everything around him, if not in himself. The man was interested in ornamental women, not pregnant ones. Like a spoiled child in a toy store, his father had gone from one woman to another, marrying some along the way. He was vaguely aware that the man's tally stood at something like seven.

Or was it six? He'd lost count. The slight smile widened on Sin-Jin's lips, curving somewhat ironically.

Not bad, Sherry thought. The man was almost human looking when he smiled. She already knew that he was handsome. That much she'd gleaned while surfing the Internet for more than two hours, trying to piece together anything she could find on the man. She'd discovered that Owen was right. There wasn't anything on St. John Adair that didn't have to do with business. It was as if he disappeared into a black hole every night when he left the impressive edifice that bore his name.

It made her feel like Vicki Vale, on the trail of Batman.

Well, Batman was smiling, she thought. Perhaps not directly at her, but close enough.

Maybe Adair had a weak spot for pregnant women.

It would be nice to be given an ace in the hole because of her condition for a change.

She took a deep breath, bracing herself. No time like the present.

Leaning around Adair, Sherry pressed the emergency stop on the elevator. The elevator hiccuped and came to an abrupt, jarring halt between the eighteenth and seventeenth floors.

The smile on his lips vanished instantly as a score of different scenarios crowded into his mind. Was he being threatened, kidnapped? There'd been two botched attempts at that in the past four years. He began to doubt the woman was pregnant. It made for a good disguise, put a man off his guard.

He was on his guard now. "What the hell are you doing?"

Sherry's smile was sweetness personified as she looked up at him. "I was wondering if you could give me a moment of your time, Mr. Adair."

Chapter 2

For one heartbeat, there was nothing but silence within the elevator. Sin-Jin stared at the only other occupant in the car as if she had lost her mind. He wondered if she was dangerous in any sense of the word.

"Who *are* you?"

Sherry was ready for him. Opening her purse, she took out the press card that she'd carefully laid on top just before entering the multiwinged building that bore Adair's name. This was *not* the time to fumble through the various paraphernalia that she deemed indispensable and always dragged along with her.

She held her identification card aloft for Adair's perusal. And watched a transformation.

The unfriendly look on his face turned to something that, in a different era and country, would have reduced pagan worshipers to quivering masses of fear had Adair been their emperor, or, more probably regarded as their god. She felt a little unnerved herself.

Sherry shook herself loose from the hypnotic effect and squared her shoulders. Fierce expression or not, he wasn't about to make her back down.

Adair's glare was hot enough to melt the plastic on her ID. "You're a reporter?" It sounded like an offense second only to being a serial killer.

Damn, but she could see how he could strike fear into the hearts of those around him. She reminded herself that she wasn't afraid of anything except a magnitude-seven earthquake.

"Investigative," she informed him crisply, as if that fact took her out of the general pool that merited his disdain and elevated her to a higher plateau.

It didn't. Electric-blue eyes nearly disappeared into small, darkly lashed slits. "All right, then go investigate something."

The growled order only had her stiffening her backbone. She met him on his own battlefield, smiling sweetly. "I am. You."

"The hell you are." He reached past her to press the elevator release button only to have her hit the red stop button again. Stunned, he glared at her. "You will stop doing that." It was a command, brooking no disobedience, no dissent.

Her smile never faltered as she met his words with a condition. "I will if you promise to answer a few questions for me."

Mrs. Farley had pleaded with him to take on a bodyguard. Had even gone so far as to line up several for him to interview, but he'd then refused flatly, thinking it a waste. Now he wasn't all that sure. At least bodyguards would keep annoying reporters where they belonged. Away.

"I never make promises I have no intention of keeping." Again he pushed the button to restart the elevator and again she stopped it. "Look, lady—Mrs. Campbell—" he amended, exasperation evaporating the very air in his lungs.

"Right in the first place, wrong in the second," she informed him cheerfully, then suggested, "Why not just Sherry?"

She didn't think it possible, but his dark expression darkened even more.

"Because, 'just Sherry,' I don't intend to get that friendly with you." He hit the release button and the elevator made it to another floor before she abruptly halted it with a counterpunch. "You keep this up and the cable's liable to break. We'll wind up free-falling the rest of the way. That might be on your agenda, 'just Sherry,' but it's not on mine."

The glare he shot her bordered on filleting her nerves. She could see his underlings scattering and running for cover like so many Disney mice before the villainous cat in *Cinderella*. The thought did a lot to calm her nerves and made it difficult for her not to grin.

Sin-Jin's eyes slid to her belly. "Are you even pregnant?" It could have been a ruse used to allow her to gain access to his floor. In his experience, reporters were capable of all sorts of devious deceptions.

She surprised him by taking his hand and placing it on her distended abdomen. "Most definitely."

As if burned, Sin-Jin pulled his hand back. Although not soon enough. He'd felt the stirrings of new life beneath his palm. The child she was carrying had moved—probably on cue, he thought cynically.

What was a pregnant reporter doing here, lying in wait for him? He thought of the meeting he'd just left. "If this is about the Marconi merger—"

Sherry cut him short. "It's not," she told him. Raising her eyes to his face, she dug up all the charm she could muster. "It's about you."

Suspicion entered his eyes. He'd never had any use for reporters, feeding off the misery of others for their own ends. "What about me?"

"That's exactly what I want to find out. What about you? Nobody knows anything about Darth Vader, the Corporate Raider."

He winced inwardly at the label. If it was meant to flatter him, it missed its mark by a country mile. The limelight had never meant anything to him. Sin-Jin didn't do what he did for any sort of recognition. He did it because he was good at it, good at trimming fat off selected businesses and getting them to run more efficiently. Once he accomplished what he set out to do and the businesses were running at their maximum peak, he grew bored with them, selling them off to other corporations while he turned his attention to something else.

That this sort of thing attracted a great deal of attention and generated an almost obscene amount of money was without question. But it was never about the money. It never had been, perhaps because there'd always been so much of it when he was growing up. Every movement he'd ever made had been cushioned in it, as if somehow money could take the place of everything else that was deemed important in life. Like parental love and warm memories to draw on when things became difficult.

He'd had the best upbringing that money could buy. All needs taken care of, everything done in a utilitarian fashion. It was the kind of upbringing that could have produced an emotional robot, which was what his enemies had accused him of being.

If no one knew anything about him, it was for a reason. Because he wanted it like that. "And it's going to remain that way," he informed her.

As he reached to bring the elevator back to life, she moved to block his access. "Why?"

For just the smallest second, he almost forgot that they were stuck, suspended between the eighth and ninth floor like a yo-yo that had gotten tangled in its own string. The annoying woman who kept insisting on getting into his face had eyes that were probably the deepest shade of blue he'd ever seen. Undoubtedly, she used that to her advantage, just as she used her present condition.

"Does the word *privacy* mean anything to you?" he demanded. "Or is that particular term missing from the lexicon distributed to the ignoble fourth estate?"

"Ouch, they weren't kidding when they said you could fillet a person at ten paces with just your tongue."

"No," he informed her tersely, "they weren't."

But rather than take offense at his words, she smiled, her face lighting up as if he'd just given her a ten-carat diamond instead of an insult.

She probably saw it as a challenge. He supposed he could relate to that. Challenges were what he responded to himself. The harder something was to obtain, the more he wanted to secure possession.

Somewhere in the back of his mind a question crept forward. How difficult would it be to possess the woman crowding him in the elevator?

The next instant Sin-Jin blanketed the thought, smothering it. She was someone else's wife or at the very least, someone's significant other. And unlike his father who reveled in it, he didn't poach on another man's land or try to win another man's woman if she captured his attention.

Satisfied that the verbal duel was over, Sin-Jin pressed the release button on the keypad only to have her reach for it again. The high school physics assurance that for every action there was a reaction teased his brain. Mr. Harris would have been happy that he'd come away with something from his class, he thought.

Rather than allow the annoying woman to bring the elevator to yet another teeth-jarring stop, Sin-Jin caught her by the wrist and held on tightly.

"The game is over."

Sherry raised her chin. The look in her eyes told him that she wasn't intimidated. He realized with a jolt that he found it arousing.

Man does not live by bread alone. Or, in his case, by corporate takeovers, he thought. Maybe it was time he got out a little instead of burning the midnight oil.

"What are you hiding, Mr. Adair?" Sherry wanted to know. Anyone so secretive had to have something he didn't want revealed. She felt her curiosity climbing. "What are you afraid of?"

Sin-Jin realized that he was still holding her wrist. Tentatively he released it, ready to grab it again if she tried to stop the elevator's descent. "Being on trial for justifiable homicide."

Humor, she liked that. Even if it was a little dark. Sherry smiled in response, aware that it threw him off. She liked that, too.

"Then I'll just have to make sure you don't do away with me, at least not until I get my story."

He edged closer to the doors, blocking any access she

might have to the keypad in case she decided to make a lunge for it. "Tempting as the trade might be, I'm not prepared to give you a story in exchange for your fading out of my life."

The elevator came to a stop. "When will you be prepared?"

The doors opened. He saw the security guard sitting at the desk in the lobby. If this hounding reporter gave him any more trouble, he could turn her over to the man. "There's an old song, 'The Twelfth of Never.' I suggest you take your cue from the title."

With that, Sin-Jin got off.

Just as she began to follow Adair, the baby kicked. Hard. It momentarily took her breath away. Long enough for Adair to get far enough ahead of her.

"You can run, Adair, but you can't hide," she called after him.

Sin-Jin never broke stride and didn't bother looking over his shoulder. But his words hung in the air as he made his exit through the revolving doors.

"Watch me."

The glove had clearly been thrown down. Owen had been right. This was a definite challenge. Exhilaration filled her.

"I intend to do more than that, Adair," she murmured with a grin.

Two hours later, drained, Sherry flirted with the thought of just going home and crawling into her queen-size bed. By her count, she was down some ten hours of sleep in the past five days because her baby insisted on kickboxing for hours on end.

But tonight was her weekly Lamaze class and she hated to miss that. If nothing else, she could definitely use the camaraderie. Not to mention the fact that Rusty, her former cameraman and present coach, would be there. She could pick his brain about Adair. The man had a way of ferreting things out. If Rusty Thomas didn't know about something, it didn't bear knowing.

The practical side of attending her class was that she was a little more than a month away from her due date. A minor sense of panic was beginning to set in at the peripheral level. She needed all the preparation for the big event she could get.

Stopping home for a small dinner and a large pillow, Sherry changed her clothes to something even looser and more comfortable. Fifteen minutes later she was on the road again, driving to Blair Memorial where the classes were being held in one of the hospital's outlying facilities.

The cheerfully painted room was built to accommodate a hundred. Twenty couples had signed up. They were down to thirteen after the instructor, Lori O'Neill, had shown the birthing movie. Apparently there were miracles that were a little too graphic for some people to bear. Sherry liked the extra space. It made the gathering seem more like a club than a class.

Entering the class, her pillow tucked under her arm, Sherry looked around the area. Almost everyone was here. She nodded at couples she recognized by sight, if not by name. They were a cross-section of life, she thought, being brought together by their mutual condition. In the group there was an independent film producer, a lawyer, three teachers, a doctor and an FBI agent, not to mention an assortment of other people.

She looked around for her group, two women she'd gotten close to in the last few weeks. Spotting Chris

Jones and Joanna Prescott, Sherry made her way over to them. They had all been introduced to one another by Lori. The incredibly perky instructor had felt that the three women would form a strong bond, given that they were all single moms for one reason or another. Lori referred to them as The Mom Squad. Sherry rather liked that label.

"So, how was your week?" Joanna asked the moment Sherry came within earshot. Of the two of them, it was Joanna who could relate more closely to the woman she recognized as the former anchorwoman of the nightly news. Joanna, a high school English teacher, had lost her job for the same reason that had seen Sherry out the door of her studio. An unmarried pregnant woman was the elephant in the living room as far as the board of education was concerned. Rather than cause problems and be in the middle of an ugly trial that might affect her students, all of whom had rallied around her, Joanna had agreed to leave.

She knew the frustration that Sherry had dealt with.

"Don't ask." Sherry sighed the answer as she did her best to sink down gracefully. It wasn't an easy accomplishment. Of the three, Sherry was the furthest along.

And the largest, she thought ruefully. These days Sherry felt as if she was all stomach and very little else.

"The Mom Squad's all here, I see." Walking up to them, Lori placed an affectionate hand on Sherry's shoulder. She nodded at the two coaches who accompanied the other two women. "Hi, Sherry, where's your coach?"

Sherry glanced toward the doorway. Two couples came in, but no Rusty.

"He'll be along," she assured Lori. "Punctuality was never Rusty's strong suit."

"Well then, for your sake, I hope this baby turns out to be late," Lori teased.

Lori shifted, trying not to look too obvious. Her back was aching. And with good reason. She hadn't told the others yet but she'd found herself in the same delicate condition that they were in. Five months along, she wasn't showing too much yet. With any luck, she'd be one of those rare women who could hide inside of moderately loose clothing and never show.

The noise at the door had her turning to look. "Oh, more arrivals." About to go off and greet the newcomers, she paused for a final word with the trio. "We still on for ice cream after class, ladies?"

Chris and Sherry nodded. "Try and stop me," Joanna laughed. "I've been fantasizing about a mound of mint-chip ice cream all day."

"See you later," Lori promised before she hurried away.

Sherry glanced at her watch, wondering what was keeping Rusty. Class was almost starting. Thinking about what she wanted to ask her former cameraman, she leaned over toward Chris. Blond and vibrant, Chris Jones was not the kind of woman who came to mind when someone said FBI agent, but that was exactly what she was, having been part of the Bureau for over six years now.

"Chris, what do you know about St. John Adair?"

"If you're asking if the man has an FBI dossier, I wouldn't be able to answer that—" And then Chris smiled. "If he did."

Sherry made the natural assumption. "Which means he doesn't."

"Ruthless takeovers aren't a crime in themselves, except perhaps to the people who lose their jobs because of them." Chris cocked her head as if curious. One by one they'd each spilled their stories over various mounds of ice cream at Josie's Old-Fashioned Ice Cream Parlor. "Why do you want to know?"

Sitting cross-legged on the floor, Sherry pressed her hand to the small of her back, wondering if the perpetual ache she felt there was ever going to be a thing of the past. "My editor wants me to do an in-depth piece on him. I actually cornered the man in his elevator today."

"And?" Joanna pressed.

Sherry frowned. "Mr. Adair wasn't very cooperative. Didn't even volunteer his name, rank and serial number. I think if he had his druthers, he would have had me up against and wall and shot."

Joanna nodded at the information. "I've never seen anything written up about him. From what I've heard, he's really closemouthed." She glanced at Chris for confirmation. "Maybe he's got some skeletons in his closet."

Why else would someone be that secretive? Sherry wondered, nodding. She glanced again toward the doorway. No Rusty. "That's what I'm thinking."

"Well, if it makes a difference, none of them have gotten there by foul play. At least," Chris qualified, "not to the Bureau's knowledge." She stopped and nodded toward the doorway. "Hey, there's your coach."

Without waiting for Sherry to turn around, Chris raised her hand and waved at the short, wiry man until he saw her. Raising a hand in response, he waved back and made his way over to the small, tight group.

Sherry sidled over to make room for him. Jerome Russell Thomas had been the first person to learn about her pregnancy, before her parents, even before Drew. They'd been out on a rare field assignment together, trying to corral a statement from a high-seated judge who had been brought up on bribery charges when she'd had to excuse herself. She'd barely made it to the ladies' room in time before her lunch, breakfast and whatever might have been left of her dinner the night before came up unceremoniously.

When she'd emerged from the ladies' room ten minutes later, sweaty and slightly green, Rusty was waiting for her just outside the door. One look at her and he'd asked her how far along she was. Her heated denial was short-lived in the face of his gruff kindness.

"My kid sister was the same shade of green that you are with her first," he'd told her matter-of-factly. "Couldn't keep anything down, not even water. Only thing she lived on was mashed potatoes and beef Stroganoff. You might want to try some."

Rusty had also stood by her when Drew had decided to pull his disappearing act on her and had been there for her when the studio had all but given her the bum's rush.

Having shown his true colors through the hard times, Rusty had seemed like the logical choice to be her coach. When she'd asked him, Rusty had protested vehemently at first, telling her that she would be far more comfortable if she had a woman as her coach. That *he* would be far more comfortable if she had a woman as her coach.

But Sherry had remained adamant, insisting she wanted him, and finally, he'd given in and agreed, grumbling all the way. She'd expected nothing less of him.

"Sorry I'm late. Had to fight off a horde of women at my door to get here," he cracked.

Given the truth of the matter, the only female in his life, other than the ones he worked with, was his dog,

Blanca. Sherry didn't waste any time commenting on
his fanciful excuse. Instead, the moment he dropped
down beside her, she hit him with her question.

"What do you know about St. John Adair?"

Accustomed to her abrupt, greetingless greetings,
Rusty paused to think.

"What everyone else knows. That he's one of the
richest son-of-a-bitches around. I don't trust a man
who looks that comfortable in a suit in ninety degree
weather." Rusty never cracked a smile. "There's talk
he's the devil. Why?"

She watched Lori work her way to the front of the
room. They were getting ready to start. "Owen's giving
me a crack at an investigative story."

Rusty filled in the blanks. It wasn't hard. He looked
at her stomach, his meaning clear. "Couldn't he have
started you out on something easier? Like finding out
where Jimmy Hoffa's buried?"

Sherry shifted slightly. As if that could hide something. "Easy doesn't put you on the map."

He shrugged carelessly. "Neither does coming up to
a dead end."

She didn't buy that. Although Lori was saying something to the gathering, Sherry lowered her voice, doing
her best to appeal to Rusty. "You know everything there
is to know about everything, including where all the
bodies are buried. Tell me how I can get to him for a
few minutes where he can't get away. Other than an elevator," she added.

"You always did know how to flatter a guy." It was a
tall order, but not anything he wasn't up to. There was
very little he wouldn't do for Sherry. In the vernacu-
lar of the old-timers who had taught him his trade, he
considered Sherry Campbell one hell of a broad. "Okay,

I'll see what I can dig up for you, although it probably won't be very much."

Sherry got herself into position, ready to begin. "At this point, I'll settle for anything. I tried to corner him in the elevator but I couldn't get anything out of him."

"Any man who can say no to you just isn't human."

Touched, Sherry leaned over and kissed Rusty's leathery cheek. "Thanks, Rusty. I needed that."

Rusty tried not to blush. "Shhh." He pointed to Lori. "Teacher's talking. You'll miss something."

She was still smiling at him. "I'll always have you to fill me in."

Rusty's blush deepened beneath the bronzed, craggy suntan.

Chapter 3

"Ladies, I have a confession to make."

Lori sank her long-handled spoon into the mound of whip cream atop her fudge-ripple sundae before looking up at the other three women seated with her in the ice-cream parlor booth.

The establishment, decorated to resemble something straight out of the early fifties, provided an informal atmosphere where they could each give voice to the concerns that were troubling them, concerns about the way their lives were about to everlastingly change because of the heart that beat beneath their own. It was something they all looked forward to far more than the classes that were to ready them for the upcoming big event.

"Let me guess," Chris interjected, deadpan. "You're not really a Lamaze instructor, you're actually an international spy." Not being able to hold it back any longer, Chris grinned as she glanced around at the others.

"Sorry, occupational habit. I've been bringing my work home with me a lot."

Joanna nodded knowingly. "Trust no one, right?" A healthy spoonful of cookie-dough ice cream punctuated her declaration.

Chris acknowledged how good it felt to laugh about her work. So much of it revolved around darker elements. "That's only a rule of thumb when you're checking out aliens on Sunday nights, Joanna."

Sherry leaned forward. They were meandering again. That was usually a good thing as far as their conversations went, but Lori looked as if she had to get something off her chest. "What's your big news, Lori?"

Lori let her spoon all but disappear into the dessert. Sherry noted that, unlike the rest of them, Lori had hardly eaten any of hers. A distant bell went off in her head, but for now she kept her suspicions on ice.

"Well," Lori blew out a breath, "I don't know if it's big—" She hesitated.

Chris was a firm believer in cutting to the chase. Even when she was trying to relax. "Sure it is, otherwise you wouldn't be hemming and hawing. C'mon, woman, out with it."

There was no putting this off. Even if Lori wanted to, it would be evident soon enough. And these women had become her friends. Initially, she'd been the one to encourage them to turn to her and one another. Now she needed them. Life certainly had an ironic bent to it.

Her glance swept around the square table. "I think that my ties to this little group are going to get stronger."

Joanna looked at her, slightly confused before a light slowly began to dawn. The light had already reached

Chris, but before she could say anything, Sherry beat her to it. "You're pregnant."

Pressing her lips together, Lori nodded.

"And you don't think you and the dad are going to get together." It wasn't hard for Chris to fill in the blanks, given the nature of the expression of Lori's face.

"Not anymore." Lori looked down at her dessert. Rivulets of light brown were flowing down along the entire circumference of the tulip-shaped glass bowl, forming a sticky ring around the base. She dabbed at them with her napkin. "My husband is dead."

Chris looked at her sharply. "Oh, Lori, we're so sorry."

"Yes, I know. So am I," Lori said, her hand inadvertently covering her still-flat stomach, mimicking a motion she'd seen time and again in her classes. She tried to sound positive. "I'll be all right."

"Of course it will." Sherry could see that the woman didn't really want to talk about it, that what she wanted right at this moment was to have the unconditional support of her friends at a time in her life that could charitably be called trying.

Reaching out, she squeezed Lori's hand. When Lori looked in her direction, Sherry quipped, "So, how about those Dodgers?"

Laughing, the others took their cue, and the conversation drifted to all things light and airy, temporarily taking their minds away from the more serious areas of their lives.

A great deal of ice cream was consumed within the next hour.

The insidious ringing sound burrowed its way into the tapestry of her dreams, shredding the fabric before

Sherry could think to snatch it back and save it for review once she was awake.

The instant her eyes were opened, the dream became a thing of the past.

The only thing she could remember was that it had created a warm haze of well-being within her. Something to do with a man loving her, caring for her, that was it. Instinctively she knew the man had been Drew during his better days, even though the face hadn't belonged to him.

Was it morning already?

The phone. That horrid ringing noise was coming from the phone, not her alarm clock.

With a huge sigh, Sherry groped for the receiver. It took her two tries to locate it. Her eyes were shutting again, refusing to surrender to the intruding morning. She tucked the receiver against her ear and the pillow.

"This better be good," she threatened.

By no stretch of the imagination was she now, or ever had been, a morning person. As far as she was concerned, God should have made sure that days began no earlier than eight o'clock, which was still pretty obscene in her book, but at least doable.

"Rise and shine, Cinderella. You told me to call when I had something."

Rusty. Rusty was talking in her ear.

Her eyes flew open. She struggled to defog her brain. "What do you have?"

"Not overly much," he warned her.

She knew better. Rusty wouldn't be calling her at this hour, whatever it was, if it was nothing. He didn't have a death wish.

"It's too early to play games, Rusty." Blinking, Sherry turned her head and tried to focus on her clock.

It was barely five o'clock. No wonder she felt like death. "God isn't even up yet. Talk to me. What did you find out?"

"There's this mountain retreat. It belongs to someone else, somebody named Fletcher, but Adair likes to go to it just after he does a takeover—I won't say a successful takeover because when he's involved, they're all successful," he commented. "Going there is his way of celebrating." The raspy sound that passed for his laugh undulated through the phone lines. "Personally, if I had his kind of money, I'd be out on the town. Hell, I'd be out *buying* the town."

Still lying against her pillow, Sherry dragged her hand through her hair. "So he's shy, okay, we already know that. Where's this retreat located?"

"At the foot of the San Bernadino Mountains, just outside of Wrightwood."

She'd been to Wrightwood a couple of times herself. It was a small town, predominantly known for its noncommercial skiing. All the dedicated skiers went to Big Bear, which was located on the other side of Wrightwood. The former offered snow and gridlock during the winter months. Wrightwood offered scenery, charm and relative isolation. She could see Adair going there.

Sherry waited, knowing, even in her semiconscious state, that there was more.

Rusty paused dramatically. "I managed to find out that Adair's going there this weekend. As a matter of fact, he's already on his way."

Sherry took it for granted that what he was telling her was not common knowledge. If it was, Adair would be on his way to a media circus camped out on the front lawn. Given his personality, that would be the last thing he'd want.

She smiled to herself. Rusty never ceased to amaze her. The man was definitely a national treasure. She blessed the day she'd gone to bat with him with their former station manager when the man had wanted to terminate Rusty, saying he wasn't a team player. It had gained her a lifelong ally.

"I know that I shouldn't be asking this, Rusty, but how did you find this out?"

She could almost hear his smile as it spread over his generous mouth. He had a nice smile, she thought absently.

"Mrs. Farley keeps religious notes."

The name was vaguely familiar, but at five in the morning, nothing was overly clear. "And she is?"

"His secretary. Has been for years. As a matter of fact, he brought her with him when he first came to Sun-Corp." That was what the corporation had been called before he'd changed the name to Adair Industries. "From what I've gathered, Adair trusts her the way he doesn't trust anyone else."

That would have been the lioness at the gate, Sherry thought. The woman who hadn't allowed her to see Adair. She'd asked the secretary for an audience with Adair before resorting to the elevator trick. There hadn't seemed to be anything remarkable about Edna Farley. Obviously she hadn't looked closely enough. "Interesting. And you got these notes how?"

"I know a lot of people, Sherry. Some of them don't stray more than five feet from their computers at any given time."

Hackers, he'd used hackers. Well, whatever made the world go around, she mused. "Got a location on this retreat?"

He chuckled. She knew better than to doubt him. "Is the Pope Catholic?"

"Last time anyone checked." Awake now, she opened the drawer of the nightstand beside her bed and pulled out a pad and pencil. "Okay, shoot."

Rusty hesitated. "Look, instead of my giving the directions to you over the phone, why don't I just come over in a couple of hours and drive you over there myself?"

Rusty had his own job. She knew for a fact that he couldn't afford to take time off. The station manager would be all over him if he did. "You've already done enough, Rusty." There'd been concern in his voice. She found it sweet but shackling. "I can take care of myself."

Rusty huffed. "In case you haven't noticed, you're pregnant."

She hated the fact that people viewed her differently because of her condition. Of all people Rusty should have known better. "Being pregnant doesn't mean I can't see over the steering wheel, Rusty, or that I've suddenly forgotten how to take corners."

He laughed gruffly. "I've seen how you drive, Campbell. They should have taken away your keys the second anyone found out you were expecting."

"Sweet of you to worry, Rusty, but I can take it from here. Just give me the directions."

He knew better than to argue with her. When it came to being stubborn, he'd learned his first week on the job that Sherry had no equal. He rattled off the directions, including which freeway exits she was to take and for how long. He prided himself on being thorough.

"If you change your mind about going alone, you know where to find me. I'll be the one on the arm of the sexiest cover model in the room."

"That's just how I'll expect to find you." Laughing, she hung up.

With a sigh, Sherry dug her fists in on either side of her and then pushed herself up into an upright position.

Adair.

The memory hit her like a thunderbolt. The face of the man in her dream, the one who was supposed to have been Drew, had belonged to Adair.

Her eyes widened before she dismissed the thought. Her brain had obviously taken recent events and combined two areas of her life. Either that, or she was hallucinating. The only thing that Adair had going for him was piles of money. Okay, that and looks, she amended. Neither of which meant anything to her. The next time she was going to trust a man, he was going to have to be strong, sensitive and caring.

A sense of humor wouldn't hurt, either. As for looks, well, she already knew what that was worth. Pretty faces, like as not, usually were the domain of shallow, vacant people. Drew was living proof of that.

With yet another deep sigh, Sherry got off the bed and went to the bathroom. The first visit of many today, she thought wearily.

He liked it here.

Liked the massive wood-framed rooms, the sparse furnishings, the wide-open spaces, both inside and out. He'd driven most of the night to get here after his late meeting with his lawyers to finalize the deal he'd been working on. It was worth it.

Sin-Jin looked through the bay window that faced the mountain and the landing pad where his private helicopter stood, waiting his pleasure. He wouldn't be using it today. He wanted nothing more than to stay here.

There was no doubt about it. There was something bracing about being alone in the wilderness.

Of course, he didn't attempt to delude himself that he was the thriving descendent of some savvy, resourceful frontier backwoodsman. He liked his creature comforts along with his solitude. Although he had to admit that he had toyed with the idea of not having a phone here. But in the end his sense of practicality had won over his need to be alone. The compromise was that only Mrs. Farley had his phone number here.

He trusted her implicitly. She wouldn't do anything to jeopardize his privacy. Privacy had become paramount for him. That was why the cabin he chose to stay in was registered to John Fletcher in the county books. No one suspected he was here today.

Mrs. Farley and he went way back. Far further than anyone suspected. Certainly a lot further than his years as a corporate raider. Other than his uncle, Edna Farley had been the first person to make a positive impact in his life, the first person who had made him feel that he mattered.

Who knew what path his life would have taken if not for her, he mused.

He owed her, owed her a great deal. Though not very vocal, he'd told her as much years ago. All she had ever asked of him was to let her earn her keep. He would have been more than willing to set her up with a life-time trust fund in any place of her choice. She would have been set for life, but she'd chosen to work at his side. That was typical of her.

He had to admit, he rather liked that. In a way she was the mother his own mother had never been, although Edna Farley never blatantly displayed maternal feelings. They were alike that way, each shut inside with their own emotions. But she took care of him nonetheless. As he did her.

Sin-Jin looked at the gray flagstone fireplace, debating building a fire. The air was nippy up here, a hundred miles away from where he usually resided. It was barely fall, but cold weather found its way faster to this part of Southern California. There was no snow on the mountains yet, but prospects looked good, he thought. The local shopkeepers would be happy.

Maybe someday he'd retire here, he mused. It would be an idyllic life. His mouth curved. As if he could stand a life with no challenges for more than a few days.

The sound of barking in the distance alerted him. Striding across the hardwood floor, Sin-Jin went directly to his gun cabinet and took out a rifle. As he moved to the front door, he loaded the weapon. That was Greta barking. His Irish setter was his flesh-and-blood alarm system and as far as he was concerned, she did a far more effective job than any state-of-the-art laser beams. There were other advantages as well. A high-tech system couldn't curl up at his feet in the evening and look up at him with soulful brown eyes that helped to ease the building tension of his everyday life.

Pulling the door open, Sin-Jin looked around. The woods were some three hundred feet to his right, but from this vantage point, he saw nothing.

"What is it, Greta?"

At the sound of his voice, the barking increased. As he listened, he placed the direction of origin. It was coming from several yards away. Sin-Jin strode toward the sound, his fingers wrapped around his weapon, ready for anything.

Anything except for what he found.

It was that woman again, that reporter who'd jumped

into the elevator with him the other day and tried to waylay him for a story.

Damn it, how the hell did she find this place?

He scowled as he went toward her. She wore a white parka that hung open around her. He doubted that she could even come close to zipping it up around her stomach.

Something Campbell, that was it. Cheryl? No, Sherry.

He grew angrier with every step he took. She had the face of an angel and the body of a lumbering bear all primed for hibernation. Why wasn't she hibernating?

"You're trespassing!" he called out to her. "What the hell are you doing up here?"

Sherry struggled to catch her breath. The all-terrain vehicle she'd borrowed from a friend had decided that it wasn't altogether happy traversing this terrain and had given up the ghost about half a mile down the road. Walking had never been a problem for her, even while carrying around the extra pounds that her baby had brought with it, but this particular half mile had all been uphill. The dog appearing out of nowhere hadn't exactly helped matters any. Her heart was still pounding wildly. Luckily the dog had decided to be friendly.

"Right now, having car trouble," Sherry managed to get out.

Yeah, right. You'd think that someone who wrote for a living would be more original than that. "If you expect me to believe that—"

"Go see for yourself." Turning, Sherry pointed behind her down the mountain. "It's about half a mile down the road."

He had half a mind to call the sheriff and have her arrested. That would put the fear of God into her. Fuming, Sin-Jin glared at her. The woman was panting. He eyed her stomach. Her whole body seemed to be vibrating from the effort it had taken to get here.

"Are you out of your mind?" he demanded. Pregnant women were supposed to stay near hospitals, not hike up mountainsides.

"Probably." She stopped to draw in more air. Her lungs were finally beginning to feel as if they weren't about to explode. She tried to smile and succeeded only marginally. "I've been accused of that on occasion."

Sin-Jin glanced down at Greta. The dog was prancing around the woman who kept insisting on intruding into his life. It was as if Greta and the reporter were old friends. The barking, now that he thought about it, had been the friendly variety, the kind he was apt to hear when Greta wanted to play. Obviously the animal didn't see the woman as a threat.

He wondered if Greta was getting old.

Sherry tried to wet her lips and discovered that she couldn't. Her mouth felt as dry as dust. "I hate to trouble you, but would you mind getting me a glass of water?"

"Yes." Disgusted, Sin-Jin paused. It would serve the woman right if he sent her on her way just as she was. He sincerely doubted that there was anything wrong with her car. But she was obviously pregnant, and there were beads of perspiration along her brow despite the cold temperature. The walk up here, for whatever reason, had cost her. He glanced back at the cabin. Sin-Jin didn't relish the idea of taking her in there. "I don't suppose you want it out here."

Sherry was beginning to feel very wobbly, as if her legs were turning to the consistency of cotton after being soaked in water. "If you don't mind, I'd like to sit down." She glanced at her surroundings and second-guessed what he was about to say. "Preferably not on a rock."

She raised her eyes to his, the blueness assaulting him. In the light of day they looked even more intense than they had in the elevator. There was something really unsettling about the way she looked at him. His thoughts came to an abrupt halt as he gazed into her eyes.

Probably just the altitude getting to him, Sin-Jin reasoned.

"What a surprise," he muttered. "All right, come on." He waved her forward. "But once you're rested, you're going back."

She didn't bother trying to keep up. Walking was now a challenge.

"My car died," she reminded him.

"I'm pretty handy with a car. I'll get it going." There was no room for doubt in his voice. He glanced over his shoulder to see if she'd heard him. Her mouth was curved. "Why are you smiling?"

"I've learned something about you already." She struggled not to huff as she followed. "I don't recall reading anywhere that you were handy with cars."

Sin-Jin blew out a breath, saying nothing. Instead he glanced at Greta, who was prancing excitedly from foot to foot as she ran alongside of the woman, only to backtrack and then begin again. She gave the impression of trying to shepherd the reporter into his cabin.

"Traitor," he muttered under his breath.

Chapter 4

Trying to contain his anger, Sin-Jin slammed the door the second the woman was inside. The Irish Setter jumped. Greta looked up at him accusingly. The feeling was mutual.

Taking out the ammunition, he parked his rifle in the corner and deposited the shells on the coffee table. "You're lucky I don't call the sheriff."

Sherry took in her surroundings. The ceiling in the living area was vaulted, with heavy wooden beams running across it. The look of massive wood was everywhere. It was a man's retreat, built by a man for a man. If Adair brought women to his friend's cabin, they hadn't left any telltale marks. Even the framed photograph on the mantel had no people in it, just a scenic panorama of what looked like the Lake Tahoe area.

She turned to look at him, fighting an odd wave of discomfort unlike any she'd experienced in the past nine months, a passage of time marked with a great many moments of discomfort. Sherry tried to focus on his face. His expression was as cold as the weather outside.

"You didn't call the sheriff because you don't want to be laughed at, Mr. Adair." She pointed toward the framed photograph. "Is that Lake Tahoe?"

"Yes." Impatience echoed in his voice. "As for calling the sheriff—"

Feeling suddenly woozy, Sherry collapsed in the nearest chair without bothering to ask if she could. It took effort to complete her thought. "Not many people would see their way clear to your feeling threatened by a pregnant woman."

He looked down at her and glared. The woman was making herself right at home, wasn't she? "You don't threaten me, Ms. Campbell, you annoy me."

As if to defuse the moment, Greta eased herself into the space formed by her arm and the chair, the setter's indication clear. She wanted to be petted. Sherry obliged the dog, taking comfort in the soothing act.

"Why? Because I'm trying to find out more about you than what can be read in those lackluster press releases your corporation issues?"

He strode into the kitchen, which was just off the living room and turned on the tap. "Exactly. This is a very public world we live in. I'm just trying to maintain a shred of privacy in it." Holding the filled glass of water in front of him, he crossed back to her. "Used to be a man's right." He thrust the glass toward her. "I'd like to go back to those times."

Feeling suddenly unbelievably shaky, Sherry took the glass in both hands and drank deeply. She started to feel better. Whatever had been wrong a moment ago had passed, thank God. She was herself again. Something, she figured, Adair wouldn't be overly thrilled about.

Her mouth curved.

"You're right—it is a public world we live in, when almost everyone's life can be laid bare with the right keystrokes on the computer. The internet is an endless font of information—yet there isn't anything about you." Her mouth dry, she took another long sip, letting her words sink in. "It's almost as if you didn't exist outside of the nine-to-five business world."

He thought about the past week. He'd barely had time to come home and change. It felt as if he hadn't slept at all. "It's hardly nine to five."

She realized that generalization didn't apply to him. "All right nine to midnight. The point is—" still petting the dog with one hand while holding on to the glass with the other, she moved slightly forward on the chair "—who are you?"

The warmth in the cabin was imprinting itself on the woman's cheeks. Sin-Jin wondered how he could be annoyed and attracted at the same time. No doubt about it, he definitely needed to get out more.

"The point is, business takes up all my time and who I am is my business."

The man was good, she'd give him that. He'd probably drive a lawyer crazy under cross-examination on the stand. "Nicely put, Mr. Adair. You know how to use words to your advantage."

Sin-Jin narrowed his eyes. "If I did, you wouldn't be here."

"Speaking of here," she gestured around the cabin, "how is coming here business?"

Enough was enough. He shouldn't even be talking to her. "I think you've asked enough questions."

It was an interesting phenomenon. The more Adair scowled, the more at ease she seemed to feel. "We'll put it to a vote." She glanced down at the Irish setter at her side. "How about you, dog?"

An unfamiliar possessiveness came over him. "Her name's Greta."

Sherry nodded at the backhanded introduction. "Even better. The personal touch." She looked into the setter's eyes. "How about you, Greta? Do you think I've asked enough questions? No?" She looked up at Adair, the essence of cheerfulness. "That settles it. The vote's two to one—I already know how you're voting—for me to continue."

Not that he wasn't amused in some strange, abstract sort of way, but it was time to cut this short. "In this case, might makes right."

She raised her eyebrows innocently. "You're planning on Indian wrestling me?"

"No, I plan on carrying you to your car if necessary, fixing said car *if necessary,* and sending you back on your way."

She twisted around to look at him. "You really know how to fix cars?"

He put his hands on the back of the chair, debating slanting it just enough to urge the woman to her feet. "Don't change the subject."

She'd come too far to be sidetracked now. Even though that strange feeling was back, she couldn't be deterred from her purpose. "That *is* the subject—*you* are the subject." He might not realize it, but she was picking things up about him. "What else do you know?"

The smattering of patience that he'd temporarily uncovered was gone. "I know when to end a conversation, something you apparently do not."

Time to switch tactics. She looked around. "Your friend has good taste."

The comment was out of left field, catching him short. "What?"

"Your friend," she repeated with emphasis. "The man who this cabin belongs to. John Fletcher," she added for good measure. "He has good taste."

The statement almost made him smile. Sin-Jin looked around, as if seeing it for the first time through someone else's eyes.

"Yes," he finally allowed, "he does." He looked at the half-empty glass of water she was still holding. "Are you finished with that?"

"Not yet." To prove it, she took another long sip. For some reason it just made her hotter. "You know, it's true what they say, about mountain water," she added when he looked confused. "I'm a tap water person myself, but there is a difference." She held the glass aloft as if to underscore her point.

Sin-Jin leaned his hip against another chair, his arms crossed before him as he regarded her. "Do you ever stop talking?"

"Feel free to jump in anytime." Her grin was wide and inviting and for a moment, managed to sneak in through a crack. He found himself being drawn in.

"I—" Stopping, Sin-Jin shook his head and laughed. She'd almost had him for a second. "That was transparent."

Undaunted, she shrugged. "Sometimes it works. Most people find me easy to talk to."

Yes, he supposed he could see that. But there was another factor involved. "When would they ever get a chance?"

She cocked her head, her eyes warm, coaxing. "All you have to do is start. Once you do, I'll shut up."

But better people than she had tried to worm their way into his world and get close to him. He'd stopped each in their tracks. Other than with Mrs. Farley, all his relationships were hallmarked by a distance, a space that none were allowed to cross.

"Sorry, Ms. Campbell, but I don't intend to tell you anything about myself."

She wasn't going to go away empty-handed, and something was better than nothing. There was no telling how one thing could lead to another. "All right, then tell me about John Fletcher. How long have you two been friends? When did you meet him? Did he go to the same school as you did?"

He felt as if he was being shelled with torpedoes. "I value my privacy and John values his." His expression was unshakable. "We're leaving it at that."

She stared at him for a long moment, reading her own meaning into his words. "Oh."

"What do you mean, 'oh?'"

"Just that. 'Oh.'"

The word was even more pregnant than she was. Visions of a headline rose in his mind. He wasn't about to drop it until she laid his fear to rest. "What are you implying?"

Her smile was easy, kind. Sin-Jin had no idea that there could be so many layers involved in such a simple action as the curving of the lips. "Now who's asking questions?"

Irritation sealed itself to frustration. "I have a right to ask questions if the subject concerns me."

"I thought you weren't going to be a subject." She would have been enjoying this more if part of her wasn't beginning to feel like a can of tuna fish being cracked apart with a rusty can opener.

He blew out a breath. As much as he hated drawing people into his life, maybe he should be calling the sheriff. "Has anyone ever told you that you're infuriating?"

If she only had a nickel...

"Occasionally," she said, tongue in cheek. "It usually happens when I stumble across a secret they don't want to let out."

"There is no secret to let out." He almost shouted the words at her.

Sherry pressed the issue just a little, although she had pretty much decided what his answer was going to be, and that she believed it. "Then you and this John Fletcher are not in a relationship?"

"No."

She was the soul of innocence when she asked, "And you're not gay?"

Damn it, just because there wasn't a string of women in his wake... "Of course I'm not gay," he shouted. "I wouldn't have found you attractive if I were."

That caught her by surprise. She hadn't felt remotely attractive for months now. Pregnant whales were not deemed attractive, except perhaps by other whales. Desperate other whales.

"You find me attractive?"

"Yes," he shouted again, then lowered his voice, "in a very irritating sort of way. Now, if you're finished with your water..." Not giving her time to answer, he took the glass out of her hand and put it squarely on the table. "I think it's time you showed me where this car of yours allegedly died."

Taking her arm to help her to her feet, Sin-Jin was surprised at how much resistance met the offer.

A beat before he took the water from her, she'd felt something awful happening. She looked up at him with wide eyes. "I don't think I can do that."

"And why is that?"

Spacious or not, the room began to feel as if it closed in on her and there was this awful pain emanating from the center of her body. "Because I think my water just broke."

He was almost disappointed. You'd really think a reporter could do better than that. "Ms. Campbell, I wasn't born yesterday or the day before that."

She was having trouble breathing. "I don't think that when you were born…is going to be an issue, but this baby…wants to be born…today."

She almost had him believing that something was wrong. Except that he knew better. He looked at her icily. "How convenient."

"Not…really." Convenient would be if she could get someone else to give birth to this baby for her.

The hitch in her voice had him pausing. He was beginning to have his doubts at how accomplished an actress she actually was. "You're serious."

She sucked air in, trying desperately to remember what it was that Lori had said. The last eight weeks of classes seemed to vanish from her brain as if they'd never taken up space there. "Yes."

"You came up here on your due date?" The woman really was crazy.

Sherry wished that she'd listened to all those people who'd cautioned her about being careful, even though it went against her nature. "No…I came up here…almost a month away…from my due day."

Okay, then they had nothing to be concerned about.

Taking her hand again, he made a second attempt to get her to her feet. "Well, then—"

She winced and collapsed back into the chair. Lift-off had existed for only three inches. She was positive that she felt a contraction. A hard one. "Apparently... they don't...issue calendars...along with...uteruses."

Since he couldn't get her to her feet, Sin-Jin sank down beside the chair, deciding for the moment to play along and give her the benefit of the doubt. No one could change color like that at will, no matter how good they were. She was definitely pale.

"Exactly what is it that you're feeling?" He wanted to know.

Words failed her. "A whole bunch...of things I'd rather not...be feeling right now." She looked at him, a mild panic setting in and rising up to her eyes. She could see he didn't believe her. Sherry pressed her lips together, doing her best to explain. "I feel like...I'm a tube of toothpaste that...someone's trying to squeeze the...last drop out of."

He laughed shortly. "If that's a sample of how you write, I suggest you change your profession."

But even as he said it, the woman squeezed his hand so tightly the blood felt as if it would stop flowing. He started having doubts that she was doing this for his benefit. Early labors weren't entirely unheard of.

Here came another one. "I'll...do a...revision...on it later. Is there...a doctor close by?" The words were coming out in short pants. She hated this.

Sin-Jin thought of the small clinic that he'd anonymously funded. Its main function was to care for injured skiers, patching them up just enough to send them on to regular facilities that were far better equipped to handle emergencies. It was run by two physicians. "There's a clinic about twenty miles from here."

She gripped his hand harder. Why wasn't that making the pain go away? "No…I mean *close*…like twenty feet…away."

Sympathy began to stir. He'd never been one not to be moved by suffering. "You're panicking."

She tried to smile. The effort wasn't entirely success-ful. "What was your…first…clue?"

He knew a little about what she was going through. "Look, if you are in labor, you've got a long way to go before the baby's born."

A lot he knew. It felt as if the baby was trying to tear its way out of her with the jaws of life. And then hope nudged forward on the wings of irrationality. "You're not…a…closet doctor…are you?"

Part of him still couldn't help wondering if she was pulling this stunt just to find out more information about him. He'd had some medical training, but she didn't need to know that. At least, not yet.

"No, but haven't you heard the horror stories about women being in labor for seventy-two hours?"

The women in her office had converged around her, sharing their experiences and making her feel that giving birth was a torture second only to being drawn and quartered during the Spanish Inquisition. Joining the Lamaze class was her way of trying to placate her own fears.

"I've got…a horror story…of…my own. Giving… birth without…a doctor."

He looked at her pointedly, his voice firm. "You're not giving birth."

"I know my…own body," she gasped. "It's expelling the…foreign body…within…in this case, a ba—BEE!"

He winced as she suddenly jackknifed forward and shouted the last syllable in his ear. Sin-Jin could see the perspiration along her brow increasing.

He looked around, thinking. "Okay, let's say for the sake of argument that you are in some kind of accelerated labor—"

She felt as if she was being crushed from several different directions at once. Was this normal?

"I...don't want...to...argue, I want...this...to be over with." She gripped his hand even harder, trying to pull together what strength she had. "Are you...*sure*....there isn't someone...you can...call?"

Sin-Jin made his decision. She was on the level. But he sincerely doubted the situation was as urgent as she believed it was.

"C'mon," he tucked his hand under her arm. "I'll drive you to the clinic."

But even as he tried to get her to her feet, Sherry's knees buckled. She wound up sinking to the floor in a less-than-graceful movement. "I don't...think there's... time."

"You're serious." This time it wasn't a question, it was a resigned statement.

She thought she knew what he was thinking, hoping. Right now she wished he was right. "I don't...want...a... story this...badly."

"Okay, I believe you." Still on his knees beside her, Sin-Jin reached over to the sofa and pulled down the blanket that was slung over the arm. He spread it out on the floor as best he could while supporting her against him. "Let's get this jacket off you." Moving as swiftly as he could, he stripped the parka from her. It was drenched with perspiration. That clinched it. It wasn't an elaborate ruse. No one could perspire like that on cue. He pulled a cushion off and placed it at the edge of the blanket for her head.

She sagged against him. "What…are you going…to…do?"

He brushed the hair from her forehead before gently moving her toward the blanket. "Nothing, you're the quarterback in this. I'm just going to be the wide receiver, catching the football when you release it."

She blew as a contraction closed its jaws around her and then finally released. "You…play…football?"

"Played," Sin-Jin corrected. As he began to rise, Sherry caught his hand, her eyes widening. "I'm just going to wash my hands."

She watched his every move as he crossed to the kitchen. She was putting her fate into the hands of a man she and the world knew next to nothing about, except that he was ruthless when necessary. It wasn't a ringing endorsement. "Do…you know…what you're…doing?"

He washed his hands quickly. "Probably more than you do." Drying off, he crossed back to her.

"How?"

He shook his head. "Don't you ever stop being a reporter?"

The contraction abated, allowing her to draw air back into her lungs. She was almost giddy from the respite. And then another began to gallop toward her, harder and faster than before. "Right now…I'm being a…scared… woman…about to give…birth…a hundred miles from nowhere…in a cabin…with a man…known as the Darth Vader…of industry."

Feeling sorry for her, he opened the door to his privacy just a crack. "I've had a little medical training."

He was trying to make her comfortable, she realized. "How…little?"

He'd been premed for a while, actually toying with the idea of becoming a doctor before he discovered that he had a truer calling. "Enough."

Sherry groped around either side of her, crumpling the blanket beneath white knuckles. "Okay...I'm going to...trust...you."

"Don't see that you have much of a choice," he told her gruffly.

He certainly wished he had. This wasn't the way he'd envisioned his day when he got up this morning. The cup of coffee he'd poured himself just before Greta had begun barking was still standing on the table, stone cold now, reminding him how, despite his best efforts, he had little control over life.

A sense of panic washed over her. Maybe this was a bad idea. What if something went wrong? This was a baby she was about to produce, not a contract. What did Darth Vader know about birthing babies? "Are you sure...there isn't...time?"

Rocking back on his heels, he regarded her quietly. "You tell me." There was another option. "I could get you into the chopper and—"

She blinked. "Chopper?"

"My helicopter." He nodded toward the rear of the cabin. "It's on a landing pad a few yards from the house."

He wasn't a man, he was a superhero. She tried to focus on his face, the perspiration dripping into her eyes making it hard to see. "You fly...too?"

"Yes." If he was going to do this, he had to hurry. "Look, no more questions. Are you up to a trip? I can have you back at the hospital—" His statement was cut short as Sherry grabbed his hand again and screamed. "I guess not. Okay, looks like the floor show's going to be here." He rolled up his sleeves. "What did you say your first name was?"

Panting again, she held her hand up until the contraction lessened. "Sherry."

"Sherry," he repeated, nodding. "All right, we're going to get through this, Sherry. Just remember, you're not the first woman to have her baby outside a hospital."

He was talking to her. She knew he was talking, but his voice kept fading in and out. Sherry shook her head, trying to focus, trying to hear what he was saying. But everything was fading, being stuffed headlong into a large, dark cylinder.

And then a curtain fell and she heard and saw nothing. Fear was her only companion and it was about to swallow her up whole.

Chapter 5

The acrid odor assaulted her senses, rudely pushing its way into the black abyss and grabbing hold of her. Startled, trying to get away from the smell, Sherry rose to the surface, aware that she was twisting her head from side to side.

She opened her eyes and moaned a second before the pain came again, twice as strong as before and three times as overwhelming.

"What happened?" she gasped, coughing.

Sin-Jin kept the opened ammonia capsule by her nose a moment longer, just in case.

"You fainted," he answered matter-of-factly. She'd done more than that. She'd given him one hell of a scare. He wasn't sure if she'd just fainted or if the situation was actually far more dire. She'd remained unconscious for almost five minutes. "Don't do that again."

With wavering strength she pushed his hand away

from her face. "I'll do...my best..." Her eyes flew open, looking like giant blue cornflowers searching for the sun. "Oh, God, oh, God, oh, God."

He tossed aside the capsule. "Another one?"

"Well...I'm not...praying to you... Don't you have... anything to...knock me out?"

"Other than my fist? No." He tried not to give in to the feeling of helplessness that was hovering over him. It wasn't an emotion he welcomed. "Hang in there."

About to prep her as best he could, Sin-Jin paused, hesitating even as he knew it was foolish. But privacy was such an issue with him that invading another's, no matter how noble the reason, just didn't seem right without permission.

As he picked up the edge of her denim jumper, he looked up at her. "Sorry."

The sentiment was genuine. In a haze comprised of pain, disorientation and jagged fear, Sherry was still moved by what she would have termed old-world court-liness in this impersonal world. Sin-Jin Adair wasn't just some coldhearted bastard who made his living gutting other people's dreams. There was far more to him than that.

If only she was in her right mind to make mental note of it.

She struggled to keep ahead of the pain that insisted on squeezing her within its jaws. Sherry bit her lip to keep the scream back, then nodded. There was a time for modesty, but she'd gone way past that now.

"Go ahead... Do what you have...to do."

Sin-Jin pushed up her jumper and got her ready to deliver her baby. The woman was fully dilated. "My God, you're crowning."

It was a familiar term, but if her soul had depended

on it, she couldn't have said what it meant. "Is that…a good thing?"

He did his best to sound encouraging. Behind him he could hear Greta pacing back and forth like a worried relative in a maternity waiting room.

"Means that this should be over with soon." Though he recalled all the particulars, he'd never actually attended a birth. He capped the uneasiness that tried to push forward. "I see the head."

A head. There had to be more, right? It felt like there was a convention going on inside of her and everyone was trying to push their way out the fire exit at the same time.

"Anything…else?"

"Not yet."

She heard him doing things but had no idea what. It didn't matter. All that mattered was getting rid of this pain.

"I'm…passing…an elephant, there's…got to be… more."

She looked fully ready to go. He glanced up at her face. "Are you ready to push?"

Push, that meant this would be over soon, right? "Ever since…this started."

Sin-Jin took a breath, bracing himself. Hoping nothing was going to go wrong. "Okay, on the count of three."

His words echoed in her head. "You're going…to push with…me?"

Even out of her head, she was still questioning things. It made him wonder how she'd gotten pregnant in the first place. "No, just take the credit when it's done."

She blinked, trying to focus on him. "A…sense of… humor?"

He lifted his shoulders in a half shrug. "I find it helps when things are tense."

Tense. That meant dangerous. Was her baby in danger? She tried to swallow, and it felt as if her throat was sticking to itself. "Are they?"

He heard the mounting panic. The last thing he needed right now was for her to give in to that. "Don't worry, I know what I'm doing," he assured her again. "My uncle was a doctor."

Had she had the energy, she would have asked about his uncle, about the rest of his family now that he'd allowed that to slip out. But her head began to swirl dangerously. It was all she could do to keep from passing out from the pain again. It was all around her now, like a giant steel vise.

Sin-Jin crossed his fingers that, like everything else she seemed to have done so far, she could get through this part quickly. "Okay, one, two, three—push!"

Gathering all her strength together, Sherry leaned as far forward as she could and pushed with all of her might. Heat assaulted her and she felt as if she was being pulled in two opposite directions. Panting, she fell back.

"Is it…out…yet?"

If only, he thought. "No, not yet."

She wanted to cry. This wasn't fair. It wasn't fair that she was going through this and the man whose baby this was, who had broken her heart, wasn't even going to feel so much as a twinge. He'd moved on to another relationship, leaving her to handle all this by herself. She wanted Drew's head on a platter.

"Why…not?"

Because didn't seem enough of an answer, although that was what came to mind. "Because it doesn't go that fast."

She struggled to get air into her lungs. "It should. Who...made the...rules? Oh, God—"

He knew the signs by now. Her body was going rigid. There was no way for her to relax, even though it would be easier on her if she could.

"Okay, again." Sin-Jin watched her face intently as he issued the order. "One, two, three—push!" Sherry was already pushing before he reached the third number. He was afraid she was going to rupture something. "You've got to pace yourself, Sherry. Push when I tell you to push."

She looked at him accusingly, her lashes damp with perspiration. Maybe he'd like to trade places. "God, but...you are...bossy."

"I'm right." His voice left no room for argument. She was stiffening again. It wouldn't be long now. "All right, one, two—"

She shook her head, exhausted beyond words. "No, I can't...I just can't."

This wasn't a time to bail out. "Yes," he insisted firmly, "you can."

How dare he stand there, issuing orders, telling her what she was capable of? He was on the safe side of this torture rack. "How...many...babies have you...pushed...out?"

"I didn't say this was easy, but you can't stay pregnant forever."

She could feel the tears gathering. One trickled down her cheek, skimming the outline of her ear. "Not forever...just a little...longer. I can't—"

Abandoning his post at one end, Sin-Jin moved until he was close to her face. He took out his handkerchief and dried the path the tear had taken.

"Yes," he told her, his voice gentle, "you can. You're

a damn strong woman, Sherry Campbell. This is going to be in your past soon enough. Now do it for the baby."

She bit her lip again, trying to hold everything at bay. She could feel forces beyond her control undulating downward. "One…for the…gipper?"

He laughed shortly. "Something like that." With that he returned to where he felt he could do the most good. "Okay, now push!"

With her last remaining ounce of strength, Sherry scooted her elbows in close to her body, propped herself up, and through clenched teeth almost shrieked out, "Okay." Screwing her eyes shut tight, she pushed for all she was worth.

His hands in position between her legs, a sense of amazement skimmed over him as the small being began to emerge. As he shared in the miracle, a sensation like no other materialized within his chest.

"You're doing great, Sherry. The head's coming." He sucked in his breath as the damp crown met his hands. "It's out!"

Just the head? Where was the rest of her baby? "Isn't…it supposed to…be attached…to something?"

She was delirious, he thought. That made two of them. "We need shoulders, Sherry."

The task before her seemed insurmountable. "Aren't you…going to…do…anything?"

Something was wrong. The baby's color didn't look right. There was no time to waste. "Push, Sherry, push." His hand beneath the small head, he looked at her, not wanting to alarm her, wanting her to cooperate. "You're almost there."

At this point all she wanted to do was die in peace. Gulping in air, Sherry shut her eyes tight and concentrated as she gave up the last of herself and pushed. The push ended in a guttural scream.

With the shoulders now out, he tugged the infant out as gently and quickly as he could. "And we have a winner."

"What…what…?"

Turning the baby over on his palm, Sin-Jin was amazed at how tiny the infant was. He patted the baby's back, doing his best to expel any amniotic fluid from the child's nose, mouth and lungs.

"It's a boy."

What was going on? What was he doing? She strained to hear the sound of a baby crying, mewling, something. But there was nothing. "I don't hear…"

The baby had stopped breathing altogether. Quickly Sin-Jin opened the tiny mouth to see if there was anything inside obstructing it. The airway appeared to be clear. But the small chest remained still. Trying to remember everything he'd learned in one year of premed, Sin-Jin placed the baby on his back and gently blew into the tiny mouth before working on the baby's chest.

A panic far greater than the one she'd experienced while in labor was beginning to overtake Sherry. Something was very wrong.

"What is it?" she demanded. "What's wrong with my baby?"

Sherry tried to prop herself up on her elbows and found there wasn't a shred of energy left. She'd used it all giving birth to her baby. The umbilical cord still connected them.

She could almost feel life ebbing away.

"Please," she cried.

The single word said it all. She was pleading with

him to save her baby. As if he wouldn't if she hadn't made the entreaty.

He ignored her question, her very presence. All his energy was now focused on bringing air back into the small life he'd helped to bring into the world. Several times he'd pushed on the small chest and then breathed into the tiny mouth.

After what seemed liked an eternity, he felt the smallest of heartbeats beneath his fingertips. Elated, drained, only then did Sin-Jin look up at the baby's mother.

The look in his eyes terrified her. She shouldn't have come up here. She should have stayed home, safe. If she hadn't been so hell-bent on getting this story, her contractions would have overtaken her in her own house, less than five miles away from the hospital. Maybe they wouldn't have come at all. Maybe it was walking uphill that had done it.

Irrational thoughts attacked her from all directions. Had she killed her baby?

Tears gathered in her eyes. "Is he—?"

Sin-Jin was afraid to take his eyes off the infant, afraid that if he did, even for a moment, the baby would stop breathing again.

"He's alive, but he needs to get to a hospital right away."

He couldn't afford to wait.

Moving quickly, Sin-Jin severed the tie between mother and child with a kitchen knife and clamped the end of the cord with a large metal paper clip he'd thought to sterilize.

He wrapped the baby in a towel, amazed at how it seemed to dwarf him, and tucked the infant into her arms.

"I'm going to fly you to Blair Memorial," he told her.

It was the closest hospital he knew of that had a neonatal section. He looked at Sherry. The placenta had been expelled, but he wasn't sure if she'd stopped bleeding. The best thing for her would be rest, not to be jostled and then flown a hundred and ten miles, but it couldn't be helped. "This isn't going to be easy," he warned her.

All that mattered was saving her son. "Don't worry about me." Emotion and exhaustion mingled in her voice.

Stooping beside her, Sin-Jin did his best to cover her and slip the parka around her shoulders before he began to pick her up.

With her free hand, she gripped his arm. "That's all right," she told him, "I can walk. Just help me up."

There was no question in his mind that if she tried to gain her feet, she'd pass out again. "The hell you can."

Without another word he rose holding Sherry in his arms as she held the baby to her.

The man was going to pull something, she thought. "We're too heavy for you," she protested weakly.

He steadied himself, then began to cross to the door. "I picked you up when you fainted. The baby was inside of you then. It's just a matter of repositioning." Shouldering open the door, he spared her a look, his expression reproving. "You have got to be the most argumentative woman I've ever encountered."

She felt strength draining from her. It was all she could do to keep her arms around her son.

Live, please live.

"Sorry to hear that."

Greta began to follow him. He paused only long enough to fix the animal with a look. "You stay here and guard the place better than you have been."

The tone of her master's voice had Greta obediently retreating.

"Good dog." Sin-Jin managed to push the door closed with his elbow. Getting a better grip on his cargo, he began walking away from the cabin.

Every step jostled her, underscoring the pain that was running rampant through her body. Her heart was pounding wildly, and she struggled to keep from passing out again. "Adair?"

He kept his eyes fixed on his target, the helicopter on the landing pad. He cursed the fact that he hadn't had the pad built closer to the cabin.

"What?"

No words seemed good enough. She went with the simplest and hoped that Adair would understand. "Thank you."

He didn't look at her. "You didn't leave me much choice."

Despite his hectic schedule, he'd always made time for exercising and keeping fit. Even so, the hundred yards to the landing pad felt as if it was ten times that as he walked with the woman and child in his arms.

When he finally reached the helicopter, he breathed a silent sigh of relief. Very carefully he eased Sherry into the passenger seat, then strapped her in. Under perfect conditions he would have had a way to secure the baby, as well. But under perfect conditions he wouldn't have had to airlift the infant to the hospital in the first place.

Rounding the front of the helicopter, he got in on the pilot's side. "Hold on, we'll be there in fifteen minutes," he promised.

As he started the engine up, Sin-Jin radioed in his flight plan, and explained his dilemma as well.

Sherry tried to listen, but the sound of the rotors

drowned out Adair's voice. Everything was swallowed up by a sea of noise.

She clutched her baby to her, looking down at him to assure herself that he was still breathing, still alive. It all felt surreal, Sherry thought. The delivery, this emergency flight, the pain she was feeling. Even the tall, dark, grim-looking man beside her—all of it surreal. There were tears in her eyes as she looked down at her son. He looked so small, so helpless.

She closed her eyes, the tears seeping through her lashes. *Please let him live,* she prayed. *You don't need another angel, but I do. Please let him stay with me. Please.*

Sherry turned to look at the man piloting the helicopter. In the space of an hour she'd shared an experience with him that had brought her closer to the man than she'd been to almost anyone else.

Who was he, really, and where did she go to find the answers?

There was an emergency crew waiting on the roof of Blair Memorial Hospital. Sin-Jin could see them as he approached the tower building. They stood clustered around a gurney and a glass bassinet, waiting for him to land. The instant the helicopter touched down, they rushed forward with the gurney and the bassinet.

"I thought you'd be a paramedic," the attending physician said, raising his voice to be heard above the din made by the helicopter blades as they came to a slow halt.

Remaining in the copter, Sin-Jin helped to guide Sherry and her baby out, gently easing them from their seat.

Sin-Jin shook his head. "Just a civilian. I got them here as fast as I could." Capable hands laid Sherry on the gurney. He saw the look of concern as her son was taken from her and placed in the bassinet. "The baby's less than an hour old. He stopped breathing right after he was born."

"How long?"

Sin-Jin got out from his side and rounded to the gurney. He anticipated the question. "A minute, maybe less."

The doctor nodded, then signaled his team to retreat into the building. Gurney and bassinet began to move. "Thanks, we'll take it from here."

It was his cue to leave. Sin-Jin had every intention of turning back to his helicopter and just taking off. With any luck he could salvage the rest of his weekend before he had to get back.

But as he started toward the helicopter, his line of vision crossed Sherry's. The look in her eyes spoke volumes. He hesitated a split second. Then, as the team hurried back to the roof's entrance, Sin-Jin found himself following in their wake.

The moment they were back inside the building, the nurse pushing the bassinet looked at him. "Are you the husband?"

He laughed dryly. No, thank God. "No, just some guy in the right place at the right time."

The elevator arrived. The team with its gurney and bassinet filled the interior almost to capacity. The doctor pushed for the fifth floor. "Lucky for the baby," he commented.

"Yeah," Sin-Jin murmured in response, "lucky." He saw Sherry lift her hand, groping for his. He took it, wrapping his fingers around hers. He raised an inquisitive brow.

"Did I say thank you?" she whispered.

Sin-Jin nodded. "Yes, you did."

Her eyes held his for a long moment, the sounds around them fading, becoming just so much background noise. "It wasn't enough."

The doors sprang open and suddenly they were mobile again. Sherry's fingers remained wrapped around his. Sin-Jin was forced to accompany her as her gurney was hurried down the corridor.

And then the team broke ranks. A nurse and an orderly were guiding the bassinet in another direction. "My baby, where are they taking my baby?" Sherry cried.

The doctor leaned over her gurney. "He's being taken to the neonatal division." His voice was soothing, reassuring. "Don't worry, he'll be well taken care of." Issuing orders regarding the nature of Sherry's immediate treatment, the doctor turned toward Sin-Jin. "If you want to hang around, you can visit with her once we've checked her over and gotten her to a room."

He'd already come farther than he should have. Sin-Jin began to back away. "That's all right, I just wanted to make sure she and the baby were taken care of."

The doctor looked unconvinced. "You're sure?"

"Oh, I'm sure."

Turning on his heel, he walked directly into a nurse. Startled, the woman backed up. Her mouth dropped open and then he saw it, that look of recognition he'd come to dread.

"Aren't you...?"

"No," he said curtly, hurrying past her toward the public elevators before the woman had a chance to ask another question.

As he turned down the corridor, he saw a cluster of reporters and camera crews camped not too far from one of the birthing rooms. He ducked his head down, but not before he'd accidentally made eye contact with one of the cameramen.

Adair. Rusty recognized him instantly. What the hell was he doing here? The man was supposed to be off at a mountain retreat. He'd sent Sherry there.

Concerned, Rusty peered after the man. It was Adair, he was sure of it. He'd been sitting here, cooling his heels for the better part of three hours, waiting for Jennifer Allen, last year's Oscar winner and this year's latest mom-to-be, to give birth. He'd been called down by the station manager and told to join Sherry's anchor replacement, a woman with air pockets for brains. Along with her fellow reporters, he and Lisa Willows were waiting to break the story for the benefit of a Hollywood-enthralled public in need of its latest celebrity fix.

If Adair was here, had he sent Sherry off on a wild-goose chase? Rusty turned and handed a dumbfounded Lisa his camera. "I'll be right back."

"Where are you going?" Lisa called after him.

"Men's room," he tossed over his shoulder. He figured that would do as an excuse.

Rusty turned the corner to where the elevators were located just as Adair got inside. "Wait up," he called.

Sin-Jin had no intentions of doing any such thing. Instead he pressed the button that closed the doors. The last thing he saw was the cameraman racing toward him.

Just his luck, Sin-Jin thought, annoyed. He would have to stumble across a nest of reporters just as he flew a new mother and her baby in. Apparently no good deed went unpunished.

As he rode up in the elevator, he wondered how long he had before some kind of trumped-up story would break. He was certain the reporters would get wind of his being here. He'd had to identify himself when he asked to land on the roof. It was only a matter of time before someone found out about the emergency flight and the baby who had necessitated it.

They'd probably think that the baby was his.

Great. He was going to suffer slings and arrows without ever having even held the woman's hand.

Well, not quite, he amended as he got out on the roof and remembered the way Sherry had looked at him. She'd clutched at his hand and he'd held hers. But that in no way balanced out what he felt certain was going to come his way. He'd had his share of media circuses.

Getting into the helicopter, Sin-Jin started the engine and then cleared the landing pad. He still had part of today and tomorrow before him to try to forget about the rest of the world. That included an overly intrusive news reporter.

Somehow he didn't think he was going to have much luck, but damned if he wasn't going to try.

Chapter 6

"What do you think you're doing, having the baby without me?"

Her eyes felt as if they were each weighted down with two fifty-pound plates. With supreme effort, Sherry fought off the drugging effects of well-earned sleep and roused herself as the familiar voice pushed itself into her consciousness.

Surfacing was not easy when every single bone in her body screamed for oblivion or, at the very least, sleep.

When she finally managed to open her eyes, she saw Rusty standing over her, his thin face looking far more drawn and concerned than she recalled seeing in a long time.

Sherry filled her lungs with air before offering a response. "Couldn't be helped." Her reporter's mind kicked in belatedly. Why had he come? Had someone called him? "How did you know I was here?"

As far as she knew, no one knew she was at Blair yet. She hadn't even had the energy to call either of her parents, or Owen. She'd planned to do that after her nap.

"I'm here with Lisa Willows, staking out Jennifer Allen." Rusty nodded toward the door in the general direction of the media circus he'd left behind. "She went into labor early this morning."

This morning. That was when she'd gone into labor. Or was that a hundred years ago?

"Small world." The statement came as a sigh.

"I'll say." Ordinarily not a demonstrative man, Rusty took her hand gently in his. He looked at her with concern. "I looked up and saw Adair walking down the hall. I got this feeling in my gut." Rusty shook his head. "More like a sick feeling, actually, because I knew you'd gone to that cabin retreat to get a lead on him… Are you all right, Sherry?"

It was the same tone he'd used when he'd found out about her quitting the TV station. This time, she didn't have to force a smile to her lips. "I'm fine, achy but fine."

"What happened?"

"I cornered him and went into labor." She laughed at the sound of that.

"But everything turned out okay." He looked at her flattened stomach. "I guess you got here in time."

The words were hard to push out, but she wanted Rusty to know. Someone should know that Adair wasn't the ogre people thought he was. "No, actually, Adair delivered my baby."

Very few things surprised Rusty, but this seemed to qualify. His mouth dropped open as he stared at her. "You're kidding. Darth Vader, the corporate raider, delivered your baby?"

She smiled. "Yes."

He peered at her face. "You're sure you're not just hallucinating? They give you these drugs sometimes—"

"No, I'm not hallucinating." The last few hours were a blur now, dotted with hazy, touching moments and covered in pain. "Adair was very competent—and gentle—from what I remember."

"How did you manage to get here? Medevac?"

"More like Adair-evac." She laughed at the look on Rusty's face and immediately regretted it. There were parts of her body that didn't welcome any kind of exertion no matter how minor. "Adair flew the baby and me here in his helicopter. I didn't realize that Blair had a helicopter landing pad."

"This sounds like one of those improbable movies."

Sherry felt her existing energy ebbing away. "It does, doesn't it?"

"Hell of an angle you got on your story, kid." He spaced his hands in the air, framing a headline. "'St. John Adair delivered my baby.'" Glancing toward Sherry, he saw her shiver. He dropped his hands, immediately solicitous. "What's wrong? Want me to get you a blanket, ring for the nurse, what?"

She groped for his hand, stopping him before he could race off. "No, I'm all right, Rusty. It's just when you put it that way, it sounds like something the tabloids would run."

"You've got a hell of a lot more finesse than a tabloid," Rusty assured her. "You'll find the right way to phrase it."

"Yes."

But even as she said it, Sherry could feel a small glimmer of doubt nudging its way forward. Adair had done something good for her, could she pay him back by doing the one thing he dreaded? Exposing his actions to the scrutiny of the general public.

Damn it, wasn't that why she went up there in the first place? And this was a good thing, it would negate his image as a cold-blooded predator. Or at the very least temper it.

The momentary mental debate tired her even more. There was time for a decision later. Right now, there were more urgent things to tend to than securing her byline in a new area.

She pressed the button on the side railing, and the upper portion of her bed rose.

"Don't tell anyone, Rusty."

"Hey, it's your exclusive, kid. As far as I'm concerned, I'm just visiting a friend."

She smiled her gratitude. "Do me one more favor."

"You caught me in a generous mood. What?"

She indicated the telephone that was just out of reach on the nightstand. "Bring the phone over closer, will you? I need to call my parents to let them know they've just entered the grand stage."

He placed the telephone on the table beside her. "Your mother's going to love that," he quipped.

She grinned. "Mom's still looking for a title that won't make her feel old."

"How about 'Your Highness'?"

"Not warm enough." Sherry began dialing. "Have you seen him yet? My son," she added. *My son.* How incredible that sounded.

"I'll do that now. Be back in a little while," Rusty promised.

Sherry nodded in response, waving goodbye as she heard the receiver on the other end being picked up. "Hi, Mom. Guess what?"

* * *

She'd left her purse.

The shapeless black leather shoulder bag was now sitting on the coffee table, silently mocking him, reminding him that he had unfinished business.

Sin-Jin hadn't seen the purse when he'd walked back into the cabin that afternoon. It probably would have remained on the floor under the table if it hadn't been for Greta. The setter had drawn his attention to it by barking at the bag as if it was some kind of dark interloper.

Stretched out on the sofa, about to finally dig into Tom Clancy's latest action thriller, he'd told the dog to be quiet. Greta had responded by placing the bag at his feet.

Looking at the offending item now, he frowned. He'd intended to have no further contact with Sherry Campbell. Now he had her purse, which necessitated interaction of some sort, even if just through a courier. He wasn't about to entrust something as important as a purse to the postal service.

For just a moment he considered looking through the purse. After all, she'd invaded his privacy. He would be within his rights invading hers. Turnabout was only fair play.

He left the purse where it was.

Fair play or not, by rifling through it he'd be sacrificing his principles, giving in to the curiosity that unexpectedly spiked through him.

So far the woman had managed to invade his life and come perilously close to sabotaging his principles.

"Looks like we're not rid of her yet, eh, Greta?"

The Irish setter barked. He could have sworn there was a sympathetic note in the sound and that she was agreeing with him.

With a resigned sigh, Sin-Jin abandoned Tom Clancy and rose to his feet, feeling too restless to settle in and give the book its due. He needed to move, to clear his brain.

"C'mon, girl, let's go for a walk." He took her red leash down from the hook where he kept it when they visited the cabin. "But if you flush out any more reporters, you're going straight to the pound where I found you." Greta wagged her tail in response, fairly hopping from paw to paw, nothing short of unlimited adoration in her big brown eyes. Sin-Jin wasn't taken in for a moment. "Don't give me that smug look," he warned.

Looping her leash over her head and securing it, he walked out the door. It was going to be a long walk.

Sherry braced her hand against the railing to steady herself and give support to knees that still insisted on being wobbly. She was in the hospital corridor, looking in through the large bay window. The neonatal ICU was located just down the hall from the regular nursery, where all the babies who didn't have problems were safely nestled—on display for doting parents, relatives and friends to come by and view them.

Here, the population was greatly reduced. There were only ten incubators in the neonatal intensive care unit. Ten little souls were born tinier than the rest, but just as mighty, just as pure.

She leaned her forehead against the glass, telling herself everything was going to be all right. She forced back tears so she could see him more clearly. Her son's incubator was positioned second from the left. Tiny baby girls buffered him on both sides. She prayed for all of them.

This was the third time she'd made the pilgrimage

today. Three times so that she could assure herself that all was well. That her son was well. Because he was hooked up to a machine that monitored his vital signs, he couldn't be brought to her, but she could come to visit him all she wanted.

Earlier today she'd actually held him for a few minutes. She'd sat down in a rocking chair while a young nurse had carefully placed her baby in her arms. His weight hardly registered. The lump in her throat felt heavier.

She had bags of sugar in her pantry that weighed more.

Holding him had been almost too much for her. Giving him back to the nurse had been harder.

He looked so tiny, she thought, lying there, one tube monitoring every breath he took, every function of his body, another allowing him to get the nourishment he needed. She should be the one nourishing him, not some tube. It hurt her heart just to look at him.

It was all her fault.

"You shouldn't blame yourself."

The deep voice startled her. It was as if it had somehow delved into her mind, into her heart.

She placed it instantly, before she even turned around. Adair.

The very last person in the world she would have expected. With effort, still bracing herself on the railing, she managed to half turn her body toward him. The casual look was gone. He was back in uniform again: an expensive designer suit, complete with a shirt and tie, the cost of which would probably feed a family of six for a month.

"What makes you think I blame myself?"

He'd seen it in her eyes, reflected in the ICU glass

as he came up behind her. "I didn't get to where I am today by not being able to read body language."

At another time she might have made an attempt to protest, but it was taking all the energy she had just to stand here. Besides, he was right. She did feel guilty. "If I hadn't gone up there after you—"

He'd never had much patience with second-guessing a situation. And hindsight was only good if it taught you something about the future, not the past. "He still might have arrived early. You didn't exactly play half-court basketball that day."

"Maybe not, but I did walk up the side of a mountain."

"Half a mile," Sin-Jin pointed out. He'd located her car after he'd returned. She hadn't lied, the car wouldn't start. The battery had been a faulty one. He'd had the local mechanic put in a new one, then hired the man's two sons to bring the car back into the city. "And you walked, you didn't hop."

That he was actually trying to make her feel better stunned her. Was this the same man who'd ruthlessly gone in and closed down a chain of discount department stores that had been around for the past fifty-one years? "Still, I can't help thinking—"

"What-ifs only make you doubt yourself the next time you have a decision to make," he informed her gruffly. "Don't waste your time on them."

"Is that the secret of your success?"

"Let's keep this friendly," he advised. "No questions."

For the time being, she retreated. Adair had delivered her son. She owed him. But there was one thing she did want to know. "Not even to ask what you're doing here?"

"I could say I was stalking you to give you a taste of your own medicine—"

Her eyes met his and she experienced a little shiver that took her utterly by surprise.

"Being stalked by a rich, handsome man, I think I can handle that." She turned completely away from the ICU window, intending on walking back to her room, but the simple motion made her light-headed. Afraid of passing out, she grabbed for his arm, her fingers digging in before she realized what she was doing. Sherry flushed, "Sorry, every time I'm around you, I seem to get light-headed."

What little color she'd had in her cheeks was draining away. "Maybe I should get you into bed," he said.

That sounded like a very good idea, but she felt the need to cover her weakness with a quip. "Why, Mr. Adair, I bet you say that to all the women you meet."

"Only the ones in fuzzy blue slippers," he deadpanned. The expression on his face was dubious. "Can you walk?"

"I can walk," she assured him with less than unwavering confidence. One tentative step later had her hesitating. "Maybe if I just held on to your arm—for good luck."

"Nobody's ever said that to me before." Sin-Jin presented his arm to her, waiting. She hooked her arm through it, trying hard not to lean on him too much. They began to walk down the hallway very slowly. "So what are you doing here, besides providing escort service to wobbly newly minted mothers?"

"I brought your purse." She looked at him quizzically. With everything that had happened, she'd forgotten all about that. "You left it in the cabin. And," he slipped his free hand into his pocket and pulled out a set of keys, "to give you this."

She looked at them, lightning striking her brain and activating it. "Car keys. Oh, God, the car—"

She looked so worried he was quick to set her at ease. "You were right, there was something wrong with it. I had it fixed and then had someone drive it down to your place."

Her place. She stopped taking baby steps and looked at him. "You know where I live?"

"I know everything."

She resumed walking. The man was coming across like a regular Renaissance man. "Delivering babies, flying helicopters, fixing cars, detective. I'm beginning to believe that you do."

He didn't want her making too much of it. It was all just common sense. "I believe in being prepared for all contingencies."

"Apparently." She stopped before the door marked 512. "This is my room."

His mouth curved in a half smile. "Yes, I know."

"Sorry, I forgot for a minute." She leaned against it rather than turn the door latch. The door gave, opening. "You know everything."

The quip died on her lips as she walked into the room. There was a large, cut-glass vase on her table, filled with a dozen of the reddest long-stem roses she'd ever seen. There were flowers in her room, several arrangements from family and friends. Even Owen had sent a basket. But nothing like this.

The roses took her breath away. "Did I forget those at your cabin, too?"

He regarded her guardedly. Was that just a slip, or was she baiting him? "It's not my cabin, it belongs to

John Fletcher and no, you didn't. I don't like showing up empty-handed when I go somewhere."

"You brought the purse," she reminded him, tongue in cheek. She noticed something else just behind the vase. "And a football." Sherry looked at him. "I'm afraid you're going to have to wait a few days before I'm up to playing."

He brought her to the edge of her bed. She sank down gratefully. "It's for your son."

Yesterday came back to her, at least a fragment of it did. "That's right, the football metaphor. You being the wide receiver." She beamed, proud of herself for re-membering.

"I wasn't sure you heard that."

"I heard everything, I just couldn't assimilate it all until later." Sitting down now, she felt almost human again.

"As I recall, you were a little indisposed at the time." He watched her toe off her slippers one at a time.

"Just a little," she agreed. And then she turned somber. What she couldn't remember was whether or not she'd expressed her gratitude. "Look, I don't know how to thank you. Nothing seems good enough."

He hadn't done it for the thanks, she'd been in need of help. He would have done the same for Greta. Faster, probably. But if she was really serious, he had a way for her to express her gratitude. "I think something will occur to you."

He was talking about the story, she thought. She really wasn't at liberty to tell him that she wouldn't pursue the story; that, if anything, his actions had aroused her curiosity. She wanted to know more about the man who was a ruthless businessman by day and a rescuing Renaissance man by night.

"What does occur to me right now is that you have got to be possibly the most well-rounded person I have ever met."

Flattery turned him off. He'd suffered too much of being pandered to by people who were stupid enough to believe that flattery made a difference in the way he viewed things, or them.

"Like I said, I like being prepared."

"There's prepared and then there's *prepared*." She studied him in silence for a moment. "Is there anything you can't do?"

He looked her in the eye. "I can't seem to get you to stop asking questions."

He didn't look annoyed, she thought. Progress. "Occupational hazard."

She still looked pale, he thought. "How are you feeling?"

She thought of her sore bottom. Stretching was definitely out. "Well, I don't think I'll be doing any intricate yoga positions for a couple of weeks, but all things considered, I'm doing great." Her smile deepened as she looked up at him. "If you hadn't been there for us—"

He shrugged off her words before she could finish. "Someone else would have."

He was really sincere about that, she realized. One of the richest men in the country resisted compliments and gratitude. Amazing. "I guess I should add modesty to that list."

That did make him laugh, however briefly. "There'd be a lot of people who'd dispute that with you."

She liked the sound of his laugh. Deep, rich, like the first coffee in the morning. "They'd be wrong."

He rubbed his chin, regarding her. She didn't seem

the pandering sort. "I don't give way before flattery, Ms. Campbell."

"And I'm not trying to flatter, Mr. Adair." Her expression softened. "I think after everything we've been through, we don't need to be that formal."

It was time for him to leave, he decided. He'd already been here too long. He'd only meant to leave her purse and the gifts. Discovering the room empty should have been a godsend. But something had urged him on to see how the baby was doing, and then he'd found himself compelled to comment once he'd seen the reflection of her face in the glass.

"Yes, we do. Well, now that you have your purse and your keys—"

She smiled, nodding at the vase. "And my roses."

"And your roses," he allowed, already withdrawing, "I'd better go."

Suddenly she didn't want him to leave. Not because he was her story, but because he was the man who'd come to her aid. Whether he liked it or not they'd bonded, up in that cabin.

"You could stay. We could talk. Off the record," she added for good measure.

Sin-Jin looked at her pointedly. "This has *all* been off the record," he informed her. "And I have a meeting to get to."

Still on the edge of the bed, she tried to scoot back and wasn't very successful at it. And then, before she knew it, Adair had placed his hands on her waist and moved her back. Before she could say anything, he threw the blanket over her legs, covering her.

"What are you smiling about?" he asked.

She wiggled out of her robe. Aware that her nightgown was slipping from her shoulder, she pulled the strap back up. "I was just thinking that you're not nearly the coldhearted man you want the general public to think you are."

He felt something stir in his gut as he looked at her. "I don't care what anyone thinks, Ms. Campbell. And I am a coldhearted man. The general public is right."

She inclined her head, knowing better but too tired to argue. "Have it your way."

"I generally do, Ms. Campbell, I generally do. You'll forgive me if I don't say, 'See you around.'"

"You don't have to say it," she told him as he began to leave. "Some things are a given."

She had the pleasure of seeing him stop for a fraction of a second before continuing on his way out. For that fraction of a second she knew she'd gotten to him. Which was only fair. Because the feeling was mutual.

Chapter 7

"What do you mean, 'The bill's already been taken care of'?"

Sherry wasn't in the mood to untangle someone else's bureaucratic mistakes. After a three-day stay at the hospital, she was finally going home. Going home without her baby. The infant was still not ready to leave the shelter of the incubator and monitors that watched over him. Sherry was having a great deal of trouble coming to terms with that.

Standing beside the wheelchair that hospital regulations dictated she use to make her exit, and buffered on either side by her parents, Sherry looked at the older woman at the cashier's desk.

The woman smiled at her brightly. "Just that, it's been taken care of."

Had she missed something? Sherry tried to remember. No, there was some mistake. "But that's not

possible. I haven't even given you my insurance card."
She held it aloft for the woman's benefit.

In the confusion of her emergency entrance, she'd just
assumed that no one had thought to take her insurance
information. It seemed rather odd to her, given what
hospital expenses were these days, but she wanted to
rectify the situation before she was discharged.

But when she'd stopped the nurse pushing her wheelchair from taking her outside so that she could provide
the necessary information, the billing clerk had politely
but firmly refused to take it down because apparently
there was no need.

Connor Campbell gently edged his daughter aside
as he leaned over the desk. A short bull of a man with
a thick mane of white hair, he had a presence that immediately gave him center stage. He smiled encourag-
ingly at the clerk.

"There must be some mistake. Maybe you have
my daughter mixed up with another Campbell. It's a
common enough name."

With a patient smile the woman retreated to her computer and reentered Sherry's information. The same
screen came up a second time. She shook her head and
raised her eyes to Connor. "Nope, says right here, 'Paid
in full.'"

Connor frowned. "Never heard of an insurance company being eager to pay out on a claim, especially before
the claim's been made."

The woman looked up at him brightly. "Payment
didn't come from an insurance company." She looked
back at the screen to double-check before she continued. "It's a voucher from Adair Industries."

Sherry's mouth dropped open. "What?"

Without waiting for an invitation, Sherry pushed

aside the wheelchair and came around to the other side of the woman's desk to look at the screen herself.

Stunned, the clerk began to protest. "Ma'am, you can't just—"

Sherry was in no mood for opposition. "Yes, I can 'just' when it concerns my bill." Amazed, vaguely annoyed, she read the notation on the screen. The woman had been right. "Son of a gun," she whispered, stunned. The payment was coming from Adair Industries all right. Which meant the money was somehow coming from Adair.

Why?

Connor raised a bemused, shaggy eyebrow as he fixed his daughter with a quizzical look. "Just what kind of secrets did you promise to bury for this man?"

Her head jerked up. She knew her father was kidding, but deception of any kind was a sore point for her. Drew had deceived her when he'd made her believe that he loved her, that there were no other women in his life. Instead the man was probably just one female short of a harem.

"None," she told him tersely. "I didn't promise to bury any secrets." And then, because it was her father, her voice softened. "He never told me any secrets."

No man was prouder of his daughter than Connor Campbell. He'd stake his reputation on her honor. Connor exchanged glances with his wife as if to wonder if there was something going on between Sherry and this man?

"Then why's he being so generous?" Connor asked.

Sherry sighed, shoulders rising and falling in a helpless shrug. "I don't know."

Her mother had what to her was a plausible explanation. "Could be the man's just got a good heart. Well, it's possible," she insisted when both her daughter and her husband looked at her as if she'd suddenly lost her mind.

Connor pressed his lips together as he shook his head. "Oh, Sheila, if you only read the paper once in a while instead of using it to wrap things with, you'd know the man's a cold devil."

The petite, trim woman remained undaunted. "Even the devil's got some good in him if you look hard enough."

To which Connor shook his head. "Incorrigible. You'd think after being on this earth for—" his wife shot him a warning look "—twenty-nine plus years," he said carefully, "she'd know that the world isn't a big sunny garden."

The soft Irish lilt in Sheila's voice became more pronounced whenever she grew adamant. "You only see the dark side, Connor, my love. I choose to see the light. I think of the two of us, I'm the happier one."

Sherry frowned. "Well, I don't care what color St. John Adair sees, there's no way I'm going to let him pay my bills for me." Coming around to the other side of the desk again, she slid her insurance card across the counter toward the woman. "Here, contact my insurance company for actual payment of the account."

The woman shook her head. "The hospital will only wind up sending it on to you." The woman gently pushed the card back to Sherry. "We can't collect twice on the same account."

Temporarily stymied, Sherry refused to give up entirely. "But you'll need the information for my son's bill. He's still in the neonatal section."

The woman typed in "Campbell, Infant," then looked

up at Sherry. She hesitated slightly before saying, "It seems that bill's covered, too."

That really didn't make any sense. "But the charges are still coming in." The doctors had told her that her son was going to have to remain here at least a week, if not two.

The woman took a deep breath, then launched into the explanation. "There's a voucher attached to the account. All expenses will be paid by—"

Sherry closed her eyes as she echoed the clerk's next words. "Adair Industries."

Connor snorted, then slipped his arm around his daughter. "Maybe helping you deliver the baby was like a religious experience for him," he offered. When she looked at him, Connor punctuated his guess with a wide shrug.

Sherry didn't know what to say, what to make of it. This act of so-called generosity was entirely against type. Although now that she thought about it, she really didn't know what "type" Adair was. She had only hearsay to act on, and that wasn't very satisfying. Up close and personal, the man certainly didn't fit into any mold that she knew of. It wasn't as if he was fearful of the press or exposure, he just didn't like the media. Not all that unusual, really.

There had to be a catch, but what?

Behind her the nurse who had volunteered to usher her out shifted. She was still holding on to the wheelchair. "I need to get back to my floor," she prodded gently. "Could we get you to your dad's car?"

Relieved that the discussion was tabled for the time being, Connor responded quickly.

"Sure thing." He patted Sherry's hand. "We'll get to the bottom of this, don't you worry, but first things first.

I'll bring it round to the entrance," he told the nurse, then turned to his wife. "Coming, Grandma?"

Sheila Mckinney Campbell drew herself up to her full five feet, squaring her shoulders defiantly as she fixed her husband with a dark look. "I'll wait right here with Sherry, and I'll thank you not to call me that, Connor."

Connor only laughed as he hurried off to fetch his vehicle.

Sherry sighed, pocketing her insurance card. There was nothing more to be done here today. Bracing her hands on both armrests, she sank down in the wheelchair again and allowed herself to be taken down the long corridor.

"You know he's just doing it to get to you, Mom." She tried not to notice the baby items that were displayed in the window as they passed the gift shop.

"I know that." Sheila patted her daughter's hand as she walked alongside the wheelchair. "I love the baby, I truly do. It's just that I don't think I'm quite ready to be called—" she took a deep breath "—that name yet."

Sherry glanced at her mother. With her flawless Irish skin and her red hair that still required no assistance from any chemical product on the market, Sheila Campbell looked more like her older sister than her mother. She could understand her mother's ambivalent feelings.

"Work something out soon, Mom. I don't want him growing up saying 'hey you' every time he wants your attention."

Sheila nodded, her red hair bobbing about her face in lively waves. "Let me think about it a little more," she murmured.

Sherry barely heard her. Her mind was elsewhere. Like a dog with a bone, she was trying to break it down into manageable pieces. Why was Adair doing this? What was in it for him?

The puzzle helped to keep her mind off the fact that she was leaving her son behind.

"He's doing very well." Moving softly, the evening shift nurse came up and stood behind her as Sherry sat with her baby, rocking in a chair the hospital provided. "If he keeps on this way, you'll be able to take him home in another week."

Another week. It felt as if an eternity had already gone by, even though it was only a matter of a few days since she had left the hospital. As she was still unable to drive safely, her parents and friends took turns bringing her to the hospital, where she remained a few hours at a time, bonding with her son. Praying. Looking forward to the day she could be around him for more than a few revolutions of the hour hand.

"That's good." Sherry bent over and kissed the tiny hand that splayed out over her palm. The baby stirred, filling her heart to maximum capacity.

"I want you home, little one."

"I know. I bet your brother'll be happy to hear that."

Sherry looked up at the woman, confused. She was an only child. "My brother?"

"Yes." The nurse paused to beam down at the infant in his mother's arms. "He's been stopping by here late every night. It's past visiting hours, really," she confided to Sherry, "but he persuaded one of the other nurses to let him in for a few minutes. Wish my brother was that attentive to my kids. I can't get him to even remember their birthdays."

It couldn't be Rusty or Owen because both had told

her about their visits. "Are you sure there isn't some mistake? I don't have a brother."

The woman looked at her, surprised and confused. "Tall, quiet, *really* good-looking." A small sigh escaped the nurse.

It had to be Adair. "Does he say why he's here?"

"Well, sure. To see how his nephew's doing. That's what he told Doris," the nurse added, mentioning one of the nurses on the night shift.

For the past few days, Sherry's professional life had taken a backseat to her private one. She was busy trying to return to normal, and spent what time she had visiting her son. But this thing with Adair was turning into a mystery. Maybe it was time to take the reporter in her off hold. "What time does he come by?"

"Nine," the nurse answered. "Every night like clockwork."

The woman made it sound as if she made it a point to be in the area, she thought. Well, maybe next time around, Sherry would, too.

Later that same day Sherry gingerly eased herself out of Lori's car. Her bottom still felt a little sore if she sat for more then ten minutes at a time. She couldn't wait to get back to her old self.

Closing the passenger door, she looked at her former Lamaze instructor. "I really appreciate the lift, Lori."

Lori was still in the vehicle. She needed to park the car. She'd just stopped at the front entrance to shorten the distance for Sherry.

"Don't thank me, I had to come here, anyway." She leaned out the window as Sherry rounded the hood of the car. "You have someone to pick you up? Because I can double back later after class if you don't."

Sherry shook her head. "I'll be fine. I'm going to call my father when I'm finished."

Lori nodded, taking the car out of Park. Her foot still hovered on the brake. "Come by and join us for ice cream next week. The Mom Squad just isn't the same without you." She did a quick calculation. "You should be able to drive by then."

Sherry missed seeing the group, especially Chris and Joanna. They and Lori had gotten together and bought her a beautiful hand-carved crib, delivering it to her parents' house the day she'd left the hospital. Her father had transported it to her house today. Her parents were there now, putting it together. If she knew them, they were butting heads as to how it should be done. She was far better off here.

Sherry smiled broadly. "I'd love to."

"Good, see you at the ice-cream parlor." Lori waved, taking off to the parking lot. "I hope they tell you that you can take him home tomorrow," she called out.

Sherry turned away and walked in through Blair's electronic doors. There was no chance of that. The physician who had come by later this afternoon had confirmed the nurse's prognosis. She'd already been by twice today, once when Owen had dropped her off and once with her mother. This time around she wasn't here just to see her son, but her son's "uncle" as well. If Adair actually showed up tonight.

She still had her doubts.

They disappeared when she stepped out on the floor and made her way to the neonatal ward. Approaching the bay window, she saw a tall man standing in the dimmed corridor light.

Adair.

Damn it, this just wasn't making any sense. From

everything she'd gleaned about him, he was an incredibly busy man who was forced to schedule every breath he took. What was he doing here?

She echoed the question aloud as she drew closer. "What are you doing here?"

He glanced in her direction as if he'd expected her to show up. Was clairvoyance to be added to his repertoire?

"It's a free country, Ms. Campbell, and I am over the age of eighteen." He turned back to look at the babies in the ward. Babies who were struggling for what everyone else took for granted. Life. "Unless I break the law, I am not accountable for my actions to anyone—" he slanted a look at her again "—not even a woman as lovely as you."

She couldn't say why the compliment didn't bounce off her the way so many others did. Instead, it seemed to find a crack and seep in, warming her when she didn't want to be warmed.

"Maybe not accountable," she allowed, crossing her arms before her, "but a few explanations might be in order."

He had to admit there was something magnificent about her when she tossed her head that way. He was reminded of a painting he'd once seen of St. Joan decked out in full battle regalia, ready to uphold the honor of God and country.

"I——"

She wasn't about to let him veer off the track and he had that look about him. Like a man who was just about to charm the socks off a barefoot woman. Suddenly, she saw what every other woman saw in him. "Like why did you pay my hospital bill?"

He shrugged vaguely, his broad shoulders moving comfortably beneath his navy jacket. "Act of charity."

He'd pressed the wrong button. Her eyes narrowed. "I don't need charity."

"Act of kindness, then." He pinned her with a look, beginning to wonder about the woman who had attempted to beard him in his den, who would risk uncomfortable surroundings just to get what she was after. "You can't tell me you don't need kindness. I'm of the opinion that most people need kindness."

The sentiment oddly echoed her mother's. Who would have thought they were of like mind? No one, because they weren't. He was after something; she was sure of it. "Like you?"

The smile slowly curved his lips. Why hadn't she noticed how sensuous they were before?

"I'm not most people," he replied.

She forced her mind back on business. That was what this man was all about, business. "But you wouldn't be averse to kindness. Perhaps you think that paying my hospital bill and my son's hospital bill will buy me off?"

His expression sobered, wiping away all traces of any smile that might have existed. "I am not in the habit of explaining myself, just as I'm not in the habit of buying people off." Feeling charitable, he shared a little of his business philosophy with her. It had stood him in good stead in his private life, as well. "People you can buy off are too cheap to want to keep."

"Very profound," she inclined her head. When she raised it again, her eyes pinned him to the window. "So exactly why did you pay my bill?"

It had been a whim, pure and simple. He had no better explanation for it. But he couldn't afford to let it get around that he was governed by things that weren't grounded in cold, hard reasoning.

"You're my first delivery. I was feeling generous." Most women would have let it go at that. "Don't look a gift horse in the mouth, Ms. Campbell."

She didn't like being dismissed. "The Trojans didn't and it got them in a whole lot of trouble."

The remark made him smile again, almost against his will. "You're not a Trojan."

"I'm also not naive, Mr. Adair." If she knew nothing else about him, she knew that he didn't do anything without a reason. She wanted to know what it was. "There is no free lunch and you can't get something for nothing. Now what is it that you want?"

No good deed went unpunished, he thought again. Served him right for being impulsive.

"Ideally?" There was a hint of sarcasm in his voice. "Peace in our time." She wanted a reason, all right, he'd give her one, even if it hadn't been the one behind his actions. "If not peace in our time, then no more of this kind of reporting." He took a folded sheet of newspaper out of his pocket and handed it to her.

It wasn't a newspaper, she realized, it was the front page of one of the supermarket tabloids she blocked out whenever she shopped. Her eyes widened as she read the headline: Adair Flies Mistress and Secret Love Child to Hospital.

Mrs. Farley had brought this to his attention. The look in the older woman's eyes had been anger. A similar one was entering Campbell's eyes. You couldn't fake that kind of a response, he judged.

"I see by the look on your face that you didn't leak the story to this rag."

Crumpling the page in her hand, she stared at him.

How dare he even think that? He dared, a small voice whispered, because he didn't know her and because she'd followed him to his haven, invading it. What did she expect?

Sherry struggled to put a lid on her anger. "I'm a serious journalist, Mr. Adair, not a gossipmonger."

He found himself wanting to hear her calling him by his first name. The thought had come out of nowhere, and he promptly returned it there.

"Serious journalist," he echoed. "Do serious journalists write about how the Hathaway twins have made good in their transition from child stars to adult sensations?"

He'd read her article? Or just the headline? In either case she didn't see him as the type to even know that section of the newspaper existed.

"They do if they're trying to work their way up into getting a serious byline. My editor gives me an assignment. I do it." She saw a hint of a smirk take over his lips. He obviously didn't believe her. "Besides, if you read the article, all my facts were correct and, unlike you, my subjects weren't hostile."

She didn't strike him as the obedient type, job or no job. "They were also young and welcomed publicity."

She gave him a long, measuring look. He was how old? Thirty-three? He made himself sound years older than that. "You're not exactly Mr. Wilson—" She could see what he was thinking. "And I'm not Dennis the Menace."

He laughed. The sound wasn't off-putting. "Matter of opinion, Ms. Campbell, matter of opinion."

She was getting sidetracked. By his laugh, by his smile and his manner. She was definitely off her game, but she intended to make a comeback. Now. "I can pay my own bills, Adair. I'm not exactly from the wrong side of the tracks."

He nodded. The mistake had been his. He should have left well enough alone. "No, you're very comfortable, very bright when it comes to investing your money. Admirably frugal, too."

Her eyes widened again. "You had me checked out?"

It took effort not to be mesmerized by the blue orbs. "How does it feel to have the shoe on the other foot? Pinches, doesn't it?"

He was comparing apples and oranges. "I don't merit national attention for doing what I do."

He could beg to differ. She'd been a local celebrity, eased out of her job, he'd discovered, because of her condition. He had to admit he admired her spirit, if not her vocation.

"And I do." It wasn't a question.

"I'm afraid it goes with the territory you've picked out for yourself," Sherry said, relenting, thinking of how kind he'd been to her while she was giving birth. Like it or not, there was a soft spot in her heart because of that. "Why do you want people to think you're this dark-hearted ogre?"

"Because people have a healthy respect for ogres." And kept a decent distance away from them, he added silently.

"That's fear, not respect," she corrected.

He inclined his head. Semantics. "That works for me, too."

"You want people to fear you?"

"I want people to keep out of my private life."

She read between the lines and placed herself in his position. She wouldn't have been able to put up with it. Her world was filled with people. People she cared about. "Must be lonely."

The note of pity in her voice took him by surprise. And offended him. The last time anyone had pitied him was Mrs. Farley. He'd been fourteen years old. "That is for me to know—and you not to find out." He had someplace else to be. "If you'll excuse me, I'm going to call it a night."

There was no hesitation on her part. She recognized opportunity even when it tiptoed in rather than knocked. "Could you drop me off?"

She'd managed to catch him off guard. But just for a moment. "You really do have a hell of a lot of nerve, don't you?"

Her smile was wide. "No argument."

"Finally." And then he sighed. "All right, come on, I'll take you home." Already on his way to the elevator, he slanted a look at her. "And I'd stop smiling smugly if I were you."

"Yes, sir."

There was a grin in her voice a mile wide. Sin-Jin didn't trust himself to comment.

Chapter 8

He drove fast. It didn't surprise her. A man like Adair—intense, goal oriented—would drive fast. He would do most things fast.

Would he make love fast, too?

The thought sneaked up on her, but she pushed it aside. It wasn't remotely part of her research. She blamed it on the song playing in his CD player and the crumpled tabloid headline in her pocket.

The music wasn't filling up the spaces. On the contrary, the interior of the Mercedes was getting smaller with each mile that passed by.

Sherry cleared her throat. "I didn't think you listened to music."

The statement brought the slightest curve to his lips. "Did you think I listened to all-news stations all the time?"

"Not while you slept."

"Culture has a definite place in the world." He spared her a glance. "It refines people, nurtures their souls."

That sounded incredibly lofty. Sherry ventured a guess. "Lulls them into a state of tranquility so that you can take them over more easily?"

"So my competitors say."

"I didn't think you had competitors."

He slanted another glance in her direction a moment before he merged into the extreme right-hand lane. "Flattery isn't going to get you anywhere."

"Not flattery, observation."

The car ahead of him was moving too slowly; he changed lanes quickly. "More flattery."

"You're a hard man to talk to."

He checked his mirrors, then changed lanes again, moving back into the lane he'd just vacated. "So I've been told."

They were almost there. She didn't remember ever making the trip so quickly. "You're going to need to take the Jeffrey Road off-ramp." It was coming up within a matter of seconds.

He was already easing onto the off-ramp. A red light at the end prevented him from making a smooth transition onto the thoroughfare. "I know where you live, remember?"

She knew he'd sent the vehicle she'd left stranded on the mountain to her address, but she hadn't expected him to actually recall what it was. "With all the things you have to remember? I'm impressed."

He shrugged off the comment. "Don't be. I have a photographic memory."

Another personal tidbit. She wondered if he realized that he was opening up to her, however slightly. She baited him, recalling a recent article she'd read.

"Scientists maintain there's no such thing, that it's simply a matter of teaching yourself how to memorize things."

The light turned green. He pressed the accelerator. The road before him stretched out with a smattering of traffic. "Scientists have been known to be wrong."

"So how does that work, you look at something and zap, it's stuck in your mind forever?"

He had no idea how it worked, only that he could recall anything at will. He used it like a tool. "Something like that."

She shook her head, trying to imagine what that was like. "Must get awfully crowded in there."

He smiled. The woman just didn't give up attempting to coax information out of him. Since it did no harm, he indulged her. "I manage."

"All right." Sherry shifted in her seat to look at him. "Let's see if it works. What's the name of the first girl you ever kissed?"

It was time to stop indulging. "Clever, but no cigar."

They'd reached their destination. He pulled up in front of her house and turned toward her. The streetlight standing before the house next door to hers scattered just enough light into his vehicle to dance along only part of her face, highlighting it. Something stirred within him, nudging curiosity forward.

Getting out of the car, he rounded the hood and went to the passenger side. He opened the door, taking her hand as she got out.

She found herself standing much too close to the man. Neither of them took a step away.

"I'd rather tell you the name of the next woman I'm going to kiss," he said.

There was something hypnotic about his eyes. "Does she know?"

His smile was slow, drifting under her skin. They both knew what he was saying. "I've got a feeling that she might have a good idea."

Sherry felt her heart accelerating. She became aware that she had stopped breathing, and forced air back into her lungs. "Doesn't that constitute bribery or conflict of interest or something like that?"

Sin-Jin moved her hair away from her shoulder, exposing her neck. "You're the reporter, you tell me."

Her heart was now doing some serious beating. She wondered if he could see it vibrating in her throat. "I suppose it could be seen as research."

"Whose?"

The word skimmed along her skin, teasing her. Tantalizing her. "Mine," she breathed.

His smile broadened. "Whatever works for you."

Sin-Jin dove his fingers into her hair, framing her face with his hands. He paused a fraction of a moment, looking at her.

"Memorizing my face?" she asked, surprised that at this point, she could even form words. Everything within her was holding its breath.

"I don't need to." The next moment, before she could ask why, Sin-Jin brought his lips down to hers.

Sherry wasn't sure just exactly what she was expecting. Maybe disappointment. No one could live up to the buildup she'd just created in her mind.

She didn't find it. Disappointment had left the building on winged feet.

The one thing she hadn't expected was to be affected, not to this extent. She'd bounced back fairly well from her pregnancy in the past couple of days, so she couldn't blame the weakness she felt in her knees on anything remotely postpartum.

She had to put the blame exactly where it belonged. On the lips of the man kissing her.

After Drew had walked out on her, she had been convinced that she would never feel anything, physical or emotional, for a man again. It was far too painful to expose yourself that way, to hand yourself up, naked and wanting, to another human being. She'd closed off all ports of entry to her soul and had thrown away the keys.

Somehow, they'd been found again.

Without thinking it through, Sherry leaned into the kiss. Into Sin-Jin. Savoring the wildfire that was suddenly ignited within her.

She knew to the moment the last time she'd been kissed.

And then she knew nothing at all.

He was a man of reason, given to doing things for definite, concrete reasons that at times made sense only to him. But he wasn't entirely sure just why he was kissing her, or what had brought him to this juncture.

He just knew he had to kiss her.

When it came to Sherry Campbell, fledgling ace reporter, he wasn't sure of anything, not his actions, not his thoughts. What he was sure of was that he was reacting to her despite all the self-imposed restraints that had been put in place over the years. The fact astonished Sin-Jin.

At a very young age he'd promised himself never to emulate either of his parents. He would never go from mate to mate, investing his soul only to be disappointed. Love, to him, was far too important a thing to tarnish, and so it was kept under wraps, hidden, never to venture out into the light of day. Or the soft, seductive rays of moonlight.

To that end he made himself far too busy to risk entanglements or to waste any time on relationships that were guaranteed an ignoble death by the law of averages he'd observed while growing up.

But there was something about this woman that made him curious, that made him want to put himself at risk. Just a little.

If he pushed aside the circumstances that surrounded their interactions, he'd have to admit that she had stirred him, twisting his gut and waking desire even from the very first.

She tightened her hands on his arms, bracing herself. Her bones were melting, and it wouldn't do to sink down here on her front stoop.

Bells, she was hearing bells. No, wait, that was a cell phone ringing.

Blinking, struggling out of her dazed state, she looked up at Sin-Jin. The words came out in a hoarse whisper. "Is that your phone?"

He found he had to swallow before answering, taking care not to lose his tongue. He wasn't sure exactly what had just happened here, only that it had never happened before.

Sin-Jin cleared his throat. "No, I believe that's yours." Releasing her, he touched his pocket to make sure. "Mine's on vibrate."

Sherry blew out a breath, feeling completely unsteady. Locking her knees rigidly to keep from embarrassing herself, she tossed her hair over her shoulder, praying for nonchalance.

"That's one way to get a thrill. Must be mine, then."

Hoping that her hands wouldn't shake, she took out her phone and flipped it open. "Campbell."

"When are you going to call for me to pick you up?"

She closed her eyes and sighed. Saved by the cavalry. Just as well. One more second and she would have permanently forgotten how to breathe.

She dragged her hand through her hair. She saw Sin-Jin looking at her, his dark eyes curious. It took effort to stop the shiver that wanted to shimmy up her spine in its tracks.

"I'm already home, Dad. Just look out the window."

When the light-gray drapes at the front window moved back, she waved. Her father, she mused, looked as if he could be knocked over with a feather.

The next moment the front door was opening. Connor Campbell filled the entry, somehow giving the impression, at five-eight of being larger than life.

"Need any help?"

It wasn't completely clear if her father was addressing the question to her or to the man standing beside her, but Sherry was the one who answered.

"No, we're fine." And then, because it was awkward not to, Sherry began to make introductions. "Dad, this is—"

"St. John Adair, yes, I know," he told Sherry pointedly.

She turned toward Sin-Jin. "Mr. Adair, this is—"

Sin-Jin extended his hand to her father. When the latter grasped it, they shook with the solemnity of two chieftains meeting on the moors. "Connor Campbell, I've read your byline."

Sherry shrugged haplessly. The awkwardness of the moment wouldn't abate. She'd just been kissed by St. John Adair. And she'd kissed him back.

"Well, I'm certainly superfluous here," she murmured to herself.

Sin-Jin dropped his hand to his side as he looked at her. He could still taste her on his lips. "I wouldn't exactly say that."

Connor looked from the tycoon to his daughter. In typical fashion, he made his assessment rapidly. He was rarely wrong.

"Why don't you come in?" He opened the door wider. "The crib's finished—"

"No thanks to your father," Sheila Connor called out, joining them at the door. Sherry was surprised her mother had held out this long. Consuming curiosity was far from an unknown factor in her mother's life. "The least handy man I've ever met." She smiled warmly at the man standing beside Sherry. "He's all thumbs."

Connor wrapped a proprietary arm around his wife's shoulders. She fitted neatly against his side. "Didn't hear you complaining last night."

Sherry made a show of covering her ears as she rolled her eyes. "I don't need to hear this."

"Of course you do, girl," Sheila told her with a laugh that was almost identical to her daughter's. "How else are you going to know that there are good relationships out there and that not all men are like that scum who deserted you?"

The last remark had been for Sin-Jin's benefit, Sherry thought with a sinking feeling inside her. It was a mistake to bring him here, and now she was paying for it.

She wet her lips, feeling oddly nervous. It wasn't a feeling she was accustomed to.

"Sorry about this, Mr.—" She caught herself and could feel a flush creeping up her neck. She prayed that he was farsighted only. "Under the circumstances I guess I'd better call you St. John."

Connor gave the man the once-over. "Huh," he snorted. "Never knew a man to live up to the title of saint." His voice had the ability to be both booming and intimate at the same time, making the listener feel as if he had become an instant friend and been welcomed into Connor's inner circle. "What do your friends call you?"

Sherry looked at him with interest, half expecting the man to say that he had no friends, or, at the very least, that it wasn't any of her father's business *what* they called him.

Instead, he responded, "Sin-Jin."

Connor cracked a wide smile. "Man named after my favorite liquor can't be all bad." He was taking Sin-Jin's arm and ushering him into the house as if it was his to do so, rather than his daughter's. "Come on in a spell, rest your feet—" he looked at his daughter significantly "—if not your ears."

"Sin-Jin has to leave," Sherry protested.

Sin-Jin looked at Sherry, wondering if she was aware that she'd slid from Mr. Adair to St. John to Sin-Jin without pause. She'd given him his way out. But he had to admit there was something oddly compelling about the couple who stood before him. About them and the daughter they had produced.

And then the small woman who looked like an older version of her daughter robbed him of his escape. "Oh, he'll stay for a cup of Irish coffee." She looked up at him brightly. "Won't you, dear?" Before he could say anything, Sheila had slipped her personality, her Irish lilt and her arm through his and was gently drawing him into the living room.

"I guess I can stay for a few minutes," Sin-Jin allowed.

Amused, Sherry watched her mother weave her magic on the man. It occurred to her that had she wanted to, her mother would have made an excellent investigative reporter. It was obvious that Sin-Jin hadn't stood a chance against her.

Maybe her mother could give lessons, she mused, following behind them. She heard her father chuckling beside her and knew he was probably thinking the same thing.

"So that's the mighty St. John Adair, eh?" Connor commented an hour later as he shut the front door. He turned to look at his daughter. "Seems rather taken with you, missy. I saw the way he was looking at you."

Oh, no, she wasn't about to let her father go off on that tangent. Even if he'd seen them kissing, which she was sure he hadn't, there was no basis to believe that Adair had felt anything but curiosity.

"I think you have your looks confused, Dad. He was blaming me for pulling him into all this." She fixed her father with a look. "You can be overwhelming, you know."

Sheila moved to side with her husband, physically as well as verbally. "Say what you will, I like him," she declared.

Connor laughed. "You'd like Satan if he smiled wide enough."

Sheila raised her eyes to his face. "As I recall, my father thought you were the devil incarnate when you first started coming around."

He waved away the story. "Well, we all know your

father was always wrong, God-rest-his-soul," he tagged on mechanically.

"Maybe that one time," Sheila acquiesced generously. There was a teasing smile playing on her lips.

Feeling suddenly drained, Sherry decided it was time for her to retreat. She stuck her hands into her pockets, about to say good-night, when her fingers came in contact with a crumpled piece of paper. Drawing it out, she remembered the look on Sin-Jin's face when he handed it to her. His expression had been carefully controlled. This bothered him, she thought.

Impulsively she made up her mind. "Dad, I want you to do me a favor."

Connor looked away from his wife. "Anything, love."

She knew how he felt about tabloid journalism. He didn't like to dirty his hands with it. But this was necessary. "I need a few strings pulled."

Independent though she'd been since the moment she'd opened her eyes on this world, he'd always made it a point to let her know that he was there, in the background, ready to do anything she needed doing. That's what made them a family. "You've come to the right man. What is it you need done?"

She took a deep breath. "Who do you know on the *Bulletin?*"

The shaggy eyebrows drew into a scowling, dismissive line. "That rag?" he hooted. "What makes you think I know someone there?"

"Because you know everyone, dear." Sheila patted his chest with the familiarity of a woman who knew her husband's every thought even before it occurred to him. "Even people who work on that rag. Like William Kelley, remember?" She turned to Sherry. "Why are you asking, dear?"

Sherry smoothed out the front page, then held it up for both her parents to see at the same time. She saw anger spring like lightning into her father's eyes. "I want this to be retracted."

Sheila took the page from her, reading the headline again in disbelief. She turned to her husband. "Oh, my God. Connor, you have to make them print an apology. We can't have Sherry's character maligned like this—"

Sherry quickly cut her off. "It's not my name I'm concerned about, Mother. Sin-Jin saved my son's life and maybe mine, as well." She'd begun hemorrhaging shortly after she'd been taken to the hospital. If that had happened while she'd been in the cabin, she might not be having this conversation with her parents now. "This is not the way to pay him back, especially considering how he feels about his privacy."

Connor plucked the page from his wife. His scowl deepened and he muttered something under his breath that was best left unheard.

"Consider it done, love. The retraction's going in the day after tomorrow. Sooner if I can get ahold of Blake Andrews," he said, mentioning the name of the managing editor.

She knew she could count on him. Too bad there were no men out there like her father. "Nice to have connections in low places," Sherry quipped.

Sin-Jin had always believed that the way to kill a rumor was to ignore it and allow it to die for lack of fuel.

The headline on the *Bulletin* he'd brought to Sherry's attention had irritated him, but he'd managed to shrug it off. He fully expected it to die like everything else. He was not about to demand a retraction or an apology.

There was no way he was about to dignify the false story with any sort of reaction on his part.

So when Mrs. Farley came into his office two days later with another copy of the *Bulletin* in her hand, he made no offer to take it from her, even when she waved it at him.

He knew she always had his best interests at heart, but there were times when she took the matter of his honor a little too personally.

"I'm really not interested in a follow-up, Mrs. Farley." Turning from his computer, he looked up at her. "I don't know why you bother with something like that."

Edna drew herself up to her full small stature. "I don't bother with it." Her tone was not defensive, just firm. "Joseph Bailey in accounting brought it to my attention. I really think you should look at page two."

He paused tolerantly. "Now why would I want to do that?"

She placed the paper on his desk, turning it to face him. "So that you can see history in the making. To my knowledge, this has never happened before in the *Bulletin*."

Amusement raised one corner of his mouth. He glanced at the headline. "They have exclusive photographs of aliens taking over Alaska?"

"Better."

When he made no effort to open the paper, Mrs. Farley came around the desk. She opened the tabloid for him. Handling the paper gingerly, as if merely touching it defiled her fingertips, she turned to the second page. Moving it before him again, she jabbed her index finger at the box on the bottom of the page.

"Read."

"Yes, ma'am," he joked. The tone of her voice placed

them back in time some twenty years or so. He was in her English class again, getting help after hours. She'd been an unrelenting woman then, as she was now.

Placating her, he looked down to where she was pointing.

Amazed, he read the four lines again. And then he raised his eyes up to hers. Mrs. Farley was smiling. She rarely did that. "It's a retraction," he said.

"Yes, it is," she agreed triumphantly, taking the paper away again and folding it back into its original position. Victory had momentarily taken away the paper's taint.

Leaning back in his chair, he scrutinized the older woman. He'd obviously underestimated her. "How did you get them to do this?"

"I didn't. I just assumed that you did."

Sin-Jin laughed shortly. "You know better than to think I'd dignify a rag like the *Bulletin* with a phone call."

Pencil-thin light-brown eyebrows drew together in confusion as Mrs. Farley mulled over the situation. "Well, if you didn't, then who did?" She frowned as she dropped the tabloid into the wastepaper basket. "I doubt very much if anyone at that establishment has suddenly gotten a conscience. The people of the fourth estate are born without them."

The fourth estate.

Campbell.

Sin-Jin thought of the look on Sherry's face when he'd handed the single sheet to her. She'd looked surprised and then angry.

And, suddenly, he thought he had his answer.

Chapter 9

Sherry heard the phone ringing from within her house as she put the key into the lock. Hurrying inside, she picked the receiver up on the third ring.

"Hello?"

"Did you do this?"

"Sin-Jin?" She tossed her purse on the sofa and kicked off her shoes before she sank down on the cushion. Her visit to her gynecologist had been uneventful. According to the woman, she was doing fine and all systems were go. She'd stopped at the hospital next to see her baby, wishing the same could be true of him. "You know, it's customary to say hello when you call someone."

"Hello." She heard something rustling on the other end of the line. "Did you do this?"

"And 'this' would be...?" She waited for him to

fill in the space. "Don't forget, I'm good, but I'm not clairvoyant."

There was a hint of impatience in his voice. The man had to be hell to work for, she decided. "The retraction in the *Bulletin*. Are you the one behind it?"

Sherry curled her legs under her. She certainly hadn't expected this kind of reaction. "You make it sound like an assassination plot. If you mean did I have something to do with having the *Bulletin* set the record straight, yes I did."

Unable to bring herself to actually buy the tabloid, she'd asked Rusty to get a copy for her. He'd dropped it by the day after Sin-Jin had given her the front page. The article, full of speculations that were guardedly phrased, had been accompanied by a couple of rather unflattering shots of the two of them, very obviously spliced together from separate sources.

"Why did you bother?"

She frowned. "A simple 'thank you' would have sounded better, but if you must know, I did it because I'm a journalist. I deal in the truth, not lies just because they guarantee sales." There was silence on the other end. "Hello? You still there?"

After a beat, he answered. "I'm still here. I'm just sitting here, trying to imagine your nose growing."

She didn't know whether to be insulted or to laugh. "I think you've made a mistake. Pinocchio's nose only grew when he lied. My nose is the same size it's always been, thank you."

And it was a lovely nose, Sin-Jin caught himself thinking. Set in an even lovelier face.

He blew out a breath, impatient with himself. What the hell was going on with him? He didn't have time for this kind of mental drifting.

She shifted the receiver to her other ear. "Have you blown down the three little pigs' houses yet, or is there some other reason that you're huffing like the big, bad wolf?"

He frowned, still looking at the retraction. It placed him in a vulnerable position. Far more vulnerable than the original, silly article had. "If you think getting this retraction somehow places me in your debt—"

So that was it, he thought she wanted something from him. It figured. "Debt had nothing to do with it. Besides, if we're talking debt, I do owe you a favor." *Or six or seven,* she added silently. There was no way to repay what he had done for her son. It went far beyond his covering the hospital bills. Those she could well handle herself. Losing the baby was another matter.

He wanted to make his position perfectly clear. "I'm not in the business of exchanging favors."

It was always about him, wasn't it? This wasn't going anywhere. "Oh, no? My mistake." She wanted to hang up. "Look, if there's nothing else—"

He'd offended her, he thought, surprised at the regret that followed in the wake of the realization. Sin-Jin didn't want to leave it that way. After all, she had done him a service. "Sorry. I guess I'm just not into interpersonal exchanges."

Sherry softened slightly. She sensed that apologies didn't come easily to him. "They're called relationships, Sin-Jin, and don't worry, you're not in one. Our paths just crossed, that's all."

"Right." Sin-Jin paused again, then added, "thank you."

She felt warmth seeping in. Damn him, but he could turn her around faster than a weathervane swinging back and forth in a gale. "You're welcome."

She continued smiling long after she hung up the telephone.

* * *

He was home; her baby was home.

Finally.

Sherry had no idea she could feel this wide expanse of emotions running through her all at once. Relief, joy, pride, love, they were all bouncing around within her, temporarily blocking out the exhaustion that stood waiting in the wings.

Ever since she and her parents had brought her son home from the hospital six hours ago, the house had been laid siege to. There had been an endless stream of visitors from the moment they had arrived, all bearing gifts, all eager for a peek, however brief, of the tiny guest of honor.

John Connor Campbell lay in the white Jenny Lind crib bought for him by the ladies of The Mom Squad and assembled for him by his loving grandparents. All five and a half pounds of him.

Sherry lost count of how many times she came by just to look in on him.

He looked like an angel, dropping by for a visit. Sherry hoped that she would never think of him any other way. She doubted that she could. He was her special miracle.

Making her way back to the living room, she watched as her mother ushered the last visitor out. Sherry sank down on the sofa. The low buzz of noise that had surrounded her for the past six hours had finally faded. Her eyes drifting shut, she demurred when her mother said she was staying the night. She should have known better.

"I'm not taking no for an answer, Sherry Lynn Campbell." Opening her eyes, Sherry saw that her mother had fisted her hands at her sides, a sure sign that she was digging in. "We can send your father home, but I'll be staying here for the night." Sherry tried to protest, but only got as far as opening her mouth. Her mother headed her off at the pass. "There's no way I'm going to leave you all alone with a brand-new baby. You'll both be crying within the hour." As the woman moved about the room, straightening, she picked up the throw that had been set aside and spread it out over her daughter's legs. "If it hadn't been for my own mother, flying in from Ireland to be by my side those first few weeks I had you, I would have fallen to pieces. The least I can do is return the favor in her memory."

Sherry knew it was useless, but she felt bound to try. "Mom—"

Sheila fixed her daughter with a reproving look. "You wouldn't be wanting me to dishonor the memory of your sainted grandmother, now would you?"

Game, set and match, she thought. "No," Sherry sighed. "I wouldn't. If you're sure—"

Her mother didn't wait for the sentence to be completed. "I'm sure." She looked at her husband. "You can make your own dinner for a change, Connor. See what I have to put up with every night."

Connor snorted. "For your information, I'll be taking my supper at McIntyre's tonight."

"Restaurant food. You know perfectly well they don't serve authentic Irish food at McIntyre's." Sheila sniffed disdainfully.

"Yes, my love," Connor replied patiently, "and if I didn't, I'd have you to remind me of it." He gave his wife his most calculated pathetic look, the one only family got to see. "But what's a poor man who can't boil water to do?"

Sherry couldn't keep it in any longer. She laughed. "Mom, let him stay for supper."

"But I thought you didn't want too many people around," her mother said.

"I didn't want to put you out," she corrected. "And Dad's not people, he's Dad. Since you're here and I know you're going to cook for me no matter what I say, you might as well throw another plate on the table and have Dad stay, too."

She'd never known her mother not to cook for ten and expect that people would just show up to avail themselves of leftovers. When Sherry was growing up, she'd been certain that she had a huge family. It surprised her to realize that there were only the three of them at the core and that all the others were just friends she'd grown up calling uncle and aunt. Friends who enjoyed the warm atmosphere created by Connor and Sheila Campbell.

"Well, if you insist, love," her father said magnanimously as he settled himself in on the other end of the sofa.

"I insist." The doorbell rang and her smile faded. She stared at it in disbelief. She'd had more visitors than comprised the populations of some small third-world countries. "I didn't know there was anyone left in Bedford who hadn't dropped by today."

"I'll get it," Sheila volunteered cheerfully. "You just rest yourself."

The instant his wife was out of the room, Connor leaned forward toward his daughter. "If she starts to drive you crazy tonight, just give me a call. I'll come for her in an instant."

It was shorthand for her father saying that he wasn't looking forward to spending the night without her mother by his side. She wondered how he'd managed all those years when he'd been sent to various places in the world on assignment. And more than that, she wondered if there would ever be that kind of relationship, that kind of love, waiting for her someday.

"The guest room's got a double bed, Dad." It was a needless piece of information. He'd seen her guest room. "Why don't you just stay the night here with Mom?"

Her father pretended to debate the matter. As an actor he would have starved, she thought in amusement. "I don't think she wants me interfering."

Her parents thrived on interfering with each other. "You can take turns changing the baby."

"Well, if you insist." He heard his wife's heels on the tile as she returned to the room. "Hey, Sheilo," he called her by the nickname he'd given her, "Sherry here says that I can stay and help if I behave. We'll take turns on the poop brigade."

"Dad!"

His daughter was looking over his head. Twisting around, he saw why Sherry looked so embarrassed. His wife was not alone.

Connor rose to his feet, extending his hand in a warm greeting. "Well, nice to see you again, Sin-Jin." He didn't bother hiding his smug expression. "Although I can't say I'm surprised."

Sherry wanted to sink into the sofa and just disappear. "Dad—"

"Well, I'm not," Connor protested. "A fella's not supposed to lie, is he?"

Sherry's father might not have been surprised to see him show up here, Sin-Jin thought, but he had to admit that he was. He hadn't expected to be anywhere near Sherry's home. But he'd gotten a call from the hospital's insurance administrator, per his earlier request, notifying him that the Campbell baby had been discharged that morning. Sin-Jin had had Mrs. Farley cut a voucher from his private funds for the proper amount of the account the moment he'd hung up. It was already in the mail.

The thought that "that was that" was somehow short-lived. It had faded in the wake of his desire to see how the child was faring.

If the mother happened to be in the same vicinity, well, so be it.

It was a flimsy excuse.

Sin-Jin realized that Connor was waiting for him to say something that would back him up. Obligingly, he allowed, "No, he's not. I can't say that I expected to be here, though." Feeling uncustomarily awkward, he looked down at the gaily wrapped box he was holding. Again, he had to thank Mrs. Farley, who knew exactly what to get. "I brought the baby a little welcome home gift."

Sherry took the box from him and removed the ribbon. And then laughed. It was a Green Bay Packers jersey, made for an infant. Even so, it looked almost too large for the baby. Something to grow into, she mused.

Tossing the box onto the sofa, she held the jersey up for her parents to see. "Green Bay?"

Sin-Jin wasn't much into sports anymore, but he did follow the team's progress when he had the chance.

"It's a feisty team. I admire their spirit." He saw the look in Sherry's eyes and knew exactly what she was thinking. That he'd opened himself up a little more. The comment hardly deserved to be guarded. A lot of people liked the Green Bay Packers.

"I was just beginning to make dinner, Sin-Jin,"

Sheila informed him. "You'll stay, of course." Sweetly extended, the invitation still left no room for refusal.

Sherry slanted a look toward him. She didn't want the man to feel trapped. Or worse, critical of these people she loved so dearly. "Mom, I'm sure Sin-Jin has somewhere else to be."

Sin-Jin thought about his own house, empty except for the housekeeper who always discreetly faded into the shadows, of the dinner he was going to partake in solitude. There was something about the way the three people in the room interacted, the body language he observed that created an atmosphere of warmth that pulled him in. It was like nothing he had experienced, certainly not within his own family.

The decision was spur-of-the-moment. "Oddly enough, I don't. Mrs. Farley thought I needed some free time."

"And Mrs. Farley is?" Connor asked.

"His secretary," Sherry quickly cut in just in case Sin-Jin was about to tell her father that it was none of his business. "She guards you with her life, you know. The first time I tried to get in to see you, she absolutely refused to allow it. Told me to call back at a more convenient time."

Sin-Jin smiled. "She tends to be a little protective. We go way back."

Tilting her head beguilingly, Sheila asked, "How far is that?"

"Far," Sin-Jin replied, amused. Apparently relentless questioning was a family trait.

Sherry grinned. "I think he's getting immune to you, Mom."

"The evening is still young," her mother replied with a wink directed at Sin-Jin. A tiny mewling sound came over the baby monitor that was placed in the center of the coffee table. Sheila exchanged glances with her husband. "I'm off for the kitchen, Connor. Think you can handle John?"

Sherry saw Sin-Jin's head jerk up at the mention of her son's name. He looked startled. Why?

"Piece of cake," Connor said confidently. Inclining his head toward Sin-Jin, he shared a confidence with pride. "See, I'm a modern man. Diapering, feeding, all those things."

"It's called teaching an old dog new tricks," Sheila said over her shoulder as she left the room, she going in one direction, her husband in another.

Alone, Sherry turned to look at Sin-Jin. He still appeared slightly bewildered. "You looked surprised."

"I, um—" Sin-Jin glanced toward the stairs.

And then she thought she understood. "I named him after you."

"Then his name is actually St. John?"

"No," she admitted. "Just John. I couldn't get myself to call him St. John, so I settled on John." Looking at him, she tried to envision what Sin-Jin had been like years ago. Probably still as formal. He probably wore crisply creased pants and blazers when he went to play. The image made her smile. "You must have endured a lot of teasing as a boy."

He looked at her blankly. His childhood had been marked with loneliness, not teasing. "Why?"

"Well, you can't say that 'St. John' is exactly an everyday name, now, can you? And kids always have a field day with people who are different."

He shrugged carelessly, thinking that perhaps he'd made a mistake, agreeing to remain. He should get going before the questions began in earnest. "I survived."

"Obviously." He looked like someone about to take flight, she thought. Probably regretting being roped into dinner. She needed to get this out before Sin-Jin suddenly made his apologies and left. "Anyway, now that you're here, I was wondering if I could ask you about something—"

All right, here it came. The payoff. He might have known there was a reason behind the invitation and display of filial closeness. She'd been setting him up for the kill. "Look, don't get the wrong idea. I'm still not going to give you an interview—"

The cool rebuff had her pulling up short. "I'm not asking for an interview."

"Oh?" He didn't know whether to believe her and feel like a jackass, or applaud the way she could shift gears in midtransit.

She wasn't about to get caught in a lie. "At least, not right now." Owen had been very clear that he wanted her to take it easy. Any stories she was on could wait. It wasn't as if any of the stories were a matter of national security. "I'm on maternity leave and I intend to make the most of it."

He eyed her, waiting to see what she would come up with. "Then what's your question?"

"Will you be my son's godfather?"

"What?" The woman took the prize when it came to catching him off his guard.

"Godfather," she repeated, enunciating the word. "You know, someone who stands up for the baby at the baptism. Technically it's supposed to be someone of the same faith as you, but Father Conway is a good guy." She had known the white-haired priest for as long as she could remember. Going to church meant seeing the small, sprightly man, who looked very much like an elderly, transplanted elf, officiating at Mass. "He'll look the other way if Dad asks him to. What really counts here is the character of the godparent."

How could she even say that with a straight face? "You don't know anything about my character." He thought of all the scathing articles he'd read about himself. "And what you do know doesn't exactly qualify me as an example for a young boy."

She wasn't about to get swayed by the reports, especially now that she had had a chance to be around him. "I know you wouldn't turn your back on a pregnant woman giving birth. That's enough for me. So will you?" When Sin-Jin didn't respond immediately, she gave her own interpretation to his hesitation. "I intend to live forever, so you don't have to worry about having to take care of Johnny, and even if I don't, my parents are ready to take him, so all that remains for you, really, is the honor of the thing."

This had to be a gimmick of some kind. "Why are you giving this 'honor' to me?"

She would have thought that was self-evident. She didn't like the suspicion in his eyes. "Because if it wasn't for you," she said softly, "my son wouldn't be here now."

Without him noticing, she'd placed her hand on his arm in quiet supplication. He felt himself cornered. And not resenting it. "You're not leaving me any space to turn you down."

She smiled, the effect hitting him right between the eyes. "That's the general idea."

"All right, what do I have to do?"

She thought for a second. "Be there at the church. Oh, and hold him while the priest sprinkles holy water on his forehead."

There had to be more. "What else?"

Sherry shook her head. "That's all."

He had no experience in these matters, but it definitely sounded too simple, too innocent. "I don't even have to buy anything?"

"Nope." She thought of her cousin who she'd asked the moment she knew she was carrying a child. Even before she told Drew. "The godmother takes care of the baby's christening outfit." She smiled up at him. "All you have to do is be there."

He wanted to leave himself a way out. "My schedule's pretty booked."

She'd already found out that he worked a full week and sometimes added on a Saturday, but he kept Sundays to himself. "It'll be on a Sunday afternoon."

She was good, he'd have to give her that. "Got all the answers ready, don't you?"

"I always try." She tried to read his expression. "So, what do you say?"

He couldn't have explained why this felt as if it was a huge commitment on his part, but it was, even though she had just told him it wasn't. He wanted to choose his commitments, not have them presented to him.

"I'm not—"

Sherry shrugged. She wasn't about to beat him over the head and drag him to the church.

"Well, the honor belongs to you. If you can't make it, my dad'll be there in your place, like a stand-in. But your name's going on the certificate. Don't worry, there're no strings," she assured him again. "We don't want anything from you. It's just my way of saying thank you."

Had she argued, he might have stood a chance. Her dignified retreat had left him with an odd feeling of guilt that he was far from familiar with. Under the circumstances, he said the only thing he could.

"I'll be there."

Hiding her triumph, Sherry only smiled and said, "That's great."

Sin-Jin couldn't have cited why, but he felt like the man who had just signed on the dotted line and handed over a deposit on the Brooklyn Bridge.

Chapter 10

Sin-Jin couldn't remember the last time that the minutes had just slipped away, knitting themselves into hours without his having monitored their departure by periodically glancing at his watch. He hadn't looked at the worn timepiece once. The company around him was too compelling.

Accustomed to conversations that dealt with fair market values of products, the international worth of the dollar and the recent history of various stocks, listening to personal stories about the woman sitting beside him and the trials of a marriage that seemed to have been made in heaven instead of hell—the marketplace of both his parents' numerous unions—was an unusual change, to say the least.

Sin-Jin found himself being reeled in until he felt as if he'd known Sheila and Connor Campbell for years rather than for hardly any time at all. And through them, Sherry.

His uncle would have liked these people.

The realization had quietly sneaked up on him from the deep recesses of his mind. He hadn't thought very much about Uncle Wayne lately. Probably because he didn't want to dwell on what his uncle might have had to say about the direction his life had taken over these past ten years or so. The world he had come to inhabit was more like the one his father existed in than the one his uncle had been dedicated to.

The thought bothered him more than he liked to admit.

"Another helping of dessert, Sin-Jin?" On her feet, Sheila was already cutting another slice of chocolate cream pie, confident of the response.

The dinners he was used to partaking of were artfully arranged meals surrounded by a great deal of plate. He'd astonished himself tonight by the amount of food he'd consumed. There'd been two helpings of the main course, followed by the same amount of servings of dessert. He was already in danger of needing the jaws of life to remove him from his clothing.

"No, really, I've eaten a great deal more than I usually do."

Connor eyed their guest, then chuckled. "You're one of those people who eats to live, aren't you?" He snaked his arm around his wife's middle, drawing her closer to him as he sat at the table. Sheila squealed, swatted his arm away. But she remained standing beside him, her expression that of a woman who was loved and pleased to allow the world to know it. "I was like that myself until Sheila here came into my life."

Sheila winked broadly at her guest. "Married me for my cooking."

"Hell, woman," Connor snorted, "if I'd just wanted you for what you could do in the kitchen, I would have hired you instead of giving you my name."

Sheila sniffed, tossing her head, the ends of her hair brushing along her slim shoulders. "You didn't give it, I deigned to take it."

Connor sighed, shaking his head as he looked at Sin-Jin. "Modern women, it's a wonder any of us men have managed to survive 'em."

"Sure I can't tempt you?" Having cut a healthy slice of the pie, Sheila now held it just above his plate, ready to set it down.

It was time for Sherry to come to the rescue before the man beside her became annoyed, overwhelmed or exploded. "No means no, Mom. Stop feeding him before we have to roll him out the door." Sherry turned to Sin-Jin. "Mom's destiny, she thinks, is to fatten up the immediate world."

Temporarily surrendering, Sheila placed the slice on her husband's dessert plate instead. She gave Sherry the once-over. "You could stand to gain a pound or seven, yourself, missy. Seems now that the baby's out, you're your former too-thin self."

"I think she looks just fine."

Three sets of eyes turned to look at him. Sin-Jin coughed, realizing that once again he'd said too much. It was getting to be an unnerving habit around anyone named Campbell.

"Would you mind if I took a peek at my godson-to-be?"

My God, one evening in their company and he was even beginning to sound like these people. He didn't dwell on how odd it felt to refer to any child as his godson. He'd long ago stopped thinking of the concept of any sort of family, even an extended one. Since he had no example to look back on, he couldn't trust himself to be involved in any relationship that wasn't doomed to fail right from the start. And he wasn't about to bring a child into the world to have only half a family. Besides, what did he know about children, anyway?

She knew a call for help when she heard one. "I thought you'd never ask." The baby had required one feeding since Sin-Jin had arrived. She'd excused herself while her father had held Sin-Jin captive with one of his long-winded stories. When she'd returned, she'd been surprised to find that Sin-Jin hadn't bolted. Sherry rose to her feet, pushing back her chair. "Right this way."

Following behind Sherry, Sin-Jin missed the knowing look that was exchanged by her parents, but as she turned on the stairs, Sherry had caught it. She knew that for once her parents, in their unfailing optimism, were dead wrong.

She opened the door to the baby's room and motioned Sin-Jin inside. It amused her that he seemed to be tiptoeing in. Leaning his arms on the railing, he looked down at the sleeping baby.

"He looks tinier than when I saw him in the hospital," he whispered to her.

The whisper, low and sexy, seemed to slip along her skin. She leaned her head toward him just a little to keep from having to raise her voice to be heard.

"That's because the crib dwarfs him." He did look tiny, she thought. She'd already nicknamed him "peanut," but that was going to have to change by the time he was old enough to understand. She wasn't about to give her child any deep-rooted psychological problems because of a pet name. "It just means he'll get more use out of his clothes."

Sin-Jin was amazed. There were people who would be beside themselves in the same situation she was in, already booking specialists for their infant. Yet Sherry seemed calm and confident. "You always think so positively?"

There was a smile in her eyes when she looked at him. "Always. Focusing on the negative never makes you anything but unhappy. It certainly never gets you anywhere."

"It prepares you for things when they go wrong."

She turned toward him. "But if they don't go wrong, think of all the time you've wasted, despairing."

"And if they do go wrong?" he challenged.

"Well," she said, shrugging philosophically, "then at least you've had a little hope in your life to make you feel better."

The woman certainly wasn't an idiot, and yet, as intelligent as she was, she still managed to be optimistic. Coming from a world grounded in reality and worst-case scenarios, he found her attitude unsophisticated—and incredibly appealing.

Maybe it was time to leave.

Sherry saw him looking at his watch and was struck not just by the fact that a great deal of time had gone by and he was still here, but by the watch itself, as well. She would have expected someone with Sin-Jin's affluent lifestyle and penchant for the finest that life had to offer to be wearing a Rolex, or at least a similar ludicrously expensive watch. Instead he was wearing a watch whose face had seen better days and whose metallic black band was worn and tarnished in several places. It seemed entirely against type.

Sin-Jin saw her looking at his wristwatch. He lowered the cuff of his jacket back into place, not to hide the watch but to protect it.

"It was my uncle's."

That was the second time he'd actually mentioned a family member to her. "The same uncle who was a doctor?"

She'd been in the throes of pain when he'd said that to her. He was amazed that she remembered. "You don't miss a thing, do you?"

Taking his arm, she led him out of the room and back to the stairs. "I try not to. Am I right?"

She fell into place far too easily beside him. Alarms should have been going off, but they remained dormant. Why was that, he wondered. "Yes, he left it to me when he died."

"Doesn't seem like much of a legacy."

He thought of the one photograph of his uncle he carried in his wallet. The man had looked like an aging hippie, long gray hair pulled back in a ponytail, a beard and worn work shirt and jeans that had more than seen their day of service. The man had meant more to him than all his other relatives combined. "His legacy wasn't in material things."

"And he was a doctor?"

Sin-Jin walked down the stairs in front of her. "The kind that goes off to practice medicine in the poorest sections of the country because that's where he's needed the most."

He didn't add that when his uncle was preparing to leave for the Appalachian area, Sin-Jin had been all of ten years old. He'd begged the man not to go, saying that he needed him to stay in his life. His uncle had talked to him for hours, finally making him realize that there were children who needed him even more than he did. It was the first time he'd been confronted with the concept of charitable giving.

Sin-Jin turned to look at Sherry, who had stopped at the base of the stairs. Her expression was thoughtful. He did what he could in the way of damage control, berating himself for having mentioned anything. "He was kind of the black sheep of the family."

Not so black, Sherry thought. And he'd meant something to Sin-Jin. Anyone with ears would know that. "What happened to him?"

Sin-Jin's face sobered. "He died."

There was a note of finality in his voice that forbade her asking any more questions.

She was curious even beyond her realm of investigative reporter, wanting to know particulars of the man's life before his death, but she wasn't insensitive. For now she let the matter drop.

"So you said. Well," she said, glancing toward the living room. They were going to have to run the gauntlet in order to get to the front door. "Let me walk you to the door and help make good your escape before my father suddenly thinks to engage you in a 'friendly game of poker.'" She saw Sin-Jin raise an eyebrow in silent query. "Believe me, it's not all that friendly. My father hates to lose. At anything. It's his one flaw."

"A lot of men are like that."

Was he putting her on some kind of notice? "Including you?"

His eyes held hers. "Including me."

She felt a shiver of electricity dance along her skin, but held her ground.

"Then you had really better not get in a card game

with him." She saw her parents already turning in their direction. "Ready?" she murmured.

She made him feel as if he was about to navigate the rapids in a paper raft and no paddle. Rather than answer, he made his way into the living room.

Sheila was the first to meet him halfway. "Oh, but you're not really leaving."

"Mom, if he stays here any longer, his people'll probably be expecting a ransom note of some kind to be delivered."

"Well…" Moving forward, Sheila enveloped him in a warm embrace that caught him completely by surprise. "If you must, you must." Stepping back, she looked genuinely disappointed that he wasn't staying longer.

Ordinarily when people tried to detain him, it was to talk about business, to try to get him to back a deal, or something equally based on money. The look on Sheila Campbell's face was rooted in emotion. It stirred feelings that he had long ago placed under lock and key, when he'd decided that he was not destined to have the kind of family he ached for.

The kind of family Sherry had.

Connor wasn't as easily put off. He placed his arm around Sin-Jin's shoulders, having to reach up a little as he did so. "Sure I can't talk you into a friendly little card game?"

Sherry quickly wedged herself in between the two men, brushing against Sin-Jin in order to do it. She seemed to be oblivious to the contact. No such lapse was experienced on his side. The lady's soft contours telegraphed themselves to him with the speed of lightning traveling up a rod.

"It won't work, Dad," she informed her father. "I've already warned Sin-Jin about your friendly little games."

Connor frowned. "Whatever she said, she was exaggerating." He nodded his head toward his wife. "Gets that from her mother, she does."

Sheila pretended to be incensed, crossing her arms over her chest, her accent thick enough to rival the pie she'd served earlier. "I'll be begging your pardon, sir, but you're the one given to blarney, not me."

Connor turned, laughing as he caught his wife up in his arms and kissed her soundly. "And you love it."

Sheila rested her head against her husband's shoulder. The two formed a contented picture. "Never said I didn't, did I?"

Taking Sin-Jin's arm, Sherry ushered him to the door. "I think you'd better go before your stomach decides to rebel against what you've just witnessed. They only get worse with encouragement."

"Sherry Lynn Campbell," her mother protested, "what a thing to say. And before a guest, too."

"True," Sherry testified, "every word of it."

Escorting him to the door, she surprised him by closing it behind them. She walked with him to his car in the driveway.

"Your parents seem very nice."

She smiled. There were times they embarrassed her, but she loved them both dearly. If they hadn't been there for her in the beginning months, she didn't know what she would have done.

"There's no 'seem' about it." She looked toward the house. "They *are* nice. I couldn't have asked for a better set—" Her mouth curved in self-deprecation as she remembered. "Something I wasn't all that sure of twelve years ago."

He took a guess. It wasn't that much of a stretch. "The rebellious years?"

She inclined her head in semiassent. "Something like that. I'm surprised they didn't raffle me off to the highest bidder."

He caught himself thinking he would have liked to have been part of that auction.

Suddenly feeling oddly self-conscious beneath his scrutiny, she ran her hands along her arms. "Well... thanks for coming by, and I'm sorry if they came on a little strong. That's just their way."

There was no need to apologize for her parents. He only wished that there had been a mold and that his could have been formed from the same one. "Actually, I found it kind of refreshing."

"Even though my dad's a former reporter?"

"Even though," Sin-Jin acknowledged. The man didn't seem like any reporter he'd ever met. But then, he was beginning to think the same thing about Sherry. All the reporters who had crossed his path were like sharks, waiting for the first sign of blood. "Besides, the key word here is *former.* Can't hold things against someone forever."

She didn't want to go inside just yet. Didn't want to see him leave. "So you hold my vocation against me?"

What he wanted to hold against her, he realized, was himself.

But he gave her the answer he knew she was expecting. The answer he would have been expecting himself—except now he wasn't completely certain of it any longer. "As long as you keep your pen sheathed, we're all right."

As a rule, Sin-Jin wasn't a man given to impulses, not since he'd walked away from his life all those many years ago and forged a new one for himself. Not until Sherry had burst into his life with the force of an unexpected squall at sea.

Impulse was guiding him now.

Again.

Maybe it was the moonlight caressing her skin. Maybe it was the warm environment he'd just left, an environment that had, however temporarily, broken down his barriers.

Or maybe it was the woman herself, half annoying, half enticing and completely exciting.

Whatever the explanation behind his actions, Sin-Jin found himself wanting to kiss her again.

And then he found himself kissing her.

The wanting didn't go away.

Sherry thought that this time she was ready. Braced. Forewarned was forearmed and all that.

It turned out to be the kind of slogan that did better inside a fortune cookie than out in the real world, because she wasn't forearmed, not in the slightest. What she was, instantly, was intoxicated.

One taste of the man's mouth had her wanting more, even though denial had been her constant companion since the last time he'd kissed her. She'd told herself then that it had just been a fluke. That having lived a life that would have bored a nun was responsible for her intense reaction to the man.

She'd told herself lies.

The moan that escaped her lips was involuntary.

Hearing it created an even greater rush in Sin-Jin's system than the taste of her lips already had. His body heating, he slipped his hands from her face to her shoulders, holding her closer to him. And then his arms went around her. Drawing her essence inside.

This had to stop.

He wasn't sure why.

Like a swimmer submerged for too long, his lungs aching, his body tingling, Sin-Jin came up for air. Taking a breath, he looked down at her. Funny, she didn't look like a witch. And then he thought of the Sirens. The mermaids who called sailors to their doom. *The Odyssey,* wasn't it? One of the books Mrs. Farley had assigned him to read so many years ago. They'd been beautiful, too. Beautiful but deadly, to be avoided at all costs.

So why wasn't he avoiding Sherry?

He had a hunch he knew why. "I have two tickets to the opening of a new performing-arts theater my company recently acquired and renovated. They're for two weeks from Saturday." Though the gala affair called for his attendance, he'd already made up his mind to give the tickets away. Until just now. "It's not a command performance or anything—"

"I'd love to." Afraid that he would change his mind before he finished asking the question, she fired her answer faster than a bullet.

He almost laughed. If he didn't know any better, he would have said she was eager. "We can have dinner first."

Sherry nodded. She knew her parents would be more than willing to babysit. They'd both been after her to resume her usual routine. "Sounds good to me."

"All right, then."

Getting into his car, he drove away. The official story he gave himself was that he was trying to cure himself of her. The best way was to sleep with her. Once the thrill of the conquest was over, he would be ready to move on. It always worked that way for him when it came to business. He saw no reason why it wouldn't work with this woman. It was a matter of self-preservation. He needed a clear head to conduct his work, and she was definitely blurring things for him. Ever since that day up at the cabin, he felt like a crayon that was continually being forced to draw outside the lines.

Sherry's heart was still pounding hard as she slipped back inside the house. Her parents were off in the kitchen and for that she was extremely grateful. She needed the time to pull herself together.

It took her a moment to get her bearings. Taking a deep breath and then releasing it slowly, the way she'd been taught to in Lamaze class, she took out the small pad she kept in her pocket. The pad she'd been carrying around ever since Owen had first given her this assignment. Drawing in another deep breath to steady her pulse, she jotted down the latest information Sin-Jin had inadvertently given her. She might be on maternity leave, but that didn't shut down the journalist in her.

"Uncle's name was Wayne. Doctor. Practiced in Appalachia."

Slowly but surely she was determined to piece together Sin-Jin's life—to form at least a shadow of the man he was. She slipped the pad back into her pocket. If she felt a little sneaky doing this, she consoled herself with the fact that he knew exactly what she was and no one was holding a gun to his head to tell her things.

Besides, she wasn't about to put this all down for Owen's perusal until she'd secured Sin-Jin's permission. When she was ready, and there was still a great deal of investigative work to be conducted, she was just going to have to find the right way to present the article to Sin-Jin.

But there was still time to worry about that.

Though two weeks away, she had to worry about

what on earth she was going to wear to a performing-arts theater opening.

She felt a bubble of excitement rising up within her. Cinderella was going to the ball. And Prince Charming was driving the coach.

Chapter 11

Cinderella had definitely come into her own, Sherry thought as she and Sin-Jin slowly made their way across the red carpet into the Bedford Performing Arts Theater Saturday evening.

The last time she'd seen so many women bedecked in diamonds, furs and designer gowns that came in the four-figure and up range, she'd been covering an Academy Awards function with Rusty for her television station. Then it had been an assignment, now she was supposedly on the inside, one of the beautiful people.

She wasn't vain enough to feel that she could carry off the pose comfortably.

For one thing her dress came with a far less impressive pedigree, an off-the-rack gown emerging from a local department store. Feeling a little self-conscious, she looked down at it.

"I think I'm a little underdressed," she whispered to Sin-Jin.

He escorted her through the door. The woman was garnering looks without even realizing it. Her strapless evening gown was high in the front, but dipped low as it made its way to her back, a perfect display of sexy modesty.

Inclining his head, he brought his lips to her ear. "From where I'm standing, you could do with a little more underdressing." She turned her head to look at him, her hair brushing against his face. He wasn't quite able to read the expression on her face. "Sorry, I couldn't resist. You look sensational."

The foyer, with its mirrors that doubled and tripled the number of people within its enclosure, added to the noise and confusion around her. His compliment surprised her. Pleasure embraced her. "I didn't think you noticed what I was wearing."

He slipped his arm around her waist, guiding her toward an open pocket of space. "Then obviously you think I'm far more cold-blooded than my rank detractors do." He allowed his eyes to travel slowly over the length of her, enjoying the journey. "An Egyptian mummy would have noticed what you were wearing, Sherry."

The shimmering hot-pink dress was only a breath away from being painted on, highlighting all of her curves and threatening to bring a lesser man to his knees. The floor-length gown's thigh-high slit didn't help his sense of concentration any.

He'd thought of her as attractive and distracting before. Now she was positively breathtaking.

And tonight, Sin-Jin promised himself, he was going to get her out of his system. After all, he was his father's son and as such given to noticing outstandingly attractive women. Sherry Campbell definitely fell into that category.

But the working rule of thumb was, once a conquest was met, it ceased to work its magic, ceased to hold its allure. He'd seen it time and again when he was growing up. His parents would become obsessed with someone, only to have that obsession fade once it became so-called permanent. He followed the same pattern, except that his passion was business. But there was no reason to believe it would be otherwise with a woman.

Still, he had to admit that he found the blush that crept up her neck vastly appealing, not to mention tantalizing. It made him want to trace the light pink path from its source.

Sherry scanned the area. Well-manicured, pampered bodies as far as the eye could see. "Who are all these people?" she wanted to know. "Business acquaintances of yours?"

He knew a great many by name and by sight. And usually felt alone at these functions. That was why he was originally going to pass on this one.

"Some are, others refer to themselves as patrons of the arts. They're here to rub elbows with other patrons, to hear themselves hailed as 'angels,' and possibly last of all, to enjoy the show."

She'd just thought that this was going to be some sort of dedication ceremony, filled with self-congratulations and adulation for Sin-Jin as the force behind the theater's stylish resurrection. "So there is going to be a performance?"

Again he inclined his head. He was watching her expression too much, he admonished himself. After all, this could be used as a time to network further. "A special, one-night, by-invitation-only, performance."

She'd yet to see anyone handing out programs. "Do I get a clue as to what it'll be, or am I going to be kept in the dark?"

He'd been informed ahead of time as to the program. He envisioned the letter he'd received several weeks ago. "Highlights of the upcoming season, performed by every famous celebrity the director of the theater could round up."

"And your company bought this theater and reno-vated it?" The structure was all glass and glitter, the architectural, futuristic vision of an up-and-coming de-signer who was already making a name for himself. She'd discovered, by doing a little preliminary digging, that rather than work with what was, Sin-Jin'd had the old building torn down and reconstructed from the ground up. The end result was a thing of beauty that in some places seemed to defy gravity.

Business, the driving force in his life, felt somehow dull and boring to him tonight. "We hold the mortgage."

She smiled at the short, staccato sentence. "Is that the collective 'we' or the royal 'we'?"

Instead of answering, Sin-Jin plucked a glass of champagne from the tray held out by a passing waiter and placed it in her hand. "Here, see if this can get you to stop asking questions for a few minutes."

She took a sip, her eyes on his. He felt that stir-ring in his gut that he was beginning to associate with being around her. "Don't you like women with inquir-ing minds, Sin-Jin?"

Actually, he didn't. Until now. She was the rule breaker. It was becoming the norm with her. "Only if I can be sure that they're asking for themselves and not a potential reading audience."

"Touché." Sherry lifted her glass in a silent toast to him before taking another sip.

"Why, Sin-Jin, you did make it after all. Good for you."

The smooth British accent belonged to a distinguished-looking man who was dressed in a formal tuxedo, complete with arm candy. The woman he'd brought was young enough to be his daughter.

Which was, Sherry discovered several minutes later, exactly who the young woman was.

For the next forty-five minutes, until they were politely requested to go into the theater proper and take their seats, what seemed like an endless stream of people flowed by them, all wanting to spend a moment with someone they deemed to be one of the most influential men in the current business world. Sin-Jin conducted himself like someone to the manor born.

He was, she noted, charming to all of them. But even so, there remained that small distance between him and whoever he was talking to, that small distance that established him as ruler of his domain and testified that anyone he spoke with was just a separate island that was drifting by.

It was clearly his evening. And he had chosen to share it with her. Pretty heady stuff, Sherry mused. Even headier was that he introduced her to people as exactly who she was, a reporter for the *Bedford World News*. That in of itself garnered her more than one surprised look.

The moment the first bell chimed, alerting them to the fact that there were five minutes until the curtain went up, Sherry felt his hand slip to the small of her back.

"Time to go in," he told her. "And none too soon," he murmured under his breath.

She wasn't sure if he was addressing the remark to her, or if she just happened to overhear him talk to himself. Was he weary of these people who tried to curry his favor? When did the attention stop being flattery and become tedious?

One of the red-jacketed ushers showed them to their seats. They were located front-row center. Sherry was duly impressed.

"Wow, it certainly pays to hang around you." Taking her seat, she looked at Sin-Jin. God, but he did have a hell of a good-looking profile, she thought. "Does everyone always fall all over themselves around you?"

His eyes when he turned them on her made her feel as if she was the only one in the room. "You don't."

"I don't want anything—" She saw his eyebrow go up. Just one. Why was that so incredibly sexy? "All right," she relented, "except for an interview."

"You might want something," he observed, "but you're not pandering."

She lifted a slim, bare shoulder, then let it drop. He found himself wanting to skim his fingers along the curve of skin. "It's not my way."

She was right. As annoyingly determined as she had come on, Sherry hadn't been about to flatter him in order to get what she wanted. Maybe that, he thought as the lights began to dim and he settled back, was why he was attracted to her.

In any case, it would be over with soon.

"You seemed to be living every beat of that music." The house lights were going up, signaling an intermission. He'd been watching her almost as much as he'd been watching the performers. He couldn't recall seeing anyone enjoy themselves as much as she was.

"I love musicals." She wasn't embarrassed to make the statement. She got her love of music from her father, who had sung with the church choir as a boy and had sung her to sleep with old beer-drinking songs he'd learned in his youth. "There's something wondrous about feeling the beat vibrating in your chest. It makes you feel as if you were part of what was happening."

The last number before intermission had been one lifted from *West Side Story.* "Doesn't seeing a gang member suddenly break into song and execute intricate dance steps offend your sense of reality?"

She had a very healthy sense of reality—and enjoyed tucking it away on occasion. "Nope. It enhances it."

"Come again?"

Unless he felt the same way, she didn't think that he could begin to understand what she was talking about, but she gave it a try anyway. "Watching things like *West Side Story* and *Riverdance* make reality bearable to me sometimes."

He shook his head, amused. "If you say so."

What kind of person was this woman sitting beside him? Sin-Jin had to admit his curiosity about her surprised him. Under normal circumstances he would have sworn he didn't have a curious bone in his body.

And yet questions about her were occurring to him at an alarming rate. Questions such as why the father of her child wasn't at her side. She'd never mentioned the man to him, or commented about his absence.

It was ironic. For all her chatter, she seemed to be as private a person as he was.

The performance, complete with one intermission and three encores, lasted a little more than three hours.

And then it took them almost another forty-five minutes to make their way out of the three-story building, even though he tried to hurry along their progress to the entrance.

Everyone, she noted, was determined to secure their five minutes with him. Twice he flashed an apologetic look in her direction. That he gave any thought at all to her comfort both intrigued and pleased her.

She amused herself by listening. When the jargon became too technical and boring, Sherry turned her attention to the handsomely bound program she'd been handed just before taking her seat the first time. What caught her attention were the last three pages. They were completely devoted to the names of donors who had given generously to the foundation that was to oversee the immediate management of the theater.

Skimming over the list, it surprised her to see a familiar name. John Fletcher was one of the chief contributors, his name printed in the group of donors who were categorized as being in the Platinum Club, reflecting donations over a hundred thousand dollars. She wondered if it was the same John Fletcher whose cabin Sin-Jin had gone to. It was obvious that the man was as wealthy as Sin-Jin.

Was this John Fletcher a boyhood friend? A silent partner?

Sherry could feel her mind waking as possibilities began to suggest themselves to her. She began making mental notes.

"Tired?"

Lost in thought, the sound of his voice took a moment to penetrate. She realized that she'd just stifled a yawn. But that had nothing to do with him.

"No, I'm fine."

"You're yawning," he pointed out.

She was trying not to pay attention to the way his breath on her neck made her skin tingle. "New mothers don't get to sleep much."

Rather than say something along the lines that it would only be a few more minutes, he cut short his conversation with the latest group of men who had tried to commandeer his time.

"Sorry, I'm afraid that Ms. Campbell needs to make an early night of it."

"That's right," she said as he took her arm and made for the exit again, "make me the bad guy." She glanced at her watch. It was just a little after midnight. "I guess I really am Cinderella," she murmured.

The air was bracing as they finally made it outside. Sin-Jin handed the valet his ticket before turning in her direction. When he did, there was amusement in his eyes. "You feel like Cinderella?"

She went for the obvious rather than tell him that she'd felt that way for most of the evening. "It's just a little after midnight."

How was it that she looked even better to him now than she had when he'd first picked her up at her home? "Does this mean that your dress is going to disappear?"

He was flirting with her, she thought. Something else she wouldn't have thought he was capable of. Sherry laughed. "Don't look so hopeful."

His look made her feel warm.

"I don't believe in missing opportunities."

The car arrived just then. She silently blessed the valet. The young man hurried out of the vehicle and went to hold the door open for her.

She slid in and waited until Sin-Jin got behind the wheel. "You were very patient tonight."

He turned the engine on, not sure what she was driving at. "With anyone in particular?"

That was just it. "With everyone."

Just what kind of image did she have of him? "Did you expect me to snarl?"

She looked at his profile for a long moment as he wove his Mercedes into the stream of traffic and they joined the slow-moving process of vehicles that were trying to make good their escape from the parking lot.

"I'm not exactly sure what I expect you to do anymore."

He kept his eyes forward. That makes two of us, he thought.

Rubbing the sleep from her eyes, Sheila looked surprised to see them walk into the house. She checked her watch to make sure she hadn't lost track of time and fallen asleep. Twelve-thirty. She felt disappointment unfurling inside her.

Getting off the sofa, she crossed to the foyer and met them halfway. "I wasn't expecting you back until two or three in the morning." She saw Sherry glance toward the stairs. It brought back memories of her own waltz with new motherhood and made her smile. "The baby's fine. I just put him down."

Sherry did a quick mental calculation. That gave her four hours before he woke up again—give or take an hour. She sincerely hoped her son was in a generous mood. Then again, she was probably not going to get any sleep tonight, not in her present wired state.

She smiled her gratitude at her mother. "I really appreciate this, Mom."

Her purse in hand, Sheila was already making for

the front door. She was obviously anxious to leave the two of them alone. "Anytime."

Sherry slanted a glance toward Sin-Jin. Rather than leave her on her doorstep, he'd come inside with her when she'd unlocked the door. Nerves began to do pirouettes through her. If her mother left, she'd be alone with him. Alone with a man who'd flattered her, who'd flirted with her, and who she found immensely attractive.

Everything in her system cried out Mayday. Sherry looked to her mother for help, knowing it was probably as futile as grabbing on to a soda straw while drowning in the ocean. "Mom, you don't have to run out the second we walk in."

Her hand on the doorknob, Sheila was already opening the front door. "Now that he's retired, your father hates to sleep alone."

Sherry frowned. The excuse didn't jibe with her mother's earlier statement. "But you just said that you expected me to be in by three o'clock."

Rather than try to regroup, Sheila merely gave her daughter a patient, loving look. "It's too late to argue, sweetheart." Crossing back quickly, she kissed her daughter's cheek, whispered, "Have fun," in her ear and sailed back to the front door. She was gone in an instant.

Sherry stared after her mother as the door closed, a sinking feeling taking up residence in the pit of her stomach. The rest of her was humming with an anticipation she was trying vainly not to acknowledge.

"What did she say?"

She turned around, a little startled to discover that there was no space between them. She didn't remember

Sin-Jin being this close a moment ago. Had the room gotten smaller somehow?

"She told me to have fun."

She pressed her lips together, telling herself she was being childish. It wasn't as if she was a vestal virgin and besides, he probably wasn't going to do anything anyway.

Nerves warred with disappointment.

"I guess she's more tired than she thinks," she told him.

His smile was slow, seeping into her system, covering every part of her like honey over ice cream. "Or more alert than you think."

Suddenly, the air around her became very still. She could hear every sound the house made. The slight creaking of the walls as the wind picked up. The sound of crickets outside the living room window, calling to one another, intent on having a mating fest.

Did crickets get lonely, too?

The single word shimmered before her. *Too.*

Her mouth had gone dry. Damn it, she *did* feel like a vestal virgin. What was the matter with her? "She always has been a sharp lady."

He threaded one hand through her hair, cupping her cheek. Making strange things happen to her insides. "You looked very beautiful tonight. Or did I already tell you that?"

It took her a moment to get in enough air to answer. "You did. Past tense?"

His smile widened, pure pleasure marking the path. He had a really nice smile, she thought, feeling herself losing ground. "Past, present, pluperfect, take your choice."

Breathe, damn it, breathe. "Are you going to kiss me again?"

He shook his head slightly, his eyes never leaving hers. "Don't you ever stop asking questions?"

"I...don't think...I know...how." The words seemed to dribble from her lips, dew slowly sliding down the petals of a rose.

"Let me see if I can help you with that." He brought his mouth down to hers, sealing in her questions and releasing a wave of excitement that felt almost over-whelming.

The kiss was gentle, sweet. The more receptive she became to it, the more it grew until it felt as if there wasn't a single space left that wasn't filled by the kiss or by the emotions it generated within her.

Sherry leaned into him, their bodies touching then pressing against each other as their breaths mingled and their tongues tangled. Desire sprang up, full-bodied and strong, embracing her.

Her eyes shut, Sherry fell headlong into the kiss, losing her bearings. Not wanting to find them again. At least, not yet.

Her heart was pounding hard as she felt his warm hands slide along her shoulders, her back. Melting her knees. Making her quiver inside.

And then there was separation. He was drawing his head back, leaving her adrift. When she opened her eyes, she saw that there was just the slightest look of uncertainty in his. St. John Adair, uncertain? It didn't seem possible.

"Maybe I should go."

No! The wave of panic almost took her breath away as much as the kiss had. "It can't be anything I've said because I think I just swallowed my tongue."

He found her honesty incredibly refreshing. Sin-Jin was beginning to think that she was a rare woman. "No, but maybe I'm rushing things." She had, after all, just given birth a few weeks ago.

Sherry placed her hands on his arms, looking up at him. It was as if she no longer had a choice in this, that her destiny was already preordained, written down in some vast book somewhere.

"Isn't that what makes you so good at what you do? You know when to rush in and when not?"

Normally, he thought. But right now, he'd seemed to have lost his instincts. They'd evaporated, leaving him feeling just the slightest bit lost. It wasn't something he was used to.

The thought that fools rush in where angels fear to tread meandered through his mind. "I'm afraid that this time I need a little input. Did the doctor say—" He never got a chance to finish his question.

According to her gynecologist after her exam, everything was back in working order and better than ever. "The doctor says I'm terrific." Sherry pulled herself up on her toes and brought her lips up to his, kissing him for all she was worth.

"Yes," he murmured against her mouth, "you certainly are."

He could feel her lips widen into a smile. A smile that imprinted itself on his soul.

"I never thought I'd hear myself say this, Sin-Jin, but you talk too much."

Sin-Jin laughed, sweeping her up into his arms. "Let's see what we can do about that."

And then the laughter faded.

Chapter 12

He was seducing her.

From the moment he first kissed her, the seduction began, enveloping her, making her tingle with incredible anticipation.

There were all sorts of things wrong with this. The words *conflict of interest* sprang up in her mind in eight-foot-high letters. This was a dalliance, a temporary meeting of bodies, for him. She knew that. It had no future, not even the hint of a promise of a future.

She had to be out of her mind.

She'd just come away from a three-year relationship that had self-destructed on her, and here she was, seeking shelter in the arms of a man who had a billfold where his heart was supposed to be.

Everything was wrong with this picture. And only one thing was right.

She wanted it to happen.

Maybe she needed to believe, just for the space of a few hours, that she was desirable, that she was wanted by someone. By a man who could easily, as she had seen tonight, have absolutely any woman he wanted with just a snap of his fingers.

So what was she doing, being the one he snapped for?

And yet…

And yet he hadn't snapped. He'd given her a way out. A way she didn't want to take.

If he was using her for pleasure tonight, well, she was using him as well, using him to feel again, something she'd thought she'd forgotten how to do. And he didn't have a billfold for a heart. She'd witnessed the actions of a kind, tender man, a man who hadn't left her side when she needed him, even though she was a stranger to him. A man who'd concerned himself with her son's health and who had, for whatever reason, chosen to pay all the hospital bills even though she didn't need him to.

It was that man she saw in her living room tonight. That man she was making love with. And to.

Her skin heated as she felt his lips lightly graze the outline of her ear and then the slope of her neck, the hollow of her throat.

Everything within her tightened with anticipation, moistened with desire. She had to keep reminding herself to breathe.

Like dry kindling, Sherry felt herself bursting in flame almost instantly.

She wanted this, needed this. Needed him, if only for the space of a night.

Live each moment as it comes, her mother had once said to her. It was never more true than now.

She threaded her arms around his neck, finding his

mouth, kissing him hard, her body so close to his the glitter from her gown scattered itself along his tuxedo, branding it.

"Where's your bedroom?" His voice was low, raspy against her ear.

It took effort to open her eyes. When she did, they sparkled with humor as she looked at him.

Had he said something funny? "What?"

"A man who asks directions." She undid his tie. "I like that."

The feel of her cool fingers against his throat made his body temperature go up another notch. Desire urgently pulsed through his veins. "That'll be the only direction I'll need."

The promise stole her breath away. Again.

She turned from him toward the stairs. Raising the hem of her dress with one hand, she took his hand in the other and led the way up. She was surprised that her knees were still functioning. She could have sworn they'd melted away in the first encounter.

"This way."

At the top of the stairs, as she passed her son's door, Sherry hesitated a fraction of a second.

"You want to look in on him?" Sin-Jin asked. He saw the question in her eyes as she looked over her shoulder at him. He wasn't a mind reader, though there were some who'd accused him of that. "I read body language, remember?"

Another man would have been in a hurry to get her to her room, to get her out of her clothes and make love with her, thinking only of himself. Sin-Jin had placed her needs ahead of his own.

He inched up a little further in her estimation.

She cracked the door to her son's room. Johnny was

in his crib, lying on his back, soft, dark lashes just touching his cheeks. An angel sleeping peacefully.

Tranquility joined the host of emotions crowding within her.

Very softly Sherry closed the door again. She turned to look at Sin-Jin.

Who are you? she wondered for the hundredth time. "Thank you."

"Don't mention it." His smile crept under her skin, heating her down to the very core.

Her room was next to her son's, done all in whites, light grays and blues. Sin-Jin took note of his surroundings. Cool, yet somehow still warm. The room suited her.

The moment she was inside, he turned her around and kissed her again, softly, gently.

Something exploded inside of her. Suddenly Sherry felt like the aggressor, eager, desirous, unable to wait for that fulfilling moment, that final release that brought with it exhilaration and peace all at the same moment.

The instant his lips touched hers, an energy filled her, governing her moves. She started with his jacket, pushing it off his shoulders, stripping it from his arms. And then his shirt. Her hands felt as if they were trembling as she worked the buttons from their holes, moved the fabric from his skin.

His chest was lightly covered with dark hair. Excitement rose up another notch, mingling with sensuality that threatened to undo her completely.

He found her eagerness endearing and igniting. The fact that he wasn't mentally standing back, that he discovered himself to be as eager as she took him completely by surprise. For the first time in a very long while, he wasn't viewing what was going on in a controlled capacity. Instead he was in the midst of it, caught up in the moment, in the anticipation and the rising passion that seemed to be hammering at him.

Caught up in the woman.

He liked to affect people, liked to leave his imprint on their lives. Here it was almost as if the roles were reversed. She was doing something to him, stirring him in ways he, with his perfect ability to recall, couldn't remember ever having been stirred.

Stirred not shaken. Well, he was both and losing all sense of time, of place, of everything but the woman who'd done this to him.

Sliding the zipper of her dress down along the curve of her spine, Sin-Jin branded her with his mouth, his excitement increasing proportionately as the gown slowly slid from her body until it was finally on the floor, leaving her dressed in shimmering stockings that came up to her thighs, a tiny white thong and high heels.

He felt a tightness all through his body. It took everything he had not to take her at this moment. But he held himself in check. Wanting the moment to go on a little longer.

Sin-Jin forced himself to back away from her as his eyes skimmed over her body. She was even more sensational than he'd imagined. "You look like every pubescent boy's fantasy."

Her eyes held his, searching for something she needed to sustain her. "And what about your fantasy? What do I have to do to be that?"

"Just be," he whispered. The words glided along her skin like a sinful promise.

Everything drifted into a blurry haze for her after that, full of flash and fire and longing. Of sharp moments surrounding heightened reactions. Each sensation took her a little farther, a little higher up the path that led to the final plateau.

She never knew she could feel like this, it was like being in the middle of a tempest, and she was both afraid and exhilarated at what was happening to her. At what was coming.

It was the difference between a song and a symphony, Sin-Jin realized as he felt her eager lips skimming along his throat, his chest.

His body hummed with suppressed urges as their nude bodies tangled on the bed, generating heat, slick with desire still unspent.

Moving over her, he threaded his hands through her hair, but rather than enter her, Sin-Jin kissed her over and over again, assaulting her mouth, her neck, the swell of her breasts, her very being.

Feeling her twist and quiver beneath him was almost more than he could resist, her hips arching in an un- spoken, urgent invitation. But suddenly, for reasons he couldn't quite crystallize, it was important to him to turn this night into something memorable for her.

And to somehow get his fill of her, though he was beginning to feel that it was impossible.

When he finally drove himself into her, the sensation was all powerful for him. The dance was short, fiery and intense. And when it was over, when he rolled off her and onto his back, completely spent, he thought he was seriously in danger of never being able to catch his breath again.

Sin-Jin waited for his usual waning of interest, of desire; the feeling that always came as a prelude to his moving on.

It didn't come.

There was no hollow feeling, no widening hole within

his being. No desire to get up and leave as quickly as possible.

All he wanted to do was hold her closer. And so he did, telling himself to be patient. She'd aroused more passion within him than any woman ever had, it was only natural that the inevitable might take a little longer to appear.

For now he could drift within this false feeling of contentment.

Sin-Jin gazed at her, wondering who this innocent-looking woman who had just rocked his world was.

His breathing only now was becoming more steady. "Are you all right?"

Her smile was dreamy, pulling him in again. If he'd had the energy, he would have been surprised.

"I'll let you know once I find out if I still have a pulse left."

Concern nudged itself forward. "Was it too soon for you?" he asked.

"I believe Goldilocks had a phrase for it." Sherry turned her face up to his and smiled. "It was 'just right.'"

He kissed the top of her head. "So is that who you are? Goldilocks?"

"Right now, if you were to interrogate me, I couldn't even give you my name, rank and serial number." Sherry raised herself up on her elbow and looked at him, her breasts teasing his skin as she moved. "Who *was* that masked man?"

Sin-Jin laughed as the contentment he didn't want to place stock in spread out a little farther within him. "If you're trying to flatter me, you've succeeded."

"I'm not trying to flatter you, I'm just trying to figure out if I was in an earthquake or a time warp." She fell back against the pillow, her hair fanning out about her like a reddish cloud. She sighed deeply. "Wow. If you raid corporations the way you make love, the world might as well give up and make you emperor now. All hail, Emperor Sin-Jin."

She was completely guileless. Was that possible for a woman? And a reporter at that? He didn't know. All he knew was that he was being reeled in and damn if he wasn't enjoying it.

Sin-Jin tucked her closer to him. "You weren't exactly shabby yourself."

She pretended to take offense. "Oh, well, that's terrific. Is that it? That's what they'll put on my tombstone? 'She wasn't shabby herself'?"

"Fantastic, all right?" He kissed her temples one at a time, arousing himself as he did so. "You were fantastic." He kissed each eyelid in turn, feeling himself begin to surge. "And besides, it's far too soon to talk of tombstones."

She sighed, weaving her arms around his neck. "Make love to me like that again and it might not be too soon at all."

He smiled into her soul, feeling his own catch fire again. "Is that an invitation?"

She rubbed against him enticingly. "Do you want it to be?"

The woman really was a siren. But for now, he assured himself, he knew just where the rocks were, and he wasn't about to be dashed against any of them. "Questions, always questions. I guess I'll have to stop you the way I did last time."

She turned toward him, her body pressing against his. She felt his response and smiled wickedly. "I was hoping you'd say that."

The crying woke him.

When Sin-Jin opened his eyes, the unfamiliarity of

his surroundings momentarily disoriented him. He was in Sherry's bedroom. The sound that had roused him was coming from the baby monitor next to the far side of the bed.

He hadn't realized that he'd fallen asleep.

Raising himself up on his elbows, he realized that what he was hearing was Johnny crying. The place beside him was empty. He skimmed his hand over it. It was still warm. A small rush undulated through him. He swept it away before it could complete its route.

Sin-Jin sat up and dragged his hand through his hair. He glanced at his wristwatch. It was almost four in the morning. Well past time to get going. He reached for his underwear and then his trousers. As he pulled them on, he thought about getting dressed and simply slipping out the front door. That way he could avoid the necessity for having to engage in any awkward conversation with Sherry. It seemed like the thing to do.

The trouble was, he didn't want to leave, didn't want to simply vanish into the darkness, like Batman.

He wanted to stay.

To see her with her child.

What the hell was happening to him?

The next moment, he shrugged. What was the harm in remaining for a few minutes, he upbraided himself. He was overreacting. All he was planning to do was be polite and say goodbye, not promise her half the kingdom.

The crying stopped. A soft, contented noise followed in its wake.

Curious, Sin-Jin tiptoed to the doorway of the next room in his bare feet.

The nursery smelled faintly of talcum powder and of the soft, seductive scent of her cologne.

Moonlight streamed in through the window, slipping

through the white nylon curtains and bathing parts of the room. Half in shadow, half in light, Sherry was sitting in a rocking chair next to the crib, holding her son in her arms and rocking ever so slightly. The infant was sucking madly on the bottle she held to his mouth.

Sin-Jin stood in the doorway, just watching them for the space of a moment. Wondering why such a simple thing could move him so much.

Maybe it was the love he felt, the love that was so evident between the mother and the child she held in her arms.

Sherry sensed his presence before she looked toward the doorway.

"Hi," she said softly. Even in the dim light of the moon, she looked radiant to him. "I'm sorry, did we wake you?"

We. As if whatever her son did was an action that she gladly shared, gladly took responsibility for. He felt envious of the baby, envious of the life that was yet to unfold before him. John Campbell was never going to lack for love, never feel that he was alone in the world.

Sin-Jin half shrugged, feeling suddenly as if he was intruding. "I heard crying."

"He was hungry." She smiled down at the little soul in her arms. "Actually, I'm surprised he didn't wake up sooner. He was giving me a break. I guess he knew tonight was special." She raised her eyes to Sin-Jin's face. "We don't usually have overnight guests."

He knew what she was saying without her stating it outright. That she didn't do this casually. That she didn't just top off the evening by taking someone to her bed.

She didn't have to tell him. He knew. God only knew how he knew, but he knew.

What the hell was he doing here standing half-dressed, barefoot in a child's nursery, watching a scene out of a Norman Rockwell calendar? This wasn't the place for him. He shifted uncomfortably. "I should be going."

She wanted to ask him not to, but that would be needy, and she wasn't about to let him think that she was the clingy sort. She knew it was wrong to hope, yet everything within her wanted him to stay, just a little while longer. To let her pretend, just a few more minutes.

"I know." When, to her surprise, Sin-Jin made no move to leave, she stopped rocking. "Would you like to feed him for a while?"

Sin-Jin unconsciously pressed his lips together. *Go, damn it. Get out of here. This isn't for you.*

"I—"

The very fact that he didn't say no, that he hesitated, gave Sherry her answer. She rose to her feet, the folds of her robe barely slipping closed.

"It's easy. Here, just hold him against you in the crook of your arm." Before he could protest that he really needed to be going, she made the transfer. "And sit down in the rocker. If you hold the bottle anywhere near his mouth, Johnny'll do the rest."

Sin-Jin did as she instructed, and the infant continued sucking on his bottle. He couldn't explain the warm feeling that originated at the point of contact between himself and the child, nor why it spread outward so quickly. Couldn't explain it and didn't want to try. It was too early in the morning to contemplate complex matters.

He just rocked and enjoyed the moment.

Chapter 13

Hints of twilight found their way through the wide bay windows of the twentieth floor of Adair Industries. This reminded Sin-Jin that it was getting late.

Within the room were sixteen of his finest people, all seated around the perimeter of the highly polished teak oval conference table he'd picked up in the Philippines on his last business junket there.

To his left was Mrs. Farley, dutifully taking down every word being uttered. On his right, appropriately enough, was Carver Jackson, his right-hand man for the past five years. Carver had come to him straight out of Harvard Business School, clutching his MBA and eager to set the world on fire. He'd never found the younger man wanting in any way.

But right now he found himself wanting. Wanting to be somewhere else other than here. It was the tail end of an excellent week that had seen significant corporate gains for Adair Industries. For once he was satisfied. It was a new experience for him.

Of late he'd found himself experiencing a great many new sensations.

There was a pregnant pause as Althea Mayfair had just finished her report. He'd hardly kept his mind on the words, but knew that her work was miles beyond competent, as was Althea.

Splaying his hands on either side, he leaned forward and looked at the faces of each and every one of them. "Go home, people."

Carver's thin brows furrowed over his hawklike nose. Startled, he glanced at his watch and then exchanged looks with Edna Farley. They'd hardly begun to dig in.

"But it's not even a school night, boss." The cryptic smile on Carver's lips gave way to a sobered look. "What gives?"

Under the watchful eyes of everyone present, Sin-Jin began returning various folders and disks to his titanium briefcase. "I thought for once everyone would like to get home before eight."

It was only five o'clock. Carver looked a little unnerved. Was this a joke? "If this is your idea of a production of *A Christmas Carol,* you're several months early."

Rather than begin dispersing, everyone around the table appeared to be sealed to their seats, their eyes trained on Sin-Jin.

A whimsical smile found its way to his lips. "This is not a test. I repeat, this is not a test, it's a genuine order. Go home."

No one moved except Carver, who rose to his feet to peer more closely at Sin-Jin's face. "Are you feeling all right, sir?"

If he felt any better, Sin-Jin realized, it might actually be illegal. "I'm feeling fine, why?"

Carver shook his head, glancing around at the others at the table. To a one, they seemed stunned. "This isn't like you."

No, it wasn't, and maybe that was the shame of it, Sin-Jin thought. "I've decided that maybe there're more important things in the world than the next corporate takeover."

Shaken, Carver looked to Sin-Jin's secretary for guidance, but the woman appeared to be unaffected by what was going on. She was even smiling. "Now I know you're not feeling well."

Rather than answer, Sin-Jin looked to the woman he'd always felt was the only one who truly understood him. It was through her that he directed his money to the various charities that he supported. He could trust Mrs. Farley to safely keep his largess a secret. She was the only one left alive, aside from his estranged parents, who knew him when.

"Mrs. Farley, help me out here."

Rising to her feet, the prim woman looked at Carver, waved her hand in a classic motion of dismissal and said, "Shoo."

Nervous laughter echoed in the room.

Carver attempted to make light of the situation, wondering if a call to 911 was necessary. "Well, I guess that settles it. Science has finally managed to clone an adult. How do we get ahold of the company?"

Sin-Jin snapped his briefcase shut. "You can put that on the agenda for Monday, no, Tuesday," he corrected himself.

Wanting in on what he assumed had to be some kind of a joke, Carver asked, "What happened to Monday?"

"It was swallowed up in a three-day weekend, Carver." Sin-Jin told him matter-of-factly. "Look at your calendar."

Carver frowned. This was becoming stranger and stranger. Several people slowly began getting their things together, all still watching Sin-Jin for any indication that this was some kind of strange prank. "We've never taken a three-day weekend."

They were a good crew, loyal to a fault. And he'd robbed them of half their lives. It was time they began having lives outside of the corporation.

"We are now." He looked at the group, sixteen of the hardest workers he had the pleasure of knowing. "Go home," he repeated for a third time.

This time the order seemed to take. Papers rustled as they were packed away in briefcases that were already crammed full of files. Cases snapped, chairs moved silently along the rug as they were pushed back.

"See you Monday, boss," Althea called out.

"Tuesday," Sin-Jin reminded her as he walked quickly out the door.

With Sin-Jin gone, the conference room emptied out in a matter of minutes. Carver remained the only holdout. He turned toward Sin-Jin's secretary as she neatly gathered her things together. Something was definitely up, and she was the only one who would know what it was.

"Mrs. Farley, just what's happened to our fearless leader?"

She smiled. "I believe *Love Finds Andy Hardy.*"

The response seemed to confuse Carver. "Isn't that an old Mickey Rooney movie?"

A smile entered her eyes as she nodded. "Among other things."

"Who, what, where, when, how?"

"All good things a reporter would ask." She looked at him. "But you're not a reporter."

Carver stood in the room, alone now, thinking. And then it seemed to hit him.

"But she is," he called out.

Hearing him, Mrs. Farley continued walking down the hallway, neither confirming or denying. Had Carver been able to see her, however, he would have seen the smile on her face and had his answer.

She'd spent part of her day on the computer and part of it on the telephone. Spurred on by personal curiosity rather than her original assignment, she'd discovered that trying to track down Sin-Jin's origins only brought her to a blank wall over and over again. He seemed to have no history until he came on the scene to spearhead a takeover of what was to become Adair Industries. Frustrated, she'd done a search on John Fletcher, thinking that if she could locate the man, maybe he would provide, however inadvertently, a few answers for her. Or at least a clue.

The cabin at Wrightwood was indeed in John Fletcher's name. The only trouble was, the address given as a permanent residence turned out to belong to a plot in Los Angeles that had long since been abandoned.

The rest of her search was equally as frustrating. The country, it turned out, had a host of John Fletchers and she was patiently trying to weed her way through them. She kept at it until four o'clock.

Temporarily giving up the quest, she turned her attention to the night that lay ahead. It was time to get ready.

* * *

Sin-Jin took the turn a little faster than he should have and cautioned himself to go slower. Five minutes weren't going to make a difference. It wasn't as if she was going to disappear if he wasn't on her doorstep at exactly the appointed time.

Carver was right, he was behaving strangely.

He didn't want to think about it, or even acknowledge what was happening, but anyone who knew him would have said that he was undergoing a transformation. He could see the amusement in Mrs. Farley's eyes when he caught her looking at him. She knew, he thought. But then, she had always been intuitive.

For the first time he was allowing his feelings to govern his actions. Why else would he have placed his private life above his corporate one? The meeting he'd abruptly brought to a close had been set to continue into the wee hours of the morning. They'd been brainstorming another corporate takeover. This time it was a failing movie studio that had overextended itself in the last few years. He had ideas, a whole spectrum of ideas on how to improve operations, trim away the fat, get the hundred-year-old enterprise back on its feet again and begin earning a profit by the end of the next fiscal year.

It wasn't for lack of ideas that he'd terminated the meeting.

But amid all these ideas that were percolating in his brain, images of Sherry kept finding their way into his mind. Sherry, the way she'd been the last time they'd made love. The way she would be the next time he held her in his arms. It made it hard for a man to think about anything but the woman who was consuming him.

He was falling into a trap and he knew it.

But knowing didn't help. He was still standing willingly within the circle of iron teeth set to spring.

Like an alcoholic in denial, Sin-Jin told himself that he could walk away anytime, close the door on what he was feeling at any given moment. Denial allowed him to believe that lingering here like this was all right.

What was the harm in enjoying himself? he argued as he drove down what had become a familiar street to him.

Sherry made him laugh, she made him feel good, and he was careful not to say things to her that he would regret the next day. Things that had to do with emotions, that had to do with his past.

As long as he remembered the rules, everything could go on the way it was a little while longer.

Stopping at home for a quick change of clothing, he pulled his Mercedes up into her driveway a shade before seven. He was dressed in semiformal evening wear. Mrs. Farley had made the reservations at the exclusive restaurant for eight. It gave them enough time to get there even in the height of traffic.

As he walked to Sherry's front door, it occurred to him that he didn't see her mother's car in the vicinity. She was supposed to babysit.

Had the Campbells come by and taken the baby with them instead? He'd been looking forward to seeing the little boy.

A warning signal went off in his head. He was displaying all the signs of a man who was getting attached to not only a woman but to her child. He was going to have to watch that.

When he rang the doorbell, she opened it almost instantly. Barefoot, she was wearing a tank top that casually flirted with the waistband of her jeans, showing off a stomach that had become flat in an incredibly short amount of time. There was what appeared to be a dab of some kind of tomato sauce on the kitchen towel she had slung over her shoulder.

She was usually very punctual. Was something wrong? "You're not dressed."

Sherry spread her hands and looked down at herself. "I'm not naked."

He'd be lying if he denied that part of him wished she was. "No, I mean for the restaurant. Did I get the night wrong?" The question was merely to be polite. He never got any date wrong.

Taking his arm, Sherry drew him into the house. "No, but I decided that instead of going out, I'd treat you to a home-cooked meal."

He glanced over his shoulder as the door closed. "I didn't see your mother's car outside."

"My home, my meal," she emphasized. "I can cook, you know."

It wasn't her cooking that interested him about her. "Why bother?"

"Because it's more intimate."

He followed her into the kitchen. There were pots simmering on the stove and all sorts of things going on on the counters. He was beginning to realize that she did nothing halfheartedly. "I didn't think we could get more intimate."

"Maybe not our bodies," she agreed, stirring the pot of sauce. "But our souls, well, that could stand a little more work."

He didn't quite follow the transition. "And that'll be accomplished by you cooking for me?"

He didn't understand, she thought. She wanted to do these things for him. It seemed somehow more real than walking into a restaurant to eat food someone else had prepared, leave dishes that someone else had to wash. "Now who's questioning everything? Open that bottle of wine for me."

"Must be the company I keep." He picked up the corkscrew she pointed to and worked it into the cork, pulling it out.

She paused to kiss him. "Must be."

Sin-Jin ran his tongue over his lips. "Mmm, what is that?"

She was already turning back to the stove. "Me, I hope."

Running his tongue over his lips again, he tried to place the taste. "Not unless your lips have suddenly gotten spicy."

"I was sampling my tomato sauce." Some of the sauce must have remained on her lips. "I think something's missing."

In reply, he turned her around and swept her into his arms. Sin-Jin kissed her again, longer this time, then pretended to taste his lips again. "Not a damn thing that I can think of."

She laughed. "You're supposed to eat the sauce off a plate, not my lips."

Pouring a glass of red wine for her, he placed it on the counter next to her, then poured one for himself. "To each his own." He leaned over and went to kiss her again.

She stopped him with a hand to his chest. "Later," she said, staving him off. "That's after dessert."

The look in his eyes was sensuously wicked. "That *is* dessert."

"You know," she said, her voice softening, "sometimes you can be awfully nice."

He paused to take a drink of his wine, then removed his jacket. It was hot in the kitchen. "Not too many people would agree with you."

She sniffed. "Then not too many people know the real you."

He came up behind her, unable to resist. Threading his arms around her waist, Sin-Jin nuzzled her neck. "Do you?"

Her eyes threatened to flutter shut. It took effort to concentrate on the meal she was making. "I'm working on it."

Kissing her neck, he released her and backed up. The least he could do, when she was going through all this effort, was not to get in her way.

He took another sip of wine, then leaned a hip against the counter and watched her work. "I let everyone go home early today."

Breaking up spaghetti and dropping it into the boiling pot, she smiled to herself, thinking of how that must have come across. "I bet that was a shock to them."

He laughed, remembering the looks on everyone's faces. "I practically had to shove them out the door."

"You've trained them well." Stirring the spaghetti to keep it from clumping together, she glanced in his direction. "I imagine they're all very loyal to you."

Was that the woman he'd made love with asking, or the reporter? "Is that off the record?"

She could almost read his thoughts. "I'm not a reporter tonight, Sin-Jin, and you're not the great corporate raider. We're just two people about to enjoy a home-cooked meal, a store-bought dessert—" her eyes glinted with humor "—and lots of red-hot loving after it's over." She cocked her head, looking at his expression. He wasn't the easiest man to read. Was she saying too much? Or not enough? "Or should I call it sex?"

The one was too hot, the other too cold. "Why label it at all?"

She found herself wanting answers and knowing that she shouldn't. If she squeezed too hard, what she held in her hand would slip away. "I thought you were the one who liked to have everything neatly labeled and placed in a niche."

He was. Until now. If he put a name to it, if he defined what was going on between them, he'd have to go. And he didn't want to. "Some things defy labeling."

Everything on the stove was going according to plan. She let the pots fend for themselves for the moment and crossed to him. "Like me?"

He smiled, caressing her face. Was it him, or did she just keep getting more beautiful every time he saw her? "Like you."

It took effort not to sigh with contentment. "I'll take that as a compliment."

"It was meant as one." He was more in danger of boiling over than the pot of spaghetti. Taking a breath, he backed off. "So, what else would you like me to do besides open up the bottle of wine?"

Everything was almost ready. She had a little time. "You could try priming the cook a little more."

He set his glass of wine on the counter beside hers. "And just how do I do that?"

"You're a very intelligent man." Her eyes smiled up into his. "You figure it out."

Sin-Jin took her into his arms. "How's this?"

The smile spread from her eyes to her lips. "Keep going, you're on the right trail."

Was he? he wondered as he kissed her. Or was he

going deeper and deeper into the woods, about to get as lost as his father and mother always had.

For now, Sin-Jin shut his mind down and let his emotions take over. There was time enough later to sort it all out.

"You know, I was also planning on taking you dancing." Rinsing off another dish, he handed it to her. Sherry placed it into the dishwasher.

That was the last of them. After shutting the dishwasher door, she switched it on. It hummed to life. Sherry stepped away from the appliance, raising her voice to be heard about the noise. "You sound as if that's not possible anymore."

It was still early enough to go out, but there was another obstacle. "Don't you have to get a sitter for the baby?"

"Why?" Her look was innocent, teasing.

She was up to something, but he played along. "Well, we're not about to go out and leave Johnny alone."

"We're not about to go out at all," she informed him mysteriously.

"But didn't you just say—"

He was really so straitlaced, she loved teasing him. "I said we can still go dancing. It's only as far away as the next source of music. Unless, of course, you're one of those people who dances to some inner tune he hears."

He shook his head. "The only thing I hear is you."

"We can change that."

Taking hold of his hand, Sherry drew Sin-Jin into the living room. She'd had this in mind all along. Everything had already been prepared before he arrived.

She pressed a button on her home entertainment unit and the air was suddenly filled with soft, bluesy music.

Turning around, she presented herself to him. "You can ask me to dance now."

He laughed, inclining his head. "May I have this dance?"

She affected a Southern drawl as she fanned herself and fluttered her lashes. "Well, I seem to have this space open on my dance card, sir, so I suppose it'll be all right just this once, even if you did wait till the last minute to ask."

Taking her hand in his, he pressed his other hand to the small of her back and began to dance to the slow song. "You're crazy, you know that?"

"There's been some talk," she allowed, still in character, "but I don't pay them no mind."

Looking up at him, their eyes met for a moment, and things were said silently that could not be said aloud. Smiling, she laid her head against his shoulder and let her mind drift away with the music.

"This is nice," he said, his breath tingling the back of her neck.

She looked up at him, her heart swelling. "Yes, I know."

Sin-Jin stopped dancing and kissed her.

He stayed the night, as she knew he would. Just as he had the other nights that he had come to take her out. And when the lovemaking was over and she lay beside him in the dark, she listened to his even breathing and thought about things.

In a distant corner of her mind, she knew she was playing with fire, allowing herself to feel things for a man who might be out of her life tomorrow, or if not tomorrow, then the day after. But it was as if she had no say in the matter. Things were happening inside her that were beyond her control.

Everything was finite and an end was coming. Knowing that it was didn't prepare her any more than lecturing to herself did.

So for the time being, she went on pretending that she was just another woman who was falling in love and that he was just another man, knowing that both were false.

Chapter 14

"For a generous man, you certainly are hard to find, John Fletcher," Sherry murmured.

She was sitting in her home office, frowning at her computer screen. Several feet away from her, Johnny was quietly sleeping in the bassinet that Owen had given her. Johnny had turned out to be the best baby ever, sleeping long periods of time and waking with a sunny disposition, but right now her mind wasn't on her son. It was on the mystery stacked up before her.

She had on her desk documentation of the charitable contributions that John Fletcher had made over the past nine years. Even without resorting to a calculator, she could see that they came to quite an overwhelming sum. Whoever this John Fletcher was, he was obviously generous to a fault. Someone like that would need to keep his identity a secret to prevent the onslaught of everyone with a hard-luck story.

Confounded by what she wasn't finding on the computer, Sherry leafed through the contributions, looking for a clue, something to go on that would take her farther than nowhere.

Was it some kind of a coincidence that the contributions began one year from the day that Sin-Jin had emerged to take over and rename Adair Industries? Or that the checks made to the charities all passed through the same bank that handled both the Adair Industries accounts and Sin-Jin's private ones?

This would lead someone to believe that John Fletcher was somehow connected to Adair Industries, especially since Sin-Jin had been using the man's cabin that fateful weekend she'd given birth to Johnny.

But if there was a connection, where was the man? It was as if he was in hiding. There were no payroll checks made out to him and no history of his ever having worked for Adair Industries in any capacity. Except for his deep pockets and his cabin, he was, for all intents and purposes, an invisible man.

Because of his connection to Sin-Jin and because of the timing of that first check, she arbitrarily placed the phantom man in an age range approximately five years younger to five years older than Sin-Jin and had begun her search there. With the aid of Rusty's friend, she tapped into restricted databases, wading through social security files of men with that name born in that particular decade.

Weeding through the various John Fletchers one by one was a tedious process that led her to premature obituaries, improbable locations, county jails and dead ends that defied breaching.

The men she actually did locate just didn't fit the profile. After talking to them or their spouses for a few minutes, Sherry instinctively knew she'd come across yet another wrong John Fletcher.

She sat back in her chair, sipping coffee that had long since grown cold and trying to piece together what she had so far—which was next to nothing.

So who the hell was he? she thought in utter frustration.

Johnny began to stir. "Motherhood first," she announced to no one and went to see to her son.

He needed changing, feeding and a little bonding. So did she, she thought. Sin-Jin was out of town for the day and wouldn't be back until morning. She tried not to miss him too much. And tried not to feel too guilty over what she was doing.

Since it was late, she put Johnny down for what she hoped was a good part of the night and then came downstairs to shut down her computer. On a whim, promising herself that this was the last one she was going to try, she keyed in John Fletcher and searched through the Nevada phone books. There was none. It didn't surprise her. But when she went to the birth and death records, she discovered that there had been a John Fletcher born in the Lake Tahoe region.

As Sherry remembered a panoramic framed photograph of the Lake Tahoe region on the mantel of Fletcher's cabin, excitement began to hum through her.

Scanning the death records, she found nothing. Working forward from his birth, she couldn't find any record of him after the age of eighteen. Nothing at all. It was as if the earth had just swallowed him up. She knew how many homicides went unsolved each year, how many missing persons were destined to remain that way forever. She might never be able to find this particular John Fletcher. She told herself to let it go.

But if this John Fletcher had no history after eighteen, where were the checks coming from? He *had* to be the right John Fletcher.

She was getting punchy, she thought, but she had nothing else, and something in her gut told her she might be on to something. At the very least, it gave her something to explore.

Adrenaline was pumping through her veins. Ignoring the fact that it was getting late, she reached for the telephone and dialed her parents.

Her mother answered on the third ring, just before the answering machine kicked in.

"Mom, it's Sherry—"

"Well, of course it is, dear. No one else calls me Mom."

"Right." She tried not to sound impatient. "Would you mind staying with Johnny for the day tomorrow?"

Sheila laughed. "That's like asking a chocoholic if they'd mind visiting Hershey, PA. Of course I wouldn't mind. Why?" Her tone ripened with interest. "Is Sin-Jin taking you somewhere?"

Sherry smiled enigmatically to herself as she looked at the information on the computer monitor. "In a manner of speaking."

After boarding an early-morning plane for the Lake Tahoe region and renting a car, Sherry had driven to the town she'd discovered yesterday—Hathaway, Nevada. Because nothing else occurred to her, she began with the high schools. There were three in the area and she'd struck out with two of them.

Paydirt came with the third.

The woman sitting behind the desk that guarded the principal's office had informed her that Dr. Grace

Rafferty was out of town, not due back until the following week. Desperate, Sherry had played a long shot, giving her credentials and telling the woman she was attempting to find a John Fletcher. The woman's face had lit up immediately. "That delightful young man just sent the school a handsome bequest. And when Dr. Rafferty offered to draw up a petition to have the school named after him, he declined. Imagine that."

Money. The key that tied everything together. He *had* to be the right John Fletcher. She needed to nurture this along. The woman, she decided, looked old enough to have been here when Fletcher graduated. "By any chance, do you remember John Fletcher?"

The woman's features softened considerably. "Why, yes, I remember John Fletcher. Outstanding student. Outstanding. But very quiet. Kept to himself a great deal." She shook her head. "Not a thing like his parents."

Sherry almost felt giddy. She was actually finally getting somewhere. "His parents?" It was hard to curb her eagerness. "Are they still alive?"

The woman, Mrs. Sellers, considered the question. "I imagine so. They're long gone from the area, of course. Given their lifestyles, they were hardly ever here at all, even when they did live here."

Sherry could feel her lead slipping through her fingers. "But you made it sound as if John was a student here for a longer period of time."

"He was. Times were that he was the only one in the house, aside from the servants, of course. If you ask me," the woman confided, lowering her voice, "they were the ones who raised him, not his parents. They were in and out of his life like tourists on a holiday. I strongly suspect the only one who had a lasting effect on John Fletcher was Mrs. Farley."

Sherry felt as if she'd just opened a door that led to *The Twilight Zone.* It seemed like just too much of a coincidence. "Who?"

"Mrs. Farley. Edna Farley. Finest English teacher we ever had." The woman leaned forward confidentially. "Not like this new crop we've been getting." The woman looked genuinely saddened as she added, "Mrs. Farley retired several years ago."

Sherry felt her heartbeat accelerating. "Do you have a picture of Mrs. Farley?"

Mrs. Sellers looked at her as if she was slightly simple. "In our yearbooks, of course."

The yearbook. Adrenaline kicked up another notch, hummed a John Philip Sousa march. "What year did John Fletcher graduate?"

"Give me a minute." Moving her chair back, she began typing on her keyboard. One screen after another opened on the monitor as she hit the appropriate keys. "There." Turning the monitor so that Sherry could see for herself, she indicated the line in question.

That would make him Sin-Jin's age. Sherry tried not to sound as excited as she felt. "May I see that year's yearbook, please?"

"Yes, of course." The woman rose from her desk. She was almost tiny in stature. Mrs. Sellers pushed up the sleeves of her sweater. "It might take me some time to find it."

The search through the bookshelves in the back of the office was shorter than Sherry expected. Mrs. Sellers triumphantly placed the volume in question before Sherry on the small desk.

"Senior photos are generally in the middle." The telephone rang. Torn, the woman had no choice but to return to her desk, leaving Sherry alone with the yearbook.

Sherry looked down at her hands. They were shaking as she flipped to the middle of the yearbook. Taking a deep breath, she found the *F*s.

Scanning one page, she found what she was looking for at the top of the other.

Her breath caught in her throat.

John Fletcher could have been Sin-Jin's younger brother.

Or Sin-Jin at eighteen.

Hoping against hope, she flipped to the front of the section, to the *A*s, but there was no St. John Adair graduating that year.

She closed the book.

"Find him?" Mrs. Sellers asked.

Sherry rose and crossed to the woman. "Yes, I did. I was wondering, could you look through your database and see if there was ever a student here by the name of St. John Adair? *A-d-a-i-r.* He would have graduated at approximately the same time."

Mrs. Sellers typed the name in, then shook her head. "I'm afraid we've never had a student by that name."

Yes you did, but his name was Fletcher then. "I didn't think so," Sherry murmured for form's sake. She looked down at the leather-bound book in her hands. "You said there were photographs of the teaching staff in the yearbooks."

"Right here." Taking the book from her, Mrs. Sellers flipped it open to the front and found the right section. She pointed to a black-and-white photograph. "There she is. Edna Farley."

It was Sin-Jin's Mrs. Farley.

She didn't understand.

It was obvious that Sin-Jin had changed his name,

that he was this mysterious John Fletcher, but to what end? As far as she could discern after spending the day here, there were no skeletons in his closet, no unsolved crimes or murders in the town that could somehow be traced to him or to his parents. Why all the secrecy?

She'd remained in the town the entire afternoon. Mrs. Sellers gave her directions to the Fletcher house, or rather, the Fletcher estate.

Located on the outskirts of town, the building could have been taken for a small castle in centuries gone by. It actually had been one once. Sin-Jin's mother had fallen in love with it on her honeymoon and his father had had it transported to the United States where it was rebuilt, stone by stone. It turned out to be the most solid thing about their lives.

Victoria and William Fletcher were the epitome of a mismatched couple. They had little in common other than a love of the finer things in life and partying. Eventually, they divorced and moved on to marry others. Many others. Both products of wealthy families, John Fletcher's parents had no vocations, no goals in life other than enjoyment. She couldn't help wondering where Sin-Jin had fitted in all this.

No wonder he'd taken so readily to her mother and father, she thought. Who wouldn't after having these two as parents?

The pair were obviously self-involved flakes, she thought as she took the commuter flight back to John Wayne Airport. Her heart ached for him, for the boy Sin-Jin had once been, living alone in that cold, gray castle.

Was he ashamed of his parents, was that why he kept his past a secret?

As the plane taxied down on the runway some

forty-five minutes later, Sherry discovered that she had far more questions now than when she had first taken off for Tahoe this morning.

Weary, confused and still feeling marginally guilty about what she was doing, Sherry wasn't prepared to see Sin-Jin's black Mercedes parked at her curb as she drove up to her house.

Her pulse began to race. Would he be able to tell what she'd found out? She angled her rearview mirror as she came to a stop. Was it there on her face?

She turned off the ignition. The professional thing would be to confront him, but she didn't feel very professional right now. Just confused.

Love did that to a person, she realized as she got out of the car and walked up to her front door.

"There she is." Sitting on the sofa next to Sin-Jin, Sheila twisted around to see her daughter walking in. She smiled a greeting.

Sin-Jin rose to his feet. Sherry saw a hint of concern in his eyes. Did he suspect where she'd been? He crossed to her, kissing her lightly.

"Hi, I tried to call you earlier, and your mother said you'd gone out."

She cleared her throat, offering up a smile. Damn it, you'd think an investigative reporter would be better at keeping cool under duress. "I had."

He heard the evasiveness in her voice. His eyebrows narrowed slightly as he studied her face. "Where did you go?"

Desperation bred the lie. She wasn't ready to tell him that she knew who he really was. Because she wasn't ready to see him walk away.

"I got together with the ladies of The Mom Squad."

She'd mentioned the group to him before and crossed her fingers that none of the women had seen fit to call her today. She glanced at her mother, but there was nothing in the other woman's face to indicate that she suspected her daughter was lying. "Lori's definitely beginning to show and I think that Joanna looks like she's going to pop any second." Given that the women had looked this way a week ago, she figured she was safe in making the comment to Sin-Jin.

"Are they coming to the christening?" Sheila asked.

Sherry nodded, making a mental note to caution the women not to say anything about not having seen her today. She sighed inwardly. This was getting complicated. "They wouldn't miss it." She turned to Sin-Jin. "How about you? Are you still coming?"

He found that he was actually looking forward to the experience. "I cleared my calendar."

"Johnny will be honored."

Even as she said the name, Sherry was suddenly struck by the irony of the situation. Inadvertently, without knowing it, she actually *had* named her son after the man who had delivered him. That was why Sin-Jin had looked so surprised when she'd told him her baby's name. He'd probably thought that she had somehow stumbled onto the truth.

She still didn't understand why he'd done what he'd done, only that he had.

Sheila picked up her purse and sweater from the sofa. "Well, I'll leave you two to do whatever."

"Mom—" There was a warning note in Sherry's voice.

Sheila was the soul of innocence. "I wasn't being specific, was I, Sin-Jin? 'Whatever' covers a huge range of things." Passing him, Sheila patted him on his arm. "See you at the church."

"Church?" he echoed, looking from the woman who'd just walked out to the one beside him.

"The christening, remember?" Sherry laughed. She kicked off her shoes. "You look like someone who's just seen a ghost. If you think she was saying something about weddings and marriage, that was far too subtle for my mother."

"I'm beginning to see that." Moving her shoes out of the way, he sat down on the sofa again, making himself at home. "I like your mother." He took her hand, pulling her toward him. "Your father, too."

Sherry slipped onto his lap, getting comfortable. "That's good, because they like you."

And so do I. That's what makes this all so hard, Sin-Jin.

Guilt nibbled away at her. She felt somehow disloyal by probing into his life this way, and yet it was her job. Owen wouldn't fire her if she didn't come through; they had too much history together. But she would be disappointed in herself if she dropped the story. Letting her feelings dictate what she did or didn't write would set a precedent, one she didn't think she could live with.

But could she live with hurting Sin-Jin? He obviously didn't want people knowing about his past, and here she was, debating exposing it in exchange for her own byline. It felt like a lose-lose situation.

Sin-Jin brushed back her hair from her face, catching her attention. "A penny for your thoughts."

"Hmm?"

"A penny for your thoughts," he repeated. He laced his hands together around her. "You look as if you were a million miles away."

"A penny, huh?" She laughed, threading her arms around his neck. "Boy, now I know how you got so wealthy. You pay rock-bottom prices for everything."

He looked at her, his eyes growing serious. "Not always."

He certainly wasn't paying rock-bottom prices for getting involved with her. It was going to require the ultimate price eventually. No matter how you dressed up the scenario, he was certain that it would end the way all his parents' liaisons and marriages had: with bitter feelings all around.

Damn it, he'd sworn to himself that it wouldn't happen to him, that he was above those kinds of needs, and here he was, up to his forehead in the very same thing. And still not willing to walk away while he still could.

He still could, couldn't he? he thought, framing her face with his hands.

He'd never been less sure of anything in his life, not even when he'd turned his back on his former life and just walked away. The only time he'd returned to the town where he'd grown up was when he'd heard about Mrs. Farley taking an early retirement from the school district. He'd flown back for her party, waited until it was over and then approached her with his proposition. She'd come to work for him the following Monday.

But except for that, he'd never gone home again.

No, it wasn't home, he amended, it had been a place where he'd grown up. Sherry's house was more home to him than that place, that castle, had ever been.

Sherry was home.

The concept scared the hell out of him.

"Okay, my turn."

Her voice drifted into his thoughts, mercifully

pushing them aside. He looked at her. "Your turn for what?"

"To offer you a rock-bottom price for your thoughts. I'll even make it two pennies." There was something in his eyes, something troubling. Something was bothering him, she thought. "You looked like you were a thousand miles away."

"Only a thousand?" he teased. "I allotted you a million."

She lifted a shoulder casually, then let it drop again. "I'm not given to exaggeration."

He raised his brow, pretending to take offense. "Oh, and I am?"

"If the shoe fits." Before he could say anything in protest, she kissed him soundly, laughing halfway through it.

He could feel the joy spreading through him. Joy that being with her created. Sin-Jin gathered her closer to him.

"I was just thinking about the christening. What is it I'm supposed to do?"

"Nothing too taxing." Her eyes glinted with humor. They'd been through this before. Where was his famous memory now? "Just hold him during the ceremony and try not to drop him in the baptismal font."

"I'll do my best."

She leaned back and studied his face. "I don't know. I think I'd better test those arms of yours out, to see if they're strong enough. Purely for the purpose of research, of course."

"Of course." He tightened his arms around her. "Strong enough?"

"Tighter."

The humor faded a little as she hoped that somehow,

if he held her close enough, tight enough, everything would eventually resolve itself. Like a fairy tale that came with a happily-ever-after guarantee.

"Tighter."

He held her closer still, rocking with her in silence. Wanting to ask her what was wrong, but instinctively afraid of the answer.

Chapter 15

Two mornings later Sherry stood watching as the priest poured holy water over her son's head and said words that linked one generation to another in a timeless ceremony. Her heart swelled as she watched Sin-Jin hold her son in his arms, a tender expression on his face.

It was in that moment that she knew.

It was gone.

Her resistance to ever becoming involved with another man, to ever loving another man, was gone.

Sherry knew that she was setting herself up to be hurt, that this relationship with Sin-Jin could not possibly be permanent. It was an interlude, nothing more. But that didn't change the fact that she wanted it to be permanent, wanted this man to be part of her life and she part of his.

But there was too much against it. Too many secrets between them.

Should she tell Sin-Jin of her discovery? Should she try to prod him for an explanation about his past, or pray that he suddenly wanted to tell her on his own? And now that they'd become intimate, why hadn't he told her on his own? Was he just passing the time with her? Was she just a filler until his interest waned?

And yet he was here and he didn't have to be. For all her pushiness, the man did not have to be here, taking on the mantle of godfather before a church full of people. That was of his own choosing.

There was no point in driving herself crazy with this, it wouldn't change anything.

And at least, she thought, smiling at Sin-Jin as he looked in her direction, she had the moment. That was all that life really was, perfect little moments strung together on a necklace of time.

She wanted more.

After the ceremony was over, she managed to herd everyone out of the small parking lot to the reception, which was being held at a restaurant belonging to one of her father's friends. Even Father Conway came along. The aging priest made a special point of singling Sin-Jin out and engaging him in lengthy conversations about the condition of business in the modern world. Sherry had her suspicions that her father had put the old priest up to it, but Sin-Jin didn't seem to mind sharing the car and his opinions, so she made no attempt to rescue him.

The party in the festively decorated banquet room continued until six o'clock, at which time a select few adjourned to Sherry's house for coffee and even more conversation.

Around eight, Father Conway said his goodbyes.

"I like your young man," he told her, his thick Irish brogue molding each syllable.

"He's not my young man," she'd protested. The last thing in the world she wanted was for the priest to get the wrong idea.

The priest looked genuinely disappointed. "That's a shame, because he's generous to a fault. Gave me a donation for the church right after the ceremony." He took out the check he'd slipped into his pocket and looked at it as if to assure himself that it was real. "This'll cover the rest of the new roof." And then he winked at her. "The Lord does move in mysterious ways." Beaming, he waved goodbye to Sin-Jin before taking his leave.

She sighed, closing the door. "That He does, Father, that He does."

It was ten o'clock before the last of her family and friends bade Sherry good-night and slipped out the door.

Exhausted, she blew out a breath. The first thing she did as soon as she closed the door was slip out of her shoes. She heard Sin-Jin laughing behind her.

Sherry turned around, looking at him quizzically. "What?"

"You always do that as soon as you're alone." Funny how he'd taken to noticing things about her. Without meaning to, the woman had managed to impress her actions on his brain.

It was suddenly very quiet in the room. She wondered if he planned to stay the night. Excitement began to slowly bubble through her. "But I'm not alone, you're here."

Yes, Sin-Jin thought, he was and he still wondered at it. Wondered how strange life sometimes was. Long ago he'd set aside the idea of ever having a family and yet here he was, being absorbed into hers and willingly so.

He slipped his arm around her shoulders. "Tired?" He kissed her temple.

All sorts of wonderful feelings began to take root within her. She wrapped her arms around him for a moment and nodded.

It had been a long day for her. "I can go," he offered.

"No." She placed a hand to his chest as he started to reach for his jacket. A warm, comfortable feeling spread out from beneath her hand. "Not yet," she whispered. Leaning her head back, she brushed a kiss against his lips. Her eyes met his in an unspoken promise of the night ahead. "Let me just go and check on Johnny."

He nodded, stepping back, getting out of her way.

Sherry rushed up the stairs.

The baby was sleeping peacefully. She lightly tucked his blanket around him, then kissed the tips of her fingers and just barely passed them along his cheek.

She had a baby she adored, a family who cared about her and a man she was falling in love with waiting downstairs. No matter what was waiting for her on the horizon, tonight she considered herself to be the luckiest woman on the face of the earth.

Walking out of the baby's room, Sherry stifled a squeal as she felt her waist caught up from behind. Sin-Jin spun her around, and before she could say anything he had her against the wall, sealing his mouth to hers. Blotting out her words, her thoughts, the very world around her.

Nothing existed but him and the fire that was instantly ignited in her belly.

The kiss, powerful and demanding, drained her and somehow energized her at the same time. She didn't bother questioning it, she just went with the feeling.

Sherry wrapped her arms around his neck, pressing

her eager body against the hard contours of his. He kissed her over and over again, raising her up off the floor. She wrapped her legs around his torso, demands running rampant through her, throbbing wildly.

She wanted him, wanted him badly. And he wanted her. She felt her blood sing as it pumped madly through her veins.

And then they were in her room, clothing flying everywhere, inert casualties to their mutual desires. Her body was on fire. And only Sin-Jin could put it out. But with each pass of his hands, each kiss pressed along her skin, the flames only rose higher.

He'd been downstairs waiting for her, debating whether or not he should just quietly withdraw and go home. He was in over his head and he knew it, was growing unnerved by it. She was changing him, taking him in directions he didn't want to go.

He'd made it all the way to the front door and then he'd thought of today, of being in the church and holding that small life in his arms, a life he'd helped bring into the world. He'd thought of the woman who had become such a huge part of his world in such an incredibly short amount of time, and suddenly desire had risen up and seized him by the throat, making it impossible for him to leave. Making even a minute longer without her incredibly hard to endure.

Acting on impulse, he'd raced up the stairs to be with her.

He knew he should go slower, savor the moment. He didn't want to frighten her. But the feelings that were ricocheting through his soul frightened him. *Frighten* was too genteel a word. They downright scared the hell right out of him.

The last time he'd been vulnerable was when he was

a very young boy, watching his father leave home, a curvaceous woman on his arm who wasn't his mother. He remembered feeling lost and alone. Abandoned. To be vulnerable, to lay yourself bare to feelings, meant not being in control, not being able to save himself.

He'd vowed then never to be vulnerable again. Yet here he was, being vulnerable. Placing his soul into the small palm of a woman whose motives were not entirely certain.

It was insane, and yet, he just couldn't help himself. The ache in his belly, in his loins, in his heart, wouldn't let him help himself. He wanted her, this moment, here and now, he wanted her.

Pressing Sherry down against the bed, he held her captive as his lips raced along her body, anointing her flesh with hot, moist kisses that had her panting and twisting beneath him. With every movement she made, she excited him more, captivating him until he was utterly and completely her prisoner.

Unable to hold back any longer, Sin-Jin drove himself into her.

Her muffled cry of ecstasy against his lips began as the heated rhythm fused their hips together. Like a man possessed, he went faster and faster. Her arms wrapped around him, she kept pace.

When the final moment came, he felt as if an explosion had racked his body and yet, it wasn't enough.

He wanted more.

Exhausted, spent, he wanted more.

Was he completely crazy?

Dragging air into his lungs, Sin-Jin slid off her. He barely had enough energy to gather her body to him. Contentment blanketed him but didn't quite manage to cover his concerns.

Her heart was beating so hard Sherry was sure it was going to leap right out of her chest at any second. No matter, this was the best way to go, being made love to by a man she loved.

Passing a hand over her eyes, as if to help them focus, she could only lie there for a moment, doing her best to regulate her breathing. When she could finally manage to form words, she turned her face toward him. "Wow, what was that?"

He laughed shortly. It momentarily depleted his growing energy supply. "I'm not sure."

She smiled to herself. It was nice to know that he was as affected as she was. "Does the government know you have this secret weapon?"

He dragged another breath into his lungs. What *was* it that she did to him? How was it that making love with her turned into an Olympic event? "I didn't even know I had it."

Gathering as much strength as she could, she rose up on one elbow and propped her head up, looking at him. Who would have ever thunk it? Sin-Jin Adair in her bed.

"If you ever tire of being a captain of industry, I promise you that you can make an incredible living as a gigolo." She spread her hand out, forming a horizon. "Women will be lining up for miles for just a sample of that."

He arched a brow. "I won't want women lining up for miles."

Her expression was the epitome of innocence. "Oh?"

He wanted to say that all he wanted was her, but that would place him at her mercy, and he couldn't allow that to happen, couldn't make himself that vulnerable.

The moment begged for something, for a revelation of some kind.

In a moment of weakness, when most of his guard was down, he told her, "That was my father's way." Tucking one hand under his head against his pillow, Sin-Jin pulled her closer with the other. He stared at the ceiling. "And my mother's."

Her heart began to hammer hard again. It took effort for her to make light of the moment, hoping that it would somehow encourage him to say more. Not because of any article she needed to write, but because she wanted him to trust her. "Your mother liked to have women line up for her?"

"No," he laughed, kissing the top of her head. And then the laughter died away as he remembered things he didn't want to. "They both liked to play change partners, though. A lot." She was quiet. Sin-Jin found her reaction unusual. And because she didn't ask, he heard himself telling her things he never meant to say. "My father was married five times before I lost count and interest. My mother, three." And he had disliked every one of the various spouses, because none of them had any use for him, making him feel more and more of an outsider in his own life.

He tried to sound philosophical. "I imagine by now I'd have to hire a stadium to properly celebrate Mother's Day and Father's Day in order to accommodate all the stepmothers and stepfathers I've acquired." His mouth curved cynically. "Not that any of them would come if invited."

They had shut him out, she thought. Sherry raised herself up again and looked down at him. "Oh, Sin-Jin, I'm so sorry."

He shrugged the sentiment away. "Don't be. Being

a distant fifth wheel made me strong. It made me determined to be my own person, to never rely on anyone else for my happiness."

Was he putting her on notice? Telling her that this was nice, but don't get used to it? Now wasn't the time to think of her own feelings, she warned herself. He was sharing something, something hurtful from a past he'd kept locked away. This was about him, not her.

"That shouldn't have been a decision made by a young boy." She truly ached for him. Sherry caressed his face, wishing she could have made things different for him. No wonder he felt the way he did. "Every child should have a warm, loving family."

He blew out a dismissive breath. "Yes, well, there seems to be a slight shortage of those. At least where I was. I decided that that kind of thing was highly overrated."

She knew that was the act of a child attempting to protect himself. And the child was the father of the man. Right at this moment she hated the emotionally crippled couple that had given birth to him.

"Money being the only stable factor in my life, I decided to make some of my own. So as soon as I was able," he told her, "I took the money that my grandfather had left me in his will, left the place that was supposedly my home and went to college." He didn't bother saying which one, but that was a matter of record. He closed his eyes, remembering how hard it had been for him. "Along the way I shed my name and my family. I don't think either one of the two principal players even noticed. They were too busy with their own lives."

He opened his eyes, staring straight ahead. He couldn't remember what his parents looked like anymore. If he passed them on the street, would he know? Or would he just keep walking?

"They always had been. Which was all right," he said a second later, "because I was busy forging mine. Making connections and reinventing myself."

When Sherry reached for him, he pushed her hand aside, stiffening. He shouldn't have said anything. What had gotten into him? "I don't want your pity."

He was shutting her out. Just like his parents had shut him out. Putting her own pain aside, she looked at him incredulously.

"Why would I pity a man who went on to become a force to be reckoned with? Who didn't wallow in self-pity but made something of himself? If anything, what I'm feeling right now is sympathy for the small boy who shouldn't have had to grow up in a house with no love. Who left home and felt that no one cared."

When he turned his face away, she physically forced his face back to make him look at her.

"Sympathy," she emphasized, "not pity. Pity is for the person who lets life knock him down and refuses to get up again. There is nothing pitiful about you, Sin-Jin. There never has been."

But there was, he thought. It was pitiful to him that he felt so lost without her, that his body was spent and all he could think of was making love with her again. Not because he had any physical needs. That would have been easier to accept. Men had needs. But he couldn't lie to himself. He wanted to make love with her because he needed and wanted this woman.

Needed and wanted Sherry.

And to need was to be vulnerable. And to be vulnerable was to be pitied.

His mouth curved slightly. "You do know how to stroke a man's ego."

"That wasn't stroking, that was the truth." And then she smiled up into his eyes. "But if you want to see stroking," she told him mischievously, slipping her hand down beneath the tangled sheet, finding him. "I can show you stroking."

Her fingertips lightly closed over him, her thumb passing over the tip of his shaft. Her hand just barely made contact as she moved her palm tantalizingly up and then down, over and over again. She felt him grow from wanting her. Her smile deepened.

"You know just how to get to me, don't you?" he breathed. Within a moment he had shifted so that he was over her again.

"Do I?" she wanted to know. Her smile faded as desire took root again. *Want me, Sin-Jin. Love me.* "Do I really?"

He pretended to breathe a sigh of relief. "Thank God, the questions are back." He laughed, and his breath tingled the skin along her throat, making the very core of her tighten in anticipation. "I was becoming worried. You didn't ask me any questions while I was telling you about my parents."

Guilt chewed at the fabric of the illusion she was trying to maintain for just a little while longer. Just for tonight. Tomorrow she would tell him the truth, that she already knew everything that he'd told her. Tomorrow, not tonight.

For tonight she sought refuge in half truths, praying she'd be forgiven. "You were telling me what you wanted me to know."

"Was I?" He kissed each of her breasts in turn, fascinated at the way her breathing became more labored.

"Or were you just pulling it out of me like the sorceress that you are?"

"Is that what you think I am, a sorceress?" She rather liked the description. One of her favorite characters in literature was Morgana Le Fey, King Arthur's half sister. Seen as evil by some, she was still a fascinating character.

"Come to your own conclusion." He paused, knitting a wreath of openmouthed kisses over her quivering abdomen. "You certainly cast a spell over me. I've just said things to you, told you things I haven't said to anyone else." She moaned as he licked her belly. A recklessness came over him. He slid his body along hers until he was looking into her eyes. "Did you know that my name is really John Fletcher?"

She didn't want to lie, but telling him the truth now would ruin everything. Would steal him away from her. She knew it.

So instead of answering, she threaded her arms around his neck and brought him down to her abruptly, seizing his lips and kissing him as hard as she could. Praying that the question would slip his mind.

The question he'd just uttered vanished in a haze of desire. He'd already talked too much. It was time to stop talking and to make love with her.

Sin-Jin gathered her into his arms and gave himself up to the demands of his body and hers.

The soft, crying sound coming from the monitor on the nightstand had her opening her eyes immediately.

The baby was hungry, she thought, sitting up groggily. She looked at the clock beside the monitor. Almost four. Just like clockwork, she thought, smiling to herself. It gave Johnny something in common with his god-father.

Last night and the wee hours of this morning came back to her in brilliant hues. They'd made love three times, each time more frantic than the last. It was as if Sin-Jin couldn't get enough of her. That made it mutual.

As her feet touched the floor, she turned to see if the baby had woken Sin-Jin.

Her heart froze.

His side of the bed was empty.

She stretched her hand out to touch where he'd slept. The sheet was cold.

And his clothes were gone.

Chapter 16

Maybe Johnny had cried earlier and she just hadn't heard him. Maybe Sin-Jin had gotten up to look in on the boy and hadn't wanted to wake her up.

Mentally crossing her fingers, Sherry hurried into her son's room.

Sin-Jin wasn't in the nursery.

Johnny was awake, fussing in his crib, trying to shove his fist into his mouth. Cooing softly to soothe him, she picked the infant up.

Slipping her hand beneath his bottom at least told her what part of the problem was. "You're wet, huh? Well, we can fix that. Just hang on a second longer, okay?"

Sin-Jin had to be in the house; he couldn't have just left without saying a word.

Could he?

With the baby tucked into the crook of her arm, Sherry went out into the hall again and crossed to the head of the stairs, hoping that perhaps he'd gone to the kitchen to make a pot of coffee.

Sin-Jin was just opening the front door, on his way out.

"Wait."

He stopped dead and looked up toward the top of the stairs. It was evident by the look on his face that he'd hoped to be out of the house by the time she woke up.

Damn it, why?

It wasn't a time for banter, but it was the only way for her to hide the suddenly panicky feeling that was clawing its way up within her. She would have come down the stairs if she could have, but her knees felt frozen in place.

He was leaving. Permanently. Think. Say something to keep him from going.

"You don't have to sneak out, you know." Sherry forced a smile to her lips. "I won't make you change his diaper."

He was behaving like a coward and he hated it. But he'd wanted to be gone before she woke up. Before she looked at him with those eyes of hers, those eyes that made him forget everything else except her.

Before he wanted to make love with her again.

It was too late for that. He could feel the stirrings beginning already. He slammed them down. The consequences of following his impulses were too costly. They were already costing him. Dearly. He'd seen that last night. Time to get out before he couldn't.

Damn, why couldn't she have slept just a little longer?

Uncomfortable, he cleared his throat. "Look, this was a mistake."

Stunned, feeling like a single-engine plane caught in a tailspin, Sherry could only stare at him. She'd never felt more isolated in her life. There were suddenly a million miles between them.

Maybe she hadn't heard right. Maybe she was stuck in some kind of time warp.

"What?" she whispered hoarsely.

"This went a little too far," he told her. A helplessness was drenching him. The frustration he felt angered Sin-Jin. "It was nice, but—"

She held her baby against her. Her eyes widened as she continued staring at him incredulously. "Nice? You call these last weeks 'nice'?"

It was a bland word, meant to be applied to a cut of clothing, not to what was happening between them.

But maybe nothing *was* happening between them, maybe it was all in her head, all one-sided. Could she be that blind not to realize?

No, it wasn't possible.

Was it?

"Yes, nice," he repeated with emphasis, wanting to be anywhere but here, anyone but him. "But I think it's over. I said some things last night..."

He stopped, not knowing how to end the sentence, knowing only that he felt threatened. And he hated to feel threatened. What the hell had he been thinking of, saying those things to her? Baring his soul to a woman he knew was a reporter? For all he knew, she might have been playing him all along.

His eyes darkened. "If I see a word of what I told you in print, your paper'll face a lawsuit the magnitude of which you can't even begin to imagine. By the time my lawyers are finished with the *Bedford World News,* it will be completely bankrupt." The words were coming out of his mouth, but it felt as if someone else was saying them. Still, he couldn't stop them. "I won't have my privacy invaded."

Numb, she felt as if someone had just ripped out her heart and left a gaping hole in its place. "Your privacy?" she echoed. "This is about your privacy?"

She wanted to scream at Sin-Jin, to beat on him with both fists until he took it back, until he came to his senses. But there was a baby in her arms and he came first, before her own feelings. Johnny was growing progressively fussier, as if he was reacting to the agitation going on inside of her. She couldn't even raise her voice. But her eyes said it all.

"Well, the hell with your privacy, John Fletcher, or St. John Adair, or whatever you want to call yourself. And the hell with you."

With that, she turned her back on him and walked back to the nursery.

He wanted to rush up after her, to sweep her into his arms and apologize. But it was better this way. Better for her, better for him.

Sin-Jin slammed the door as he left.

As she laid Johnny in his crib, the sound vibrated within her chest. Sherry caught her lower lip between her teeth to keep from crying.

He waited for the story to appear in the paper. For ten days he waited. Each day that it didn't, he grew progressively more restless, progressively more uncertain of his actions. Had he been wrong to end it?

No.

Yes.

He didn't know.

Sin-Jin threw himself into work, arriving early, staying late. His temper shortened, his disposition deteriorated, and his fuse became nonexistent. He caught himself snapping at everyone and regretting it, but lacking the ability to right the situation.

He was a man in hell.

And then, after what seemed like the umpteenth sleepless night, he came to terms with his demons and began setting his house in order. The first order of business was to call Sherry and humbly apologize.

She wasn't home.

He kept calling, getting her answering machine and growing progressively more and more irritable.

Ten calls later he was sitting at his desk at work, debating whether or not he should go over to her house in person and set siege to her door. He'd taken over entire corporations with less difficulty than he was having trying to find this woman.

Another futile attempt had him slamming down his phone receiver. Where the hell *was* she?

He heard the slight tap on his door and knew better than to hope that Sherry would be standing on the other side. He did, anyway.

"Come in."

Mrs. Farley walked quietly in and placed a single printed sheet on his desk, then took a step back.

Disappointed, Sin-Jin frowned at the paper without picking it up. He didn't recall asking for anything. "What's this?"

Mrs. Farley laced her hands together primly. "I believe if you read it, you'll see that it's a letter of resignation."

He felt as if a bomb had just been detonated beneath his feet. "Yours?"

She inclined her head. "Mine. Although," she said, "it will probably be the first of many."

Picking it up, he scanned the sheet without really seeing it. This had to be some kind of mistake. Mrs. Farley was the most steadfast part of his life. "I don't understand."

"Neither do we, John." If the letter hadn't gotten his full attention, her addressing him by his real first name would have. Mrs. Farley rarely ever called him that. When she did, it was because she was deadly serious and meant business. "Ever since last Monday, you've become this surly, unapproachable man whose only order of business seems to be biting people's heads off."

He'd been like a man who could not find a place for himself within his own skin. It had taken him almost two weeks of grappling with his soul, with the past that he'd wanted to keep buried, to come to the conclusion that he had allowed ghosts to rob him of his only happiness. The specter of his parents' failed liaisons had egged him on to sabotage his one true chance at happiness.

He realized that what he had failed to take into the equation, on that morning he'd run for his life, were the personalities of his parents and of the people they chose to have their relationships with. Not a one of them was equal to Sherry.

And he was not his parents. For as long as he could remember, they had been comfortable coasting through life, never contributing, never attempting to leave a mark or make the world even a minutely better place than they had found it. That wasn't him. The contributions he made to various charities attested to that. Since he couldn't care for one person, he'd cared for many.

But now it was time to take the training wheels off. To care for the one. Because she had finally come into his life.

Looking at the letter of resignation, he knew he'd already made up his mind to go to Sherry and get on his knees if he had to, to get her to forgive him his temporary foray into the land of the insane.

But first there was a fire to put out. He raised his eyes to the thin, regal-looking woman standing by his desk. "I'm sorry, Mrs. Farley."

She sighed delicately. "And so am I. You're a good man, John." Her eyes narrowed behind her glasses. "Whatever's wrong in your life, fix it."

That was exactly what he intended to do. Sin-Jin smiled at her as he crumpled up the letter of resignation. "Absolutely." He held up the ball of paper. "May I throw this out?"

She paused. Married at twenty-three, childless and widowed at thirty, she had always regarded the man at the desk as the son she would have loved to have had.

"If you promise to stop this nonsense and go back to being the man I've always been proud of, yes, you may throw it out."

"It's a deal." He pitched the wadded-up resignation into his wastepaper basket. As he reached for the telephone to try one last time to get through to Sherry before he went to her physically, it rang beneath his hand.

Ever the guardian, Mrs. Farley moved his hand aside and picked up the receiver. "Adair Industries, Mr. Adair's office." She paused, listening, then placed the call on hold. "Are you in for a Rusty Thomas? He says he's a friend of Ms. Campbell's and that this is urgent."

Something suddenly tightened in his gut, stealing his breath away. Sin-Jin extended his hand for the receiver. "Give it to me. I'll take it."

He barely had time to say hello before the man on the other end began talking.

"Look, Mr. Adair, I'm a friend of Sherry's," Rusty told him. "She'd kill me if she knew I was calling, but her son's in the hospital."

Sin-Jin was on his feet instantly. "What hospital, where? Why?"

For once in his life, Rusty had very little information and it confounded him. "Blair Memorial. There's something wrong with his heart and—"

Sin-Jin hung up. His face was ashen as he looked at Mrs. Farley. "Have my car waiting by the time I get to the lobby," he requested, hurrying out the door. "And tell Carver to take over."

He's back, Mrs. Farley thought, dialing. She crossed her fingers that everything was all right.

Sin-Jin didn't remember driving. He remembered getting into his car and then arriving at Blair. The way to the hospital was a blur of twists and turns and yellow lights he just barely squeaked through.

There was something wrong with the baby and she hadn't called him.

Damn it, didn't she know he'd be there for her? For the baby?

How the hell could she? he upbraided himself. The last thing he'd done was threaten her with a lawsuit. You didn't turn to people like that in your time of need. You did your best to avoid them. He knew that.

He cursed himself savagely.

Not bothering to search through the lot for a space, Sin-Jin surrendered his Mercedes to the parking valet at the hospital's entrance. Tossing the keys toward the attendant, he raced through the electronic doors.

He'd barely made it inside when he heard the valet calling after him. "Hey, mister. Mister! You forgot your ticket."

The attendant ran after him. Sin-Jin paused only long enough to grab the ticket that the red-vested man thrust at him. "Thanks." The valet looked a little wary of him as he stepped back.

Sin-Jin caught sight of his reflection in the glass doors. He looked like a madman. He did his best to pull himself together. Frightening hospital personnel wouldn't help him find Sherry and the baby.

The information desk was immediately to his left. "I'm looking for a Sherry Campbell," he told the woman behind the desk. "No, wait, I mean John Campbell. He would have been admitted sometime today, yesterday, I'm not sure," he confessed.

"What for?" the woman asked kindly.

"He's an infant," Sin-Jin began, realizing that his thoughts were scattered like so many raindrops in a storm. "Heart trouble," he clarified. "I'm sorry, I really don't—"

"Right here," the woman informed him softly, her finger isolating the baby's name on her screen. "He's in the neonatal section. Admitted last night."

Last night. While he had been calling her. Guilt twisted inside of him.

"That's on the—"

"I know where it is," he said, cutting her off, then adding, "Thank you," before he turned on his heel.

As he began to hurry down the corridor that eventually led to the tower elevators, something made him look toward his right, toward the small, serene room that served as the hospital's chapel.

She was there.

His heart stood still. Walking to the entrance of the small room on someone else's feet, he called out to her, his voice throbbing with emotion.

"Sherry."

At first she thought she only imagined his voice. Kneeling, her head bowed, Sherry had been praying so hard that she'd lost track of her surroundings and the time. She'd left her parents upstairs with the baby and had come down here to ask for help.

Almost afraid, she turned away from the cross on the wall. He was standing in the entrance.

Sin-Jin.

He looked like an answer to a prayer.

She rose to her feet in slow motion. Her first impulse was to throw herself into his arms, to sob her heart out and somehow have him take the pain away.

But she'd been so hurt, felt so abandoned when he'd left, she couldn't bring herself to risk being rebuffed again. When Drew had walked out on her, she'd been devastated, but that feeling didn't begin to compare with the way she'd felt when Sin-Jin had left her that morning. Like there was no reason to go on.

But there was a reason, there was Johnny. She needed to go on, to be strong for him. And now her baby was ill. She didn't know if she could bear it.

"What are you doing here?"

Her voice was cold, distant. He knew he deserved it, but it still hurt to hear her like that. Hurt to think that she was going through this without him. "More important, what are you doing here without me?"

Feeling lost. She tossed her head, trying hard to look strong, to look as if what he had done to her hadn't gutted the very foundations of her world. "Doing the very best I can."

He made his way into the room slowly, invading her space an inch at a time. "Why didn't you call me?"

How could he even ask her that question? "Why?" she echoed incredulously. "Because you made it perfectly clear that you didn't want me in your life."

"I was an ass."

The bluntness of his admission took the wind out of her sails. Her hastily newly reconstructed defenses slipped. "Nobody's arguing."

"Look." Taking her hand, Sin-Jin sat down with her in the pew. "It doesn't really justify anything, but there's a lot of baggage in my life, a lot of emotional scarring. I was afraid to get involved, afraid to allow myself to love someone because I didn't want to get on that merry-go-round that my parents were on." He looked into her eyes, praying she could understand. "Didn't want to have my heart ripped out of me."

She shook her head. She understood in theory, but not in practice. How could he think that of her? "Did I look like the kind of person who goes around ripping people's hearts out for a hobby?"

He couldn't help smiling at the ludicrousness of the image. "No."

Sherry threw up her hands helplessly. "Well, then?"

He could only resort to the simple phrase, meaning it from the bottom of his heart. "I'm sorry."

Her world had been tipped over in the past twenty-four hours, ever since she'd taken Johnny in to his pediatrician, her mother's instinct telling her that something was wrong with her baby. He'd been too listless lately.

She hated being right.

Sherry shrugged, looking away. "Doesn't matter, anyway."

Sin-Jin took hold of her hand, forcing her to look at him.

"Yes, it does," he insisted. "It matters a great deal. It matters to me. For what it's worth, Sherry, I love you and I want to take care of you." He'd never meant anything more in his life. "You and Johnny."

She drew herself up, unconsciously still leaving her hands in his. "I don't need anyone to take care of me." Didn't he understand? "I need someone to be there, that's all."

He intended to do whatever it took. "Then I'll be there," he swore. "And I'll help take care of Johnny."

Emotions warred within her. She was afraid to believe him. Afraid and, oh, so tired. She felt as if the past twenty-four hours had been an eternity. "Don't put yourself out."

"I'm not, damn it. I want to." He struggled to contain his temper. "I will do whatever it takes to make you forgive me." He was pleading now, fighting for his very life. She had to forgive him. "You want me in a hair shirt, you got it. You want it in skywriting, you got it." His voice became deadly serious. "You want to publish that article, you got it. I'll even give you details. It'll be your exclusive."

The article didn't matter. It'd stopped mattering the night of her son's christening, when he had let her into his life, however briefly. She knew she couldn't betray that trust, no matter the professional cost.

She shook her head. "All I want is for my son to be all right."

He felt his heart twisting in his chest, wishing he could take the burden off her shoulders. "What's wrong with him?"

There was a long, technical name for the condition. Dr. DuCane had been very patient, very kind as she had explained it to her. She'd called in a heart surgeon, a Dr. Lukas Graywolf, and between the two of them, they had gone over everything with her and her parents. It had all boiled down to one thing for her: Johnny's heart had a slight tear and needed to be operated on. If it wasn't, he might not make it to his fifth birthday.

"He needs corrective heart surgery. He's in surgery right now." She looked up at him. "And I am so scared."

He took her into his arms. "So am I." She looked at him, stunned by the admission. "But he'll be all right. I swear to you he'll be all right. He'll have the finest doctors in the world. Whatever it takes. And when he gets through this—and he will—he can be our ring bearer."

"Ring bearer?" Her mind felt like a vast wasteland. She tried to focus and make sense of what he was saying to her. "He's only two months old."

He had that covered. "Mrs. Farley can push him in a carriage. We'll run a string through the ring and attach it to his hand. Greta will even trot at his side. It'll work."

She stared at him, dumbfounded. "Are you—are you proposing to me?"

He knew he was making a mess of it, but this wasn't an area he had any experience in. "Badly—but this is my first time. My only time," he amended. "Unless you say no, then I plan to ask you every day of your life until you say yes."

And suddenly she knew. It was going to be all right. Everything was going to be all right. She smiled at him. "I guess it would save us a lot of time if I said yes, then."

He breathed a sigh of relief. "Definitely more efficient."

She pressed her lips together, suppressing a giddy laugh. "You're an idiot, you know that?"

Twice in one day. "Mrs. Farley already beat you to

that description. Not in so many words, but the general gist was there."

She allowed herself a moment longer in his arms. "Why, did you ask her to marry you, too?"

"No, only you." He rose from the pew. "I know that I probably don't deserve you two, but I want the three of us to be a family. You, me and that wonderful son of yours. I want him to be my son, too." A part of him thought that he probably had all along.

"I guess, since you were the first one to hold him, it's only fair."

"That's all I want, my fair share of you." He kissed her and she clung to him. It took them both a moment to realize that they weren't alone.

Sherry's eyes widened with fear as she looked at her son's heart surgeon. "Is he—" She couldn't bring herself to finish the sentence. Her heart wouldn't let her.

Tall, stately Lukas Graywolf was quick to set her at ease. "Your son pulled through with flying colors. He's going to be fine." He smiled. "Your mother told me where to find you. Whatever you two said in here—" he nodded toward the altar "—obviously worked. He's in recovery right now, but you'll be able to see him when they bring him back to the intensive care unit—just a precaution," he explained when he saw the look on her face. "I'll be by later."

She clasped his hand. "Thank you, Doctor."

"Just doing my job." He hurried away.

Sherry took the handkerchief Sin-Jin held out and dried her eyes. "I guess you brought us luck."

He took her into his arms again. "That goes double for me."

As he kissed her, Sin-Jin knew he wasn't alone anymore.

Epilogue

"My God, Sheila, there's enough food here to feed the city of San Francisco." Walking into the kitchen, Connor Campbell shook his head at the wealth of plates spread out on the kitchen table. His wife had added two extra leaves to it just to accommodate all the various items.

Sheila continued arranging the various trays. "Better too much than too little. We don't want to run out on your grandson's first birthday party, do you?"

Connor came up behind his wife and wrapped his arms around her waist, hugging her to him. "So, you're finally okay with 'Grandma'?"

"As long as it's Johnny who's calling me that, yes. But don't you be getting no ideas that you'll be referring to me that way." She turned around to face her husband, a look of warning in her eye. "Or you'll find yourself sleeping on the couch, Connor Francis Campbell."

"Uh-uh." Sin-Jin walked in to join them. "Three names, sounds like she means it, Connor," he teased.

Connor locked his arms around Sheila again. "Go tend to your own wife," he said to his son-in-law. "I'll handle mine."

Sin-Jin was the soul of innocence. He indicated the empty bowl he was carrying. "Just came in to refill the pasta salad bowl. They're eating as if they've been starved for three days."

Sheila was looking at her husband, her hands on her hips as she wrestled out of his hold. "'Handle' now is it?"

Connor raised his hands in abject surrender. "Just an expression, love, just an expression."

Sin-Jin laughed as, bowl refilled, he made his exit from his in-laws' kitchen to the living room.

Sherry saw him laughing as she approached. "What's going on in there?" She nodded toward the kitchen.

"Just your parents clearing up some semantics." Putting the bowl down on the buffet table, he looked at the crowded room. Between Sherry's friends, the people his in-laws had invited and the selected few he'd asked from his office, there was hardly any space to move about. His son, the guest of honor, was in the middle of a group of loving admirers. He'd recovered with remarkable speed from his surgery and was the picture of health. Mrs. Farley was holding him, beaming. It was a nice look for her, Sin-Jin thought.

He nuzzled Sherry. "Think we have enough people?"

She laughed, loving the feel of his arms around her. It was something she knew she would never take for granted. Her son was healthy and happy, and Owen had just told her that he was promoting her to investigative reporter, even though the article on Sin-Jin had never materialized. Life just couldn't get any better. "We could always send out for more."

"Actually—" he brushed a kiss against her hair "—I was thinking of slipping away myself."

"Not before the cake," she warned. "Mom worked on it all day."

Sin-Jin smiled down at his wife. "I've already got my cake. And I'm thinking of nibbling on it, too." He kissed her ear.

"I'll hold you to that." Taking his wrist in her hand, she looked at his battered watch, marking the time. "At twenty-two hundred hours…bedroom."

He looked down at his watch. It was only four in the afternoon. An eternity away.

"You're on, Mrs. Adair."

Sin-Jin began counting down the minutes.

* * * * *

ROMANTIC
SUSPENSE

USA TODAY BESTSELLING AUTHOR

MARIE FERRARELLA

Brings you another exciting installment from

CAVANAUGH
JUSTICE

A Cavanaugh Christmas

When Detective Kaitlyn Two Feathers follows a kidnapping
case outside her jurisdiction, she enlists the aid of Detective
Thomas Cavelli. Still reeling from the discovery that his
father was a Cavanaugh, Thomas takes the case, thinking
it will be a nice distraction…until Kaitlyn becomes his
ultimate distraction. As the case heats up and time
is running out, Thomas must prove to Kaitlyn that he is
trustworthy and risk it all for the one thing they both
never thought they'd find—love.

Available November 22 wherever books are sold!

www.Harlequin.com

HRS27753

Enjoy this sneak peek from A CAVANAUGH CHRISTMAS
by Marie Ferrarella, coming December 2011
from Harlequin® Romantic Suspense.

"**B**oy, some guys sure get all the luck."

Detective First Class Thomas Cavelli's looked questioningly with his blue eyes at his partner.

"Now *that* walks into your life," Angelo LaGuardia said, clearly envious as he gestured toward the tall, leggy redhead who had just entered the squad room.

It was all Tom could do to keep his mouth from dropping open. The woman moved with precision, as if each step had been measured out. No doubt about it, she was exceedingly beautiful. She was also as serious-looking as a judge rendering the date of a convicted killer's execution.

"From where I'm sitting," he observed, his voice deceptively mild, "she's walking into the squad room, not my life."

LaGuardia ignored the protest. "But she is heading for you."

Tom turned to look at his partner. "And you know this how?" he challenged.

"Overheard her talking to the Chief of D's himself," Angelo confessed, lowering his voice as if to keep this source between the two of them. "She went straight to the top to get her information."

"And she asked for me?" He didn't know who the woman was, and he sincerely doubted if she knew him. This had to be LaGuardia's lame idea of a joke.

"When she talked to your new uncle, she asked for the person with the best track record for finding missing children."

"Best" in this case was still not good enough in Tom's opinion. "Best" to him would have meant that he located the children every time instead of only seventy percent, which was where his record stood at the moment.

That was something to be proud of, his father had told him. But he had no patience—or the time—for pride. There'd be time enough when every child's file that came across his desk was marked "closed" and had been resolved with a happy ending.

And a happy ending only occurred when the child was found.

Alive.

Tom's doubts as to the veracity of LaGuardia's claim began to dissipate as the tall, willowy redhead drew closer. Apparently the woman *was* heading straight for his desk.

*Who is this mystery woman
and what does she want from Tom? Find out in
A CAVANAUGH CHRISTMAS,
by* USA TODAY *bestselling author Marie Ferrarella,
available December 2011
from Harlequin® Romantic Suspense.*

HSCEXPHSEF1011